The Wall at the Edge of the World

Damion Hunter is a pseudonym of Amanda Cockrell. Along with the Centurions Trilogy, she is also the author of *Pomegranate Seed*, *What We Keep Is Not Always What Will Stay*, the historical trilogies *The Deer Dancers* and *The Horse Catchers*, and *The Legions of the Mist*, a Roman historical adventure novel. She lives in Roanoke, Virginia.

Also by Damion Hunter

The Legions of the Mist
The Wall at the Edge of the World

The Centurions Trilogy

The Centurions
Barbarian Princess
The Emperor's Games

THE WALL AT THE EDGE OF THE WORLD

OF THE WORLD

AMANDA COCKRELL *writing as*

DAMION HUNTER

CANELO

First published in the United Kingdom in 2020 by Canelo

Canelo Digital Publishing Limited
31 Helen Road
Oxford OX2 0DF
United Kingdom

A CIP catalogue record for this book is available from the British Library.

Print ISBN 978 1 80032 026 0
Ebook ISBN 978 1 78863 715 2

Look for more great books at www.canelo.co

Printed and bound in Great Britain by Clays Ltd, Elcograf S.p.A.

For Tony

Wherever the Roman conquers, there he dwells.

—Seneca

I. Home Posting

"It appears that you are behind on your drill, Surgeon Corvus." The camp optio bent to wave a records tablet in front of Postumus's nose in the dusty surgeon's quarters next to the fortress hospital. A bugler on the mud and stone rampart sounded Change of Sentries, and a smell of burning cereal drifted lightly on the wind from numerous cookfires. The Roman fort at Palmyra, on the emperor's service in Syria, made ready for the morning.

"I've been sewing up the results of yesterday's outing," Postumus protested.

"If you mean the one who got rolled on by his horse and the one who stabbed himself with his own pilum, they seem to be alive at the moment." The optio's stance indicated he had no intention of moving until some agreement was made. He had records to keep and the medical officers were always trouble. Surgeons held rank equivalent to a centurion and were supposed to earn it with regular weapons drill and marches. They generally considered evading that an ongoing sport.

"Tribune Balbinus is taking a patrol out this morning. You can catch up by going along. It's a lovely day."

"Won't that be nice," Postumus muttered but he got up and collected his armor and let the optio tut at him because it needed polishing. He shrugged on his tunic and harness skirt and then the segmented plates of his lorica, fiddling with his scarf until it kept the plates from rubbing his chest. He fastened his greaves, inspected his helmet for scorpions, and jammed it on his head. He picked up his sword and shield, a long flat oval bearing the wave insignia of the Ulpia Dacorum, and glared back at the optio. One of the few privileges of the Medical Corps was not having to wear armor except on the march or on parade.

Tribune Balbinus was mounted and waiting at the Dexter Gate with three centuries of the Ulpia Dacorum who garrisoned the fort. Postumus saluted him, fist to chest, and thought, *On a horse. Of course you are.* Tribunes generally came from senatorial families, destined for careers in politics after a stint with the Army. They were not career soldiers and not inclined to travel by foot.

Balbinus gave the signal and the men lined up behind the standard-bearer, Postumus beside the centurion of the First Century. The optio was right; it was a nice day. A march would blow the dawn cobwebs out of his head, no doubt. They headed out of the gates at a standard pace, rising sun glinting off pilum points and the century standards. To one side they could admire the gardens and columned grandeur of Palmyra, and to the other the lion-colored hills of the Parthian Empire.

After centuries of on-again, off-again warfare, Rome and Parthia were ostensibly at peace, a peace maintained by frequent border patrols on either side. The oasis city of Palmyra itself was prosperous, a stop on the Silk Road to the East, traded back and forth between Rome and the Parthian Empire for centuries and generally content with either as long as no one was laying siege to the city.

Once past the city the land was drier, shading into desert hillside. Smaller tracks led through dusty scree upward from the stone-paved Roman road. One of the

Palmyra patrols' functions was to discourage the bandits that preyed on travelers along the border. Goods from the east were a mainstay of Palmyra's trade and a sore temptation to the thieves of the hills.

Tribune Balbinus signaled to the standard-bearers to turn the column southeast onto an unpaved track and the centurion beside Postumus swore, ducking out of line to trot beside the tribune's horse. He spoke too softly to be heard, but Postumus was reasonably sure he knew what he was saying. This was too close to the border and they hadn't enough men.

Balbinus shook his head. "That's what we're here for, isn't it? All right then. Column right!"

They swung onto the track into the hills, dust rising from mailed sandals that slipped a bit in the scree. The centurion slid back into line, his mouth grim. "He's likely to get more than bandits, the fool," he said and then snapped his mouth shut. Criticizing a senior officer, no matter how misguided, was never a good idea.

Postumus found that he was wide awake now. He had not managed to get out from under the optio's eye without bringing a pilum along to carry and was beginning to think better of his objections. He could feel the tension in the officers next to him, and feel it run along the column. They were moving farther up the track, farther into hills that hid their line of sight, farther toward the Parthian border with its own patrols and maybe no more sense than the tribune had.

The chink and rattle of their own armor blocked the sounds of the horsemen until they were on them. At least a hundred Parthian cataphracts, men and horses, both plated with coats of scale, and fifty more horse archers poured over the ridge above them.

"Form up!" The patrol scrambled to form battle order, the signifers at the front with their centurions, the tribune's horse dancing under him as he shouted orders.

The cataphracts made the first charge, with their mounted archers on the wings. The Roman front ranks locked their shields together, Postumus with them, and hurled a simultaneous flight of pilums, the deadly spears whose iron heads went halfway down their length. The pilum tip was tempered but the mid-length of the iron head was not, so that it bent as it pierced its target, heavy enough to drag a man from his horse if it lodged in his shield. The Ulpia Dacorum centuries formed up with a shield wall on three sides and backed up slowly as the leading cataphracts went down under the rain of iron. Only the hillside terrain kept them from being completely surrounded. Loose horses began to career through the Parthian ranks and the cataphracts struggled to close up again. Postumus, fighting desperately with a dismounted Parthian commander, thought that the Parthians might have been surprised as well. The cataphract had lost his spear along with his horse, and swung a vicious straight-bladed sword at him. Postumus blocked it with his shield and closed to slide his own short sword under the man's guard, trying to pierce the coat of plates. The cataphract went down and another took his place as a loose horse galloped by them, streaming blood. It leaped over the wounded man and collided with the tribune's mount. Both horses went down. Postumus, fighting frantically in the front line, could only take note from the corner of his eye before another cataphract, this one mounted, was on him. Postumus ran his sword into the horse's belly, the only vulnerable place, and stumbled back as it went down too.

The cataphracts were trying to regroup, and the horse archers on their wings were keeping their enemy pinned down as much as possible while they did so. In a momentary breathing space, he saw Tribune Balbinus writhing under the weight of a downed Parthian horse and all its armor. As Postumus watched, he went still.

"Help me!" Postumus grabbed an auxiliaryman by his chain-mailed shoulder. He stumbled toward the tribune with the infantryman behind him, shields over their heads, and they heaved at the horse's flank. Around them the Parthian archers were raining arrows down on the patrol.

"Lift!" The horse was dead, which was better than alive and kicking, but armored it was almost immovable. "Just try to lift it long enough for me to get him!"

Two more soldiers took it by the hooves and began to heave and Postumus, abandoning his shield and sword, reached under the belly to drag Balbinus out. He got him clear just as an arrow took the soldier at the horse's head in the thigh and he felt another go into his own arm below the shoulder plates. It had just caught the flesh, protruding from the opposite side, and he yanked it all the way through in a flurry of bloody feathers rather than pull backward on the barbed head.

"I have him!" Postumus gasped. "Get to the rear!" He lifted Balbinus, trailing blood, and stumbled backward through the Roman ranks while the wounded man limped behind him. The three centurions had collected their men into formation again and the Parthians were drawing off, under cover of a final deadly rain of arrows.

"Form up! Stay sharp!" They stood gasping, waiting to see if the Parthians would attack again.

Postumus set the tribune on the ground before his grip gave out. His arm was pouring blood now.

"Mithras god, is that the tribune?" The centurion of the Third Century bent over him.

"It is." Postumus pulled his scarf from under his breast-plate and knotted it around his arm with the other hand and his teeth. "Give me yours."

The centurion handed it over. Postumus rolled the tribune carefully onto his back and worked the scarf around his leg, tying it in a loose knot. The leg was scored and bloody and very clearly broken. "That's where you don't touch him, got it?"

The centurion nodded. The First Centurion shouted the order to Fall Back and they began to move down the track, four men with the tribune's limp body between them. Halfway down they found his horse, unhurt but reins tangled in a thicket of scrub. Postumus collected him and they put the tribune across his saddle.

In the Palmyra hospital, Postumus set the tribune's broken leg and taped his broken ribs while his own arm dripped blood. Afterward he lay down and gritted his teeth while his surgeon's apprentice poured vinegar through the wound and tied a clean cloth around it. That night he slept in the surgery where he could watch Tribune Balbinus, who miraculously did not die.

–

Six days later Postumus sat in the open door of the surgery office with the surgery cat on his lap. There was nothing he need do this evening. The tribune's leg had not become infected, also miraculously, and most likely would not require amputation. Palmyra's new surgeon would make the rounds tonight. Postumus had packed his kit, his baggage and library, introduced the cat to his successor, and made his farewells among the men of Palmyra Fort. He was twenty-four years old and he was going home.

There had been little enough to pack, he thought, to mark six years in the Army – spare tunics and undertunics, a game board and counters and a pair of green glass cups, a folding instrument case, tattered copies of Celsus and Dioscorides, and a small store of Eastern drugs that might be hard to come by in the North.

And the silver Valorous Conduct bracelet on his arm, as brightly new as the waxing moon, his ticket home – home and a fat promotion. A well-earned honor, the commander had said, when he snapped the silver band on Postumus's arm: senior surgeon and a post in Britain, at Eburacum Fortress. Postumus had saluted, the commander had saluted, and Postumus had turned at parade quickstep back to his place.

–

The Valorous Conduct band winked in the last glow of sunlight, and Postumus polished it gently with the hem of his tunic, while the cat yawned, stretched, and pricked up his ears as a brisk little wind came up with the falling twilight. A moment later he was gone, trotting purposefully past the hospital, tail erect and eyes wide at whatever scent came blowing along on the night wind. Postumus watched him as he walked out of sight and then swung his legs down from the desktop. Perhaps there were farewells to be made after all, if only to the relatively tranquil contentment of his Palmyra posting. It would keep him from thinking about how much he wanted a home posting and how little he wanted it to be at Eburacum.

II. Childhood's Close

Postumus Justinius Corvus had been named, after the manner of his people, on the ninth day after his birth. If the slight-framed, sandy-haired centurion who had come home on leave occasionally to bounce him on his lap and applaud his first tottering steps bore a name totally unrelated to his, no one saw fit to mention the fact. He was eight years old before it occurred to him that his name didn't match his father's, and then the idea terrified him nearly into incoherence. Roman children always took some form of their father's name. That was how you know who was whose – and who you were.

"That's because he's not your father, dummy," his brother Justin said as they sat on the blue-tiled edge of the atrium pool and dabbled their bare feet in the water. "Or mine either, of course. Not really. Here, don't cry," he added. "I thought you knew. I've known for ages."

Postumus, his whole safe, orderly world pulled from under him, scrubbed at his eyes with the hem of his grubby tunic. "N-no," he managed to say. "Why didn't anyone tell me?"

"Probably because they thought you weren't old enough," Justin said, with the superiority of nine-and-a-half. "That's why Papa is Marcus Constantius Hilarion, but I'm Marcellus Justinius Corvus and you're Postumus Justinius Corvus, and our real father was Somebody-Else

Justinius Corvus. He died just after I was born and just before you were. Why d'you think you're called Postumus anyway? You were the last. That's what it means."

"B-but Mama—?"

"Oh, she's our mother all right. Don't be silly. Did you think the fairies left you under a cabbage?"

"I don't know!" Postumus wailed.

"Well, if I'd known you were going to take on like that, I wouldn't have told you," Justin said. "If you don't shut up, Januaria will hear you and then we'll get smacked for putting our dirty feet in the pool. They are, too," he added, wiggling his toes and observing the small brown cloud that drifted around them. He cast a wary glance over his shoulder but there was no one there, only the household cat in a cushioned chair, cleaning her ears in the shaft of sun from the skylight. They weren't to play in the pool or put frogs in it. There were probably other things they weren't to do, but they hadn't thought of them yet.

Postumus sniffled and was silent. Justin didn't seem to mind, so maybe it wasn't so bad after all. "Who was he?" he asked finally.

"He was a cohort centurion, like Papa. In fact, he was a friend of Papa's, and Papa married Mama after he was killed because he'd said he would take care of her. I think that's kind of nice."

Postumus wondered if Papa and Mama had thought it was nice, but he didn't say anything. But you could tell they liked each other, he thought, and they'd had Marcus and Constantia together.

"He had a cohort in the same legion as Papa," Justin went on.

"In the Second?"

"No, I don't think so," Justin said, considering. "And it wasn't the Sixth or the Twentieth either, because Papa's never been in them. I heard Papa say something to Uncle Licinius once about the Ninth. And then they saw me and shut up."

"But there isn't any Ninth Legion," Postumus said.

Justin looked thoughtful. "No, but I think there used to be."

–

Postumus mulled this information over in private for the next few months, hesitant to ask any more questions for fear of getting even more frightening answers. He wasn't who he had thought he was. And if he wasn't, what if nobody else was either? Mama, for instance. Postumus knew she was British; not just native-born like himself, but really British, although of course she was Roman now – you always were if you married a Roman, and Mama, it seemed, had married two. But that was all he knew about her. Up until now she had just been his mother, not really a separate person at all. And what if there was something else awful there too, that nobody had told him about?

In the end he worked up a full-fledged case of nightmares that woke him screaming, and half the household along with him. Justin, who always slept like the dead, was still snoring obliviously in the next bed, but his mother came flying down the corridor with an oil lamp, Januaria two paces behind her.

"My darling, what is it?" Gwytha, his mother, scooped him up and cuddled him in her lap, while Januaria, their nurse, clucked about them, her bulk encased in a volu- minous nightshift and a hastily caught-up cloak pinned sideways.

Postumus rubbed his eyes and tried to remember what he had dreamed, but it was fading fast in his mother's comforting embrace. "I'm not sure," he said. "I think – everybody went away."

"Hush now, nobody's going anywhere," his mother said softly. "Januaria and I are always here, and Papa too, even when he's with his legion."

"Me too." There was a pit-pat of small feet on the tile floor and five-year-old Constantia slipped her hand into his. "Was it an awful dream?" she inquired solicitously. She ignored Januaria's cluckings about the dangers of night air and snuggled up onto the bed beside him in her nightshift.

"I think so," Postumus told her seriously, pulling the checkered woolen blanket around her, "but I can't remember it."

"Well, you mustn't have it again," she said firmly, and then, taking a good look at her mother and Januaria, began to giggle. Both women had their long hair neatly braided for the night, but their front hair, cut short, was rolled and tied with rags which stuck out wildly in the lamplight, like starfish.

Postumus, his nightmare receding before their female solicitude, started to laugh too, and in a moment both children were clinging to each other and laughing hysterically.

"We are glad to have afforded you so much amusement," Gwytha said when they had finally subsided, and Constantia began to giggle again. Her own sandy blond braids were parted in no-nonsense fashion down the middle and no such adult vanities adorned her freckled brow.

"Bed for you, miss." Januaria picked her up and draped her firmly over one shoulder. Constantia grinned conspiratorially at Postumus and waved one small pink hand as she was removed from the room.

Gwytha lingered for a moment, her eyes grave, watching her son. "You were talking about your father when I woke you," she said gently. "Do you want to hear about him?"

–

Postumus learned a lot that night, which at least put him one up on Justin, who had slept like a pig throughout the whole story, as Postumus informed him the next day as they collected eggs from the flock of speckled chickens that clucked and muttered in the farmyard.

Besides Papa's mother, they had another grandmother who had died the year after Postumus was born, and who had lived at Antium, which was very fashionable and near Rome itself, and her husband, their grandfather, had been an Army officer too.

"The Corvus family goes back at least seven generations in the Eagles," Postumus said proudly, and Justin nodded. That would stand them in good stead when they came of age for the Centuriate, which Justin was already planning on.

"But I don't much mind not having known her," Postumus added, looking in the hedgerow where the black hen insisted on hiding her eggs. The reason that Mama hardly ever mentioned her was that she had been furious when her son had married Mama, because Mama had been a freedwoman, a former slave, and not good enough for the family. Looking at it from a Roman point of view, Postumus could see that, but it didn't seem fair all the same, because Mama had been a chief's sister's daughter, which meant highborn in her tribe, when a slave trader had caught her out alone one day. (That was illegal, Mama had explained, but it happened all the time anyway, if no one powerful enough to do anything about it took your side.) And the reason that they never saw Mama's people was that her tribe was the Iceni and they had hated Rome and anything to do with it since Boudicca, the last of their great leaders, had rebelled and slaughtered a legion and three cities before Rome, which never forgives, had come with an avenging army and burned their land from one end to the other. An Iceni woman who married a Roman, for whatever reason, would find small welcome. And so she had never gone back. The black hen appeared and pecked at his ankles and Postumus broke off a branch and waved it at her.

Justin, with small Marcus and Constantia, who had followed to hear the tale, listened wide-eyed. Mama had led a far more exciting life than any of them had realized. In the Iceni chief they had less interest. Almost all Army families had tribal blood somewhere along the line, in these days when new citizens were created in each new conquered territory. The imperial policy for many years had been to settle its veterans on grants of land in the provinces to further the stability of the government (Papa's family had Rhenish blood). But it was generally the Roman men who married foreign women (there were always too many women among the losers in a war) and gave to them and their children a Roman name and Roman customs. Gwytha's children had never thought of themselves as anything else.

But it was what Postumus had learned about his father's old legion that he saved for last, and to this only Justin paid much attention. Constantia was really too young to understand how you could have two fathers anyway, and Marcus, as Justin said disgustedly, must have been a changeling because he spent his time naming the chickens, and didn't seem interested in playing Army at all. So while the young ones sat quietly under the hedgerow and tried to behave themselves under Justin's glare, Postumus told him about the Ninth Hispana, which had come to Britain with Claudius Caesar's invasion force more than eighty years ago, and had been the garrison legion at Eburacum in the wild lands to the north, before the Sixth Victrix. It was the legion that Boudicca slaughtered before her rising was put down and it was said that she had cursed it before she killed herself. The legion had been reconstituted but the shame of that defeat had marked it.

In their father's day, the Ninth Hispana, by then under-manned and too long from Rome, had finally gone down in another tribal rising that had spread to mutiny in the legion itself, and swept the few loyal cohorts into the whirlwind with it. One of those cohorts had been their father's, and he had died when the last of the legion had made its desperate stand at the abandoned fortress of Castra Pinnata at Inchtuthil in the far north, where now Rome didn't even patrol. And the Senate had considered and spoken, and the Ninth Hispana had become a dead legion, with even its number blotted from the master Legionary List in Rome.

It seemed that everyone they knew had somehow paid for the wreck of the Hispana. Mama, who had loved their father so much that even Postumus could see it when she spoke of him (although he didn't say that, because of Marcus and Constantia); Uncle Licinius, who was really a courtesy uncle and had been Senior Legionary Surgeon to the Ninth, and was invalided out with a bad knee and a criminally small pension when the Senate broke the legion; his wife Aunt Felicia, whose own father had been the Ninth's last legate; Papa, fuming because they had taken his cohort and left him behind to command Eburacum's handful of troops, transferred and demoted, tarred with a guilt by association that had continued to follow him and stalled his career, so that even now after fifteen years' service he hadn't risen farther than command of the Fifth Cohort. And of course their father, dead at Inchtuthil.

"He was called Justin too," Postumus said, when he had finished. "Mama says we look like him."

"Mithras god," Justin said, and didn't even look around to make sure that no one heard him swearing a grown-up oath.

That was the day on which Postumus and Justin began to grow up. In Justin, the story of the lost Hispana seemed to make him even more determined to follow in his father's and Papa's footsteps and make himself a career in the Eagles that would give the lie to the emperor and the Senate that had broken their legion. But in Postumus it marked a turning point of another sort, and the road marker was Licinius.

–

"Take these to Aunt Felicia, dear, please." Gwytha handed Postumus a wicker basket of eggs. "The young ones are starting to lay and with Papa at the fort, we'll never eat all these."

Postumus suspected that meant the older ones were going to be soup, but that was the way with chickens. He took the basket and set out carefully ("Don't run!"

Gwytha called after him) across the meadow that ran between their house and Uncle Licinius's farm, skirting the pond where Cook was raising carp and frogs. The sun was out and it wasn't raining for a change and the new grass felt lovely so he took his sandals off and put them in the basket with the eggs. He stopped along the way to peer into a badger's burrow – carefully – and pat a black horse that stuck its nose over the pasture fence, and feed it a handful of clover, and then went in the kitchen door of Licinius's house, stopping to make his respects to the household snake who lived under the sill. He gave the eggs to the cook and looked at her hopefully.

Cook produced a piece of cake from the cupboard. "Thank your mother for us. This is for you. And take your sandals out of the eggs, please." She glanced over her shoulder at the gridiron on the hearth where something was boiling furiously. "I need to pay attention. No more children in the kitchen, please. Mistress has taken ours to the village to buy new boots but if you go down to the barn, I think you'll find that the master has a new foal you could look at."

Postumus nodded and put his sandals on again. The children of the two families were much of an age and had run tame in each other's houses since Postumus could remember. He went down the path to the barn, cutting through the kitchen garden and then through the buzz of bees in the apple orchard to the stone and timber barn below the house.

Licinius was in the barn, but the foal wasn't there yet. The sorrel mare lay on her side in the straw, flanks heaving and foamy spittle coming from her mouth. Licinius, in just an undertunic, was flat on the stall floor behind her.

He looked up when he heard Postumus, his face dripping sweat and covered in blood and muck from the stall.

"Should I go away again?" Postumus asked him, a little frightened because Licinius looked so grim. His graying dark hair was plastered to his forehead.

"Yes! No. No, wait. Come here."

Postumus edged closer.

"Get down here with me." It was clear that it was a command. "You have little hands. One foreleg is bent and it's stuck. It's caught on her hip bone. We need to push the foal back in until the leg comes loose. See if you can get your hand in there and shove."

"Inside the horse?"

"Yes! Inside the horse! I need help. Like this, only my hands are too big." Licinius pushed his hand in beside the one small hoof that appeared from the mare's back end. "I can't get far enough up." The mare's flanks heaved again and she tossed her head wildly. "We're going to lose them both if I can't get it loose soon."

"All right." Postumus knelt down and slid his hand up inside the mare where Licinius showed him. It was warm and sticky and felt so alive it startled him. He had never thought about what was inside of things before. What felt like another soft unformed hoof pushed against his fingers. "I can feel it. I think."

The mare strained again and the muscles contracted around his arm like a vise.

"Push it back in," Licinius said when the muscles relaxed.

Whatever he was touching wasn't a leg. It had two small holes and he realized it was the foal's nose. He could feel the mouth working. There was another horse in there, inside, alive, if he could just help it out. The thought was overwhelming. He shoved against it and felt it move. A little more. Between the mare's straining, he let his hand do the thinking – that seemed to be the way, since his eyes couldn't see inside the mare. A little more. Suddenly two tiny hooves were in his palm. Then the mare gave a huge heave and the whole foal slid out almost into Postumus's hands.

"Good boy!" Licinius sat up and began to clean the foal while the mare lay breathing hard. Postumus sat in the straw, staring at his hands and at the foal. It was a sorrel too, with a huge white blaze down its nose and one white sock. After a moment the mare heaved herself up as the afterbirth came out too. She settled, forelegs bent under her chest, to nuzzle the foal. Licinius reached behind him for his surgical kit, tied off the umbilical cord and cut it. Then he rolled over in the straw and lay on his back, panting. Postumus stretched out beside him and they lay there silently watching the swallows building a nest in the barn roof and listening to the mare murmur horse things to her foal.

"We had better get you a wash and a clean tunic," Licinius said finally and sat up, and Postumus followed him, ready now to do pretty much anything that Licinius suggested.

Afterward they sat in Licinius's surgery office, Postumus in the visitor's chair in an old, much-too-big tunic of Licinius's, with a plate of buttered buns and a green glass cup of very watered wine beside him.

"You have a good touch," Licinius said. "I owe you for that. She's my best mare." He pointed at the green glass cups. "I don't bring these out for just anybody."

"Mama said you were a surgeon in a legion," Postumus said.

"I was."

Postumus wondered if he should have asked that. Was there something else awful no one was telling him? But he had had his hands inside an actual horse and now there was a live foal when there mightn't have been one, and that had somehow opened up an entire new world, where you could make things live instead of killing them or ordering them around, which seemed to be what the Army did. For the good of Rome, of course.

Licinius fiddled with a stack of meticulously kept records folders, the ingrained habit of his Army years, and some scent of the old days came back on a little sigh of the wind.

"I was," he said. "I understand you've been wanting to know things."

Postumus nodded. He wanted to know more things now, like how you knew what was inside of something and how to fix it. People, horses.

Before he could ask anything, there was a light tap on the doorframe. "There is a person to see you, master." Theodore, who was the house steward and had belonged to a legionary legate's household before Licinius married Aunt Felicia, had certain standards and it was evident that the person did not meet them.

Licinius sighed. "Very well, youngster. I'll answer any questions you can think up, but you'll have to squeeze them in between my other crises. In the meantime, you can play fetch-and-carry. My knee's giving me trouble after this morning's adventure and Theodore feels that an orderly's work is beneath his dignity."

Licinius walked with a slight limp, testimony to the bad knee that had kept him from marching out with the Hispana on its last campaign. He had been one of the best surgeons in the Eagles, Gwytha had said, and a medical Unfit for Service had been an easy road for the Senate to take when it broke the legion. Now he was a civilian physician and the villages surrounding the fort at Isca Silurum brought him everything they couldn't treat themselves, from wolf bites to lung fever and the occasional sick pig.

The current specimen was a local of uncertain age and cleanliness who had laid his leg open with a scythe and then nursed it himself until it was properly inflamed.

"Old bastard brought me his damn cow the same day when she cut her hock," Licinius muttered. "And then he lets himself get like this. This is the third time I've dressed this, and it's finally coming along."

He cleaned and re-dressed the wound, pointing out to the fascinated Postumus where the flesh and muscle were beginning to knit together, and the infection subsiding. The old man sat stoically throughout the process and when Licinius had finished, nodded his thanks. "I'll send my woman with some eggs," he announced, and departed.

"I just brought you eggs," Postumus said indignantly. "Mother sent them over. Don't they *pay* you?"

Licinius washed his hands in the surgery basin and grinned at him. "Sometimes they don't even pay eggs."

"Why do you let them do it?"

"I can't let the old fool die of an infected leg because he's too pigheaded to pay me. And he paid for the cow."

Postumus thought that over.

"It gets bred into you in the Army," Licinius said. "Half the time you'll spend treating the natives. They'll bring you their wounded – some of whom got that way fighting your lads – and their babies, and even their livestock. Anything their priests can't touch, they'll hand to you and stand back and wait for a miracle. Sometimes you can even give it to them."

Postumus took a bite out of his bun and a sip – very carefully – out of the fragile green glass cup.

"And if you can't manage it," Licinius added, in case Postumus was giving him too much credit, "and whoever it is dies, they'll spread it around the local beerhouse that you poisoned their grandfather."

That was the day that Licinius became a real person to Postumus, a three-dimensional being rather than merely the misty figure of another grown-up; a man with a whole world's knowledge to offer, who could see what was wrong with someone and make it right, or at least know why he couldn't. Even the fact that Licinius had known and loved his father took second place to that.

Thereafter Postumus spent every minute that Licinius would allow him in the surgery, grinding herbs and patiently scraping verdigris for ointments, learning to make a proper distillation, and best of all, discovering the wonderful intricacy with which the gods had fashioned all living creatures. After a while Licinius showed him how to kill a frog and then dissect it.

"I can't bring myself to murder anything besides frogs, or a fish," Licinius said. "But if you find a dead bird or we have a barn cat meet an untimely end, I'll show you those too."

They inspected the insides of chickens bound for the pot, to Cook's dismay, and a lamb that died at birth. They always poured a bit of wine into the grave – or the pot – afterward to thank the shade of the creature for its help.

"What about people?" Postumus asked. "How do we know about people?"

"The gods forbid that," Licinius said. "Or so the priests tell us. That is a thing you cannot do."

"What, look inside dead people?"

"Precisely. For fear of offending the gods or stirring up a vengeful shade. So we learn by looking at live people who have had the misfortune to have already been cut open by somebody else."

Postumus suspected that Licinius would have cut up a dead person at the soonest opportunity if he thought he could have gotten away with it, but Licinius also made it clear that this was a frightful crime and the punishment would be equally frightful.

"Go into the Medical Corps and you won't find a shortage of things to look at," Licinius informed him. "The Army provides the best anatomical research you'll find."

Postumus thought there was a note of sarcasm in that, but also that he was probably right. If there was another war in the north like the one that had destroyed the Hispana, there would be plenty of material to study.

In the meantime, Licinius began lending him his medical texts to stumble through, with many questions, and they had a fine time with the bones of a dead cow, which the vultures had obligingly cleaned for them, reassembling it – the foxes had gone off with a few pieces – and naming all the bones in reference to their human counterparts. Licinius's son Felix was showing no interest in anything but the horses, although he was fearless there, so Postumus had him to himself.

All of this Postumus explained in lurid detail to Constantia, who was the only one in his own family who showed any inclination to listen. She would cheerfully have let him bore her to death on any subject for the sheer pleasure of his presence.

Grateful for her quiet interest, Postumus talked to her about his father and the strange, unquiet feeling that still lurked at the back of his mind of not quite knowing who he was.

Oddly enough, Justin, once he had absorbed all the relevant information about their father, seemed unaffected by it, other than to regret that Hilarion, whom he adored, would never rise higher than a mid-level cohort command and a retirement on the family farm, and all because of the wretched Ninth Legion. Hilarion was an able commander, but there would be no legate's post for him, no chance for glory and a famous name. As far as Justin was concerned, he was Hilarion's son, accidents of birth aside, and the one qualm he had harbored was laid to rest the day he somewhat hesitantly asked Hilarion why, when he had adopted them, he had not also given them his name, as was the custom.

"I thought your father should have that much monument," Hilarion had said, putting his arm around him. "Rome has done its best to bury even the memory of the Ninth and anyone who served in it. The least I could do was leave him his name."

Justin, after thinking it over, had decided that seemed fair, and had ceased to trouble over it. But for Postumus, it went deeper than that.

"Maybe it's because Justin knew our father," he told Constantia. "Even if he was too little to remember. But I was born after he died, and sometimes I feel like I don't belong to anybody."

"You belong to me." His sister slipped a small, slightly grubby hand into his. "Would you like to tell me about the insides of a frog again?" she asked hopefully, searching for some way to comfort him.

III. The Peace of the Frontier

In the end, it was the Army that gave him a home, not so much a place as a calling, a work to be done regardless of location or blood tie, despite the fact that the Army had also done its best to keep anyone associated with the tainted Ninth out of its legionary ranks. Justin, for instance, who found when he was of age for the Centuriate that despite letters of recommendation from both Hilarion and Licinius, or perhaps because of them, that there was an excess of applicants that year and while Justinius Corvus the younger was of course excellently qualified, there just did not seem to be a place for him. He would, the Army was certain, find a suitable spot in one of the auxiliary regiments. Postumus, too, was posted to the auxiliaries, but medicine was much the same in any fort.

After the terrors of his training year at a field hospital in Dalmatia where, upon his arrival, a short-lived local rebellion provided more than sufficient bodies on which to learn his craft, he served a second season as a surgeon's assistant in Achaea, arduous mainly for the boredom of what was essentially a bureaucratic outpost rather than a military occupation. After that, a long leave and enough left of his pay, supplemented by the bonus paid the Empire's soldiers on the accession of its new Emperor Antoninus, allowed a first visit home. The journey made part of a circuitous route to his next posting with a Gaulish cavalry regiment in Germania, if the posting wasn't changed in the meantime, and he would not have been surprised if it had. The Emperor Hadrian had died only a year ago and no one knew then quite what Antoninus was going to do.

As it happened, he and Justin had leave at the same time, and Gwytha invited Licinius and his family to a celebratory dinner. Constantia had touched up the dining room mural of herons and carp in a lily pond with fresh color in their honor, and Januaria had recruited the gardener's boy as well as Theodore and Licinius's cook to pass trays of pastries, fish, tiny roasted birds, and cups of Hilarion's best Falernian wine. Justin and Postumus wore their uniform tunics, the blue and brown of the auxiliaries, and Justin's belt buckle identified him as the new commander of the First Thracian cavalry, currently stationed on the Rhenus.

Now that they were grown, Postumus and Justin looked much as their father might have, according to Januaria, including the light brown eyes, almost amber, the sharp angled brows, and the nose that Marcus claimed made them look like someone on a coin. Tonight Postumus wondered if there were times when their mother looked right through them and found their father somewhere on the other side.

She reclined on a couch opposite theirs and beamed at them impartially, content in their homecoming. Constantia was beside her with a tame hedgehog curled in the folds of her gown. Marcus, on her other side, had maintained his utter lack of interest in the Army other than as a market for meat and cavalry horses, and was a stocky nineteen-year-old with Gwytha's red-brown hair and a no-nonsense look about him that made Postumus think of a herd dog.

Completing the circle, through the center of which the servants passed tray after tray, were Hilarion, Licinius, and Felicia, with Felix and his little sister Aurelia. Felix looked like his father but Aurelia was a beauty, somehow favored by the best aspects of both her parents. She didn't seem to notice it yet, but everyone else did.

"Do you two have any sense of what Antoninus is likely to do?" Hilarion asked, as a tray of prawns in lovage and pepper went around – the question that had been on everyone's mind. When Trajan had died and Hadrian succeeded him, he had consolidated the provinces, pulled back troops from an ill-fated campaign in Parthia, and brought the British legions up to strength, just a little too late. The worry in everyone's head was that Antoninus might undo all that.

"The whole Empire has been bubbling since Hadrian died," Justin said. "But what it will come to is anybody's guess. There are a lot of opinions, most of them constructed of wishful thinking."

"Or nerves," Postumus said. "I wish we knew which was which."

"There are always bubbles for a new emperor," Licinius said. "In the most part they bubble back down again."

Postumus lifted a pastry-wrapped bundle from the tray offered to him by Theodore. "Mother, what *is* this?"

"Dormice, Surgeon," Theodore said in a tone that might as well have been addressed to the small Postumus of twenty years ago.

"They're lovely, dear," Gwytha said. "Try one."

"They're very fashionable," Aurelia said. "Theodore has been fattening them since we heard you were coming home. In jars," she added. "Theodore chased the snake out of the kitchen with a broom and Cook said that was bad luck."

"The snake was probably confused," Licinius said. "His job is to eat mice."

"The snake and I have an understanding," Theodore said, and Cook made a hissing noise and the Sign of Horns. Theodore gave her a look that plainly said that her opinions were not required.

Postumus took a bite, wondering if there were bones or not, while across the circle Felix mimed slipping something into the folds of his tunic.

Theodore had belonged to a senatorial household and had opinions on suitable menus for dinner parties, which he didn't get many chances to exercise in West Britain. Postumus had thought him stiff-necked when he was small but had learned that Theodore had followed the legate's household across the Empire and was capable of producing a four-course dinner on a camp stove.

"See what you've been missing?" Constantia asked him, feeding bits to her hedgehog.

"It's quite good," Postumus said, swallowing, still not entirely sure what else had been in the bundle besides dormouse.

"Ooh, spiced lamb!" Aurelia stretched a white hand out as the gardener's boy came around with another plate. She helped herself while he gazed longingly at her until Theodore took him by the ear and turned him in Hilarion's direction. Januaria came around with the water and wine in silver pitchers while Felicia kept a careful eye on the proportions in Aurelia's cup.

Hilarion smoothed the folds of his white woolen tunic as if wondering what he was wearing. The civilian clothes of retirement still sat uneasily on him. "The new emperor has sent a good man here, at least," he said, circling back to what was on most people's minds. Lollius Urbicus had been appointed Governor of Britain the year before.

"We may need him," Licinius said.

"This is the first real news of home we've had," Justin said. "What has been happening here?"

"The Selgovae have been making trouble north of the Wall."

"I thought we'd given up on Valentia," Postumus said of the billowing acres of heather and moorland that swelled unendingly above the Wall. The Wall was the late Emperor Hadrian's work, a massive 73-mile-long fortress cutting across the midsection of Britain, fencing off the rebellious tribes of the Selgovae from their equally dangerous kin, the Brigantes. It was those two tribes who, with the Picts from the north, had staged the tribal rising that had wrecked a legion; and for the past twenty years the Wall had stood between them, and marked the farthest reach of Roman rule. Beyond it the Selgovae, in the old abandoned province of Valentia, were bound to Rome solely by treaty and a dubious promise of good behavior. They did not seem to have been extending this behavior to their neighbors.

"The Votadini have formally requested our help," Hilarion said. "Brendan of the Selgovae has been raiding rather hard into their territory and they're afraid he's got his eye on more than just the occasional head of cattle."

"Does he?"

"I don't know. I do know he's unsettling the North, though, which may be his plan. He's getting up in years and he may be trying to consolidate some power for his heir's sake. At any rate, Governor Urbicus is putting affairs in order to show him the error of his ways – and it looks like he may open up the Wall to do it."

"Open up the Wall!" Constantia sounded shocked. Since any of them could remember, the Wall had been there, solid, defensive, a line between civilization and the halls of the barbarians.

"You forget, my dear, that the Wall isn't much older than you are," her father said. He looked down at his hands. "I helped build it. And there is fort after silent fort beyond it."

Forts that had once housed troops of the Eagles, Postumus thought, before the wreck of the Ninth. He watched a wave of pain go across the faces of the elders, including the servants. And now Brendan, one of the leaders in that long-ago war, was threatening to stir it all up again.

"Will they open up Valentia again, do you think?" he asked.

"I rather think Valentia will open itself up," Hilarion said.

The dormice and spiced lamb were followed by a stuffed hare and a fricassee of pork with apricots, and then stuffed dates and an egg sponge with honey. The conversation wandered to the prospects for selling the new cavalry remounts at a better than usual price, given the governor's plans, to the new crop of lambs on the farm, to the midsummer festival in the village and whether Aurelia was old enough this year to go to it with only her brother for escort. It was clear that no one but Felix and Aurelia thought so.

After dinner Licinius had invited him to ride home with them in the lingering twilight, all gray-green shadows and owl hoot. Postumus had forgotten how much he missed that landscape. "There's a foal with a quarter-moon-shaped mark I want you to see. My head groom thinks it's an evil omen and the cook's girl, who claims her aunt was a sorceress, says it's lucky. I'll let you vote."

The foal, a filly, licked his hand when he offered it, so Postumus voted for good luck. "Call her Imperatrix," he suggested, "in honor of the new emperor."

–

He put in two more years as a junior surgeon, the second of them with an auxiliary cavalry ala in Syria, followed by a series of small Syrian surgical commands – all single cohort forts of cavalry and auxiliaries – learning his craft the way all military surgeons did, half by what he'd been taught, half by what some new skirmish or training mishap forced him to devise.

He came of a letter writing family, and Constantia as well as his mother and Hilarion kept him abreast of affairs in Britain, news that he read always with the tug at the heart of the native-born. He had expected to miss his family, but he had not known how much he would miss the Silure Hills. He saw Licinius once when he came East to look for breeding stock to improve his horse herd, and Postumus showed him proudly around the mud-walled hospital, the first to which he had been assigned as senior – and sole – medical officer. They sat in a pair of decrepit camp chairs in Postumus's office and drank bad wine together from the green glass cups that had been Licinius's commissioning gift to him, and Licinius filled in the gaps between letters from home.

Governor Lollius Urbicus was pushing the Selgovae hard to the north of Britain. He had opened up the Wall, and spanned the ditch that paralleled it with bridges broad enough for a cavalry troop to cross. The supply depot at Corstopitum south of the Wall was being enlarged, and the old fort of Trimontium in Valentia was a legionary base once more.

"Can we hold Valentia, do you think?" Postumus asked.

"Well, we couldn't the last time we tried it," Licinius said. "That's why they built the Wall. But it's caused more frontier problems than it's solved. It cuts right through some tribes' land. And we can't keep control beyond it. They're going to have their hands full reoccupying Trimontium."

"You and my father were there once, weren't you?" Postumus asked.

"Yes, the year before the rising. I remember the camp surgeon's office was filthy and half the drugs had been pilfered. I was going to make his life a burden to him for it – and they told me he'd gone Unlawful Absent a week since."

Postumus glanced at the dusty office with its collection of military trappings – standard issue supply chest and desk, records shelves, his instrument case with the Medical Corps insignia – all the things that made one military surgeon's office much like another the world over. Licinius's office in the legionary fort at Eburacum would have been a bit grander than this one, but still much the same.

"Will Urbicus make a peace that lasts this time?" Postumus asked.

"Maybe."

How many times had that question been asked on the edges of the Empire, including after the wreck of the

Ninth, when the Wall was built? It was supposed to be a permanent frontier.

"Apparently not everyone wants to walk in our footsteps." Postumus picked a small gnat out of his wine. "Why are we surprised by that every time?" His mother's people, for instance, who wouldn't let her come back to them. Her own mother might still be alive. He found that notion unutterably sad.

"Well, to be fair, I don't think we are," Licinius said. "That's the public line. Every empire claims it's all for the benefit of the people being ruled. It's the nature of man, I suppose, to justify what he wants. And there are, of course, a few times when it's true."

"In the long run, I suppose. After we've changed them in ways they can't undo. And how are the children? I should have asked sooner."

"Aurelia, as you may have noticed, is turning out to be a stunner and I am falling over her suitors daily, from the reasonable prospects to the utterly unsuitable. Felix is turning my hair gray as usual, but he has a miraculous hand with a horse. He can ride anything Neptune Equester ever put breath in."

Postumus remembered Felix as a carefree grin, curling dark hair like a faun's, some four years younger than himself. "I take it he's not militarily inclined?"

"He'd be cleaning latrines on half-pay within five minutes of joining the Army."

Postumus's amusement was cut short by shouting from outside.

"Surgeon Corvus!" A breathless cavalryman halted in the doorway, saluting briefly. "It's Sergius – kicked bad!"

"I told him that accursed horse would kill him!" Postumus pointed at the orderly, already hovering in the

33

doorway. "Get the surgery set up. And send someone with me to carry him!" He turned out the door with Licinius jogging at his heels, conversation forgotten.

Sergius lay facedown in a pool of his own blood just inside the schooling ring. A dun mare, wild-eyed and foam-flecked, trotted nervously back and forth at the far end of the ring with two wary cavalrymen in pursuit.

"Everyone from the commander on down warned you about that she-demon," Postumus murmured, turning the still form over, "but you wouldn't listen, would you?" He wiped the dirt from the boy's face. "Oh, Typhon!"

The dun mare's hoof had turned Sergius's face to a mangled wreck. His nose was flattened and twisted sideways, and one eye hung horribly from a bloody strand of tendon. A gaping cut ran from his temple to his chin. Postumus ran a hand down the boy's chest and winced again. There were three broken ribs, jagged and deadly, enclosing the fluttering lungs and the faintly beating heart. She had trampled him as well.

"Help me get him on the stretcher," he said to Licinius. "You've just been conscripted for the duration." And to the orderly and a white-faced cavalryman, "When you get to the surgery just put the whole thing on the table. Don't try getting him off again."

In the surgery, they set the stretcher on the operating table and pulled the poles from the pockets in its sides. Postumus cut Sergius's tunic off and wrapped his ribs, lifting him carefully and making as certain as he could that none of the organs had been punctured by a jagged end of rib bone. ("Lucky," Licinius said briefly.) Then they turned to the boy's shattered face.

"He's left his beauty under that devil's feet," Postumus murmured. "I'll be glad if we can save the eye." If they

34

couldn't he would be invalided out, Unfit for Service and half-blind in the bargain.

"Ever put an eye back?" he whispered to Licinius.

"No, but I know the principles involved. And I did it on a dog once."

"Wonderful."

Postumus worked as gently as he could, washing the dirt from the slashed face with vinegar and clamping the larger vessels to stop the bleeding.

"Ephedron," he said to the orderly and the man handed him a small vial. "I want to be able to see what I'm doing." He dusted the wound with the powder and the blood which seeped up from the smaller vessels began to slow.

Sergius's good eye fluttered open suddenly and he started to sit up.

"No!" Postumus held him down. "Lie still, it's all right."

The eye widened, panic-stricken, but he subsided.

"You have broken ribs. Don't move. And I have to work on your face, so you must lie still and not fight me. Can you swallow if I give you something to drink?"

The boy nodded, and Postumus carefully measured poppy into a cup of wine, added a curved metal straw, and held it to his lips.

Licinius watched as the boy managed to get it down. Like all painkillers, poppy was tricky stuff, and its results were erratic. It was also addictive, although less dangerous than henbane, providing it need only be administered once. Some surgeons held to the theory that pain was necessary to healing, and it was better to let the patient simply grit his teeth and endure. "That," Licinius had said once to Postumus, "is because they aren't doing the enduring, and they've never had a man die in their hands because he couldn't endure." The poppy that Postumus had given Sergius would not erase the agony of having his broken face repaired, but merely make it possible to bear it.

They waited while the drugged wine took its effect, and Postumus spoke softly to the boy, telling him what he was going to do. He nodded at the older man. "This is Gaius Licinius Lucanus, and he was the best surgeon in the Eagles. Can you be still for us, do you think?"

"Yes, sir." The boy licked his lips, and the fear in his eyes was apparent through the haze of poppy.

They worked slowly, searching for the right edge of the torn flesh to suture to the next one, while Sergius quivered in a cloud of poppy and pain. They shifted the broken nose gently to where it should be, and mercifully he fainted with the last movement of the nose before they had to tackle the eye. Postumus looked at it dubiously. He scanned the tray the orderly had set on the stand beside him, muttering, "We should be allowed to *learn*, not experiment on some poor bastard that's the first one to come our way." The orderly looked mildly shocked and Postumus snapped, "Get some more light over here!" He poured clean water over the eye, having no idea what vinegar might do to it, and selected the smallest forceps and a fine suturing needle with a length of human hair attached. Licinius also took a pair of forceps.

"Aesculapius help me. I should have gone into the cavalry." While the orderly adjusted the lamp stand and brought up another one, Postumus maneuvered the eye and the bloody mess it hung from slowly into position, praying silently as he did so, while Licinius kept the surrounding tissue retracted.

What seemed like eons later, he laid down the suturing needle and wiped his brow. "If this works," he said to Licinius, "and Charon ever asks me of what use I was in this world, I shall have something to tell him."

He nodded to the orderly to clear up, and gently spread a clean blanket over the sleeping form. "Get the stretcher poles back in and put him on a bed."

Licinius sailed the next week from Tyre with a string of Arab breeding stock, and Sergius survived with his eye intact, at least to all intents and purposes. It had an odd cast and if he couldn't actually see out of it, he didn't mention that. The last Postumus saw of him, as he left for a new hospital two months later, was his slight form, rope in hand, crooning softly to the murderous dun mare.

And then one spring day he ran in under a rain of enemy arrows to drag out a man whose life was ebbing away too fast to wait. For which Rome praised him, saluted him, fastened a Valorous Conduct around his arm, and named him senior Legionary Surgeon, assigned to the Sixth Legion Victrix at Eburacum.

IV. Rutupiae Light

"Wake up, sir! The troop's ready to ride and their decurion says if you're going with them you've got till he counts to two hundred."

Postumus opened one eye, and then the other, and focused reluctantly on the figure before him – a youthful orderly with jug ears and a worried expression. "You're a rude awakening," he murmured, running a hand through his hair and sitting up to feel with his bare feet on the floor for his sandals. Maybe he had said a bit too much goodbye the night before, sorting out how he actually felt about going home with a flagon of mid-level wine.

"How long, did you say?"

"Till he counts to two hundred, sir, that's what the decurion said, and he wasn't too happy about it."

"Go tell him that if he doesn't exercise a little more respect toward the Medical Corps, the Medical Corps will refuse to treat his saddle boils, and then his ass will fall off." Postumus splashed cold water from a pitcher over his face, and then with a grimace stripped off his undertunic and poured the rest of it down his body. He doubted that the decurion was actually counting. He rubbed himself dry, pulled on the undertunic and the scarlet folds of his uniform, shaking it carefully first, and the skirt of red leather strips that went under his lorica. He buckled the segmented plates of his lorica, knotted his sandals, which had somehow tangled their laces in the night, and strapped on greaves, groping for his belt and sword. The orderly found them and held them out, along with the plain, uncrested helmet of the Medical Corps. Postumus gingerly shook a scorpion out of his parade cloak, jabbed home the point of his cloak pin, adjusted his helmet and picked up his rolled-up kit. The fort optio would send his trunk along after him. It might even catch up to him before Saturnalia.

"Thank you." He nodded at the orderly. "Behave yourself and mind the new surgeon, and you'll rise to be emperor someday." He stepped blinking into the sun and regarded the cavalry troop outside his door with distaste. "Do I have time to take a piss, Naevius," he inquired, "or shall I just hold it until we get to Tyre?"

He didn't wait for an answer, left his kit on the ground and turned down the alley toward the latrine. When he returned, the kit had been strapped behind the rear saddle horns of a led horse and Decurion Naevius proffered the reins with a touch of malice. "Careful. He's a bit frisky, like."

The horse, a chestnut with a white blaze, rolled one demented eye and pawed the ground, and Postumus laughed. "I remember this one. He's the one you use to terrorize recruits. I'll be lucky if I can get him into a trot." He swung into the saddle and jabbed his heels into the chestnut's flanks. The horse slewed its head around and regarded him with surprise.

Naevius nodded and the man next to him raised a curved cavalry trumpet to his lips. It rang out clear against the morning air as the troop swung around at a trot, behind Naevius and the standard-bearer in a wolf's-head hood, the green silk of the troop's dragon banner snapping in the breeze of their own making. Postumus jabbed his heels authoritatively into the horse's flank and they swung down the Via Principia, drawing up with a flourish before the Principia itself to salute the cohort standards. The trumpet sang again and they clattered down the Via Praetoria and through the Praetorian Gate onto the Tyre road, helmet and harness catching the rising light. After a moment someone started to sing, a rude ditty about a tribune and his horse, to the rhythm of the hoofbeats on the road, and Postumus lifted his head and caught, faint on the wind, the sharp familiar scent of ocean.

–

The last leg home was aboard the liburnian *Nereid*, out of Gesoriacum on the Gaulish coast, and she pitched and rolled on the sort of malignant sea that often boiled up in the Channel in spring. Postumus watched as a huddled figure at the port railing moaned once and threw up his breakfast into the slimy green depths below.

"Is the bastard gonna pitch like this all way to Rutupiae?" the dripping figure inquired of the unsympathetic marine standing watch beside him in the rain beneath the reefed sail, and the marine shrugged.

"Like as not."

"Oh, Mother." The legionary closed his eyes to the heaving seas. "What do you do for the sickness?"

"Not much. You'll get used to it after ten or twelve trips."

Nereid heaved once more and the legionary abandoned further comment to clutch the railing. Postumus crossed his arms on the starboard rail, watching the approaching coastline and the wheeling shapes of the gulls. Their sharp thin cries made counterpoint to the hortator's mallets setting time below deck while the oars dipped and rose. There was much to be said for having grown up close enough to Sabrina Channel to have acquired his sea legs young, and he could have as easily gone below and out of the wet. But as the twin pharoi on the headlands at Dubris came into view through the rain, the pull of home kept him on deck. The sky began to clear and he could see Rutupiae Light rising in the distance. Rutupiae Light, and the beacon that had preceded it, had guided ships into harbor in Britain for a hundred years, ever since Claudius Caesar's time.

By the time *Nereid* came waddling into port, sidling her way between quinqueremes and triremes of the Fleet and harbor boats, the legionary had recovered somewhat although he was still the color of bad milk and his pale hair hung over his eyes like dispirited moss. *Nereid* backed her starboard oars to come alongside the jetty, and he jammed his helmet, adorned with a centurion's crosswise crest, onto his head.

"Where are you bound?" Postumus asked him as sailors in naval green let the plank down and they disembarked. A flock of gulls squawked and fought over the detritus on the docks. The air was heavy with the scent of pitch, and the noise of the naval yard where the masts of new ships rose like trees was deafening. Rutupiae was home port for a sizable portion of the Fleet.

"Eburacum, Sixth Victrix, Seventh Cohort," the centurion shouted over the noise. He introduced himself as Appius Paulinus. "If I live till tomorrow." He nodded at Postumus. "Surgeon?"

"Postumus Corvus, and bound for Eburacum too, once I visit my family."

"This is a home posting? Lucky you. Mine are at Moguntiacum. I got an hour with them on the way here. The new emperor seems to be stiffening up the troops in Britain. I was told to catch the next coastwise ship up to Eburacum." He winced. "I'd rather just go Unlawful Absent."

"There are bound to be troops going north you can ride with," Postumus said, taking pity on him. He looked as if the prospect of another sea journey would do him in. "Ask the port commander." He watched another ship, a cavalry transport, unloading hysterical horses onto the dock.

Beyond the port proper they passed beneath the Agricolan Arch that spanned the road northwestward to Londinium, adorned with marble facings and bronze statues of Julius Agricola and the Emperor Domitian, a commemoration of the victory at Mons Graupius and the campaign that had taken the north of Britain. For a while at least.

"You are now in the province of Britain," Postumus told him. "There are other ports, of course, but under Agricola's Arch is the official entrance."

"Don't suppose we'll get an arch for our efforts," Paulinus murmured.

"Doubtful. But you can have oysters – Rutupiae is famous for them." A man with a barrel of them in sea water was hawking his wares beside the road, and a sign on an inn wall advertised oyster stew, fresh raw oysters, and oyster fritters. The town beyond Agricola's Arch was a thriving bustle of inns and shops and housing for the port officers. Postumus pointed at a squat tile-roofed compound. "You'll probably find the port commander in there."

Paulinus saluted his thanks, fist to chest. "Until Eburacum," he said, looking marginally less morose at the thought of oysters.

–

The boar had been running since midday, through the scrub and woods of the wild hills, pursued by yelping hounds and men on foot and horseback. Galt, reining his horse slightly around a clump of thorn, thought that he would be brought to bay soon. He was nearly done. The High King's men and the warriors of Dawid's hold had taken it in turns to harry him, and now the king's men would bring him down, most likely with Bran at their front. Bran needed to kill something, Galt thought. He rode up beside the king, because he was still leader of the king's household, a heavy boar spear and two light throw-spears lashed to his saddle.

It was late in the long summer day, the shadows like fingers across the slate blue moorland below and a cloud of starlings undulating across the graying sky. Bran looked over his shoulder as Galt brought his horse up even with the king's. Bran's corn-colored hair was bound back with a braided leather thong and the gold torque around his neck gleamed dully in the slanting light. He rode easily on a roan pony, one hand clasping the boar spear, bound below the blade with strips of red leather and tied with hawk feathers.

"He will turn soon, I'm thinking," Galt said. A clean kill would take the king's restless mind off other things, perhaps, and they would move on to the next hold without a quarrel in Dawid's.

The boar crashed through the brush, snorting, foam-flecked now, with the riders crashing behind, the spearmen on foot abreast of them now, and the hounds circling, baying. Where an outcrop of stone and a lone contorted elm blocked the path, he turned. He was a thick, humpbacked beast, with vicious curving tusks. The king moved up to take him, Galt and his men behind him, spears in hand now. They went gingerly because there is always some price to be paid for a life, and with a boar the price was often uncertain.

The king leveled his spear and as he did a young hound streaked between the ponies' hooves, his master shouting after him. Dawid's gray stumbled on a stone, staggered against the king's man Rhys and Rhys went down in the trampled brush and last year's leaves. The boar fixed its eyes on him. Rhys tried to get up and his ankle folded under him.

The hounds held the boar back, barely, until the hunters could close around Rhys. The ground was uneven, studded with stones and fallen branches of the elm. The boar feinted left and right, uncertain, exhausted and furious. The air was rank with its scent. The king drove his spear into its right flank and it staggered left, gathered its haunches under it and charged at the closest of its tormentors. Galt's spear went into its ribs at the same time that the boar's weight took him off his horse and its tusk went into his right thigh, halfway up its length before the boar fell away and lay bloody and twitching in the leaves.

–

They brought him back to Dawid's hold riding double, clinging to Dawid and blood dripping from the rag tied around the wound. Dawid's wife Brica cleaned the wound and said firmly that they were to send for the High Priest. "I have washed this out, but it needs more than that. I don't like the way it goes in so deep. I want Talhaiere."

Galt, gritting his teeth, didn't argue with her, as he had no intention of being a hunt sacrifice just now, and so one of Dawid's human hounds, the boys of his clan who were in warrior training, was sent with Dawid's best chariot team to the king's hold for Talhaiere while the king paced.

"You could leave me," Galt said. "Dawid was my fosterling. I will do as well here."

"That is not fitting. I do not leave the chief of my household. These are Council matters that we talk of with the clan chiefs."

Galt was silent. They would all say, *What does Galt think?* He knew that, and the king wouldn't like it, particularly not when the issue was the Romans at the fort of the Eagles to the south. "Talhaiere is ancient," he murmured. "He will take days to get here, even in a chariot, and complaining all the way."

"Nonetheless," Bran said.

"And what's more," Brica said, fussing over him when Bran had gone, "you need bathing. You smell like the boar. I will do that since you haven't ever had the sense to marry." She rolled up the woolen sleeves of her gown and took the thong out of his pale hair. "We'll wash this too, since you're so proud of it."

Galt smiled. He was accounted the best warrior in the tribe still, and so could afford to be vain. His hair and mustache he bleached regularly to white gold and his taste for jewelry was legendary. "There was a reason for that," he said, "that I didn't marry, that there be no temptation not to give over power when the king was of age. And how is Rhys?"

"He has sprained that ankle, I think, but it will mend well." She paused.

"I, on the other hand?" Galt said.

"I have asked the Mother and the Sun Lord both," Brica said. "But we need Talhaiere."

When she had left him, washed as well as she could with a basin and a clean cloth, and with a bandage over the thigh wound, he lay back on the bed in his chamber and thought. This room in Dawid's hold had been Galt's since Dawid was of age, furnished for him and kept for his visits alone. It was pleasant here, more of a home than his own holding or the High King's. He moved his right leg a little, to see how much more that made it hurt. A lot. But he hadn't been killed outright so it wasn't his fate but only bad luck. A man making the hunt sacrifice knew what he was doing, and his death bought something. Galt had thought of it once, when the drought went on and on and there was sickness and the children began to die. But he had been regent then, and held that power for the clans of the Brigantes. Now the power was given over to Bran, with the King Mark on his brow, and if Galt had died when Bran was small, Bran might not have survived to be king, and so he had weighed the choice and made his decision. It hadn't been an easy one.

Galt lay back and closed his eyes and put certain memories away as he had taught himself to do.

–

It was late at night and a pale moon rode just above the trees by the time Postumus turned his horse through the

46

stone gates of the family farm and set him at a trot up the road toward the house. The horse, a livery animal exchanged for his previous one at Aquae Sulis, caught scent of the other horses in the barn and lifted his head in a whinny. Where there were horses there would be grain and all stables were home to him. Postumus had thought of staying the night in a comfortable bed in Venta and pushing on the next day, but southern roads were safe enough even at night and after he had persuaded a grumbling ferryman to take him across the Sabrina to Venta in the dusk, he had ridden on from there. A light flared up outside the darkened house and then bobbed through the inner gate and steadied as a cloaked figure hung it on a nail in the gate post.

"Papa?"

The figure at the gate paused to sheathe a businesslike short sword, all too visible in the lamplight, and Postumus chuckled.

"I'm not a sea raider."

"I was thinking more of a fox in my henhouse," Hilarion said. "But you're more welcome than either. You didn't tell us you had leave."

"The letter would have got here when I did." Postumus slid from the saddle and dropped his voice as they walked toward the barn. "It's not leave, exactly."

"I do presume you haven't gone Unlawful Absent?" his stepfather inquired.

"No, of course not. I'm posted here. Promoted, too." He stripped off the saddle and set about rubbing the horse down while Hilarion took a bucket to the grain sacks stacked against the wall. He emptied a measure in the livery horse's manger, and his own animals stuck their heads over the loose box doors and whickered hopefully.

"That's gratifying," Hilarion said as he returned the bucket to its hook. "What's your posting?"

"Senior Legionary Surgeon. Eburacum." Postumus waved his right arm at his stepfather so that the silver bracelet caught the light and then, pick in hand, concentrated on the horse's off rear hoof.

Hilarion took the bucket off the wall, turned it over, and sat on it. "Congratulations. I know that was well earned." He was clad in an undertunic and an old and much-patched military cloak, his graying hair tangled about his ears.

"It's why I didn't write," Postumus said. "It didn't seem the news for a letter."

"The Army was never known for its sensitivity."

Postumus snorted a half-laugh at that. "It was an honor," he said ruefully. "I really don't think they knew."

"Maybe not," Hilarion said. "Once they got through rerouting Justin's career into the auxiliaries. They've tried hard enough to forget us. Bureaucracy so often depends on the bureaucrat. Someone retires and the next man doesn't know because no one talks about it, so he doesn't bother to check your name against the roster of the Ninth. If it's even in existence." Hilarion studied him. "Have you ever been to Eburacum?"

"No."

"I didn't think so. We've avoided even setting foot in it, all of us – your mother and Licinius and Felicia and me. Maybe it's just as well you're posted there. It'll lay a few ghosts to rest for the lot of us. And maybe answer a few questions of your own." He stood up and dropped a hand on Postumus's shoulder. "Come along. Your mother will be thinking it was sea raiders after all. Let's go and gratify her maternal heart with the V.C. *Then* you can tell her about the posting."

They picked their way across the moonlit terraces and through the shadowed kitchen garden to the house. As they came into the atrium, Gwytha appeared in the corridor opposite, a lamp in one hand, brushing the sleep from her eyes with the other. She held the lamp toward them. "J-Justin?" The moonlight through the atrium skylight washed her face with silver.

"No, darling, it's me." Postumus came forward and took the lamp, which was in danger of spilling, and kissed her on the cheek.

"Postumus dear." She smiled at him sleepily. "I am sorry. But you're very alike in the dark… and I wasn't expecting you home." Justin was also stationed out of Britain, and Postumus wondered briefly if it was really his brother that she had mistaken him for. In any case, she seemed awake enough now, and she slipped an arm about each of them, drawing them back down the corridor with her to the chamber she shared with Hilarion. She climbed back onto the bed and sat with Hilarion's faded red military cloak about her shoulders while Postumus stretched himself out in a chair by the brazier and Hilarion set about warming three flasks of wine.

There were wide bands of gray in Gwytha's chestnut hair, over the temples and in the braids that hung past her shoulders, and her face was marked with the lines that the birth of four children had left on it, but she was still beautiful, he thought. Her eyes were the clear bright blue of a summer pond, and her skin a soft buttermilk white that even Aunt Felicia couldn't match. She smiled at him across the bedcovers as Hilarion handed each of them a flask of hot wine. "If you're going to try to tell me you were sent home in disgrace, I think I should mention I saw the V.C. when you kissed me," she said affectionately. "We're very proud of you, darling. How did you get it?"

Postumus explained with as much modesty as he could muster while they nodded approvingly. "The only fly in the wine cup," he murmured, peering into his own, "is the posting. I've been shipped home, Mama. To the Sixth."

He saw a sort of shadow slide across her face, but only briefly. "To what rank?" she asked.

"Senior surgeon," he said. "Strange. I'll have Licinius's old hospital."

She sighed and drew Hilarion down on the bed beside her, her head resting on his shoulder. "You must go over and tell Licinius in the morning," she said, and then the talk turned to other things, the new crop of lambs, and the need to mend a wall in the lower pasture, how Justin did with his cavalry troop and how he had had another promotion too, and Marcus's plan for raising goats, which everyone else in the household regarded as a dubious idea, and how best to spend the precious ten days left of Postumus's leave. No one mentioned Eburacum or the war that Governor Urbicus was fighting in the north. Time enough for it later. Homecomings in an Army family were brief and precious.

Contrary to his expectations, Postumus slept well into the morning in the room he had shared with Justin from boyhood. When he arose in search of breakfast, and to pay his respects at the shrine of the household gods, he found Marcus coming in from the pasture with sheep on his mind and fire in his eye because a herdsman had let three of the fools stray and the wolves had been out and about this year.

"Which means I've got to go tramping all over Lower Hades looking for them," he said disgustedly while the mottled brown hound at his heel waved his tail happily at the prospect. "Hello, Postumus, it's good to see you." He gave him a brotherly hug. "What do you mean, skulking home in the middle of the night? Come out with me tomorrow after you've done the polite with the family, and take the rust off your hunting spear. We're going to have to put the fear of the gods in that wolf pack or we won't have a lamb left. Oh, and congratulations," he added. "Mother told me about the V.C. See you at dinner no doubt, if I'm not still counting sheep." He snapped his fingers to the dog and headed for the kitchen in search of a portable lunch.

Marcus was an anomaly in a family that went back generations in service with the Eagles, and it was probably just as well. A farm never prospered without the land-holder there to take the reins. Postumus suspected that all that had saved the place in the beginning had been his mother, a woman strong-minded enough to cope with crises as they came, and British-born. But she had had no more knowledge of farming than Hilarion at the start, and it had been touch-and-go for a while. Fortunately, as Marcus got older, it had become obvious that this farm was bred in his bones in the way that the Army was in Justin's, and the place had begun to prosper as soon as he was old enough to take charge.

Postumus foraged in the kitchen for a breakfast of honey cake, kissed his mother, got under the feet of the cook who was masterminding that night's celebratory dinner on short notice, and stopped to pay his respects to Januaria where she was sewing winter leggings for someone in a chair in the courtyard. Constantia, who had also heard the news, came up from the henhouse and hurled herself at him in an undignified fashion and then had to put her hair up again. "I'm to help with dinner," she said, a red chicken feather drifting about her ears. "Cook is having a spell over the sauces." She trotted off toward the kitchen.

From there Postumus set out across the meadow that marked the boundary between their land and Licinius's. It was a glory of a day, the meadow painted with daisies and buttercups and springy with grasshoppers zinging from under his feet. A lark wheeled in loud, joyous acrobatics on the updraft above him. He remembered carrying eggs through the meadow on the day he had helped Licinius deliver the foal. If people had individual days they would remember forever, he thought that was one of his, more than the day he had rescued the tribune and earned a Valorous Conduct. The foal seemed far more valuable to him than the tribune. It was like a second homecoming to top the rise on the far side of the meadow and see the white lines and red tiled roof of Licinius's house bright against the valley floor. Aunt Felicia was in her vegetable garden on the edge of the apple orchard, shelling peas into a bowl in her lap. She handed the bowl to a boy pruning shrubbery when she saw Postumus and said, "Take this to the kitchen and then tell Master that Surgeon Corvus is here!"

The air was clouded with the scent that drifted from her rose garden and she had tucked a knot of them into her black hair. Postumus complimented the effect as he kissed her.

"Aurelia will be glad to see you," she said as Licinius and his daughter appeared. Aurelia had the delicate grace of a flower carved from onyx and ivory, in a grass-green gown, and Postumus inspected her with pleasure. "No wonder Licinius is worried. You'd better marry her off fast before she starts a riot."

Aurelia laughed and hugged him, and Felicia looked at him hopefully – she liked Postumus – but it was obvious that his admiration was mostly aesthetic. He patted Aurelia on the cheek, ruffled her dark curls, and turned away to greet Licinius.

In his surgery office, Licinius handed Postumus a cup of wine, leaned back in his chair and observed the Valorous Conduct with the flick of one raised brow.

"Are you going to tell me about it or does modesty prevail?"

"Not in the least. I was heroic, I can tell you," Postumus said. "Killed fifty of 'em with my bare hands. Actually, I hauled a tribune out of a bad spot because he looked like he'd be dead before his troops finished fighting their way out of the mess he got them into in the first place. I got a home posting, a V.C., and this." He exhibited the healing puncture in his arm. On nights when he couldn't sleep, Postumus could feel the whirr in the air as the arrows went past his ears and the unpleasantly gelatinous feel to the tribune's leg as he dragged him from under the horse.

"Useful to have a tribune pleased with you, all the same," Licinius said.

It was clear to Licinius that over the past years, like all the rest of his kind before him, Postumus had left his youth on a surgery table. But when Postumus said, with an odd inflection in his voice, "I got more out of it than a nice shiny bracelet, too – Senior Legionary Surgeon, or I will be when my leave's up."

Licinius looked at him suspiciously. "What aren't you telling me?"

"Sixth Victrix," Postumus said briefly, and Licinius said, "Oh, Typhon," and after that there wasn't much else to say, so they drank another three cups of wine each while Licinius harkened to whatever ghosts fluttered at his ear, and Postumus solemnly contemplated his own achievement in gaining senior rank at an earlier age than most men came by it, and thereby plunging everyone else into a nightmare of remembrance. He was one step shy of a fine state of self-pity when Licinius looked up and said with some surprise, "D'you know how long it's been since I really tied one on? Gives you a sort of perspective. Come along, let's go and get sober and I'll give you the run-down on Eburacum. The Sixth is a good legion. One to build a loyalty to. They just should have sent it to us sooner."

Felicia, pottering among the new lettuce in the kitchen garden, was startled to see two figures weaving unsteadily through the onion beds, and to hear her husband's voice, off key but enthusiastic, raised in a tune she remembered dimly across the years.

Come you bold fellows and join the Ar-mee,
To slaughter the Pict and the heathen Parsee,
And maybe, just maybe (the chances are small)
But maybe you'll rise to be emperor of all!

Roma, far Roma, we list to your call,
Townsmen of Italy and farmers from Gaul,
We've bought you an Empire from Britain to Crete,
With the boils on our backsides and the sores on our feet.

Some of us turn home with twenty years' pay.
At the end of the long march and — some of us stay.

So when you have climbed to the emperor's throne,
Remember the Eagles who'll never fly home.

–

Into the next ten days Postumus put all the home-coming he hadn't had in four years. He hunted wolves and counted lambs with Marcus, talked late into the night with his parents, lounging beside the pool in the atrium, and coped with the everyday crises of country life with Licinius in the surgery. Tired of the mounts assigned him by the Army, which inevitably turned out to be iron-mouthed and rattle-gaited specimens that the cavalry troopers didn't want, he bargained for a horse from Licinius's stock, a red roan named Boreas.

On his last night they dined with Licinius and Felicia, setting out in the gold-washed light of a summer dusk and returning in full dark to the bob and swing of lantern light and the call of a nightjar somewhere in the meadow.

There was another guest that night, Claudia Silva, a woman of about Postumus's own age, the widow of, and now successor to, a dealer in architectural and landscaping supplies. She had come from Lindum personally to super-vise delivery of Licinius's birthday gift to his wife, a half dozen rare rose bushes. As her firm also supplied the army of Governor Urbicus with the little building material that wasn't legionary-made, the talk turned naturally to the campaign in the north.

"So we open up the old wall for the building of the new," Hilarion said. Governor Urbicus was stringing a series of frontier forts across his new lines from Credigone in the east to the mouth of the Clota in the west. The wall which would join them would complete the fencing-in of Valentia.

"That still leaves the Picts on the far side," Gwytha said. "And the Painted People have never paid much heed to a wall. Will it hold?"

"I think it can," Claudia Silva said as Theodore passed a plate of small pastries. She took one and bit into it appreciatively. "These are lovely. The forts will be closer together than the southern wall – no more than two miles, and with no other gates between. Also it will be shorter, almost by half."

She had evidently accompanied her own supplies on at least some of their journey north and Postumus pricked up his ears. He would be posted wherever the bulk of his legion went, and right now that would mean the northern lines. He took a better look at the visitor.

Claudia wore her dark hair pulled up into a plain knot at the back of her head, a severe style that accented the fine bones of her face. Her rust-colored gown was of good material but of a plain style suitable for traveling, while one of the finest rubies Postumus had seen gleamed on the finger of her right hand, dark as the wine in her cup. She was handsome enough, although in the same room with Aurelia's flower-petal beauty and Constantia's urgent vitality, no one was likely to notice. There was an observant look in her blue-green eyes, and self-assurance in her low voice. She looked, Postumus decided, like someone who knew what she was doing. At the moment she was engaged in kindly squelching Felix, who was making flamboyant overtures to her while his father watched with mounting irritation. Felix was obviously merely stirring things up for his own amusement, and Theodore paused to fix him with a knife-like glare. Postumus heard Constantia whisper, "Shut up, you ass!" and Felix subsided with a grin. Claudia appeared unruffled.

"Do you go north often?" Postumus asked her. "What is the talk in Valentia? I'm posted to the Sixth Victrix, but I've been out of Britain so long…"

"Half the rebels in Valentia appear have taken refuge with the Picts, to bide their time," she said. "They can strike when it suits them, from there, you see. They've lost more men in the building camps than I like to think about."

"And the Selgovae who are left?"

"They stay to harry the Army's back in the hope that the rest of the tribes will rise behind them," Claudia said. "No one travels in Valentia unguarded even now."

"Why do you go then, if it's that dangerous?" Aurelia asked.

Claudia was silent a moment, polishing off her pastry and licking her fingers. Thinking, Postumus decided.

"The trade prospers when I keep an eye on it," she said finally. She stretched out her hand for a peach from the silver bowl that Theodore presented and took one of the small knives that were offered.

Interesting, Postumus thought, watching her peel it with quick graceful movements. *And what do you know that you aren't saying?*

The subject dropped as the wine and water pitchers came around again and the mood lightened to the silliness of a family gathering. Constantia presented him with a wreath of privet and guelder rose from the hedgerow, which he wore rakishly over one eye, and Aurelia also made much of him, questioning him eagerly about Army life and demanding to know when Justin would also be coming home.

It had been a fine leave, he thought, as the family rode home by lantern light, even if Aurelia's attentions had been largely motivated by the hope of news of Justin. He wondered if Justin had any idea. He doubted it.

V. Eburacum Fortress

In the morning he was back to the Army again, trotting out of Isca on Boreas's back with a troop of auxiliary cavalry bound for the troubles in Valentia. Six days later, they left him at the Praetorian Gate of Eburacum Fortress with a mocking salute of cavalry horns (embarrassing the regular legions was one of the cavalry's main amusements) and were on their way with a flourish and a cloud of dust. Postumus sheepishly gave his name to the grinning sentries and headed for the Principia to report. All Roman camps, from single cohort frontier posts to stone-built monsters like Eburacum, housing a full ten cohorts of 480 men each and their attached auxiliaries, were laid out on the same grid, so that no soldier was ever lost in an unfamiliar camp at night. A marching camp could be built in an afternoon and dismantled as easily next morning, but the pattern remained. In Eburacum, sprawled over some fifty acres of granaries, drill field, armorer's shed, hospital, and baths, the pattern formed a city in itself. All it required from the town that lay beneath its walls on the banks of the adjacent rivers were the amusements of its off-duty hours – wine stalls and fishmongers, shops peddling love potions and cure-alls or liniment for aching muscles, unofficial "married quarters", and temples to gods imported from every outpost in the Empire. It had been settled long enough that the six roads that converged there were lined with cemeteries. Roman law decreed that the dead be laid outside inhabited areas and their grave markers stood like milestones, not of distance but of time.

Eburacum was a beautifully kept up fort, obviously a legion's pride. All the streets were swept and the plaster freshly whitened. But the fortress had a hollow feel to it and the orderly streets were nearly deserted.

Postumus stopped outside the Principia, the legionary headquarters, to salute the standards. The Eagle of the Sixth Victrix loomed over him, its great gilded wings outstretched. It perched on crossed thunderbolts with the legion's honors hung on the staff below it. There were only three other standards, he noted – the personal banner of Aelius Silanus, Legate of the Sixth, and two cohort standards. A cavalry wing banner flapped beside them.

Inside he saluted again and handed his orders to the optio who passed him on to the legate, a spare brisk man with a brush of graying hair mashed sideways by the helmet he had apparently just removed. He inspected them and said, "I hear you are British-born. That makes this a home posting. Most men don't make that privilege so young. Or Legionary Surgeon either. Well, Corvus, I hope you live up to your reputation."

"So do I, sir." Aelius Silanus looked like someone who would let you know, painfully, if you didn't.

"In that case," Silanus said, "please present yourself to the surgery and see what state your predecessor has left it in. You've a pair of junior surgeons here, but one of them needs to be posted to the wall camps, whichever you think, and you will be too, shortly." The legate nodded his dismissal and Postumus saluted, fist to breastplate, and left.

The hospital sat to the left of the Principia, and by the time Postumus arrived at its imposing columned entrance, nearly as grand as the Principia's, the hospital optio was waiting for him. "I'm glad to see you, sir. We're having a bit of trouble."

"Oh?" And of course, on his first day.

"Nothing young Lucian can't handle, I expect, but a senior hand would be welcome."

The optio led him down the interior corridor to the sounds of voices. A harassed young man with a thin, intelligent face and the insignia of a junior surgeon stood facing a belligerent legionary across an examining table, while a trio of soldiers in the corridor were apparently making book on the outcome.

"Is there some difficulty?" Postumus inquired. "I'm the new senior surgeon," he added as the legionary fixed him with an irritable stare. "I've just arrived."

"Well, Typhon take you and the donkey that got you here," the legionary said and returned to his confrontation.

Lucian cast an exasperated glance at Postumus. "He passed out on the parade ground in the middle of drill. I wish you'd listen to his chest, sir. I've checked him three times at three-day intervals, and I hear the same thing every time."

"You couldn't check your own ass with both hands!" the legionary exploded.

"You shut up," Postumus said. "I'll deal with you in a minute." He turned to Lucian. "What are you hearing? Heart flutter?"

Lucian nodded.

"This bastard wants to certify me Unfit for Service. With ten years behind me! It was the heat, that's all. Or something I ate, maybe."

Postumus was sympathetic. The pension for a solider invalided out was only a fraction of what he would receive as a time-expired man. But someone who passed out at drill had no place in a cohort. Too many other lives depended on it. "What's your name?"

"Tertius." The legionary glared at him. He was a wiry man, and battle scarred, with mouse-colored hair and a missing front tooth.

"That's 'Tertius, *sir*,'" Postumus said. "Very well, Tertius, have you been having any chest pains? Sweating?"

"Course I been sweating. We've been drilling, haven't we?"

"Chest pains?"

"Something I ate, I told you."

"Right. Now do me a dozen fast push-ups and then stand still and behave yourself." Postumus could hear the odds being adjusted in the doorway behind him.

When Tertius stood up, panting, Postumus sat him on the examining table and pressed his ear against the man's chest. The skin felt wet and clammy. And yes, there it was: a wildly erratic beat intruding itself every few seconds, and the lungs rattled with edema. Postumus sighed. No one knew what caused that, or exactly what it did, but when a patient had it, the results weren't good. He wished once again for a magical window through the chest wall.

"I'm sorry, Tertius, but I'm going to have to certify. I agree with Lucian. You must have known something was wrong."

"The gods damn you both," Tertius said bitterly. "What does that leave me now?"

"Have you thought of applying for non-combat status? The Medical Corps has always needed more orderlies than it can get," Postumus added, with some reluctance because

Tertius would undoubtedly be a pain in the ass. He might fall down dead tomorrow or he might live for years, but either way he wouldn't endanger a whole cohort.

Tertius looked as if he was about to spit. "I'm a soldier! What do orderlies do – slop about with a bucket, washing things!"

"They knock people like you down and sit on them when I tell them to," Postumus said, and an orderly across the room nodded appreciatively.

"I'm not that desperate yet." Tertius glared around the room. "I didn't sign on as a nursemaid. There's the arena, isn't there? The frontier towns aren't choosy. I ought to be good for a few turns, and a present now and then from the ladies."

"Don't be a fool. If you're careful with yourself, you'll do much better."

"I was a fool when I joined up," Tertius said, and strode out.

Postumus whirled on the three bookmakers in the doorway. "Get yourselves out!" he snapped.

Lucian dropped into a chair. "Thank you, sir," he said wearily. "I've never been so glad to see anyone. I just didn't seem to make any headway with him. It was like talking to a bad-tempered rock. And I did feel for him."

Postumus sighed. "That sort of thing never comes easy. Don't blame yourself. We'll just hope he doesn't do anything stupid."

"What else is there that he *can* do?" Lucian inquired.

Postumus was silent. The invalid's pension had always been criminally low – even for Licinius, and he'd had senior surgeon's rank. For a rank-and-file man it wouldn't even be subsistence level. "The patients that die aren't the only ones you lose," he said. They contemplated that morosely, listening to Tertius shouting furiously in the street, until Postumus said, "Well, you may as well show me the place."

With Lucian he inspected the wards and well-stocked dispensary, the surgery, the smaller examining rooms, the sunny inner courtyard, and the office that would be his. Lucian hastily swept his possessions off the desk into the corner of his cloak.

"We weren't quite sure when you'd arrive, sir," he apologized. "The old surgeon left two months ago. He was retiring and felt no great need to hang about, since Gemellus and I were here. Gemellus is your other junior."

"You seem rather short of patients at the moment anyway."

"Most of the legion's in the north with Governor Urbicus," Lucian said. "You've two apprentices and another junior surgeon up there with Urbicus's field hospital. I expect they'll send you on up too, with the legate. He's only here for a few days to let the local tribes know he still has his eye on them."

Postumus supposed that Appius Paulinus had been sent on his way north to the Seventh Cohort already. He would wait until he had met Gemellus before deciding which of the juniors to take with him. When Lucian had gone, he leaned back in the chair and propped his legs up on the desk. He might as well enjoy Eburacum's comforts while he could. The legionary hospital of the Sixth Victrix was impressive. The walls were spotless and each room displayed the legion's badge, a charging bull, over its door, presumably to encourage the patients to get up and get going again. The dispensary was organized, the medicines were fresh, and there were bunches of herbs hanging in the drying room that could only have been gathered yesterday and argued for the presence of an excellent hospital garden somewhere. The little shrine to Aesculapius in the courtyard had been well kept. Lucian was evidently a conscientious sort, with an inquiring mind – there had been a jumble of notes on native plants and their possible uses among the clutter he had removed from the desk.

The surgeon's office walls were whitewashed and the desk had been freshly sanded and oiled, but along the edge Postumus noticed a series of small nicks such as might have been made by a fingernail – a habit of Licinius's when he was thinking some problem out. So this had been his desk. There was still a ghost or two in the shining modern fortress that the Sixth had made of Eburacum.

He swung his legs off the desk and began to prowl, looking for... well, looking for what? For some trace of the old inhabitants, of a dead legion? He stopped. Well, maybe he'd better not find it, if it was there. He turned instead for the main surgery, collected his kit, and set off for the housing block that Lucian told him held the senior surgeon's quarters.

Outside, he could hear the sounds of an armorer's hammer, a distant cavalry drill, and a centurion barking orders to what few troops were left on the parade ground. A wagon full of grain was coming in through the Praetorian Gate, unloaded from the supply ships that came upriver from the corn country of the Iceni to the south.

Like most of the native-born, Postumus was multilingual, and the voices of the unloading crew on the dock floated over the fortress walls. He realized with a small shock that this was the dialect that his mother had spoken to him in his earliest memories. On impulse, he mounted the steps to the south tower and stood, arms crossed, on the parapet, face-to-face with yet another unknown side of himself. The cadence of her speech had never matched that of West Britain and now he knew why. These were her people, the other half of him.

He leaned on the parapet, absorbed in the prospect below him, until the last of the ship's hold had been unloaded of grain and clay amphorae of wine and oil and olives, and the cut brush that cushioned them. The members of the crew who had leave scattered into the town in pursuit of amusement while the remainder, under the hawklike eye of the captain, marched sullenly back on board to take up their posts. A flock of gulls squabbled over their leavings. The captain was most likely an ex-officer of the Fleet and knew better than to leave any ship of his small flotilla unguarded so close to a town, or worse yet, an Army post. On deck, the watch crew began to sing. It was in his mother's dialect and Postumus tried to follow the words, something about a sailor and a mermaid.

He jumped as he discovered that a dark man in the scale armor of the cavalry, who apparently moved exceedingly quietly, now leaned on the parapet beside him, and followed along a scant half-beat behind the singer in the ship. A half dozen decorations were strung on a leather strap across his chest, including the golden oak leaves of the Corona Civica, awarded for saving the life of a fellow citizen. A commander's helmet was tucked under his arm.

"Don't mind me, young Aesculapius," he said to Postumus. "Although I'll take myself to the other side of the gate if it gets on your nerves. It's a way to learn a tune when you happen on a good one."

"I don't mind," Postumus said. "I was just wondering how you did it."

"It's easy enough once you have the hang of it," the cavalry commander said unhelpfully. He resumed his song almost in mid-beat. When the melody ended, he turned to Postumus and sketched a half-salute. "Thank you for putting up with me. That's a fine song. Something to keeps the lads amused of a night, and out of trouble."

Postumus laughed. "If you can keep a cavalryman out of trouble with a song, you have godlike powers."

"Well, the Dacians are a cocky lot and like to make a noise. One way or the other." He smiled and settled himself on the edge of the wall, tossing his cloak back from his shoulders. "My name's Valerian. Third Wing, Dacian Horse. And you'll be the new surgeon, I'm thinking." He eyed the twin snakes of Aesculapius on the surgeon's belt buckle. "Bit young, aren't you?"

"Getting older all the time," Postumus said.

"Well, you'll be an improvement on old Fabius. Could barely see his hands in front of his face at the end, I thought. Made the lads a bit nervous in surgery. Now he's off to Aquae Sulis to spend his declining years and give learned advice and pot up skin cream for the magistrates' wives."

Postumus, mentally shuddering, thought that Licinius had made the better choice, and he would keep that in mind himself. "Retirement comes to us all. Or do you still plan to be leading a cavalry wing in, what, ten years?"

"Me, I plan on being emperor by then." Valerian hopped down from the wall. "Have you seen the place yet? It's impressive. Come along and I'll take you round. Only five sesterces for a tour of the famous monuments."

Postumus followed him down the tower stairs while the cavalry commander chatted over his shoulder. "We'll be off again next week. The governor's had me pulling my lads out of most of the forts hereabouts for the better part of a month. I hope the Brigantes stay quiet – we've left half the forts in their hills naked. I've got a few days rest-and-repair in Eburacum to knock them together into a good wing again, and then we're off north to keep the Picts out of the builders' hair. It looks like we may winter there too, may the Shining One help us. Valentia has too much rain, bad inns, and goblins, or so I'm told. I don't know what the governor wants with it."

"Peace?" Postumus suggested.

"We'd have that if we'd stuck to the old wall. Probably political mostly, as most things are. He's already declared himself Imperator and had the coin struck."

Postumus laughed. "Yes, my sister sent me one for good luck. I expect he needs a military credit with an imperial salutation to satisfy the Senate. I've heard he's a bit of a homebody."

"I'd say that's to the good if he leaves the campaign to the generals," Valerian said.

"The problem with that is that then the generals get to thinking they might be emperor. As you mentioned."

They paused at the foot of the stairs while a cavalry troop clattered past, stopping in some confusion to salute their commander.

"Very nice," Valerian commented. "Except for the fool in the rear rank with his helmet off."

The decurion of the troop whirled around with an awful eye and the offender hastily jammed his helmet on his head.

"See that he wears it to bathe in for the next few days, Decurion," Valerian said. "It will serve to fix the idea in his mind." The troop saluted and moved on, the unfortunate cavalryman brick red under the offending helmet.

Valerian turned back to Postumus. "I expect you'll want to dump that kit first thing," he said. "The surgeon's quarters are quite luxurious, thanks to old Fabius."

The cavalry commander proved to be right. The senior surgeon's quarters consisted of a pleasant suite of lime-washed rooms with hunting scenes painted on the office walls, where Postumus found his luggage from Syria, miraculously delivered, along with another desk and a leather-covered records chest. An apple orchard and an enthusiastic gathering of nymphs and fauns adorned the bedroom. The southeast window cast a slanting light on a decent bed and a clothes chest.

The third room Fabius had used as a study. He had apparently laid out a good sum of his own money to improve on the Spartan surroundings considered suitable by the Army. One wall here was painted with Europa in a thoroughly diaphanous gown, being carried off by Jupiter in the form of a bull, and a second had been fitted with shelves for scrolls and manuscripts. The study chair must have been the old surgeon's personal property, as it was nowhere to be seen, but Valerian obligingly filched one from the unguarded room of a cohort centurion currently in the north. He settled himself in it while Postumus unpacked his belongings, and they made the interesting discovery that they were both native-born.

Valerian, wiry and dark with flying black brows and the heavily muscled legs of a horseman, came from the Silures and had partly grown up near Isca, the usual mixture of an Army father and a native mother.

"I've been back about a year," he said. "I spent most of my time holding up the emperor's honor in Dacia with a couple of troops of Asturian Horse. When the troubles started up north, I called in a few favors and told them all what a prize I'd be to the Dacian Horse out here, being fluent in British *and* Dacian. I didn't ask for a wing command, but my speech impressed them so much they gave me one anyway." He grinned at Postumus. "Or they were just getting desperate."

Postumus, eyeing the Corona Civica, decided that the command must have been long overdue.

"Turned out to be a good thing," Valerian said. "The last Wing Commander hadn't troubled himself to learn any Dacian, figuring he could leave that to the decurions. And of course the men had enough Latin between them to say 'payday' and 'woman'. He must have had a bit of trouble rallying the troops and it showed by the time I got them. But they're coming along nicely now. I scared the liver out of them when I chewed them out in Dacian." He smiled reminiscently, and then fixed his curious gaze on Postumus. "What about you? To look at you, I'd say you had 'Centuriate' written on your forehead."

Postumus weighed his dog-eared copy of Dioscorides's *Herbal*, trying to decide whether it would be of more use here where he would have the leisure to read it, or in the surgery where he was more likely to need it… and to decide how much to say. Finally, he said, "That's my brother Justin. He has a regiment of Thracian cavalry. I was inclined to medicine myself, probably because I had an uncle who was a surgeon. He let me help him when he retired and went into village practice."

"Do you know," Valerian said, and Postumus couldn't tell whether he thought that was the whole story or not, "I've watched a good surgeon work, and it strikes me that there might be more to knowing what's wrong with a man, and seeing your way to fixing it, than there is to hacking a hole in him for his own surgeons to put right."

"Don't overestimate us," Postumus said. He folded his spare dress tunic and laid it in the clothes chest in the next room. "We can close wounds, but we don't know what else is going on inside a man most of the time, and if he dies his shade can't tell us. A lot of knowledge goes up in the smoke of a burned corpse."

"I suppose that's an unholy opinion, but I can't disagree," Valerian said. "I don't see how it's all right to kill them but not to look inside afterwards. My maternal grandfather had a whole pile of his enemies' skulls stacked up like so many melons in his hall. And nothing fearsome happened to him as a result, except maybe for the skulls' relatives now and again. And the Egyptians, now, they hadn't any such laws until we came along and they know more about anatomy than anyone."

"Of course, they're still prescribing fried mice for a toothache," Postumus said. That had been one of the more esoteric remedies found in Licinius's library.

"What?" Valerian looked revolted.

"Drop by next time a tooth hurts," Postumus said, sorting undertunics, "and I'll fry you one. I need to look up whether you swallow it or just pack it on like a poultice."

"I'd wear it for an amulet maybe," Valerian said, "but that's as far as I'd go. Or it might be an offering. That would make more sense. Is there a god that likes mice?"

"Bastet, I should think," Postumus said. "And this is why I don't talk shop with people."

VI. Galt

He held his first sick parade the next morning, a motley assortment of coughs, sniffles, pulled tendons, malingering, and a young Dacian cavalryman with a swollen jaw who eyed the surgeon dubiously, his commander having solemnly passed on this piece of ancient Eastern wisdom.

Postumus got out his forceps and dosed the cavalryman, who looked as if he would clearly have preferred the mouse at that point, with enough poppy tears to take the edge off.

"Hold him still, please." The burly orderly got a good grip and Postumus wiggled the abscessed tooth loose and gave it a good yank before the cavalryman could change his mind. Lucian and Gemellus, the other junior surgeon, watched appreciatively.

The patient howled and slumped in his chair while Postumus reflected that speed was probably the most important talent a surgeon could develop. He drained the abscessed cavity, rolled a ball of lint in a saucer of honey and packed the sticky mixture into it. "You'll do fine. Stick to soup for a couple of days and try to swallow on the other side of your mouth. If you let any food get in there and rot, it'll abscess all over again."

Postumus stuck his instruments' blades down in a jar of vinegar and signaled to the orderly to clean up the mess. He wanted to talk to Lucian and Gemellus and get

72

a sense of which of them he should send to the frontier. Lucian was the steadier of them, he thought. Gemellus was younger and appeared to be possessed of obvious good intentions and very little skill. Postumus would have to do something about that after the campaign was over, but for the time being, Gemellus was probably better off in Eburacum. The three of them were going over supply lists with the hospital optio when there was a discreet cough at the office door and a sentry stuck his head around it.

"Excuse me, sir, but there's a Briton at the gate, insisting that he's got to see the new surgeon. We tried to shoo him off, but he won't go."

"From the town?" As Licinius had said, a military surgeon spent a lot of time treating the civilian population. It helped promote peaceable relations.

"No, sir, a tribesman from off in the hills somewhere. Tattoos on his face and he smells like a goat."

"Well, I expect you're no nosegay to him either. Every tribe has its own smell – you just don't notice your own." The sentry looked indignant. "Never mind. Bring him into the surgery." Postumus rose, nodding to Lucian to follow him. "Always keep your doors open to the local folk."

A double escort of sentries produced the Briton, and stood in the doorway, arms folded. Postumus raised an eyebrow at them. "Surely you don't think he'll try to take the fortress single-handed?"

"No, sir, but we don't want him nosing round either. He's a Brigante and they've been trouble since Claudius Caesar came."

The Brigantes had begun the war that had wrecked the Ninth Hispana. Postumus took a closer look at the man. He was tall and his woolen shirt and breeches covered the heavily muscled body of a fighter. His cheekbones were tattooed with intricate blue patterns that marked him as a warrior, and his mustache and fair hair were bleached almost white after the fashion of some of his tribe. He regarded the surgeon with an almost equal reluctance.

"I am sent," he said in the tones of one who would not otherwise have set foot in a Roman camp if the hounds of Erebus had been after him.

His speech was akin to that of the southern tribes and Postumus understood him fairly well. "To what purpose? You look well enough to me."

"We have heard in the heather that there is a new healer in the fort of the Eagles, one with more skill than the old one, and who is native-born and will understand what is said to him."

"Your sources are remarkably accurate, considering that I only arrived yesterday. What do you want with me?"

"I am sent," the man repeated, as if to disavow any agreement with whatever was afoot. "I am to take you back with me if you are the one we have heard of."

Postumus was beginning to feel a little out of his depth. "Have you no healers of your own?"

"There is one with a leg that does not heal. And because he is a harper and a great warrior, the High King has said that he is to have the Roman healer if he wants him." The messenger's expression made it clear that *he* wouldn't want him.

The High King. The patient was someone of importance then, and harpers generally commanded a good deal of respect. A look at the inner councils of the Brigantes was an opportunity that might never come again, and could well be useful. Or so Postumus told himself, well aware in the moment that if it had been any other tribe he would not have been as interested. But they practically made a habit of rebellion, as the sentry noted, and the governor had left a lot of deserted forts behind him in their territory. There was surgical staff available, from the Second Augusta at Isca and the Twentieth out of Deva, to man the governor's field hospitals, and he was sending them Lucian. Postumus made a decision.

"Very well, I will come, if my legate agrees. You must understand, of course, that I must take an escort with me and that any, uh, accidents which might befall me would have very dangerous consequences."

"We are warriors," the man said coldly. "We fight only warriors. But as to the escort, that is agreed."

–

Two hours later, having consulted with the legate and received a list of things concerning the Brigantes which the legate burned to know, they careened along the northern road through a rolling landscape at once wilder and more open than that of West Britain. Postumus braced himself against the rock and sway of the messenger's chariot, a medical kit with everything he could think of that he might need at his feet. The Britons built their chariots of wickerwork and leather, lithe, whippy things that could handle the roughest road, or none at all. Postumus had ridden in them from childhood, and even driven one in the highly amateur competition on Race Day at Isca, and could appreciate the skill required to keep it upright and drive the two highly strung ponies that pulled it.

Behind them clattered a dozen of Valerian's Dacian cavalry, resplendent in polished scale and red and yellow saddle trappings, with their helmet plumes nodding in the wind. He could have ridden with them, of course, but there was some high ground to be gained, he thought, by proving that he could remain on his feet in his escort's chariot.

Past Isurium Brigantum, the nominal tribal capital of the Brigantes, they swung off the main road onto a lesser track that led north and west into the low hills. Isurium still housed the official king's hall of the tribe, but it was a thriving Roman colonia these days, and for many years the High King had seen fit to take his principal residence elsewhere. By the terms of the twenty-five-year-old treaty, official business was conducted at Isurium, and the king kept council there for a specified number of days each year, but it was suspected that the real business of the tribe went on well away from the eyes of Rome.

Postumus looked about him with interest. This was farther north than he had ever been, a wild blue-green landscape of open moors and rolling hills bright with poppies, building to a central range that formed the spine of Britain. A curlew wheeled on the air currents above him, its thin haunting cry barely audible above the hoof-beats.

They halted for the night at the edge of a small meadow where there was graze for the horses and an outcrop of rock to shelter a makeshift camp. Valerian's Dacians were well trained. They threw up a short line of ditch and earthwork on the exposed flank of the camp and posted two of their number as pickets. The Brigante warrior watched them sardonically.

"I have told you, the escort is for your own pride only. None will offer harm to one who rides at the High King's word. And if they did, a ditch isn't likely to stop them."

If this was a tribe supposedly at peace with Rome, no wonder the legate was nervous.

"No, but it shortens the odds somewhat," Postumus said. "They are warriors also."

"And not, I think, of the Roman kind."

"No, they are Dacians, a province far to the east of Rome. A highly skilled horse people who provide some of Rome's best cavalry." In truth, the native Roman standard of horsemanship in general was so abysmal that the Army generally relied on the Empire's allies and provinces to make up its cavalry, but Postumus saw no need to mention that.

The Briton watched as the Dacians loosed their horses into a makeshift corral staked out in the long grass and then turned to their own dinner of military biscuits and shreds of dried meat from their saddlebags.

"I will return," the Briton said shortly, and disappeared into the tangle of undergrowth behind him before Postumus had a chance to speak.

"I don't like that." The decurion in charge of the escort dropped down into the Briton's place, jerking a thumb over his shoulder. "What if he's just gone to let 'em know we're set up like ducks on a pond?"

"I doubt it," Postumus said placidly, fishing in his own kit for a piece of barley bannock and a sack of dried plums. "Surgeons aren't in great demand as battle trophies." He remembered the Britons' aversion to cereal as a dietary staple. "I expect he's just gone to look for dinner."

The decurion snorted. "The commander says 'don't trust anyone,' and I don't trust that one." He applied himself to a handful of rock-hard squares of military bread, pausing every so often to inspect the hillside slope behind him. He rose up some time later, sword in hand, when the Briton returned, catfooted and silent, with a hare in one hand and a light throw-spear in the other, then sat again, grudgingly impressed.

The Briton settled a few paces away, and began to skin the hare with easy, professional strokes. Having gutted the carcass, he selected a forked branch with some care, sharpened the ends, and jabbed the hare onto the prongs. He adjusted it over the campfire without comment, and squatted down beside while it cooked.

It was full dark now, with a thin horned moon hanging low over the hill and the night sounds of the country beginning to start up. The meadow was alive with the chirp and whirr of insects and the rustle of field mice. The faint hoo-hoo of an owl sounded from the wood behind them. On the far hill, a wolf signaled the awakening of the wild lands to the night's business.

The nights were still fairly warm in late summer, and Postumus slipped his cloak back from his shoulders. This part of Britain was alien to him, a wild and untamed world as far from the green hills and river valleys of his youth as the blistering heat of Syria had been; a country where Rome's hold was still precarious and the power of the barbarians made the civilization of the southern territories seem unstable. A shadow swooped silently over them, sank into the meadow and rose again with a mouse in its grip.

—

In the morning they were off again along the ancient track into the hills that had been a path of the first peoples of Britain before the forefathers of the Brigantes had come north across the Channel. Small villages of round, thatch-roofed huts appeared now and then along the way. At mid-morning they trotted up a banked track that switchbacked along a steep hillside and through the first of three gates to a holding perched on a sharp rise above heather- and bracken-covered slopes. Three rings of turf wall topped with stone encircled it, with turf-roofed timber huts, storage sheds, and cow byres within the walls. Reinforced timber gates between stone gateposts led through the last wall into the inner courtyard. Even this space was large enough to draw the whole clan in from the outer villages. A besieging army would have a hard time.

A group of children at spear practice beneath the inner wall regarded their arrival wide-eyed until the weapons master brought their attention back to business with a sharp word. It was obvious that they were expected, if not welcome.

Their taciturn guide drew rein before the main hall, a timber building of respectable size, surrounded by kitchens, a pony shed, and a smithy. The cavalry escort, Postumus noted, was attracting attention. The troopers sat self-consciously in formation while two elderly men lounging beside the well eyed them balefully. A trio of women just turning from the right side of the main hall stopped short, whispered, and then burst into laughter.

"Evan!" the driver called, and a small sandy-haired boy skittered up, eyes bright with excitement. "See to my team, and to the surgeon's watchdogs."

The decurion of the escort drew his horse up beside the chariot and bent down, as conspicuous as a tropical bird. "Hadn't I better stay with you, sir?"

"No. I rather think this is to be a private audience," Postumus said.

"Very well, sir." The decurion's glance strayed upward to where a grinning skull adorned the lintel of the hall. "It's your head."

"I fervently hope not," Postumus said, thinking of Valerian's grandfather. "Go along, Decurion. They didn't drag me all the way out here just to start a war. There are plenty of easier ways."

The decurion saluted and signaled his troops and they moved away in parade formation behind the sandy-haired urchin as a flock of chickens clucked and grumbled themselves out of their path. Postumus picked up his medical kit and followed the driver into the hall.

In the shadowed and smoky depths, ill-lit by one open window, two figures came into focus. The younger wore a shirt of soft dyed leather decorated with a complication of interlocking knots and spirals that echoed the patterns pricked into the flesh above the open neck of his shirt and the triple spiral on his forehead. A finely wrought circlet of gold shone against his corn-colored hair, a gold torque encircled his throat, and a heavy ring set with an enormous uncut emerald gleamed dully on his right hand. The driver bowed to him, and he nodded, but his gray eyes regarded Postumus without expression. Bran, High King of the Brigantes. It was unlikely that he was anyone else.

The other, a man in his forties, sat with his leg propped on a stool on the banked hearth before him, and a blanket over his lap. He had a delicate fine-boned face that must have been beautiful as a girl's in his youth and his mustache and the hair that fell about his shoulders had been carefully bleached. He wore a drop of amber in one ear and a torque of gold and carnelian around his neck, and both arms were clasped with enameled gold bands of intricate workmanship. His face was slightly flushed beneath the tattooing on his cheeks, and he was wrapped in a cloak of green and brilliant blue. He directed a level gaze at Postumus and said, "My thanks to you, Healer of the Eagles. I am grateful for your presence. Although the High King my fosterling" – he nodded at the younger man – "would have it that I grow foolish with age." There was a note in his voice that was obviously meant for the king.

"The gods' greeting to you, and to you, Lord of the Brigantes," Postumus said, setting himself to be polite. "May the sun shine always on your path and the winds blow softly about your door." He made a formal bow.

"The winds that blew in with the Roman kind," the High King said, "have ever carried evil on their wings." He turned to the other. "Galt, if you are determined that a Roman knife can do what our priests cannot, I will leave you to it." He stalked out, taking the driver with him.

"Bran has little reason to love the Roman," the elder man observed. "Yet I still carry a certain amount of weight in some things. Enough to get a Roman healer when I want him."

"I am senior surgeon to the Sixth Legion Victrix," Postumus said. "But I expect you know that. Your messenger seemed remarkably well-informed."

"I have a liking for new information," Galt said. "And there is always news blowing in the heather." Postumus wondered what particular wind had blown through Eburacum with his posting on it.

"What is the matter with you?"

"A boar's tusk rammed halfway up my thigh." He winced and pulled the blanket away so that the shaft of sun from the window fell on his bandaged leg. "But see for yourself."

Postumus shed his lorica and helmet and knelt beside him in the light. Galt put a hand out to his shoulder, turning him round to face him. "What are you called?"

"Postumus Justinius Corvus. My mother came from the Iceni, but we take our fathers' names."

"Yes," Galt said. "So I had heard."

"You aren't likely to find an Army surgeon who's *all* British," Postumus said shortly. "Count yourself lucky to get half a one." He unwrapped the strips of linen as gently as he could – they were stuck to the wound in places. Galt kept silent but it was obvious that he was in some pain. The wound was badly infected, a deep gash that began just above the knee and ran upward for nearly a foot, deepening as it went. The surrounding skin was an angry red, and it was suppurating badly. There was no evidence of gangrene, although, Postumus thought grimly, that could well be next. And other complications were alarmingly possible.

"How long ago did this happen?" he asked.

"Some fourteen days," Galt said.

Well, at least if the patient were going to get lockjaw, he would have it by now. "What has been the treatment?"

"It was washed and medicinal herbs were put in. What they were, I couldn't tell you. I am not a healer."

"Many of your healers have much skill," Postumus said truthfully. "And many herbs are beneficial. The problem is the nature of the wound. It deepens at the top, and becomes more a puncture than a gash. Whatever it was washed with may not have got clear inside, and there was probably Aesculapius-knows-what on the end of the boar's tusk. I'm going to clean it again and then treat it with something a little stronger. I'm afraid you aren't going to like it," he added apologetically.

Galt shrugged. "I don't much like it the way it is, either. And I like even less the idea of having my leg taken off at the hip."

Postumus rocked back on his heels and looked him in the eye. "There is always the chance of that. If it becomes gangrenous, it will be necessary."

Galt nodded. "That is why I have sent for you now. We are a horse people and I have been astride or behind one from the day I could walk. For thirty years I have commanded the High King's household warriors."

Postumus realized what the loss of a leg would mean to him even in times of peace. And he likely wouldn't survive the amputation.

"Very well," Galt said. "And after you have dressed the wound?"

"Then we leave it alone for a little, and let it drain. After that, treat it with honey to prevent a new infection, put some stitches in, and hope that it will heal without further trouble."

"And if it does not?"

"If it does not, it comes off," Postumus said. "If you wish to go on breathing."

"I have every intention of it," Galt said. "Get on with it."

"I shall need someone to help me. To hand me things when I need them and keep my instruments out of the dirt. Someone who won't get hysterical and decide I'm trying to poison you," he added.

"Rhys!" Galt called out. The warrior who had brought them north from Eburacum appeared in the doorway. He had obviously been stationed just outside it. "Bring me Dawid. What else will you need?"

"A bowl of clean water, and another one empty. Vinegar. A clean cloth for the bed. And some clean bandages."

"Very well. Rhys, do as he says."

The warrior vanished again and in a few minutes a brown-haired man with a pleasant, worried face appeared carrying the water, a ewer, and a dry bowl filled with strips of linen, a folded cloth under one arm.

"This is Dawid, cousin to the High King, and also my fosterling," Galt said.

"I would like to take Lord Galt to his own quarters, if that is possible," Postumus said. "He should not be walking around on that leg for some days yet."

"And have I not been saying that?" Dawid said. "Bring the bowls and your instruments. I will carry him."

"Never yet have I been carried like a fainting maiden to my bed," Galt said. "And I do not propose to start now."

"Then you may thrash me when your leg is healed," Dawid said. "I expect you still can. In the meantime—" He scooped Galt up from his chair and ducked through the leather flap of a doorway at the far end of the hall, while Postumus followed. It was obvious that the two held each other in some affection, a bond noticeably absent when Galt was with the High King.

Galt's chamber was a chaos of broken harp strings and harness straps, with a jumble of hunting spears piled in one corner. The half-eaten remains of a meal lay on a low table. A beautifully worked harp case of soft gray leather stitched in gold lay on the closed lid of a carved chest. The bed was piled with furs and Postumus spread the linen cloth over them.

Dawid laid Galt gently on the bed and began fishing in a clothes chest for a clean shirt. "We may as well put you in this now. Then, when the surgeon has done with you, you may sleep. Which is what you should have been doing before now."

"You act like a mother sparrow with one lone cuckoo chick," Galt said disgustedly, but he held up his arms and let Dawid draw his shirt over his head. His arms and chest were crossed with scars, Postumus saw; thin, pale lines that cut across the faded blue spirals of the Spear Pattern. Clearly the man was a warrior, despite the fine-boned face and the taste for gaudy jewelry. And a good one, if he had held the king's household troops, the elite of any tribe, in check for thirty years. Bran couldn't be that old. Galt must have served the old king as well.

"My nursemaid allows us to begin," Galt said, when Dawid had slipped the clean shirt over his head, and unfastened the arm bands and torque and put them away.

"I will need wine also, or a cup of beer."

"Here." Dawid poured a cupful from a pitcher on the table. Postumus tipped the contents of a small vial into it and handed it to Galt, who eyed it suspiciously.

"Drink it, please."

"I do not need poppy, or whatever that is, to have a wound cleaned out."

"You sent for me," Postumus said, "so do as I say. You are weak enough already from the infection in that leg. I'm not going to have you go into shock while I'm cleaning it."

Galt shrugged and drained the cup. "Do you always drug your patients?" he asked, settling back on the bed.

"When at all possible," Postumus said. "They are more cooperative."

"We are taught that enduring pain teaches a man familiarity with it, and hence contempt for it," Galt said.

"You'll have a chance to do your enduring later. That leg's going to hurt like Hades for a while, and I can't keep you doped up very long. This stuff will make you sick when you stop it if you take it for too long." What he had given Galt wasn't the wild poppy tears he had dosed the cavalryman's tooth with, but a dose of the far stronger cultivated poppy. He waited until he could see that it had taken effect, and then began methodically to clean the wound, dropping each reeking swab into the empty bowl as he finished with it. He could see Galt gritting his teeth even in the dreamy trance of the drug, but he took his time – there wasn't going to be any third chance for Galt's leg. At the top of the wound he found it necessary to make a small incision in the infected flesh in order to clean it properly, and he could feel Galt's whole body quiver as he drew the scalpel blade across. Behind him, Dawid flinched in empathy with each touch on the wound but continued with stoic concentration to hand him scalpel and swabs as soon as he asked for them.

When the cleaning was finished, Postumus rocked back on his heels and pushed the hair from his forehead with his arm. "Bring me a clean bowl of water and then take these out and burn them." Postumus indicated the bowl of used swabs. While he waited, he kept a wary eye on Galt – he was still flushed but he seemed to be breathing easily enough. Despite Galt's opinion, the fact remained that great pain was a danger to a weakened body.

When Dawid returned, Postumus washed his hands and began to apply a greenish dressing composed mainly of verdigris in an excipient mixture of resin, oil, and vinegar. That done, he set small stitches in the incision he had made near the top of the wound and covered it lightly with a clean cloth. He eased the now bloody sheet out from under Galt. "I don't want to bandage this further until it has had a chance to drain and the infection has subsided somewhat. The cloth is mainly to keep the flies away. He'll have to stay lying down and I want both him and this room kept spotless. Now burn those swabs, and scrub out the bowls I've used and set them in the sun for at least a week. Wash the sheet and hang it out too."

"What then?"

"Then we wait," Postumus said tiredly.

Dawid, his arms full of bowls, turned round at the doorway. "Why do you do this?"

"Because I was sent for."

"No other reason?"

"Many others. But let that one suffice you."

In a few minutes, the boy who had taken charge of the chariot ponies came to show Postumus to the quarters allotted him, and he followed gratefully.

"What's your name, child?"

"Evan, lord. I don't live here all the time. I'm one of the High King's hounds," he said proudly. "He brought me with him when he came to take council with Lord Dawid – this is his holding. We'd have been on to the next one long since if Lord Galt hadn't been hurt. Is he going to be all right?"

"I hope so," Postumus said gravely. "I think so."

"He's just got to keep that leg," Evan said, frowning. "He couldn't drive without it."

"I'll do everything I can, I promise you. Now tell me, small hound, what have you done with my escort?"

"They're in the Guest Hall. I sent one of Lord Dawid's hounds to see to their dinner. I shall bring you yours myself." The hounds were the boys of the tribe, apprentice warriors who took their training in the halls of their chieftains. Apparently the social strata of the tribe was reflected in the hounds, since Evan ordered Dawid's about with a free hand.

"Thank you. And would you tell Lord Dawid, please, that someone should sleep in Lord Galt's room with him, and that I am to be sent for if he shows any sign of complication?"

When Evan had gone, Postumus lay back on the bed. The frame was wood, and the mattress straw, with some scented herb – rosemary, he thought – mixed in, covered with a native rug. He was tired, but his impression of the Brigantes ticked over in his mind regardless. Bran was a conscientious king who made regular rounds of his chieftains' holdings. He seemed to feel a sense of duty toward Galt, who had apparently been his foster father, but whether any real affection lay in the bond between them, Postumus couldn't tell. Bran, he thought, hated Romans with something bordering on a mania. Oddly enough, Galt did not. All of which would no doubt be interesting to the legate. Unlike the peoples of the south, the Brigantes were much as they had been before Claudius Caesar's invasion force had begun to wipe out the old ways in front of the twenty-mile-a-day march of the new; they were only nominally Roman. The Silures of West Britain had been like that seventy-five years ago, before Agricola, when Valerian's grandfather was decorating his hall with enemy heads, some of them almost certainly Roman.

The old ways appeared abruptly in the person of young Evan bearing a platter of steaming pig's meat and a hefty two-handled jug of native beer. To one several years accustomed to an Army diet, or even his mother's household cooking, this was heady stuff. Postumus ate hungrily and then lay back again with the uncomfortable sensation of having eaten far too much of something his stomach wasn't used to.

He left the pig's meat to argue with the beer and settle down of its own accord while he studied the room around him. It was a pleasant chamber, the timbers smoothed and darkened with age, the plastered walls painted a pale yellow. The walls and doorway were covered with hangings of soft leather adorned with graceful leaping beasts and borders of interlocking knots. How did they work out the pattern, he wondered, following the baffling pathways with his eyes. The floor, packed earth rather than tile or stone, was strewn with dried grasses and herbs that gave off a pleasant scent underfoot. There was a small, smoke-stained hearth, a table and two stools with legs of carved shale, all decorated with the bronze heads of an animal that only an artist could have thought of, a clothes chest with ivory inlay and bronze hinges and hasp, and a small bronze mirror affixed to the wall. The furniture was that of someone well born among his people, bought from traders rather than home-fashioned. The Brigantes were a wealthy people even if most of their gold had once gone to buy weapons in the last rebellion. Now some twenty-five years later, they again bought lavishly of the luxury goods that came from the south. But the air was thick with woodsmoke and the heady smell of many bodies. In all, it was as alien an environment as the landscape had been. He closed his eyes and tried to will his mother's half of him to take over and find familiarity in these surroundings. The end result was that he went to sleep.

He awoke some four hours later in the gray-gold summer dusk, and someone was tugging urgently at his shoulder.

"What?" Postumus groped automatically for the dagger at his belt and small Evan's voice said exasperatedly, "If I'd been the Painted One, I could've cut your throat with a rusty spear blade by this time. *Will* you wake up! Something's wrong with Lord Galt!"

Postumus sat up and shook the sleep away at that. He straightened his tunic and grabbed for his kit just as Dawid also appeared in the doorway, his face chalk white and close to panic.

Galt lay on the piled wolfskins of the bed just as Postumus had left him, although his chamber had been aggressively tidied to the point that he probably wouldn't be able to find anything. But the slim, inert form was burning hot to the touch, and although the pale lashes fluttered occasionally, there was no sign of true consciousness.

"Get me some cloths and cool water," Postumus said. "And an extra hanging for the doorway. I'm going to try to bring the fever down, and I don't want a draft." When Evan had hurried away, he knelt and put his ear to Galt's chest.

"What is it?" Dawid asked.

"His body is fighting the infection in that leg, and maybe one or two more as well." He picked up Galt's wrist and found the pulse. "When a man is weakened by one illness, it lets the door open to others. His natural resistance has no strength to keep them out." Or so he had been told at his training. As usual, he wondered if they actually knew.

"What do we do?"

"Pray," Postumus said shortly. He didn't know who the Brigantes worshipped, besides Lugh Shining Spear. The Mother, of course, and no doubt various local spirits, some left over from the Old People who had been here before them. "To anybody you can think of."

VII. The Corn King

It was almost dark-of-the-moon and what little light there was flickered from the tallow dips set in bowls by the bed. The night sounds came clearly through the stillness – the lowing of a cow; the stamp and whuffle of the cavalry ponies on their picket line and the chariot ponies in their barn, speaking horse talk to each other; the sharp bark of a fox; all punctuated here and there by voices in the main hall and once an aged grumbling in the corridor outside the door, cut short by the sharp voice of Bran. The healer priest, no doubt, Postumus thought, convinced that the Roman was murdering his patient.

He only hoped he wasn't. Not enough was known about infection, he thought, sponging cool water across Galt's face and chest. He had managed to get a decoction of willow down him, even half-conscious, in the hope that it would help. And why didn't they know? After all this time, why was medicine still half guesswork and half prayer? He felt as if he was pounding his head against a stone wall, in the hope of leaving enough of a dent for the next man to carry on. He touched the back of his hand to Galt's neck. The fever seemed to be dropping, if only a little.

If Galt died... Postumus wondered if the legate had sufficiently considered the possible consequences when he had decided to use him as a medical spy. And if he himself had, setting out on a mad trip to acquaint himself with the people who had broken his father's legion, Galt most likely among them. The Brigantes were half-kin to the Selgovae, and with a long history of rebellion. And the forts in their lands were empty, and possibly waiting for a good excuse.

Galt stirred. Postumus looked at his flushed face and the tangle of flaxen hair spread on the gray wolfskin and desperately willed the man not to die.

"Aesculapius, healer, help me," he prayed, one hand on Galt's pulse. And then, because Galt was a warrior, and so was Postumus, surgeon or not, he said another prayer to Mithras, the Lord of Light, the god of the soldier.

And then, practical, he wrung out a clean cloth in the cool water and wiped it over the fevered body. Neither god looked kindly on the man who sat back and tried to let the god do his work.

The thin moon made its brief rounds and the sun was beginning to steal into the chirruping of birds when Postumus laid his hand along Galt's forehead and then sat back. He was cool to the touch and sweating. The fever had broken.

Postumus flung the cloth into the bowl of water and rubbed his knuckles across his eyes. Galt shifted – for the first time, voluntarily – and, turning somewhat to his side, burrowed deeper into the wolfskin bed covering. Postumus drew a light blanket up over him. He sat for a long time watching the sleeping form.

Finally, he got up and pushed back the heavy hangings in the doorway. The room was stuffy with the smell of sickness and a little air would do no harm now. He stretched, rubbing his eyes. Small Evan was curled outside in the corridor, and Postumus sent him to say that Lord

Galt was better and should be left to sleep. Then he made his way back to his own chamber and, like his patient, slept the day through.

After another meal delivered by Evan and eaten in solitude, he received a visit from the decurion of his cavalry escort – just to be sure, he told Postumus, that his head hadn't become part of the chieftain's household decorations. The decurion's helmet and riding crop were tucked under one arm, and he looked like a man who wanted to be on a horse and gone.

"How long are you like to be stuck in this heathen outpost, sir?" he inquired.

"That's hard to say," Postumus said. "I want to stay until I'm sure that leg is healing and the local priests aren't going to let it get infected again out of sheer spite. Are you so anxious to get back to your nice war?"

"It's the men I'm thinking of. I can't take them out for drills in front of the locals and they haven't anything else to do except sit around getting soft. And the locals don't like 'em much, which makes for trouble. They make signs behind their backs when they see us. And there's a damn sight too many women about too, running about with a damn sight too few clothes on." He nodded toward the open window where a group of girls in short tunics could be seen running through weapons drill with the boys. "All I need is one idiot to stir up a whole hornet's nest of trouble."

"Don't tell me the girls are giving them the come-on."

"Hardly. They'd just as soon spit on us. But my lads aren't used to women running around like men. They think it means they're easy."

Postumus thought it over. There were all the ingredients necessary for real trouble. "I see what you mean. The legate wants information, as I expect you realize. And they aren't going to open up around me much with a dozen bodyguards cluttering up the place, not to mention if one of them tries to go after a girl. He'll probably get killed and then we'll have a diplomatic crisis all our own. I think you'd better take your men and head back, and let the High King give me an escort back to Eburacum."

The decurion looked dubious. "I don't think the legate's going to like that, sir. Frankly, we haven't enough good surgeons as it is."

"The legate sent me up here," Postumus said. "He's going to have to let me handle it as I see fit. Tell him he can expect me in about two weeks, and he can leave my orders at Eburacum." He hoped the orders wouldn't include a posting back to Syria as a camel vet.

—

Galt, apprised of this change in plan while Postumus redressed his leg, seemed amused. "Are you always so free with your commander's orders?"

"The legate has a war in the north to keep him busy. I'm not going to have some damn fool from your men *or* mine start something that the Army's going to have to finish, and hand the legate a war on his hearth as well. Your leg is looking much better. If it stays clean tomorrow, I'll stitch it."

"I shall enjoy that, I feel sure."

"You won't, but you'll have less chance of a permanent limp that way." Postumus spread a clean cloth over the wound and knotted a bandage lightly around it at either end.

"You have the healer's touch, I think," Galt said. "I find that odd in a people so given to conquest as yours."

Postumus rolled the clean dressings and bandages up and thought that one over. "And from whom did your people take this land?" he asked finally. "And in any case, my family have always followed the Eagles. I merely took a different form of the service."

"I have heard that your own people in Rome think all physicians are charlatans and that the true healers come from Greece or Egypt," Galt said idly.

Postumus raised an eyebrow. Galt seemed an unlikely candidate for such thorough knowledge of the Citizenry's opinions.

"We become more worldly-wise," Galt said, interpreting his reaction correctly, "with each year we live beneath Rome's hand."

"Then you will also know that it is only civilians and the old nobility who think that way, and that that is born of the days when we had no healers of our own," Postumus said. "For the last two hundred years, almost every advance in surgery has come out of the field hospitals of the Eagles."

Galt's tired eyes watched him narrowly. "A true child of Rome and none of the Iceni, are you not?"

"I suppose not. Rome is all I've ever known. My mother is Roman now, and the Iceni wouldn't have her back, having no love for Rome themselves. You can't live in two worlds."

"No. Our people tried it once, a hundred years gone, when our own queen made us vassals of Rome. There were those who did not like being sold so, and thus there was a rebellion which was put down by Rome, none too gently. It has been an uneasy balance since."

Postumus didn't answer, thinking of the last time the balance had tipped.

Galt seemed to know that. "And you are no child anyway, are you? You must forgive me. I see all men of your age as children. A sign I grow old, I expect."

"Even the High King?"

"No," Galt said slowly. "He is the life of the tribe, and they are the power in him. No man can view a High King as a child. But the High King his father, who was my brother in all but blood, died in a war with your Eagles when this one was a babe in arms." Galt's eyes were focused on the middle distance now, on some memory long gone by. "There was a good chance that some of the babe's kin might not let him live to reign, seeing their own chance, without a strong hand about him – and one with no inclination to the kingship," he added wryly. "There had been a regency when the High King's own father, grandsire to this one, died, and it took a tribal war and much blood to win back his birthright. And so we made sure between us that Fate would not spin the same thread for his cub."

"And now?"

"He goes his own way now. And I am glad enough to let the power go with him. A kingship has never been something I wished to take on my own shoulders."

Postumus wondered again whether there had been anything but stark duty to hold Galt to the king all those years. It must have been an odd, uncomfortable arrangement on both sides. Still, whatever love or lack of it Galt held the king in, whatever path the High King took, Galt would follow if he couldn't stop it. Whatever vow he'd made to the old king would hold.

Postumus packed his ointments away, light from the tallow dips throwing his sharp angled profile into relief on the wall beyond. Galt lay watching him silently until he had rolled up the kit and tied it. "Postumus—" It was the first time any of the Brigantes had called him by name, and he looked up, surprised. "Stay yet awhile tonight."

"You should sleep."

"I have slept all I can. And I am not going anywhere."

"Most certainly you are not, if you wish to keep your leg. But you don't need me just now."

"I am curious. I will make you a bargain. Your left-hand heritage for your Roman one."

This man is dangerous, Postumus thought. "To what purpose?" he asked, and chose his words carefully.

"For you, because you are half Iceni whether your mother is a centurion's lady or not, and I think that half begins to call to you somewhat."

"And for yourself?" Postumus watched the light flickering on the fine-boned face and the pale pool of his hair.

Galt raised himself up on one elbow. "I find Rome hard to understand. To me, it is a world of straight lines and harsh light, like a thrown brick, crashing into things, but we must understand it if we are to survive." His blue eyes were narrowed and intent and he caught Postumus with them and held him. "All the Britons were kin to one another when the world was young, but tribe has fought tribe ever since. When your Claudius Caesar first came, we should have united and pushed Rome back across the Channel. And when your general Agricola drove farther into our land, we should have done the same. But we did not, and now it is too late for that. An enemy who comes only to raid and take tribute is one thing. An enemy who has put down his roots in the land, him you must learn to live with, or go under as the Old Folk of the hills did when my people first took their holdings here, as you said. Rome is bred in the bone of too much of Britain now."

98

"We who have put our roots down," Postumus said, "for us this is our land too."

"Then we will talk," Galt said, "your world and mine." He smiled tentatively, and Postumus found himself smiling back.

In the end they talked until the dawn began to slide like a sea mist under the hangings that shielded the room's one window. Galt spoke of Britain as far back as the tales of his people could recall it, with what he knew of the Old Folk who had come before them thrown in for good measure. And Postumus, who had never seen Rome, tried to explain the gilt and marble magnificence of that city and the ties that bound those born of her far-flung Empire.

Afterward he took his meals in Galt's chamber, rather than alone in his own, and the talk went on, confined mainly to such harmless topics as the proper design of a chariot or the intricacies of Roman plumbing, or Postumus's mad desire to bathe daily in the river, but touching now and again on the cold iron of the Roman presence in Britain, and, more to the point, the evacuation of Rome's forts in these hills. Postumus was never sure, when that came up, who was sizing up whom.

As Galt grew stronger, Postumus, whose musical ability extended to the fact that he could generally carry a tune, heard for the first time the music of his mother's people in the hands of a man who possessed both training and a great gift. There was some old magic in the songs that legend said had first come from the Old People of the hills, Postumus thought, while Galt, his bad leg propped awkwardly on a pillow, took his harp from its embroidered leather case.

Afterward, Postumus would lie wakeful, staring at the roof beams and counting over the past unsettling days. What the legate needed most to know – the stability of the Brigantes – was still uncertain. Bran regarded him with the cold and unwinking hostility of a basilisk; Rhys, the driver who had brought him, remained polite but aloof; and it was plain that he was an irksome and unwelcome embarrassment in their midst. Dawid, who was the chieftain of the clan whose lands marched nearest to the fort at Eburacum, was friendly enough, but clearly interested only in Postumus's usefulness. Dawid's wife Brica, when he encountered her, was briskly pleasant, plainly concerned with Galt's well-being. She was a small freckled woman with long brown braids and most often her hands full of some task or other, an apron tied over her gown. Like Dawid's, her clothes were of fine wool embroidered with bright colors, and her belt was sewn with small bronze bells. Constantia would like the little bells, he thought. Except for small Evan, to whom no man was a stranger, the rest of the Brigantes simply ignored him; if the Lord Galt wanted the Roman, that was his business, but they made the Sign of Horns behind their backs when they saw him, and the High King regarded him as he would an adder in his boots.

Once the stitches had been put in, the leg healed rapidly, to Postumus's silent relief. He prescribed fresh air and some mild exercise and went along to make sure that Galt didn't overdo it.

"You are a surgeon. I do not require that you serve also as a nursemaid," Galt said somewhat querulously.

Postumus suspected that the newly healing leg was paining him more than he had bargained for. But when he pointed out irritably that since no one but Galt was willing to tell him which way was north on the best of days, he had little else to do with his time, Galt laughed and shouted for Rhys to harness the black ponies.

"If I brace my leg thus" – he demonstrated with a chair – "I may ride in state and you be my driver. That is, if you think you can keep them to a walk."

Since Postumus was aware that the black ponies were a pair that were used to teach children to drive, he agreed that he probably could. He suspected that it was a compliment to be allowed to drive at all.

The chariot that Rhys brought was a much finer affair than the one in which he had driven Postumus from Eburacum, and obviously Galt's own. The wooden framework was painted deep blue and the wicker body was lashed to it with thongs of red leather. Bright medallions of bronze and silver hung along the sides and the wheel spokes had also been inset with bronze. There was an empty socket in either wheel hub and Postumus realized that beneath the fancy trappings this was a war chariot. Those sockets were made to hold the wicked double-bladed knives that could slice right through a man when the wheels were turning.

The black ponies were biddable enough, having encountered worse drivers than Postumus, and Postumus had schooled enough of Licinius's ponies and driven enough Race Days to make a fair showing. He said as much to Galt when the harper unexpectedly complimented him.

"I thought this uncle raised cavalry remounts," Galt said, eyeing Postumus's hands on the reins. "I've seen some fancy tricks with burning hedges and the like, but never a cavalry pony schooled to harness."

"Licinius sells the best ones to the officers for their own use, and a few good chariot pairs to the civilians. It does no harm for his stock to win a race or two now and again."

"Licinius," Galt said, and his voice took on an odd, careful note. "I knew a healer of the Eagles once, who had that name."

Postumus made an exasperated gesture that sent the blacks leaping wildly in all directions like hares. "Of course you did," he said, self-consciously getting them under control. "He served at Eburacum with the Ninth Hispana, and so did my father and my stepfather." He kept his attention on the ponies' pricked ears ahead of him. "I wondered how long it would take that to come out. Are you sure you want to go on, now?"

"Are you?" Galt asked.

Neither spoke, Postumus imagining the slow black dance of carrion birds over Inchtuthil, once Castra Pinnata, something that no doubt Galt had seen in person. He kept the ponies headed away from Dawid's holding and west along the track that led to the summer pastures. At the foot of the hill, the road was wooded, thick and secret, oak and elm and ash spotted with the fading white flowers of rowan, the ponies' hoofbeats hushed by last season's fallen leaves.

Finally, Galt spoke. "Do you want to know what it was like, for us, afterward?"

"Yes."

Galt braced his back against the gentle motion of the chariot. "The year after the High King died was a bad one. We had beaten the Army of the Eagles, but we had also destroyed and shamed a legion, and that, Rome does not forgive. I forced peace on the tribe, and on the Selgovae, because I saw that while the old emperor of the Eagles had left Britain much to its own devices, and taken its troops to fight in another war somewhere else, the new one who had just been made was sending a new army here to take back what had been lost, and they would take revenge for that dead legion. And so we made peace while we were still strong, for the better terms. But there were still terms – taxes, and young men conscripted for your auxiliaries, and veterans settled on our land – and there were many who felt that their dead had gone for nothing."

"And would have thrown more dead after them?" Postumus asked. "For honor's sake?"

"It would have been worse if we had fought on, or at least I thought so, but there is no way of proving a thing that has not happened. There were bad crops after that – six in a row – and many of the cattle died, and then there was sickness among us. Mainly the children, which is always heartbreaking, but the queen died also, and we came close to losing the young king. And the priests, who sometimes show more wisdom than others, said that it was the fault of bowing to the Romans, that we had angered the Sun Lord, Lugh Shining Spear, and also the Mother, for leaving the Roman kind alive to trample her land."

Postumus was silent. When Boudicca of the Iceni had risen in rebellion eighty years ago, she had laid waste to three cities and a legion – the Ninth. Why did things always come back to the Ninth? That rebellion was put down mercilessly. Gwytha had told him that her own mother had been a small child then, and she remembered buildings in flames and men on horses riding down whoever was in their path. It had marked her, Gwytha said. "It's why I can't go back. Not having lived among Romans," she had said softly.

"I understand better than you might think," Postumus said finally. He turned the ponies around, feeling that enough of a strain had been put on Galt's leg, and the peace of mind of them both, for one day.

–

Still, after that they rode out often, although Postumus insisted that Galt do his own walking for part of the way each day, to strengthen his leg.

"I told you, we are a horse people," Galt said disgustedly, as they strolled at the ponies' heads. "No warrior of the Brigantes has ever walked when he could drive or ride."

"You should march with a legion someday," Postumus said. "Twenty miles a day, and a marching camp to build at the end of it. Twenty-four if you're in a hurry."

Galt grimaced. "Thank you, no. I destroy my credit sufficiently just being seen with you."

They walked on in companionable silence. Something that Postumus couldn't put his finger on had happened after that first drive, and now they no longer fenced with each other, as if by laying bare the past they had opened some gate between them as well.

As his leg strengthened, and the pain in it eased, Galt's taste for bright finery made a reappearance. The plain tunics and cloak that had served in his convalescence disappeared to be replaced by breeches and shirts in bright colors, intricately patterned, made brighter by a collection of arm rings and cloak pins that would have done credit to a dancing girl. He was still accounted the best, and most dangerous, of the tribe's warriors and could afford small vanities.

Bran had left at last to visit other holdings, after a short and furious quarrel with Galt, which Postumus was aware he was not meant to have overheard. It was happenstance – mostly – that he had been standing in the shadow of the pony shed while they quarreled inside.

"It is beyond foolish to let the Roman run tame among us! I have told Dawid this, but he won't go against you." Bran's voice was biting. "I am not your fosterling anymore. And I tell you to send him away. Now!"

"You were my fosterling for the love I bore your father," Galt said quietly. "And as you say, you are no more. I will keep him by me until I am sure I will not lose my leg."

"The love you bore my father! I know what kind of love you bore my father!"

"You know nothing." Galt's voice was dangerous now. "And you are hot-headed."

"Because I see a chance to free us of the Romans' yoke!"

"Precisely. It may be that I have learned things from this Roman that you would do well to hear."

"And what has he learned from you?"

"Nothing that they don't know already, I expect."

"Don't give me reason to doubt your loyalty, Galt! You are not regent now."

Postumus slid away before they could finish their quarrel and find him. Bran and his retinue rode out the next day, and only small Evan bade Postumus farewell.

He had learned one thing of interest: the tribe was not a legion. Bran might be the High King, but he did not wield absolute power. He could command, and if the council of chieftains thought it unwise, they could decline. If Galt had kept them from an ill-thought-out rebellion during his regency, then he plainly had influence. That was something to take back to the legate, and Postumus knew it was time to go, although he found himself oddly reluctant.

Just now, having walked the prescribed distance, they mounted the chariot again, Galt leaping into the driver's place with no sign of pain. He shook out the reins and the ponies flew like arrows down the narrow track. Galt's hair was freshly washed and bleached and it streamed out behind him like sunlight. He leaned over the chariot rim and crooned to the ponies, his own team this time. They lengthened their stride still further and ran like the steeds of Dis, taking a turn on one wheel before they nearly overset an ox-drawn wagon coming from the hay fields. The driver, a stumpy man with the iron collar of a slave, made a furious gesture.

Galt pulled up and looked repentant and the ox cart made its careful way past them.

Poppies flickered on the hillside and above them a cloud of birds swooped joyously on the warm updraft. Postumus eyed them regretfully, thinking of the bleak lands to the north, and the frontier hospital he should have been riding for days ago.

Galt, watching him, loosed the reins and let the ponies drop their heads to crop the summer grass. "My leg is as close to healed as it needs to be," he said quietly, echoing Postumus's thoughts. "You are leaving."

"I have to. I'm needed in the north. I've outstayed my orders as it is. Not to mention my welcome."

Galt was silent for a moment, watching the careening birds.

He minds, Postumus thought, surprised.

"We've built an odd peace, for two men intending to spy on each other," Galt said lightly. "I only hope I have proved as unuseful to the legate as you have been to the High King."

"I'm afraid so," Postumus said. Although he thought that if he had given Galt enough reasons to forestall a rebellion, he would count that as useful enough.

–

Postumus lay somewhat wakeful that night. It was close to Lughnasa and the cutting of the Corn King, and there was a certain amount of pre-festival merriment going on by moonlight outside. The women had been berrying all day, coming back purple-stained with baskets of fruit, and the great fires were already laid. On its surface, midsummer belonged to the Sun Lord Lugh, but it had been the Mother's once and she was still the earth that took in the corn and made it grow. The Corn King, cut from the last stalks and given to the fire, had been human once, cut down by the new king.

He shifted under the blankets, wondering how long it had been since a Corn King had died in these hills. The Old People had belonged to the Mother, as the Picts still did. Not all that long, maybe. It was even said that the last independent king of the Silures had died in some such fashion, in Agricola's day.

A bank of cloud moved across the moon that slanted past the window's edge and the room deepened into blackness. Postumus sighed and turned over again. Tomorrow he would be back to the Army, a more cheerful thought to sleep by than the Corn King.

It might have been that the Corn King got into his dreams anyway, because toward morning he found himself riding a dark pony down the twisting road from Dawid's hold, through the three gates and the outer courtyard, holding a burning stalk of grain that bit at his fingers until he dropped it and woke.

There was only the faintest brush of movement that might have been a mouse. Postumus stiffened, awake now, foggy-headed but knowing from the pricking on the back of his neck that it wasn't a mouse. He lay still, fingers closing around the dagger under the blankets, and waited to see what happened.

Something that might have been a breath in the dark. Postumus kept his eyes half closed, letting the darkness lighten as they became accustomed. He sighed and shifted and looked asleep again. Another breath, and the faint glint of light off a knife blade. He could see it now, just barely, but barely was enough. Whatever was in the room raised its arm to strike and Postumus rolled out from under the knife that embedded itself in the straw. He was up and had the man by the shoulders from behind before he could turn. The man pulled from his grip, flailing with the knife, and Postumus raked his own dagger across the knife hand and heard the rattle as it fell. They grappled blindly in the dark until Postumus caught the man's arm with his left hand and twisted it behind him. He pushed him flat to the floor, knees on his ribs. His right hand still held his dagger, unpleasantly close to the man's ear.

"Who sent you?"

"No one!"

Postumus snorted and dug his knees a little deeper into the man's ribcage. "I can break those," he commented.

"No one! I only thought to rob you." It sounded like an afterthought, and farfetched at that.

"You planned to rob Lord Dawid's guest? And leave his body in the bed?" Postumus pushed on the shoulder where the arm was pinned behind his attacker, where he knew it would be most unpleasant. "I don't possess anything that would be worth that."

The man was silent. It was too dark to see his face clearly, but Postumus supposed it probably didn't matter. He weighed his options. He couldn't sit on the man all night. And killing him did not seem like a good idea, however tempting. What wasn't wanted just now was trouble between Rome and the Brigantes. It seemed likely that was what had been intended. "You had a shot at me," he said. "Another try would be a bad idea. I am leaving tomorrow, and I think I shall sit up the rest of the night." He lifted his right hand to touch the dagger to the man's throat, and took his forearm in his left. "Get up now and remember that I can pull this arm from its socket, or cut your throat, whichever you prefer." He shifted off the ribcage and the man stood with a moan of pain. Postumus shoved him through the door. "If I've broken a rib, you should ask someone to tape it for you before it punctures your lung," he said to the footsteps stumbling down the hall.

–

The next day Postumus rode back into his own world again, flanked by half a dozen of Dawid's men, bare chests and arms displaying the blue spirals of the Shield Pattern and the shining bronze arm rings and torques that marked them for free men and warriors. None seemed to have a cut on his hand.

Galt, with a cacophony of gold bracelets rattling at his wrists, limped out to the gate to say farewell. He pulled off an arm ring of gold, embellished with blue enamel in the shape of running horses, and put it in Postumus's hand.

"It is an insult to speak of payment to a hearth guest," he said quietly before Postumus could speak. "This is a gift." He paused. "If for some reason you should ever need to, show it to a man of the Brigantes and you will find that it is also not without power."

Postumus nodded and slipped it on his arm. "You should know that there was someone with a knife in my room last night," he said quietly, too low for anyone else to hear.

Galt snapped his head up at that and met Postumus's gaze. He made no other response but said, "May the Shining One keep you in his hand," and then he was gone into Dawid's hold, and the little cavalcade was flying out along the downhill track toward Eburacum.

–

Galt shifted in his chair to ease his right leg. "And what does Lord Galt think?" Dawid asked, as Galt had known he would, and the High King smacked his fist on the arm of his chair at the head of the Council table. The rest of the Council, clan chiefs of the Brigantes, listened warily.

"If Brendan of the Selgovae has sent an emissary to the clans of the Brigantes" – Galt nodded at the man who sat at the far end of the table, opposite the clan chiefs – "then I think that we will listen when Brendan himself comes."

"The Warlord of the Selgovae is old," the emissary said.

"Precisely," Galt said.

"He is still warlord." The man held up his right hand and the gold signet ring of the Selgovae lord gleamed on his forefinger in the firelight.

"Enough!" Bran snapped. "I will hear Brendan's emissary, whatever the Lord Galt thinks. Or Dawid."

"My lands run nearest to the Eagles at Eburacum," Dawid said. "I must think of them before I think of Brendan."

"The Eagles' fort is nearly empty."

"So I believe it was when we made war the last time," Dawid said. "I was young, but I remember." *As the king cannot* was unspoken. Dawid was cousin to the king and could push things farther than most, but not that far.

The emissary of the Selgovae had come to the High King's hold bearing a green branch as the Lughnasa fires burned down, and the king had summoned all his Council to hear him. Galt wondered if it was some kind of curse to be able to remember the last such council so clearly. It had been Vortrix in the king's chair then, with Galt beside him. And there was still the other matter to be dealt with.

"The peace that was made still stings," the emissary said. "We are a free people and not lapdogs of Rome. When he meets Lugh Shining Spear, he would go as a free man."

The rest of the Council were silent. Rhodri, the youngest, deferred generally to the king. Conor was of the royal house in his mother's line, which still carried power. Duncan had been in the old war and survived it, as had Conor. None, including Dawid, would have willingly been vassal clients of Rome. All, including Dawid, would take the chance to hunt the Romans down again and cleanse their hills of them. The question was whether Brendan of the Selgovae had the power to offer it. He had been flirting with war with the Romans for a year. Conor found that foolish and said so.

"Brendan would do better to bide his time rather than poking at the Romans with a paring knife until they know exactly how many men he has and where they're laired."

Bran nodded at that. He had been tempted himself, but Conor was right.

Galt watched the king be persuaded by Dawid and Conor, saying the same things that he himself had said. It didn't matter so long as he listened. At some point he wouldn't. And perhaps by then the Roman strength would have been drained off again, as the emperors kept their armies flowing like the tide to try to keep so much territory in their hands. They would decide again eventually that they could turn their backs on Britain.

Bran stood up and the clan chiefs rose as well. Galt waited until they had left the chamber and they were alone before he turned on Bran.

"You would kill a man who was a guest in the house? In *Dawid's* house?" Galt had arrived that morning, driving furiously along the chariot track between Dawid's lands and the High King's hold. This would taint them all, possibly even Dawid.

"Did someone try to kill the Roman? That would have been most welcome, but it was not my hand on the knife," Bran said.

"It was your word that sent it! I am not a fool, Bran. Rhys has a cut on his knife hand. I wondered why you left him behind."

"To do what you should have and get you out of the Roman's lap!"

"You are a fool. Now you will have to go to Talhaiere and make amends. I doubt you'll like it." Galt looked disgusted.

"He isn't dead, unfortunately." Bran shrugged. "And in any case, it wasn't my knife."

"If the High King thinks that trying to murder a guest at secondhand is something the gods will overlook, then

112

the High King is more foolish than I thought," Galt said. "Your father killed a man on his own hearth, knowing what the punishment would be, and he went to his purification willingly, for the good of his people. That is the least you can do for yours, or evil will come of it, to be talking of war with that on your soul."

"Don't talk of my father to me!"

"Your father knew what was owed the kingship, and he paid it more than once."

"Then run and tell tales to Talhaiere if you will." Bran turned to Galt so that the triple spiral of the King Mark on his forehead was plain in the light from the lamp. "But I will not make penance for a Roman spy."

"Then you will make something worse," Galt said and turned on his heel.

VIII. Claudia Silva

Postumus stepped down from the chariot driven by the captain of Dawid's household in the shadow of the gray stone bulwark of Eburacum Fortress. Conscious that the manner of his arrival was creating some to-do, he saluted the sentries at the northwest gate and stepped through briskly, but just inside he turned back to watch the little knot of chariots heading north again, growing smaller along the road.

The great fort was almost empty. Postumus, stopping in the Principia for his orders, found a very junior centurion in charge, and the legate of the Victrix and almost every man in it who could carry a pilum already in the north this past week. His orders consisted of a testy note from the legate that Postumus's information had better be good, and a request that he report to the secondary field hospital at Castra Damnoniorum on the northern frontier immediately, on pain of some dark and unnamed retribution. He took a day to get a decent bath that wasn't in a freezing stream, to see how Gemellus was getting on, and to supervise the loading of replacement supplies, for which a mountainous stack of requisitions had arrived by military post that morning. He set out for the north the next day on Boreas, with a cavalry troop for escort, yet another contingent of Valerian's charges rousted out of the comfort of their hillside forts. They made slow going of it, from having to keep pace with the mule-drawn wagons, and Postumus, as the senior officer present, found himself dealing with crises that rarely came his way as a surgeon. An apparently undying enmity between a mule driver and a cavalry trooper, conceived on the first day out, was among them. Postumus and the cavalry decurion, who were younger and stronger than either, dealt with this by knocking their heads together and promising a repeat performance accompanied by stopped pay for both at any time that either started up again. This tactic halted further physical combat and left them confined to muttered insults about each other's sisters.

Worse was the cavalryman who decided to show off for a farmer's golden-haired daughter and took his troop horse over a thick hedge which proved to have a rocky ditch on the other side, and broke both its front legs. Killing a horse was a miserable occupation, but Postumus and the decurion did it anyway, in the certainty that the shaken trooper would botch it. Then they argued with the farmer about leaving a dead horse in his field and gave him a goodwill payment that the decurion furiously announced would come from the trooper's pay, after he had paid for the horse. It also rained a good part of the way.

It was in no good frame of mind that anyone rode into the supply depot at Corstopitum, south of the old wall, where they would add another mule train to their caravan, and double their cavalry escort. Postumus's mood was not improved by the depot commander informing him that the second cavalry troop had yet to arrive and that in any case the extra wagons wouldn't be loaded for three days. When Postumus complained that he was needed in the north now and not next Saturnalia, the depot commander said so were the wagons and he didn't have any spare men to waste protecting one lone surgeon from the Selgovae. Postumus saw the justice of this, stabled Boreas, and stalked off grumpily to find something to do for the next three days.

When the southern wall had been built twenty-five years before, Corstopitum had become a lazy, orderly place, keeping supplies moving east and west along the Wall's length with calm efficiency. Now it was once again the last major supply depot before the front lines, the jumping-off point for troops and grain wagons, and cart-loads of pilum points and newly fletched arrows. There was even a disassembled catapult, each piece numbered and tagged, in one wagon. Carts were coming in from the south or barges upriver from the coast to unload, military transport mostly, with a few civilian merchants thrown in. Postumus jumped back out of the road as a load of clay roofing tiles lumbered by.

He found the fort baths, where he oiled himself and scraped off the road dirt. There was no one else there at mid-morning except the statue of Fortuna at the end of the warm pool, and he spent an hour soaking there with just his nose and eyes above water like a crocodile until he was in a better mood. He persuaded the hospital laundry to do something with his travel-stained tunic, and with a clean one under his lorica and leather uniform kilt, set out to explore.

The fort itself was being rebuilt in stone, and Postumus skirted around piles of rubble and cut stone apparently left where they would be most in the way by the workmen swarming about them. Outside the gates, as Corstopitum's military population had exploded, so had its civilian one, swelled by the entrepreneurs who gathered in an army's wake. The market stalls by the public fountain were doing a brisk business in trinkets and souvenirs, and a number of shops advertised perfume, bath oil, and grooming kits for the discerning gentleman, the small luxuries that would grow scarce beyond the Wall. The Army was getting its fill of other luxuries as well. Six new wineshops and two new whorehouses had opened up in the last week, the hospital orderly had informed him. Business was booming in Corstopitum.

Postumus wandered idly through the crowded streets, wondering what to do with himself. He inspected a souvenir shop and moved on, having no great desire to own a pottery plate with the likeness of the Corstopitum Basilica embossed on it. He resisted also a jug with the emperor's visage, an array of sticky sweets, and the blandishments of a woman selling dubious bits of unidentified meat on a stick. A ragged urchin with a basket of rapidly wilting roses tugged at his belt.

"Ah, come on, commander. Buy a flower for your lady." The child gave him a pleading blue-eyed stare that somehow made him think of small Evan, and Postumus gave in and reached for his purse.

The child pocketed the coin and trotted off in search of a new customer, leaving Postumus to contemplate his purchase. Now what was he supposed to do with it, stick it behind his ear?

He moved on, and at the end of the street found himself at the gates of the Corstopitum arena. There was evidently a show in progress, judging from the jostling crowd outside the gates, and the shouts of approval from within. Ordinarily he had no taste for arena games, having been brought up with the conservative notion that pitting two men against each other to the death for amusement was a barbarity unworthy of a soldier. But gladiators were hard to come by in frontier towns and it was unlikely that there would be any death-matches unless someone had paid well for them. He shrugged and went in, pushing his way through the throng to a seat near the magistrates' box in the first tier. The arena attendants were raking the sand smooth for the next combat, and the crowd had begun to chat among itself while the food-sellers made their rounds. A crew who were probably time-expired sailors from the Fleet scrambled about overhead in the rigging of the red and green canvas awning, adjusting it for the angle of the sun. A banner across the arena wall announced that the games were made possible by the generosity of Rutilius Paulus.

Postumus saw a woman in the magistrates' box beside him turn to signal to a man with a tray of spiced pears, and realized that it was Claudia Silva, the contractor's widow who had dined with them in Isca Silurum. He caught her eye and she nodded in recognition.

Postumus stood and edged a few seats down to lean an elbow on the box. "Greeting to you, Lady. You're a pleasant sight to see so far north." As an afterthought he presented her with the rose. "Here. I've been looking for someone to give this to."

Her mouth twitched as she introduced him to her companion, who proved to be the generous Rutilius Paulus, senior magistrate of Corstopitum, but she made no move to prolong the interview. Postumus had the impression that he was somehow an embarrassment to her.

She was dressed more finely than he had seen her before, in a gown of canary-colored silk and a gray-green mantle worked along the borders in gold thread. She wore the same dark ruby he had seen on her hand in Licinius's house, and pearl drops in her ears and on pins in her hair. All in all, a fairly extravagant outfit to pack for a business trip. It couldn't be to impress the senior magistrate, who was twice her age and unprepossessing as a toad. At least he hoped not. He was mulling over the additional question of why his presence seemed to discomfit her when the arena trumpets sounded and the gladiators' gate at the far end swung open. Eight men emerged, blinking in the sunlight, each with his horsetail crested helmet beneath one arm. The crowd caught its breath.

They were paired two-and-two, four sword-and-buckler men and four with net and trident, moving with a practiced swagger toward the magistrates' box to give the salute. And then Postumus also caught his breath and swore, because the third sword-and-buckler man was Tertius. He marched across the fresh sand in the cocksure style of the arena, strutting a bit for the benefit of the crowd, while the spectators cheered and pelted their favorites with flowers and a little rain of coins.

Claudia and the magistrate had turned their attention to the arena, and Postumus slipped back to his own seat, cursing. A woman in a blue gown and an improbable cluster of red ringlets tossed a gold and amber brooch to Tertius, who caught it neatly in his upturned helmet with a rakish salute of thanks. She settled back in her seat, contentedly sucking a sweet, and made ready to cheer on her favorite. How many times had he done this, Postumus wondered. And how many more times before the inevitable happened?

They raised their arms in a salute to the magistrate, and the inevitable reached out its hand for Tertius. The upraised sword thudded in the sand at his feet and he toppled down across his shield.

The crowd was silent for a moment and then its voice swelled in outrage, cursing the fallen man, the woman in blue as loud as any. The arena mercuries came running with hooks and chains to drag him away, and the magistrate was furiously calling for a replacement.

Postumus was on his feet before the mercuries in their winged caps were halfway across the field. Pushing his way to the retaining wall that supported the tiers of seats, he swung his legs over it and dropped onto the sand. Tertius was limp as he turned him over and he was pale and sweating, but he was breathing. So far.

"Go away, damn you, he's not dead yet!" The mercuries halted uncertainly. That generally didn't matter.

Above them, the senior magistrate was losing ground and the crowd was throwing things. Rutilius must have been disinclined to let the mercuries manhandle a senior officer to whom he had just been introduced, but the crowd was turning nasty. He shouted again for a replacement, but he signaled the mercuries to stay where they were.

Postumus got Tertius half upright and staggered to his own feet. "Get him out of here," he said to the mercuries. "And carry him! If you touch him with those hooks, I'll skin you!"

At a nod from the magistrate, they took Tertius by the shoulders and feet, and Postumus followed across the hot sand, ducking as a ripe peach sailed by his ear. The arena master charged through the gate at their approach. A rotten plum caught him on the back of the head and he retreated into the passage.

"Get him inside and set him down!" Postumus snapped to the mercuries. He turned to the arena master. "He's no more fit for this work than he is to fly! Who's the jackass who let him in the arena?"

"And who are you?" The arena master glared at him furiously and Postumus pulled rank.

"I'm the senior surgeon of the Sixth Legion Victrix, where this man was enrolled, and if you weren't too cheap to hire one who knew anything…" The mercuries dragged Tertius into an ill-lit room off the passage under the stands and Postumus trailed off as his temper dissipated. "Oh, never mind. You take what you can get, I expect."

The mercuries set Tertius down, none too gently, on a bench. Postumus crouched beside him. Tertius's breath was still ragged but some color was coming back to his face. The arena master picked up a bucket of water and threw it over him, and then he glowered at Postumus.

"Now look here—"

Postumus was regaining his composure. "I'm a surgeon," he said again. "I certified this man Unfit for Service a month back. He's no business in the arena." He felt for Tertius's pulse. "Was he fool enough to sell himself in, or is he under contract?"

"Contract," the arena master said shortly. "We prefer to purchase in – makes them more contented, like – but he wouldn't have it."

"How long did he contract for, and what was his fee?"

"We don't contract for more than three months at a time," the arena master said. "It doesn't pay."

"How much?"

The arena master named a sum. "And now I'm out all that silver. I reckon the Army owes me for that."

"The Army owes you a kicking with hobnailed sandals for being a thieving fool."

"Half of that." The halting whisper came from Tertius.

The arena master, at a disadvantage now that his employee was conscious, conceded that he might have miscalculated the price.

Postumus considered. "I'll give you a quarter of it to buy him back out."

The arena master protested indignantly.

"He's no use to you now," Postumus said. "He'll just have another attack and spoil your games all over again, and probably die. Listen to those ghouls out there. They still haven't settled down."

There was a bit more haggling while Tertius, breathing more easily now, watched them with curiosity. In the end the arena master capitulated at a third of the original contract price, after pointing out that he could still use him "to clean up and such," and stomped disgustedly out to the arena to see that no further disasters occurred.

Tertius lay flat on his back. "It was just another fainting spell," he said, and Postumus considered just taking him back out to the arena and letting the crowd have him.

"I warned you, you know. We don't certify a good solider Unfit for Service on a whim. You may be good for years yet if you lead a quiet life." Probably not, but there was no point in saying that.

"I can't pay you back, you know," Tertius muttered.

"I didn't ask you to, you know," Postumus said.

A mercury ducked through the arena doorway. "You'd better clear out. The lads are coming back in for the intermission, and the fans won't be far behind. Get him out of here before they spot him." Arena spectators had little mercy for the fallen.

"Can you walk?" Postumus stood up and gave Tertius his hand.

"I'll have to, won't I?" Tertius said. He gave the mercury a salute, arena fashion. "A short career and sweet. Keep my place warm for the next poor bastard."

The mercury laid a hand on his shoulder. "Head up, man." He propelled him into the corridor that led from the arena gate, with Postumus following. It ended in an immense chamber located beneath the highest tiers of the arena seats. The walls were lined with racked weapons, and life-size wicker targets leaned drunkenly on their support posts. Tertius looked around him for a moment. "It was almost like the legion," he murmured. The double doors swung closed behind them, leaving them blinking in the sunlit street.

Postumus put Tertius's arm around his shoulders. "Lean on me. There's an inn not far down the way, and you need rest and sleep more than anything."

"And if I don't want it?"

"Then I will hit you on the head with a rock and see that you get it."

Tertius managed a wry smile at that. The missing tooth made it wolfish and not altogether friendly. "Aye, that would set me up fine, wouldn't it?"

The inn was appropriately called the Net and Trident and Postumus paid the proprietor, a grizzled man with the look of an ex-legionary about him, for a week's meals and lodging.

"I told you, I can't pay you back," Tertius hissed. "I spent my contract money."

"And I told you, no one's expecting you to. I'm the one who certified you unfit and then didn't chase you down when you talked about the arena. Allow me to salve my conscience with this at least."

Tertius considered this. "Aye, well somebody some-where owes me something. It might as well be you. Now go along back to where you were going. I'll do well enough."

"And no more arena?"

"How do I know what I'll be doing when the money runs out?" Tertius said, suddenly angry. "Go on, get lost! Thank you very much but get lost!"

The last sight Postumus had of him was his thin, wiry figure hunched against the doorpost, eyes focused bleakly on the world that strolled past the inn door and that now had precious little use for him.

–

The transit barracks at Corstopitum had been built to hold no more than a cohort at a time – an army on the march carried its own camp with it – and they were full past bursting. Overflow officers not traveling with their units had been quartered about the town, to mixed reception from the residents, while the troops and mule drivers being funneled through raised their camps outside the walls. As a senior officer, Postumus had been given his choice of a tent with the cavalry escort or a billet in a small town house that had been commandeered for the dura-tion. Foreseeing a future all too full of tents, he had opted for the town billet and now found himself the possessor of a down-at-the-heels chamber adorned with the flaking remains of an old mural and a mosaic floor that was missing every other tile. A straw mattress was laid on a bed which appeared to have one leg shorter than the rest and the only other furniture was a single precarious-looking chair. His fellow residents, absent when he had left his kit there in the morning, proved to be a fleet officer bound for Credigone, a legionary cohort centurion newly posted to the Second Augusta, and an officer of the Frontier Scouts returning from a month's leave – a hard-won one, judging by the healing scar on his left calf.

They had been there for several days, left like Postumus to cool their heels until an escort was available heading in the right direction; no one traveled the northern roads alone those days.

The house had been untenanted for at least a year, they informed him – that was why the Army had got it cheap – and the hypocaust was clogged with debris and wasn't working.

"But there's a brazier in your chamber," the frontier scout said, "and it doesn't smoke *too* badly if you leave the window open. Unless, of course, you've a mind to dig the dirt and dead rats out of the furnace, in which case we'll be glad to come and cheer you on."

Postumus declined, saying that if they hadn't seen the need for it, neither did he, and retired to his room, leaving them to their interrupted dice game in which the frontier scout was eagerly fleecing the young centurion while the fleet officer watched with detached interest.

The day's ride and the arena episode had taken their toll, and Postumus was asleep almost before he touched the bed, which didn't give him time to worry about what might be living in the straw. He slept late into the morning and was awakened only by the frontier scout, who poked his face, bleary-eyed, through the doorway to inform him that he had a visitor. "And not bad either, for your first day in," he added, shaking his head in admiration.

Postumus shrugged his tunic on over his head and ran his hands through his hair, and over his chin. He was looking vaguely around for his comb and razor when the door opened again and the frontier scout executed an elaborate salute before disappearing.

"I told that drunken idiot not to wake you up, but he seemed to think we had an assignation," Claudia Silva said. "*Are* you awake?"

"Close enough," Postumus said, wondering what she wanted and how on earth she had found him.

"I asked your whereabouts of the fort commander," she said, apparently reading his thoughts. "I came to ask how that man is, and why on earth you jumped into the arena after him. Rutilius Paulus thinks you're mad."

Postumus explained his bout of conscience. "The policy on men invalided out is brutally unfair. I only hope he doesn't do something worse next time."

"Poor man. Is his condition chronic?"

"Yes, I'm afraid it is." Postumus was trying valiantly to wake up.

"If he wants a job, you may send him to me. I'm camped outside the walls with our wagons. We shouldn't be hard to find." She pulled off her mantle, a cloak of gray-green edged with a finely embroidered russet band. "May I sit?"

"Of course, if that thing doesn't collapse under you. Camped with your wagons?" There were much better lodgings available and she could clearly afford them.

"Since my husband died, I have had to learn to run a business in earnest, and one of the great principles of that is that the boss must be in evidence. You have no idea how much stock loss and general hanky-panky that puts an end to."

Postumus was impressed, and curious. Generally, the law didn't give women property rights as such, not to run a business; there would have to be some sort of male guardian. On the other hand, that was a bit more loosely enforced in Britain, where women of the tribes had given up their earlier rights grudgingly or not at all.

"I'll pass your offer to him." He hesitated, looking for a tactful way to ask the next question. "Can you hire him? On your own, I mean?"

"Do you mean do I have a guardian?" She smiled. "I do not. My husband was much older than I was and I realized quite early on that I was likely going to be a widow. If I wasn't going to have my life hobbled with trustees and guardians, I had to be able to convince a court that I could manage my own affairs. It also allows me to give the boot to the men who every month or so kindly offer to take all this off my shoulders."

Postumus considered this. "If I told you that trying to run your business ranks right up there with having all my nails pulled off, would you trust me enough to dine with me tonight?" She was bound to be better company than his housemates. He ran his fingers through his hair again in an attempt to subdue it without the aid of a mirror.

"Thank you," Claudia said. "I should be charmed." She settled her mantle about her shoulders once more. "You may call for me at my camp at the twelfth hour. The tent with the ram's head banner. Until this evening, then." She smiled pleasantly and rustled out, her thin slippers whispering against the ragged floor.

Postumus located his comb, repaired his hair and knotted his scarf around his neck, deciding to go to the public baths and get a better shave than he could give himself in honor of the evening. An interesting woman, but there was something that either she wasn't telling him, he thought, or that he wasn't seeing, some kind of imbalance between Claudia's public face and what-ever wasn't public. And also not his business, of course, although she and Tertius would be material for a letter home.

Another knock rattled the door and Postumus turned around exasperatedly. Like most of his family, he was never fully functional when first awakened unless there was an emergency, in which case he was, and irritable into the bargain, and he was not in the mood for a second visitor.

"You're a popular lad this morning," the frontier scout said, poking his own unshaven countenance around the doorframe yet again. "I'da sent this one on his way, but seeing as the lady's left – but the next visitor is yours, whatever it is. I'm going back to bed, and not all the fiends of Ahriman, or anybody's light-of-love, is going to get me out again."

"Hold on a minute," Postumus said. The frontier scout gave every evidence of a man in pain. If he was that hung over, Postumus could only imagine the state of the centurion. "Mix this into a little beer, if you can stand it. It may help."

The frontier scout focused his eyes with effort on the packet of herbs that Postumus handed him. "Thanks. It can't hurt." He managed a sketchy salute and withdrew as a second figure pushed in behind him.

"I've come to take you up on what you said a month back," Tertius said. "That is, if you were meaning it."

"Meaning it…" Postumus tried to remember what he had said a month back. "You mean about a non-combat posting? Here, for the gods' sake, sit down. You shouldn't be running about loose."

Tertius sat. He was still pale. "I thought you'd likely be gone north by the time I'd had some rest."

"You're in no state to travel now."

"I'll serve in *your* hospital or not at all," Tertius said, "so you'll have to arrange it."

Tertius was beginning to feel like a complication growing more unwieldy all the time. The hospital laundry orderly had seemed disapproving of the fact that Postumus didn't possess a slave to do his wash, and Postumus had replied that if he wanted extra nuisance and responsibility trailing after him on a campaign, then he'd be sure to purchase a slave. Tertius seemed to be filling the same role without the advantage of laundry.

"I got you the promise of a job you could do with someone in Corstopitum already," Postumus said hopefully.

Tertius was silent.

"Are you sure you want to go back in the Army?"

Tertius regarded him stonily. "Yes, sir."

Postumus sighed. "Very well. But only if I have your oath you'll stay here a full week, and stay out of trouble. After that, you can catch the first escort going north to Castra Damnoniorum, but if I see you any sooner, I'll pack you right back south again. I mean that. And you realize that once you're back in, you're in. You can't change your mind."

"You can't change your mind when you carry a pilum in a cohort, either," Tertius said. "Sir." He stood up. "The Army's all I know. I didn't want out in the first place."

Postumus sighed. "Yes, I remember. You were a fine introduction to a new posting. Very well, I'll talk to the legate, and square it with payroll until your orders come through. I expect we'll need every man we can lay our hands on in the hospitals." All the same, he gave him directions to Claudia's camp in the event that he suddenly developed good sense.

–

Claudia said much the same thing that night in one of Corstopitum's overflowing inns. Unlike the basic bed and fare that Postumus had bought for Tertius, the menu painted on the wall outside the Dolphin offered hare in pastry, fresh oysters in brine, and wine from Gallia Narbonensis – Postumus doubted that was true, but it would probably be respectable. Corstopitum was enjoying the late daylight and the long summer twelfth hour, and there were tables set on the street outside as well as crowding the lamplit interior. Inside, the air was thick with the smell of the ovens and of cauldrons of stew, and the aroma of too many bodies, perfumed and otherwise. Claudia's chair was pushed right against the wall under a painted scene of Bacchus enjoying the Dolphin's fare, and the table had to be moved to allow her to sit down. Jammed against Postumus's back was a merchant with a wig of pale curls. He was buying dinner for a dark-haired boy who couldn't have been more than fourteen, and their arrangement was revoltingly obvious. On their other side a pair of legionary officers were arguing tactics, demonstrating their respective theories on the table with pieces of bread and a pepper pot. The innkeeper's slaves circulated, grumbling, with pitchers of beer and plates of food, threading their way among the tables. Every so often the crash of breaking crockery and a muffled curse cut through the jumble of voices. Postumus and Claudia leaned across the table toward each other to be heard.

"It's probably just as well that your man chose the Army," Claudia said. "I doubt that what I could offer him would have held him for long."

"Tertius is a born fighter," Postumus said dubiously. "I'm not sure I admire that temperament, but I do have a respect for it. I wonder what he'll do the first time he sees his legion march off without him. I don't think he's thought of that yet."

"Where are you posted to?"

"A secondary field hospital. They're calling the place Castra Damnoniorum, since it's in their territory. One of Agricola's old forts, I think. I don't know what it used to be. There are camp hospitals in all the forts, of course, and a main hospital at Credigone, under the governor's field surgeon, but the camp hospitals can't cope with everything and they were losing men carting them to Credigone, so they've opened up another one now. My junior surgeon's in charge of it at the moment, I believe."

"I hope there's a good garrison at Castra Damnoniorum then," Claudia said. "The Damnonii are half-kin to the Selgovae, and probably half Pict, and those western forts with no outposts beyond are prime targets."

"You're comforting," Postumus said, poking a knife at his hare and finding it edible. She was right, though. The western forts were open to any rebels hiding out in the north, as well as any southern forces of the Selgovae.

"You were born in Britain, weren't you?" he said. "Where are you from?"

"Lindum." She smiled. "My father was an aedile, and managed the city drains and water supply. I was his only child and my mother died when I was young. There is very little about aqueducts and plumbing that I don't know."

"Is he still living?"

"Alas, no. He had a wasting condition of the lungs and so made sure first to marry me to a situation that would suit us both – for him, a prosperous match, and for me—"

"One that might leave you widowed?" Postumus suggested.

"Am I that obvious? Yes, I fear so." She fished out a small moth that had dropped from the oil sconce above their heads into her wine. "My husband wasn't dreadful, but he treated me as if I was five, all the while leaving me responsible for managing a hundred slaves and freedmen. When something went wrong, I was to blame for it, being female, and when things ran smoothly, as they generally did, it was due to his sound judgment and superior knowledge."

"No wonder you don't want to marry again." Postumus finished his hare and pushed the bowl away from him. He wiped his fingers and eyed her empty plate. "If you have eaten, let's get some air." The room was growing progressively stuffier.

She nodded. He dropped a coin on the table and they edged their way to the door. Claudia took a deep breath in the purpling dusk. "I find that my tolerance for my fellow man increases greatly with my distance from him. And if we had stayed longer, I would have wanted to stab the man with that poor boy."

Postumus offered her his arm and they strolled through the twilight into the courtyard of the basilica and perched on the fountain's edge. A marble fish with a small imp on its back spouted water from its open mouth and Claudia dabbled her fingers in it idly. It was a moonshot night with rolling clouds above them. A troop of the Watch paraded once around the square, lanterns swinging, and were gone.

They watched the pattern of the water in the fading dusk, and Postumus watched his companion with more curiosity than was probably polite. "Where do you go from here?" he asked her after a silence.

"Oh, north to Credigone with my supplies," she said lightly.

"No farther?"

"Farther? What in Cybele's name would I be doing going farther, even if the governor would let me, which he wouldn't?"

"I don't know whether he lets you or not," Postumus said quietly, "but you do go, don't you?"

"And what makes you think that?" Claudia's face was shadowed by the folds of her mantle which she had drawn up over her hair, and her eyes shone almost silver in the moonlight. He could feel a growing tension between them, like a tautened wire. Perhaps not surprisingly, it carried with it a more physical urge as well. Postumus wondered if Claudia felt that too, but her silvered eyes gave away nothing. "And also what makes it any affair of yours?" she asked.

"I'm a soldier. When I suspect someone of slipping through the lines, it becomes my affair." He remembered the magistrate, a Briton, with whom she had sat at the games. The rebellious tribes of Valentia had sympathizers south of the old wall as well.

"I assure you, I am no spy for the Painted People." Like Postumus, she spoke in Latin, but she gave the Picts their British name.

"Then what are you?"

"A woman with a business to see to." She stood up. "And we move north in the morning, so you had best take me back to my camp."

Postumus escorted her without comment to the ring of wagons encamped by firelight south of Corstopitum's walls, but he drew her up short before they reached the first guard. "Now listen to me."

She stood, head thrown back, and waited.

"I don't know what you're up to but I'm beginning to have an idea, and I'm going to give you a piece of military advice: always have a backup plan, and then back *that* up. And that's straight from Julius Caesar."

Suddenly she smiled at him, a smile that made him think unsteadily that Helen must have had a smile like that, before he got a grip on himself.

"I'll remember," she said, "and thank you for dinner." Then she was gone into the firelit circle of her caravan.

IX. Trimontium

Postumus saw her the next morning standing in the rutted road, her brown gown girdled up above the mud, briskly giving orders to her drivers. The silver-shadowed figure had vanished with the sunrise and Claudia seemed again a prosperous merchant, despite her sex, businesslike as any who passed through Corstopitum. He waved as he strode past on his way to the baths, and she waved back but seemed intent on her wagons.

Postumus and his housemates got their own orders the next morning and departed gratefully from Corstopitum. A mile beyond loomed the great Wall of Hadrian, eighteen feet high and stone-built, topped with a parapet walk broad enough for two men abreast. Below it on the southern side was a flat-bottomed ditch, the vallum, thirty feet wide and seven deep, with embankments on either side made from the upcast from the ditch. They crossed the vallum on one of Governor Urbicus's newly widened bridges and passed through the Wall itself by the gate of Onnum Fort. Beyond the bulwark of the Wall was another ditch, even broader than the vallum and V-shaped, and here too the roadway had been widened and the ditch filled in to a width a cavalry troop could cross. At each milecastle between the forts the gates had been taken from their hinges. The Wall, which had been a solid barrier for most of Postumus's life, no longer marked the northern frontier of Britain. It had become a gateway through which flowed the traffic of reconquest.

Beyond it, the abandoned province of Valentia, now reclaimed, wore its new status with sullen acquiescence. Across the wild undulating landscape that stretched beyond the Wall, there was no sign of extant human habitation except the hand of Rome. There were fresh scars in the turf where the engineers had built their bridge and repaired the old road to Trimontium, but as they clattered along its newly paved surface, the only other sound was the sigh of the wind in the tussocky grass and the cries of the curlews overhead. They passed scattered empty holdings, some with the dark scars of burning; and once a ring of standing stones circled above a pair of ancient barrows, hollow chambers built by men now lost in the mists of history; but no living human of the Selgovae or the few clans of Brigantes whose holdings lay north of the Wall. They had vanished as completely as if they had disappeared into those hollow hillsides.

Or more likely into the halls of the Picts, Postumus thought. Those who were left would be lying low, but they weren't gone. The size of the supply train's escort testified to that. They would reappear soon enough if they saw the chance to take payment for the burned steadings and ravaged fields that Lollius Urbicus had left behind him.

Pacing themselves to the precious supply wagons, it took three full days to reach Trimontium, a fifty-acre fort of red sandstone built beneath the three peaks that gave it its name. Remembering Licinius's description of the last time he had seen Trimontium, Postumus looked about him with curiosity. Everywhere there was evidence of new repair. Trimontium was a fortress of the Eagles once more, polished and humming with military efficiency. Lollius Urbicus had indeed swept clean, including through the nearby hillfort of Brendan of the Selgovae, now standing empty, its outer walls tumbled by the stone-throwers of the artillery.

Postumus was grimy from the march and he headed gratefully for the baths, accompanied by most of the cavalry escort. The one luxury to which a Roman soldier was most addicted, and which a marching camp could not provide, was a proper bath. They scraped themselves clean and then soaked contentedly in the hot pool. Sounds of a brisk game of water tag floated over the partition from the adjoining cold bath, but as the senior decurion remarked, sinking blissfully into the hot water until only his nose and eyes showed, he'd bathed in enough cold rivers lately to last him a lifetime.

Afterward, scrubbed and brushed, Postumus went with a handful of other officers to make his sacrifice at the Temple of Mithras outside the fortress walls, as Hilarion and Licinius and probably his father had done before him. Mithras was a soldier's god and he commanded a soldier's strongest loyalty in a time of war.

The temple, built by a long-ago commander of Trimontium who had set his name and rank into the cornerstone, also showed signs of recent repair. Others had paused to make sacrifice on the road north and had paid their respects by restoring the dignity of the place. It was small and cave-like, so that the head must be bowed to enter, and two rows of benches lined the nave. At the far end, one small window in the roof lit the double altars of the Bull-Slayer, and between the twin torchbearers shone the carved relief of a great bull with the figure of the god astride his back – Mithras, the guide and mediator, whose word was Light.

Those who followed Mithras formed their own priesthood, and in the absence of formal ritual, they mimed the pouring of the wine and pricked their fingers over the altar for the sacrifice.

Postumus stepped forward into the pool of light. "Mithras, Unconquered Sun, Redeemer..." The others took up the invocation in turns.

"Grant us your aid and intercession..."

"And take our pleas before the Lord of Boundless Time..."

"As you slew the Bull..."

"For our sake..."

"Take now our sacrifice, freely given..."

"And grant us strength."

Postumus rubbed the blood from his pricked finger into the altar stones and as he did so, instead of the usual sense of kinship and comfort that always came with the sacrifice, he felt a cold cloud on his skin. It was so startling that he almost gasped. There was a dark splash of old blood across the altar where he knelt and as he touched it, it seemed to grow wet again. He knew, suddenly and surely, that it belonged to the last man who had made sacrifice at Trimontium in the old war, and that there had been something unspeakable in his soul then.

Postumus shuddered and pulled his hand away but the cold, dark cloud still clung, and it seemed to him that he was alone in the Mithraeum and it was his own blood that poured out across the altar. If there were ghosts anywhere, they were here at Trimontium, seeping up through the new stone of the rebuilding.

"Mithras, Lord of Armies" – his voice had become urgent and panic-stricken – "grant us peace and lift the desolation from this place."

The face of the god wavered before him in the shadows, and the shadows too pushed in around him until he was fighting for breath. He forced his eyes to those of the god and for a moment, he thought that two living eyes looked back at him from their smooth stone depths. And then the cold began to ebb away and the shadows drew slowly back to their accustomed places.

About him his fellows were completing their worship, and he rose and followed them out into the bright sun. He stood leaning against the outer wall until he felt the pounding in his heart subside. "What happened here?" he whispered, shaken.

"I thought you looked like something was getting to you," a gray-haired centurion from the Twentieth said. "You mean you didn't know? The whole garrison went over the wall one night in the last war. Bolted the gates on the inside and went – the whole garrison. They never found them. They were auxiliary troops, of course, but that was just before we lost the Ninth and I've always thought it had something to do with it. Trimontium's accounted unlucky now. The Senate wanted to pull it down nail by nail when they found out, but fortunately someone with more sense got hold of them."

"Or we'd all be busting our asses to build it back up again," a young auxiliary officer said, grinning. He looked at Postumus. "You don't look so good. You'd best come and eat something. You're right about that temple, though. There's a nasty feel to it."

So Trimontium too had gone into the pit that under-manning and neglect had opened up for the Ninth

Hispana. Postumus wondered how enduring the lesson of that horror would be. "We're at the edge of the Empire," he remembered Licinius saying. "When it's a choice between us and the southern provinces, it's our troops that are drained off first." Would the troops that Lollius Urbicus had brought with him be allowed to stay this time, to see that their work endured?

–

In the morning they were on the march again, on the northwest road to the western edge of the old frontier – and the far edge of the Empire. Postumus, the soldier son of a long line of soldiers, was not easily unnerved, but he turned his back on Trimontium gratefully.

As they pushed north, the traffic on the road grew greater, and newly built signal stations rose less than a day's march apart along their way. Couriers, also heavily escorted, passed them in both directions and twice they were overtaken by mounted troops in the flamboyant armor of the auxiliary cavalry, heads thrown back and singing as they went. For now, at least, the best that Rome could send was traveling the roads that Agricola had carved into the highlands over sixty years ago.

Agricola had fought his way around the Bodotria Estuary, secured his work with a naval station at Horrea and a legionary fortress at Castra Pinnata, and then pushed his army north along the eastern coast almost as far as Taezalorum Head before the Emperor Domitian had recalled him and Rome had begun to drain off troops from Britain to fight for more profitable conquests in the East. Now along the walls and ditches of Agricola's deserted camps rose the new forts of Emperor Antoninus Pius and Governor Lollius Urbicus.

The garrison at Damnoniorum was an auxiliary cohort of the Nervii out of Belgica, although as with most of the auxiliaries, their senior officers were Roman. It had been built on the remains of one of Agricola's old camps and the present commander had even known where to dig for the supplies those long-ago troops had not been able to take with them when the evacuation order came. Like the building of a fort, its evacuation followed a certain pattern from which future garrisons might benefit. Their excavations had turned up a hoard of iron nails which the building crews had seized upon, but better yet, to Postumus's mind, was the bundle of copper scraps, left by some long-gone surgeon to form the verdigris used to halt infection.

The hospital was situated in its usual spot beside the Principia in the center of the compound, and Lucian met him in the portico, wiping his hands on a bloody apron and looking overworked. Postumus thought furiously of the time he'd spent kicking his heels in Corstopitum and then, guiltily, of the extra days he had remained beyond absolute necessity in the Brigantian Hills.

Lucian saluted, bloody hand to the bloody apron covering his chest. "Disgusting way to greet you, sir. All the same, I'm glad to see you." His thin face looked worried. Lucian was solitary by nature, Postumus thought. He wasn't ready to command the frantic pace of a field hospital, but he had had no choice. Fortunately, despite Lucian's bloody appearance they were, he said, in a lull at the moment. All the blood had come from a soldier who had cut his foot with a builder's adze. "The commander will want to see you when you've settled," he said. "I'm going to bathe."

The hospital itself followed the usual pattern of four wings around a courtyard, but it had been rebuilt in timber over the remains of the old Agricolan hospital, unlike the smooth stone and tile roofs of the hospital complex at Eburacum. Inside, the walls were plain Army whitewash and the floors were oiled wood. The dispensary cupboards were ample and well stocked, and their doors had been prudently secured by iron locks to which he was handed the key. The locks had been recently oiled and the key turned without protest. Postumus breathed in the familiar sharp scent of herbs and unguents and the sticky sweetness of the poppy cakes.

Castra Damnoniorum, like its sister forts a few miles to either side, was overlooked by a stretch of hills still in Pictish hands, and a double row of ditch-and-rampart works had been raised around it, over the remains of what had once been an annex to the fort. Beyond this perimeter blossomed a field of "lilies," sharpened stakes sunk in circular pits and masked with brushwood. Beyond that line, to the north, the ground was strewn with caltrops.

It looked very much as if they were expecting trouble and indeed, they had already had trouble enough, as Centurion Frontinus, the battle-scarred Damnoniorum camp commander, informed him at his briefing. Frontinus had a graying brush of hair and a scar that ran from his brow down to the bottom of his mangled left ear.

"The minute we lighten our guard or cut back our patrols by so much as half a mile, they come swarming down out of the hills like flies out of a carcass," Frontinus said. "We haven't the men to take out after them until we've finished settling the Selgovae's hash at our backs, but we've got to hold till then, or there's the whole frontier to retake."

"How big an army has Brendan got left to him?" Postumus asked.

"That's just the trouble. We don't know for sure. Report has it that his army's massing for a final push this season, but where is another matter. There's a lot of Valentia to hide out in, and a Briton practically melts into the ground when you look at him."

Before they could go further, the commander's briefing was interrupted by shouting outside the Principia and a wagonload of wounded, the ragged remains of a cavalry patrol sent out by the next fort to the west. They had beaten back their attackers, but only when a second patrol had crossed their trail and ridden to reinforce them. Makeshift field aid had been applied and they had left their emergency cases to the single surgeon at their camp hospital and sent the rest to Castra Damnoniorum. Postumus began checking them as the orderlies lifted them from the wagon.

"Get a better tourniquet on this one until I can get to him," Postumus said. "Lucian, start one of the apprentices on this one. I think it's going to take a 'spoon' to get that spearhead out so tell him to go carefully."

The next man was covered with a light blanket, leaving only his sandaled toes exposed. "There won't be much you can do for that one," the man with the broken spear in his shoulder said tiredly, and Postumus almost gagged as he saw that the body had no head.

He dropped the blanket down again. "Identify him before they burn him," he snapped at the orderly standing at his elbow. "He'll have to go on the Dead List with the rest. But don't bring him in here." The head, he knew queasily, would be tied to some Selgovae warrior's belt.

Postumus, Lucian, and Flavian, the other junior, plus the apprentices, worked for the better part of the day over the nine living bodies taken from the wagon, while the tenth was identified by a retching comrade from the troops that had ridden in with them.

"It's the head, sir," he apologized to Frontinus, who also looked a little sick. "If it wasn't… gone… it wouldn't be so bad. Poor old Crispus. Do you suppose he'll get his head back in the Otherworld, sir?"

Frontinus scratched his own head, possibly at a loss for words for the first time in his career. "I expect so," he said, and laid a hand on the trooper's shoulder. "Now get along back to your camp. Take him and light his pyre with his own men around him."

Of the nine wounded, Postumus was cautiously hopeful that they had saved six, which as he said to Lucian afterward, wasn't bad, considering. One had been dead when they got to him, one had a spear clean through his chest and had bled to death despite everything, and one was in shock and they had never been able to bring him out of it. He didn't survive the amputation of the leg that had been crushed beyond repair by the iron-bound rim of a chariot's wheel. Cinnamus, one of the two apprentices, had pulled the spear from his patient's shoulder with the long-handled Spoon of Diokles, which encased the barbs of the spearhead and drew them out without tearing the flesh, and it looked as if the shoulder muscles were going to heal cleanly. But Postumus had spent three hours stitching the intestinal wound of a man who had taken a vicious spear thrust in the belly, and Lucian had worked himself to exhaustion over the man with the crushed leg, only to lose him in the end.

Postumus, checking the man with the belly wound the next day, was grimly afraid they were going to lose him too, and three days later this foreboding proved right. Lucian found him outside the ward, slamming his fist against the wall.

"You know if you keep that up, you won't be able to operate at all," Lucian said. "Do I remember you telling me, when that amputation case died, that I had better learn I couldn't save them all if I ever wanted to make a good Army surgeon? Sir," he added as an afterthought.

"It never occurred to me that you'd throw it back in my face," Postumus said truthfully. "Come on, let's make the rounds and go get some dinner. Flavian has duty tonight, and he's got Cinnamus and young Quintus. Unless there's a night attack somewhere we should have some peace."

After a dinner of camp fare cooked over the fire in Lucian's rooms, and left wakeful by the past days' effort and the still, something's-going-to-happen feeling of the frontier at night, they wandered into the room off the Principia that served as a communal gathering place for the officers of Damnoniorum. Their numbers were not great – Frontinus, the camp commander, and four senior centurions of his cohort (the fifth had been killed the week before chasing a Pictish raiding party that had led them into a walled valley and then fired the heather behind them); four cavalry decurions posted from the elite Ala Petriana; Postumus, his junior surgeons and apprentices; and the occasional officer of the Frontier Scouts, who kept no regular post but went mainly where they could keep an ear to the wind in the heather and give the most annoyance to the Pict.

One of the scouts was there tonight, busily teaching a British board game, which seemed to be compounded mainly of inspired cheating, to one of the commander's centurions. "The bastards'll slip your tunic off under your breastplate," Frontinus muttered, watching his junior officer being expertly fleeced by the scout.

"There's not much else to do up here, sir," Lucian said, with a fascinated eye on the game. He pushed his hair back from his face – despite all efforts it resolutely refused to curl, hanging instead despondently over his ears. He sat up as the beaten centurion threw up his hands. "Here, let me try. I think I've got the hang of it."

"Uh, Lucian… I wouldn't," Postumus said, but Lucian shook his head.

"Don't worry, I think I see how it's done." He took the centurion's place.

Postumus winced. The scouts doubled their pay on people like Lucian, he thought, remembering his house-mate in Corstopitum. "Don't gamble with the scouts" had been Hilarion's parting advice on his stepson's departure for the Army.

Lucian smiled at the frontier scout. "Come, friend, show me the rules."

–

"What in Fortune's name are you doing in the Medical Corps?" Postumus inquired admiringly as they made their way back to their quarters, Lucian cheerfully jingling the coins in his purse. "You ought to be fleecing the tourists in Aquae Sulis."

"Actually, I thought about teaching mathematics at one point," Lucian said, "but it seemed so dry compared to medicine. That game's not particularly difficult. It's a matter of getting the moves right, and then remembering them. That and knowing the odds, of course. It's a lot like latrunculi."

Since latrunculi was a hideously complicated game of military tactics at which Postumus couldn't have beaten an eight-year-old, he refrained from comment, merely making a mental note of his junior surgeon's uncanny ability, for possible future use. No wonder the boy was so fascinated by research. A mind like that had to go somewhere. He really belonged in one of the old teaching hospitals at Alexandria, but these days Army medicine probably came the closest, although admittedly it was practiced in the face of much distraction.

This was brought home to Postumus once again the next morning, when an optio hauled him out of surgery and, loudly protesting, off to the commandant's office in the Principia. Postumus shucked off his bloody apron and found Frontinus, looking somewhat harassed, seated at his desk, and before him, in a cross-legged chair, his helmet with its eagle feather crest on a table beside him, Aelius Silanus, Legate of the Sixth Victrix. He had a young tribune in a purple-bordered tunic with him, a staff officer doing his year in the Army; he couldn't have been more than nineteen, Postumus thought from his lofty vantage point of twenty-four.

Postumus swallowed and eyed the legate warily, but Silanus appeared to be in a reasonably good mood. "Well, Corvus, you took your sweet time getting here," he said briskly. "I hope your information justifies it."

Postumus blinked. "The Brigantes, sir?" Two-thirds of his mind was still on his surgery and how well young Cinnamus was doing with the feverish thigh wound that Postumus had turned over to him at the optio's insistence.

"Of course the Brigantes! Who do you think I sent you to spy on, the governor's horse?"

"I beg your pardon, sir," Postumus said. "I'm somewhat distracted at the moment. The man I was working on – if that leg gets infected—"

"He can die secure in the knowledge that his sacrifice has been of service to Rome," the legate said. "Sit down, Surgeon Corvus, and stop blithering. Your junior surgeons are perfectly capable of handling that wound. I know, because I told the optio to wait, if you were engaged in repairing an essential part of anyone's anatomy, and I'm not used to being disobeyed."

"Yes, sir." Postumus sat.

"Now tell me what you've been able to get on those demons."

"Enough to make me nervous, sir," Postumus said frankly. "As well as one or two things that I found reassuring. Rather a mixed report, I'm afraid."

"Explain." The legate folded his hands on the gilded metal of his breastplate and leaned back in his chair.

"The man I treated was Galt." Postumus struggled to put his memories in report form. "He was regent for the tribe for probably fourteen years after the old king was killed, and he was the one who signed the treaty with us." Postumus paused. "And then there's the High King, Bran. He's about twenty-six, which means that he's held his own power for a dozen years – boys in these tribes become men at fourteen. He doesn't like Rome or anything smelling of it."

"But Galt does?" the legate asked.

"Not like, no," Postumus said, "although he is willing to make use of us when it suits him. He's merely more practical than Bran. Also, I think that what concerns Galt most is that the tribe itself should survive."

"Whereas Bran would dance on our graves and let the future take care of itself," the legate said. "Someone should remind him of what happened to the Iceni after Boudicca did that."

"I expect Galt has," Postumus said, "but I doubt that Bran is thinking in those terms. If he wins, he assumes it won't come up."

"His father didn't win," Aelius Silanus said, "not in the long run. And Bran won't either if he tries it. I looked up the old records when trouble first started stirring. The only reason the Brigantes didn't go the way of the Iceni was this Galt's diplomacy, and there are a lot of people who still think we owe the Brigantes one. Rome gets very vindictive when we lose an Eagle."

"How much influence has Galt got?" Frontinus asked.

"A fair amount in most things," Postumus said. "He is well thought of in the tribe, he was the old king's hound and leader of his household warriors, and he holds the same post for the new king. That may be only because as regent he kept the young king on his throne. I'm not sure there is any love between them, but it will take some strength of will for Bran to go against Galt's advice. If it comes to starting a war, though, Bran will have the final say as long as his clan chieftains go along."

"And if the High King is muddleheaded enough to do that?" the legate asked. "What will Galt do?"

"He'll follow him, if the Council votes for war," Postumus said. "He won't go against the Council."

The legate muttered something irritable and indistinguishable, and then his questioning turned to the Brigantes' weapons and how many men they could field in a war, which Postumus answered as accurately as he could, with no real certainty; and to Bran's relations with Brendan of the Selgovae, on which subject Postumus could supply nothing more than a vague suspicion based on past performance. Which put him, as the legate said, about even with the rest of the Army.

"The Brigantes and the Selgovae are kin to each other," Silanus explained to the tribune. "And it's the Brigantes who are sitting in our laps around Eburacum. If they go, we've got trouble."

"They've allied with the Selgovae before, of course," Frontinus said. "That was one of the main reasons for the southern wall, to break that up."

"Which left the Selgovae free to keep up their acquaintance with the Picts." The legate tapped his fingers on his breastplate. "Or at least with the Caledones, which means two-thirds of the most powerful Pictish clans. Fortunately, the Picts and the lowland tribes hate each other almost as much as they hate us."

"Why is that, sir?"

"The Picts give their first worship to the Mother and the lowland tribes to the Sun Lord. They'll only ally when it gives them a good shot at Rome. When Galt and Brendan made treaty with us, the Caledones walked out of the council, and when our army went after them, the lowland tribes sat tight and waved us on our way. Lately they've been getting entirely too chummy again. That had more to do with our opening up the Wall than any amount of petitions from the Votadini."

"And what are the Votadini doing all this while?" the tribune asked.

"Paying their taxes and behaving themselves. All they wanted was for us to get Brendan out of their hair. The

Selgovae are a lot bigger and stronger than the Votadini and they've been encroaching on their territory for years. The Votadini decided a long way back that their best chance lay with Rome and they've stuck to it. When Brendan began lifting their cattle a little too heavily, it gave us a chance to show that we protect our own." The legate's voice was slightly cynical. "And, incidentally, a good excuse to tone down Brendan's sphere of influence." He flicked at the ends of the white general's sash that was knotted about his spare middle. "We've a good idea that Brendan was after the Votadini to ally with him in an uprising, and when they wouldn't go for it, he stepped up his raiding to put pressure on. The Votadini aren't saying, for fear we might think they'd have gone along with it."

"And then there's the Damnonii, the local folk around here," Frontinus said. "They're behaving for the moment, but then they don't like the Pict, and they live a lot too close to him for comfort. And the Novantae in the southwest of Valentia might just as well be lumped in with the Selgovae. They're more a subgroup of the Selgovae than a separate tribe anyway, and they follow the Selgovae Warlord when it comes to a fight."

The tribune listened to this reckoning of old feuds and blood ties with a certain amount of confusion, and Postumus gave him a sympathetic glance. "The situation up here is nothing like what you've seen in the south," he said. "I was born in the south and it might as well be a different country. The southern tribes have been part of Rome since Agricola's campaign and they've lost a lot of their territorial distinctions. They're urbanized, modernized. They're Roman. Mostly."

"It's the civilian influence that does that," the legate said, "once the Army has made it possible. The tribes here in the north have very little civilian influence to alter their structure. Even the colonia at Isurium Brigantum has made little difference. They're a warrior people and strongly independent. Their way of life is fighting. If there's no common enemy, they fight each other."

"Shouldn't that make it easy enough for us to pick them off one at a time?" the tribune asked.

"It does and it doesn't," Silanus said. "That's exactly what we have done, but occasionally a king comes along who's powerful enough to fight the lesser tribes around him and overrun them completely. Then he draws all those tribes under his standard as well, and becomes a force to be reckoned with."

"I've been told their warriors are highly undisciplined," the tribune said.

"As a general rule they are," Postumus began. "But—"

"There's always a 'but' when you're dealing with Britain," Frontinus said. "The most you can be sure of is that most things that happen will not be what you were expecting."

"I'll remember that," the tribune said. "That in itself is a useful piece of information."

The legate rose. "Now I am going to perform the unexpected, in the form of a short-notice inspection of my legion's garrisons between here and the coast. The governor's headed this way, which should terrify all of us."

X. Samhain Wind

As if the legate's visit had signaled some change in the wind, the tempo of life in Castra Damnoniorum picked up from then on, even while the casualties decreased. It was the changing time of year when summer gave way to autumn and dark clouds scudded across the sky, driven on an increasing wind. Postumus, waiting for Tertius to appear, was concerned when he did not, but there was no way to do more than wonder if he had decided after all that he could not bear to be an onlooker when his legion marched.

Couriers came and went daily and the Frontier Scouts shifted back and forth like smoke across the lines. Troops were shifted and re-shifted according to the latest reports, and suddenly, for reasons best known to the generals, the main army moved westward away from Credigone, to camp just slightly to the south of Castra Damnoniorum. With them came Aelius Silanus and the Sixth Victrix; the Second Augusta, Hilarion's old legion, most of which was also attached to the northern army; and a sizeable detachment of the Twentieth Valeria Victrix out of Deva. The governor was also with them, but all anybody saw of him was his angular form and purple cloak riding beside Silanus as the army marched in.

Appius Paulinus, the centurion from aboard the *Nereid*, arrived with the rest of the Sixth and found his cohort assigned the unenviable task of helping to calibrate the catapults. The governor had brought an onager, the monstrous stone-thrower designed to break walls in a siege, and two bolt-throwing scorpions that could wreak havoc among an attacking force. It would take a whole day to set them up, calibrate the right and left tension to an equal force, and make note of range and impact for each trajectory. The torsion springs were made of animal tendon and varied in their elasticity, and unequal tension could throw the stone or bolt off-center. Paulinus was less than delighted – catapults often had a mind of their own and could easily take a finger, or someone's head, off. Lucian, on the other hand, was enthralled, and hung about in the open plain below the camp while the torsion springs were wound up, offering advice and annoying the engineers. The legate also had a tendency to get in the works and everyone was terrified of killing him by mistake.

Valerian's cavalry wing had also made its appearance, along with two others, and Valerian rode up to the hospital at Damnoniorum in the evening to renew his acquaintance with Postumus and see if anybody there knew anything more than his lot, which was not much.

Postumus, grateful for a break in the waiting, which was beginning to stretch everyone's nerves thin, took him off to his quarters and produced a hoarded jug of good wine.

"You can't know less than we do," Postumus said. "I've had orders to get this hospital ready to be moved – but where I'm to move it to, no one has seen fit to mention." With the arrival of Silanus, his hospital command was formally transferred back to the Sixth Victrix.

"Knowing Urbicus, you'll have an hour to do it in, when you *are* told," Valerian said, taking an appreciative sip out of one of the green glass cups. "He's holed up in his tent, interviewing scouts. There were two who looked like rag-and-bone sellers, one that I would swear was either a Pict or a man who'd had an argument with a vat of blue dye, and tonight a Briton who turned up with his cloak over his face and a governor's pass in his hand, and nipped off again an hour later. It's all a matter of where the Selgovae are, of course. I expect he's got wind they're in this part of the woods somewhere, but there are so many paths through the heather you'd think they had the fay folk on their side."

Postumus considered that. "If we don't catch them by the end of autumn, it'll all be to do over in the spring, won't it?"

"Most like," Valerian said. "And then there's the matter of the Pict. We've played will-he-won't-he over him for so long, we're all sick of the subject."

"Ally with the Selgovae, you mean?"

"Mmm. The Pict is a wily beast. Just because he's let some of the Selgovae take refuge in his hunting runs doesn't *necessarily* mean he'll cross the frontier to fight for them. On the other hand, of course, he might, if the mood strikes him and there's something in it for him. Still, if I was Brendan, I wouldn't hang my hopes on the Picts without a damned good assurance. And then I'd move in a hurry. Alliances with the Picts don't often last very long. There's too much old enmity there."

Postumus poured them both another cup of wine and then sat looking at his. Brendan's last alliance with the Painted People had lasted just long enough to destroy a legion. He was obviously still negotiating this one or he would have moved before now. "Well, let's hope we can find him before he gets it settled," he started to say when there was a hurried tap at the door and Lucian stuck his head in.

"We're moving, sir!" he said, excitement in his dark eyes. "They've just sounded Turnout for Parade and it looks like the governor's camp sat on an anthill."

Valerian stood up and jammed his helmet on his head. "Any bets we've found Brendan?" He grinned. "It looks like that Briton had more in his hand than a governor's pass. See you in the wars, friend." He caught up his cloak and was gone.

Outside, the whole fort was astir. The speech that Aelius Silanus gave the Sixth was brief and to the point: They moved out in the morning, all upcoming leaves were cancelled, and any man who wasn't ready to march by first light could expect awful retribution. He ended with the usual evening prayer before the legion's Eagle and the cohort standards, but tonight it took on a more urgent meaning. Afterward each man went to pray to his own gods against the morning, and Postumus, with Frontinus and Paulinus, made his prayers to the God of Soldiers at a makeshift altar in the camp commander's quarters.

Optios, mule drivers, and quartermasters hustled back and forth through the fort and the extended camp beside it. Civilian hangers-on were shooed away. Officers delivered last-minute speeches to their troops. Frontinus's sentries at the Dexter Gate dragged in a trio of cavalrymen who had been located in one of the wine stalls that trailed the Army. The night was clear and cold as jet and trailed with stars, but to the north Postumus could see a thicker charcoal tone to the sky – and no stars. There was a storm building somewhere in the north, over the hunting runs of the Painted People. He wondered if it would bring that mysterious enemy with it on its heels.

Then he was caught up in making ready for battle, as so many times before in so many other provinces, and the familiar stomach-twisting uncertainty as to how many men would be beyond his help at the end of it, and how many of them would be his friends. He stood briefly before the little statue of Aesculapius that he kept in his kit and said a prayer there too.

In the morning, with the field hospital packed into its wagons and the remaining patients left behind in the charge of one unnerved apprentice, they moved out to the south in the wake of the Sixth to swell the ranks of Lollius Urbicus's avenging army. They marched in battle order, auxiliaries to the front and rear, the hospital and baggage wagons tucked under the protective wing of the three legions that formed the bulwark of Urbicus's troops. The staff of the eastern field hospital, consisting of the surgeons of the Valeria Victrix and the Second Augusta, with Governor Urbicus's field surgeon in command, marched with them. Postumus, with Lucian and Flavian in attendance, sidled up beside the Chief Surgeon's horse and made introductions, while Cinnamus waited a respectful few paces behind. Calpurnius Aquila, the governor's surgeon, was a squat, balding man with a paunch and one wildly skewed eye. Postumus, who knew him by reputation, saluted him with some awe while he glared at them from the saddle. Aquila was generally credited with the highest surgical skill and the vilest temper in the Empire. The other two senior surgeons, Postumus noted, seemed well under his thumb.

Aquila looked Postumus up and down with the steely eye of a quartermaster inspecting a side of meat and finding it wanting. He eyed the insignia on his belt and snorted. "How did you come by seniority while you're still in swaddling bands?"

"The wisdom of the Army, which I do not question," Postumus said. "I'm accounted a fair surgeon by such of my patients as survive," he added.

Aquila lowered a pair of brows like hedgerows at him. "Don't frighten you, do I? Well, brace yourself, sonny, because I'll scare the shit out of you later."

"Yes, sir. I don't doubt it, sir." Postumus saluted and backed Boreas away.

Lucian and Flavian, sticking to his side like glue, looked utterly unnerved.

"Good gods, sir, is he always like that?" Lucian asked.

"From what I've heard of him," Postumus said, "he's a good deal worse."

"What do we do?" Cinnamus whispered, fixing a terrified eye on the substantial bulk bouncing in the saddle ahead of them.

"Speak when you're spoken to," Postumus said. "And learn everything you can from him. The old bastard's accounted the best surgeon in the Army."

They pushed on until evening at half-quick march. The assembled catapults loomed over the baggage line, strapped in their wagons. The light cavalry fanned out ahead of them, Valerian's heavy troops guarding their flanks. They circled wide once to avoid a holding of the Damnonii. The Damnonii might be at peace with Rome, as the Augusta's surgeon remarked, but they wouldn't like having their fields trampled and it wouldn't do to encourage some helpful soul to go inform Brendan that Rome was on its way to make mincemeat of him. When the scouts found ground to the governor's liking, they made camp.

A Roman marching camp duplicated the plan of every fort in the Empire. Before the tail of the marching army had even approached, surveyors had laid out the streets and the spot for the commander's quarters in the Praetorium tent where the Via Praetoria and Via Principalis crossed at right angles. It was immediately surrounded by ditch and rampart on all four sides, dug under the eye of the engineers while the cavalry and half the heavy infantry kept guard, pulling back century by century, as the rampart went up, to work on the remainder. In the morning it would all be pulled down again and even the ditch filled in so the enemy couldn't circle behind them and make use of it.

The next day they were on the march again, this time at full double-step, before the weird light of dawn had given way to the true paling of the eastern sky. Dawn, when it came, was closed and ominous, the dull steel gray of a winter sea. The air was oppressive, as if the gods were out and about in it, and Postumus tied his cloak to his saddle back and twitched uncomfortably at his scarf. His skin itched under his helmet and breastplate.

A scout on a lathered horse dove through the ranks of the vanguard and they halted with a suddenness that almost sent the troops behind them crashing into their rear. The scout wove his way unchallenged through the First Cohort of the Victrix and halted before the legate and the tall angular man beside him.

"Coming from the south," he gasped, pointing. "They have scouts in front. We killed four but I think there was another one who got away."

"Well, I expect it will save us the trouble of announcing ourselves," Lollius Urbicus said. He turned to an aide beside him. "Every commander, up here to me now."

The governor's standard-bearer swung his banner overhead and they came at a gallop, saluted, and sat at parade rest, awaiting the orders that most of them could have predicted. "The Selgovae are a mile to the southwest," Urbicus informed them. "They know where we are too. By my best information, the chances are nine in ten that the Pict is not on our tails. You will remember that other chance, however, and act accordingly."

The commanders saluted and dispersed, and soon the whole column of the army began to shift itself into a new pattern. The hospital was to stay where it was, with the baggage carts forming the outer perimeter and the reserves circled around that. Postumus, as usual, was left to watch his friends march out and to wonder how many of them would march back again with a whole hide. He saw Appius Paulinus at the head of his cohort, his shield newly painted with the bull and thunderbolt insignia of the Sixth. Valerian gave a mock salute and whistled "All's Well" as he cantered by, the horsetail crest on his helmet flying, and Frontinus grinned and gave the thumbs-up sign when his cohort swung past. Calpurnius Aquila, rendered even more irascible than usual by the impending battle, was ordering the set-up of the hospital and Postumus turned hastily to help him. They had the tents up and half the supplies out before they heard the first trumpet sound the Advance. Around them the reserves were erecting their own ditch-and-wall amid much grumbling about playing nursemaid to the baggage train. Calpurnius Aquila dispatched an orderly with arms like an ape to request their silence, and quiet fell.

They were in open country bordered by a low wooded ridge, beyond which, according to the scouts, lay the war host of the Selgovae. A wide track through the woods showed signs of recent use, and on the scouts' advice Urbicus had decided to take advantage of it, and beat them to the best ground, counting on the unexpectedness of their arrival as insurance against ambush.

The army moved forward into the green-gold dapple of the trees, a sea of steel and scarlet following the gilded Eagles of three legions and the Eagle-bearers in their lionskin hoods. The great catapults towered over them as they rumbled up the track. The dragon banners of the cavalry filled with air as they rode, and snapped open, writhing above their bearers. As the vanguard came out of the woods on a slope above a rolling moor, Valerian, on the flank with his Dacian horse, saw the assembled war host of the Selgovae gathering. They numbered in the thousands, with more warriors on foot behind the massed front line of chariots. The chariots were freshly painted, their ponies hung with gold and silver trappings that caught the rising sunlight, their drivers' bare chests blue with war paint. Valerian narrowed his eyes.

"Go back and tell the governor that Brendan has women in his battle line," he said to the trooper next to him and the trooper spun his horse around.

British women were warrior-trained along with the men. They could fight and drive as well as the men. But no war leader put either his women or his mares into battle without desperate need. This was Brendan's last stand.

It was clear that the Roman excursions of the last few years had diminished Brendan's numbers only somewhat, but if there were women in the line, then this was all he had. The sun danced on the pony trappings and the wicked little knives that extended from each chariot wheel. When they saw that the Romans were going to halt on the high ground, they came forward with a rush, howling like wolves up the slope, each eager to be first in the battle line. The auxiliaries in the Roman front line greeted them with a rain of flung pilums and then knelt, locking shields in a solid wall from shoulder to knee, while the men behind them flung theirs in a second deadly rain of iron. The heavy points drove through shields and chariots and the untempered shafts bent, embedded, pulling shields away and tangling wheels. The Roman line rose again and braced itself behind the shield wall, men behind moving up to fill any gaps as the chariots came on. A chariot charge was a terrifying sight, but the infantry had learned that if they put up their shields in an apparently solid barrier, the horses would mostly stop before it. It was difficult to force a horse to crash into what looked to it like a solid wall. The front chariots tangled and their horses reared and struggled through the chaos, running loose as riders fell.

The bolt-throwing scorpions on the ridge flung their iron missiles over the Roman heads into the middle of the Selgovae war band. The chariots came on, buffeting themselves against the Roman line, breaking through in places, before the next man stepped up to lock shields with those beside him. The scorpion bolts tangled men and chariots until the scythe blades on the wheel hubs were as deadly to the chariot ponies as to the enemy. They abandoned their chariots then, the warriors leaping down to fight on foot, pushing against the Roman lines with the massed foot warriors behind them. As the auxiliary line began to buckle, the scarlet weight of the legionary troops behind them moved up, step by step through the wreckage, and the cavalry came flying down the slope on either side to hit the enemy flanks.

The governor, from his vantage point on the ridge, took note of Valerian's message. "They won't surrender," he told his tribune. "Not with women in the line. That's a last-ditch tactic. We'll have to fight them till they drop." He looked up grimly and a raindrop hit him in the eye.

The sky above had darkened as they first crested the ridge and now it was ashen. Another drop fell and the governor swore.

Valerian, slashing his way through a tangle of broken chariots and Selgovae warriors now on foot, saw the field turning to mud as the skies opened. A boom of thunder shook the air. His standard-bearer's horse skidded in the slop and went down and a Briton ran his spear through the standard-bearer's chest. The next man in line snatched the standard up. In the infantry lines, the shield wall was moving forward now in lockstep, the dogged formation that made use of the wicked Roman short sword that could reach inside a longer sword's arc and make it useless. Stab and take a step; stab and take a step, the formation that was the core of Roman military discipline.

–

In the hospital tents, all they could see of the battle was the faint haze of dust in the heavy air, which was growing thicker by the minute, the sky ominous. Calpurnius Aquila stuck his head out of the main tent, glanced up briefly and spat with disgust. Postumus refrained from comment, but the old surgeon's thoughts were plain. The prospect of operating in a late summer thunderstorm was daunting. It could well work to the Army's advantage, however, if the Britons' chariots got mired in the mud. They waited tensely for some word of the battle, the hospital staff with their breastplates and helmets discarded and heavy canvas aprons over their tunics, the reserves at parade rest before the outer wall. A fly landed on Postumus's neck and he slapped at it jumpily. The Advance sounded again beyond the hill, and once the sharp notes of Fall Back and Regroup. The dark clouds rolled in above them and faintly through the woods they could hear the roar and swell of two opposing armies locked in desperate battle for far more than one wooded hill.

Then the roar of the battle was drowned in a roar of thunder and the heavens opened like a waterfall as the first of the wounded came streaming back through the trees with a light-armed escort pushing its way through the torrent that fell around them.

The orderlies scrambled out to bring them in, heads down through the driving rain, and Postumus saw one of the escort flash a thumbs-up and then make an encircling motion with his hands before he plunged back into the trees again. The incoming wounded confirmed it – the governor's army had broken Brendan's war host but they were fighting like demons.

"Women! Selgovae witches," the legionary on the table before Postumus said through gritted teeth while Postumus tried to save the tendons in his leg. He had been caught by a chariot's wheel blade and had taken the driver through the throat with his pilum as he went down, but he had been carried to the hospital across a cavalryman's saddle and it was likely he would never march out with his legion again.

Postumus stitched him up and then turned to the next, another leg wound, this one past saving. Postumus doped the cavalry trooper up as stiffly as he dared and proceeded to take the leg off above the knee. Calpurnius Aquila, probing a spear wound at the next table, glanced up now and again but offered no comment. When Postumus had finished, the hideous sound of the bone saw still grating across his mind, he nodded at the orderly to take the man away. The memory of those empty sockets in the wheel hubs of Galt's blue and red chariot rose in his mind. He washed the blood from his hands in the basin the orderly held out, and looked up to catch old Aquila's jumpy eye on him.

"Pretty fancy job," the chief surgeon said. Postumus couldn't tell whether it was a compliment or not. He picked up a pot of wound salve and went back to work, grateful that the soldier awaiting him, another cavalryman, had nothing more than a nice clean sword cut on the fleshy part of his thigh.

After that they came too fast for further thought, and the rain that was still pouring down began to run under the tent walls, turning the canvas floor beneath them into a sticky mess through which the walking wounded and the hospital staff squelched miserably. The senior surgeon of the Twentieth had begun to sneeze, while outside the thunder boomed and rolled and the surgeon of the Second muttered a brief prayer against lightning.

There was another crack of thunder, and then, as if in echo, the triumphant sound of a cavalry horn singing the Pursuit. A minute later an optio of the reserves ducked his head into the hospital tent, rain streaming from his helmet.

"The commander's compliments, sir," he said to Aquila, "and we've got them on the run, what's left of them."

Aquila jabbed a pair of forceps at the optio. "Spare me your compliments, you damn fool, and get the wagons out there for the rest of the wounded before they drown!"

–

The wind in the heather to which Lollius Urbicus had listened had spoken the truth. The Selgovae, with their hapless allies the Novantae, had staked everything on this battle and lost. And the Picts had not ridden to join them. They had sat instead in the fastnesses of their highland holdings and watched an old enemy go down before the swords of a new one, knowing that whichever side emerged the victor would also emerge weakened by the battle.

Only a score of chariots out of all the thousands had clawed their way out, and Brendan's had been one of them, only to have the chieftain dragged from it alive on order of Valerian, who had recognized the gold fillet around his head and the seven-pointed flower of the Selgovae lord on his forehead. He was now, hands tied behind him, in the governor's red leather tent while the governor thought about it. But the Novantae's chieftain lay flung across the front of his broken chariot, his head against the haunches of his dead horses, and blood thick in his hair, his daughter dead beside him.

The Selgovae and Novantae had paid in full for trifling with rebellion, but in one thing the Picts had miscalculated. The whisper that had come down from the heather had given Rome the advantage of surprise, and her losses had been minimal. Even considering the men killed mopping up fools who should have surrendered, the Dead List was short. Two days later, when the Roman bodies had been gathered and burned and the Britons stripped of gold and left to the reivers of the forest, the governor's army marched out. The legionary troops, with the auxiliary infantry and the hospital staff, marched north for the frontier again, while the governor, with Valerian's cavalry wing and a few other mounted detachments, swung south to put the iron grip of a Roman peace on the rebellious territories. The day they left, the first pale gold leaves were showing in the woods on the ridge above the battlefield, and they rode in some haste, with winter on their tail.

The forests of Britain had begun their yearly dance with death, the leaves warming slowly to fire and drifting on the autumn wind. In the south, Postumus's family would be putting up the shutters and laying the garden down under straw. The Army, on the other hand, oblivious to the slow charm of the year's end, gloomily stocked its storehouses and braced itself for the stifling boredom of winter quarters. The merchant ships and the quinqueremes and triremes of the Fleet came in to ride out the coming storms in harbor.

The governor's troops swept south along the coast and then eastward through the Selgovae lands on the edge of Votadini territory, ripping the fortifications from such hill forts as had been rebuilt since the closing of the southern frontier along the old wall. Rome wasted very little. Any men of fighting age found were conscripted for the auxiliaries in the East, the cattle and grain taken to feed Rome's army, anything yet unharvested trampled or burned in the fields, and the youngest and strongest of the women marked for the slave market. They left little behind them but burned holdings and old men.

Brendan also was old, his flaming hair almost blanketed with gray and the bitterness of defeat lying heavy on him. He had been allowed to retain his chieftainship for that reason, being deemed more useful to the governor in that guise than as a prisoner in Rome with a strong young chieftain in his place in Britain. Let him stay, shamed, to rule over what was left him – it was not much.

Brendan sat in the remains of his home hold on Eildon Hill, that the Eagles called Trimontium, amid the rubble of stone and timber which the Romans had further pulled apart with teams of draft oxen, and made his last council.

The Novantae woman had gotten past his Roman guardians with a tale of being a dealer in small cures, she said. Everyone's eyes hurt, or their head, or their genitals. She had sold eyewash to the legionary in charge.

Now she told him, "We are few. My father is dead and my sister beside him. Now before we decide our course, we must know yours. The Romans keep you as surety, do they not? Your life for the peace of the frontier?"

"My sons are dead," he said. "Cadal is of the chieftain's line. He will take what is left of my people north to the Picts if he can. I have told him this, before we fought."

"You would die, then?" The woman cocked her head at him, dark braids over her shoulders and the gold drops in her ears glinting in the firelight. He had a square face like an old bull and arms that had been powerful once but she could see the muscles beginning to slacken with age. "They will kill you if the rest break the peace. And not easily."

"It comes often enough for a chieftain to die," Brendan said. "I would prefer it not be at the Romans' hand. I will

168

forestall that if I can. But if the chieftainship has gone to Cadal, and they will not be able to put their lapdog in my place. We will not be vassals, and when I ride Epona's mare into the night, I will ride as a free man. The Novantae must do as they please."

"I will tell them."

It was the end of October and almost Samhain when the governor's vengeful troops came riding back to winter quarters at the new frontier. The governor, who was not a superstitious man, as regarded British superstitions anyway, made a push nonetheless not to be on the march that night, when the spirits of the Otherworld were free in the land and the dead returned to the paths they had walked in life. The tribes would be keeping to their halls, and no one but the wolves would be out after sunfall, and they were half-kin to the Otherworld anyway.

Valerian, who loathed this kind of mopping up operation, returned in no very good frame of mind, although as he admitted to Postumus, sitting by the brazier in the surgeon's quarters at Castra Damnoniorum on Samhain night itself, it had been necessary.

"They had to be broken," he said sadly, "or they'd have been raising another army in a few months. Brendan's been a thorn in our side for years. We couldn't hold Valentia without crushing him. I wonder, though, if we got them all, and I think the governor does too."

Postumus's brows rose in surprise.

"Well, we never could get a good count of his army to begin with," Valerian said, "although we had a pretty fair idea. Most fought to the death. We knew they would, if he had women in the lines. But there were some who hadn't ridden in yet or he'd have been on the march already. They may well have nipped back to Pict country ahead of us, or just dodged us in the heather."

Or ridden south to their kin, the Brigantes, Postumus thought, but he didn't say it. Valerian, let alone the governor and Aelius Silanus, was sharp enough to pick up on that unassisted. There wouldn't be enough of them to make trouble unless they enlisted some other tribe in the making of it.

"A good heavy draft went to the auxiliaries, though," Valerian said, "and I don't envy the commander who gets the training of them. It's a point of honor to be in the first charge, and if you get killed, which is likely, you'll get a grand reception in the Otherworld. And these already tried to get killed once fighting us. The only prisoners we took we chased down. None of them would surrender even with a spear at their throat. Britons like to fight — when they aren't fighting us, they fight each other — but they don't like waiting for commands."

The cavalry commander, whose own troops never twitched a hair without orders, looked so disgusted that Postumus laughed and reminded him that they were both half-British themselves.

"Ah, but we had Roman fathers," Valerian said, stretching his booted legs closer to the brazier — the night was cold and the hypocaust channels under the stone floor weren't keeping up with it. "We were brought up right. My mother's father, now — the old boy with the heads in his hall — he was just such a one. He was killed in a local war, the silly old fool, when my father was stationed in Gaul and not around to keep an eye on him, and all because some other old fool told him he was too old to carry a spear. It wasn't even his own clan that was fighting. My mother was furious, but I think even she was rather proud of him, and she'd been married to a Roman officer for fifteen years."

"Old ways don't die out right off just because you've passed a law against them," Postumus said. "Look at the Druids. They're still around, just with a different cap on. The old boy who'd been treating my Briton's leg, for instance. Every time I crossed his path, he muttered something that I would swear was a curse and it made the back of my neck itch every time."

Valerian laughed. "See now, if you'd been all British, it would have got you."

"Valerian's theory of the relative efficacy of curses, moderated by relative distance of bloodline. Lucian would like that. How long does it take, I wonder, to absorb and change a whole culture?"

Valerian looked up suddenly at that and this time it was he who raised one flyaway black brow. "I've wondered that myself," he said, his dark eyes thoughtful. "Give me some more of that disgusting wine and I'll tell you a ghost story."

Postumus refilled his cup without comment and drew the oil lamp closer. A feeling of unease had crept into the night air that wasn't just the Samhain wind. Valerian ran his fingers over the leaves of the Corona Civica that dominated the medals strung across his chest. It was the first time Postumus had seen him take any notice of his decorations at all, other than strapping them on with the rest of his gear like so many pieces of his uniform. Valerian tapped the wreath with his forefinger and seemed to study it as he spoke.

"How long would you say to absorb and change *us*…
how long for the death of all this?" Valerian brushed a
hand lightly across the gilded honors.

"I don't know," Postumus said slowly. "As an individual, or as a nation?"

"*I* don't know," Valerian countered, his eyes still down-
cast and his face shadowed by a fall of black hair, longer
than usual after two months' campaign. He took up the
poker and jabbed moodily at the coals in the brazier.

Postumus, having taken about as much of this as he
could stand, abruptly said, "Spill it!"

Valerian tossed the poker into its stand with a clatter
and sat up straight. "Right, sorry. Nobody's talked about
it, because nobody wants to *think* about it, but I saw
something this tour that's enough to bring the Deified
Augustus gibbering up out of his grave. It was the Selgovae
dead and the ones we conscripted – this is the first time
we've laid our hands on them in large enough numbers at a
time for it to show – but, Mithras grant them peace, there
were men among them who were *wrong*. Young men, and
born to the tribe – tattooed and all. They don't do that
unless you're born to it. But *wrong*. Shorter than the rest,
a few of them, but all of them too dark. The Selgovae
are of the Golden People, fair-skinned and blond or fox-
haired mostly, like your mother, I expect." He glanced at
Postumus's chestnut hair. "The Silures, now, a lot of us
are dark – there's old blood in the Silures. But not the
Selgovae."

Postumus shifted uncomfortably in his chair. Young
men, born after the last rising. "Go on," he said, although,
with a creeping horror, he found that he knew what
Valerian was going to say.

"They carried Army swords, a lot of them. Cavalry long swords mostly." He glanced at his own. "Too many to all come from a reived battlefield, and too many of them among the dark men. But the worst thing was the torque on a man I killed at the tail end of the fight. I took it because it had a familiar look to it somehow, and when I got a good look, I almost threw it back." He slipped a silver circle from his own harness and held it out to Postumus. "I don't know why I put it on... to see if anyone would notice, I suppose. No one did. *He* had it round his neck, of course."

Postumus took the proffered torque gingerly. No one would be likely to notice it among Valerian's other decorations – it was standard Army issue, silver capped with gold knobs at the ends.

"Look inside," Valerian said, his face shadowed again, although Postumus could see the grim twist to his mouth.

Postumus held the torque to the lamplight. To his disgust, his fingers were shaking. He gritted his teeth and steadied them. The incised lettering was worn but legible. *Ulpius Reburrus, of the Third Cohort of Asturians, won this for distinguished conduct in battle in the Nineteenth Year of the Emperor Trajan*. He handed the torque back to Valerian as if it had burned him. "Trimontium," he whispered. "So that's where they went."

Valerian nodded. "I think so. I wasn't sure you knew about Trimontium," he added. "I served with the Asturians in Dacia, and of course we all knew. It was the family disgrace, so to speak."

Postumus was silent, staring blindly at the inkpot on his chamber desk. Trimontium, the great red sandstone fort in the lowlands whose entire garrison had gone Unlawful Absent in the space of one dark night twenty-five years ago, while the flames of the rebellion had flared around them. Trimontium, where the Mithraeum was haunted. "Yes," he said at last. "I knew. My father... had a cohort in the Ninth Hispana." There was a short, startled sound as Valerian drew in his breath. "He died at Castra Pinnata," Postumus said, and Valerian let out his breath again.

"I didn't think—"

"Of course you thought," Postumus said, picking up the wine jug from the floor again. "I would have, too. There were enough who did run. It's the first thought anyone has for a man who served with the Ninth. That's why I'm a surgeon and Justin's in the auxiliaries. We weren't welcome in the Centuriate." He set the jug down again. "They sent a burial party up there, afterward. They found his body in the fortress. Someone had laid his cloak over him. One of the Brigantes maybe. They are odd that way." Hilarion had told him that, years ago, and Postumus had found it oddly comforting.

They were both silent while the coals in the brazier popped and sank, and the wind came up with a rustle of dead leaves outside the window. Valerian picked up the torque again, but he didn't slip it back on his harness with his own honors, turning it instead in his hands while he thought. Postumus refilled their wine cups, the green glass cups that had come from Licinius, another who carried the scars of an old war and a dead legion.

"How many years for the death of a world?" Valerian whispered.

How many years before the men who had served at Trimontium could forget that they had ever followed the Eagles? How many years before they could give their sons a Roman cavalry sword to fight Rome with, and their sons could wear an Imperial Distinguished Conduct torque as if it were a piece of jewelry?

"The old men?" Postumus asked uneasily. "Did you see the old men?"

"By and large, we saw them in plenty," Valerian said. "But none that could have fathered those boys, no. Maybe there was enough of the old loyalty left to keep them out of the battle. Or Brendan didn't trust them." Valerian drained his wine and set the cup down on the table, with a hand also somewhat unsteady. "And maybe they ran, in case we thought of Trimontium."

Postumus let out his breath, relieved. If Rome had found them, Rome would have to notice them, and he knew all too clearly what Rome would have done to them.

Valerian nodded. "I think the governor was relieved not to have to face that. The Ninth is dead. Better let it lie."

They sat in silence while the Samhain wind came up again with the uneasy ghosts of Trimontium on its wings.

XI. Beltane

In a month it was winter on the frontier, the dank kind that ate into the bones. Postumus felt as if his feet would never be dry again and his fingers were constantly cold and he dropped things. And he couldn't get Trimontium off his mind. The hospital was peopled by a parade of lung disease and chills and general winter malaise. Valerian, Frontinus and the other commanders dealt with the sulks and grumbling and occasional outright insubordination of an army in winter quarters on a hostile frontier. When the first signs of spring poked their green noses from the ground, it was an almost overwhelming relief.

Postumus, who had accumulated more leave than he had been allowed to use between his Syrian posting and his appointment to the Sixth, promptly put in for it, and, discovering that Valerian apparently had never taken leave at all and had enough coming to him to make a world tour if they had let him, suggested he come along.

"Londinium," Valerian said, his mood brightening.

The minute the first road was clear enough, they were packed and saddled, with strict instructions not to overstay their time. As soon as the ground was thawed, the new wall would begin to rise.

At Credigone, on the east end of the frontier, they wangled passage on a trader optimistically named the *Zephyr* going south along the coast to the mouth of the Tamesis and upriver to the provincial capital. For Postumus this meant a chance to prowl the Londinium potion-sellers' stalls and the cluster of dubious warehouses by the docks where the Eastern medicine merchants had their stores: cavernous, shadowed buildings thick with the scent of poppy cake and pungent herbs. The drug-sellers' domain gave Valerian much the same uncomfortable feeling that hospitals did and he looked dubiously at Postumus, deep in conversation with a cadaverous Alexandrian merchant who rattled spiderlike among the shadows of his baled wares. In the end they parted company with an agreement to meet at the horse market in two hours' time.

Afterward they visited the city baths and lounged comfortably in the steam room while attendants scraped their skin clean and rubbed it with sweet oil, then spent the rest of the afternoon unashamedly cheering a naval spectacle in the arena and exploring the city's bustling market district. They bought raw oysters from the fish-mongers who hawked their wares up and down the streets, and Postumus posted two flasks of Arabian perfume by messenger to his mother and sister. With Constantia's, he included a souvenir stylus that bore the message A GIFT FROM THE CITY: A POINTED REMINDER TO WRITE TO ME.

They stayed in the best inn they could afford, which boasted a courtyard with a cherry tree, tolerable plumbing, and a mosaic on the floor of Ethiopians hunting lions. At night from their window they could see the lights of Londinium Bridge strung like dew on cobwebs across the Tamesis. A crowd of laughing theatergoers passed by, and then a lady shielded behind the curtains of her litter, and a troupe of jugglers. Somewhere off to the right came the sounds of a cither and a drum and the jingle of coins from a dancer's belt. At night the city glowed as golden as a new-minted aureus and seemed to Postumus almost a dimension in itself, a strange jumping-off point between civilization and the bloody realities of the frontier.

Valerian knotted his neck scarf with a practiced hand and twitched the gold-bordered folds of his parade cloak into place. He inspected his reflection in the little mirror from his kit and turned to Postumus. "Dinner first, I think. After that, there's a pair of dancing sisters at the wineshop two streets over that are worth watching. In fact, I just had a word with one of them this afternoon and she seemed to think her sister might take a liking to you. Especially after I promised her you were rich as Croesus and handsome as the Sun God."

Postumus suspected that the rich as Croesus part was the enticement, although that was relative, but he followed Valerian cheerfully down the stairs. After that the evening passed in a haze of lobsters, fresh asparagus, and good wine, and dancers who flew like gaudy birds through a veil of drifting, sandalwood-scented smoke. He awoke in the morning to find one of the dancing sisters curled against him in the rushes of her bed. She had wrapped herself in all the covers like a cocoon (it was the cold that had wakened him) and she snored softly, but she looked cute and he gave her a kiss and left her enough money, Valerian said afterwards, to keep her in finger-cymbals for the rest of her life.

They took the sisters to the theater that night, to see a farce by Plautus, and bought them dinner afterward, followed by a late breakfast the next morning. When they left, neat and relatively sober in riding kit, the sisters watched them wistfully, with earnest wishes for their speedy return. Gentlemen who were handsome *and* open-handed were rare in their experience.

They returned overland on cavalry mounts to let Postumus inspect the hospital at Eburacum while Valerian descended on the undermanned forts in the Brigantian Hills, with the intention, he said, of shocking the liver out of anyone foolish enough to assume that a war on in Valentia was an excuse to get sloppy in Brigantia. Trimontium had been on his mind too.

On the road north, spring unfolded behind them as they rode. The air softened, the land greened, and the fenlands around Lindum were dotted with sheep on the higher ground. An otter poked its head up from a streambank as they passed and a heron picked its way through the marsh, each foot lifted with slow deliberation like a pantomime dancer.

Postumus found the Eburacum hospital in reasonably good order, and Gemellus, the junior surgeon he had left in command there, seemed to be doing all right. Fortunately, there was very little for him to do.

He rejoined Valerian at Isurium, which had been the tribal capital of the Brigantes in the days before Agricola's army had razed its walls. These days it was a Roman colonia, supervised by togaed magistrates and policed by civil cohorts of the Watch. The walls that had risen since guarded against little more than wolves, and the city's defenses were the strength of Roman civil law and the soldiers stationed in the great fortress of Eburacum less than a day's march away. It remained, however, the nominal capital of the Brigantes and to it their king and his Council were required to come to dispense such justice as Rome allowed them, from the marbled halls of its basilica. Where the question before the court was purely a native matter and touched only on such tribesmen as held lands outside Isurium, Rome stayed clear. The presence of the king and his Council in Isurium, where they could be observed occasionally, was the point.

Valerian was bringing another of his Dacian cohorts north to the new wall forts and he and Postumus trotted through the open gates of Isurium accompanied by their scarlet and yellow splendor. It was Beltane and obvious that a court was in session. Clusters of hillmen were gathered on the basilica's marble steps while a clerk wove back and forth among them, taking statements and checking cases against the tablet in his hand.

Postumus leaned forward as a figure emerged from the basilica and stood blinking in the sunlight. It caught the white gold sheen of his hair and the bright gold and glass bracelets that clustered at his wrists. The slight limp did not disguise the catlike gait, and the long eyes and fine-boned face beneath the blue spirals of his tattooing were unmistakable.

"Hold a minute." Postumus reined in his horse and pulled his helmet off.

Valerian threw up a hand to halt their escort, with a glance at Postumus as he swung down from the saddle.

"I've seen someone I know."

Valerian nodded at the escort to stay where they were and dismounted also, throwing the reins to a trooper behind him.

Postumus was tall for a Roman, half a head above Valerian, and Galt spotted him almost immediately, his face breaking into a smile as he came forward. He limped but it was obvious that the leg was as sound as Postumus could have hoped for, and he said so.

"Well enough to beat the puppies at the Spring Races," Galt said. He coughed and turned away for a moment.

Postumus could see his shoulders shake with the cough. "Are you ill?"

"Winter cough. Old Talhaiere's herbs and steam haven't chased it off, but now that spring is here…"

"That often cures it," Postumus said. "I spent all winter treating the same. Woodsmoke makes it worse. Stick your head out the door when you can."

Galt nodded and Postumus saw him eyeing Valerian with interest, so he introduced them.

"Does the High King hold his court this Beltane?" Valerian asked, nodding at the activity outside the basilica.

"Yes, we smooth out old quarrels and try to avert new ones," Galt said, with another cough. "The day the Briton learns unity is the day Rome may begin to beware."

"If, for instance, the Brigantes had answered Brendan of the Selgovae when the call came," Valerian suggested.

"I grow too old for such hostings, Wing Commander," Galt said lightly, turning it to a joke. "I am become an elder statesman, an old hound kept to cuff the pups into good sense."

"The High King is still a pup, perchance?" This also, softly, from Valerian, and Galt stiffened.

"Perchance," Postumus said, putting one mailed sandal down hard on the cavalry commander's toes, "but a pack leader since he was weaned, I think."

"Indeed," Galt said, and they talked carefully of the weather and the spring crops for a few minutes until a young hound appeared from the basilica and bowed to Galt.

"The High King sends me to tell the Lord Galt that the court is ready to hear the next case."

Galt nodded. "I must go and decide whether old Anwen was entitled to steal Cormac's cow because Cormac stole Anwen's three goats after Anwen stole Cormac's wife. Or some such. There will be much shouting and threats but after we decide, at least they won't feud." He held out a hand to Postumus. "It was fine to see you again. If you should stay for the Beltane fires tonight, we may talk." He nodded politely at Valerian and strode back into the basilica, the pale hair that fell down his back bright against the white and russet pattern of his cloak.

"I liked your harper," Valerian said, "although I would walk warily of him if I commanded here."

"For which reason you decided to dig at him about the High King?" Postumus asked.

"Essentially."

"And did you gain anything useful?"

"No more than you've told me already, but we should stay for the fires tonight. It's late to be on the road again and I haven't danced at a Beltane fire in years. I'll leave him to you."

"And you think he'll tell me something while you're off getting drunk on native beer?" Postumus asked.

"Quite possibly."

–

Beltane was another of the great festivals that marked the wheel of the year in Britain, midway between the spring equinox and the summer solstice, when the land began to grow green again. Household fires were doused and the New Fire kindled with a fire drill. From it, one child in each house took the New Fire home, and two great bonfires were lit for the cattle to be driven through to make them fruitful. Couples hoping for the same might run between the fires as well or jump the embers.

In a colonia like Isurium Brigantum, not everyone followed the old ways, but the festival itself attracted most of the citizenry with food and drink and general carousing. Postumus stood on the edge of the crowd around the dark circle where the New Fire would be kindled by friction. In the colonia, there were still a few lights burning but outside the east gate, on the gentle slope above the river, there was pitch darkness. Two men knelt above a small twist of tinder and spun the fire drill in it and Postumus could feel the held breath of the crowd, waiting for the spark, the New Fire, entwined with the old fear that this year, this time, the light might not come again, there might be no spark. It would be easier to fear that in the hills than outside a colonia where the more Romanized inhabitants were eating their dinner by the light of oil lamps, and no one would think of putting out the fire that fueled the hypocaust, but the darkness here discouraged disbelief. Not for the first time in his life, Postumus felt one foot in some other world.

The crowd let out its breath as a spark rose in the tinder, and then another. The keepers of the flame fed it small bits of kindling, shielding it from any stray breeze. If the New Fire went out and had to be rekindled, it was a bad omen. The fire grew to a handful of flame, and then enough to shed light on the faces around it. Postumus was startled by a woman's face that came suddenly into the light and then flickered away. It had looked like Claudia. He could have sworn he had seen her at the theater in Londinium too, in the seats to his left, beside a tribal-looking escort with an impressive mustache. If it had been her, she had made it clear that she did not want to see him, and turned away so that her veil hid her face. The little dancer beside him had taken his attention, bouncing in her seat with excitement and wheedling him for sweets, and when he looked back, the woman was gone. Postumus wondered if it had been her either time, or if he was developing an unhealthy fixation.

The New Fire blazed up and a group of boys clustered around it with torches to light from the flames. They set out at a run toward their homes, the light streaming behind them.

"A time of new beginnings," said a voice beside him, which was definitely Galt. "It always gives me hope."

"What do you hope for?" Postumus asked him.

"For this to last for a while, perhaps. Our old world, our old ways."

How many years for the death of a world? Without thinking it over, Postumus said, "I know where the men from Trimontium went. The deserters from the last war."

Galt coughed and said, "My people would have killed them. I thought then that Brendan was asking for ill luck."

They watched the bonfires being lit, and then the cattle running between them, lowing, chased by small boys with sticks. Sellers of meat and beer began to appear and the solemnity of the fire ritual faded into merrymaking.

"Valerian told me," Postumus said. "After the governor's mopping up campaign last Samhain."

"Did any of them come back to you?" Galt asked, and Postumus couldn't tell whether he was serious or not.

"After I heard that, I was British enough not to go out in the night."

Galt nodded. "It's odd. Once I wished that someone would come back. I waited each year for three years, for some sign, some feeling in the air, the touch of a different wind. I wouldn't have been afraid of him. He was the other half of my soul."

"The High King?"

Galt nodded again.

"And you don't wish for war now, to avenge that?"

"Even if we could win, when Rome is beaten, she waits. Your foothold is too strong here."

"Is that what you told him, the first time?"

"No," Galt said slowly. "But I was younger then, and he was my spear brother, my blood brother – some things I could not see clearly."

"And if you had?"

"Would I have said as much to him – to see him alive still, growing old with honor, among his people? Yes, I would have spoken."

"And would he have listened?"

"No." He watched the boys dodging among the cattle, driving them between the fires. "We were too young then."

XII. The Wind in the Heather

From Isurium, they rode northwest to Luguvallium and across the old frontier into Valentia, coming on a mid-May evening to the far side of the divide between home and service – the raw scar across the land where the new wall would run.

The wall would rise from east to west, as the forts had, and here, more than halfway down its length, the only sign as yet to be seen was the turned ground where the surveying crews had marked its path. Valentia was reasonably well pacified now, except for isolated raiding bands of the Selgovae who had fled into the heather to the north after last autumn's battle. But they were making a wonderful nuisance of themselves, and it was now strongly suspected that there might be more of them lairing in Pict country than had at first been thought. In addition, the Picts showed ominous signs of movement to the north. The western garrisons had orders to hold their ground at all costs until the last gap of the wall was spanned.

The bulk of the Sixth Legion was some miles to the east, at work on the wall, and Valerian rode out to rejoin his cavalry wing and keep the Picts off their tails, while Postumus made a quick and unnecessary inspection of the Castra Damnoniorum hospital, which Lucian had kept in excellent order, and then a tour of the smaller fort hospitals to the west. There were few casualties to deal with as it was more profitable for the Picts to harry the vulnerable building crews, and the first part of the summer passed in relative tranquility. Centurion Frontinus and the other western commanders kept their forts lynx–eyed and watchful and the Pict kept clear.

Lollius Urbicus rode through periodically and when he did, there were generally scouts about, cloaked in disreputable anonymity and passing in and out of the camp with little more than a password to mark them as men of the Eagles.

Postumus was occupying the first hour of the night with answering a letter from Justin by the light of the dispensary lamp when an optio tapped on the door and informed him that the governor wanted to see the senior surgeon, please. Now, he added firmly, as Postumus glanced at the dark sky outside the window, if it was quite convenient.

"If it's convenient for the governor, I expect it had better be convenient for me," Postumus said. "I didn't know he was in camp."

"He's not. So you'll keep mum, sir, if you please. And you're to bring your kit, sir," the optio added.

"All of it?" Postumus inquired, waving a hand at the stocked shelves and the array of surgical tools in their cases against the wall. "It would help if I knew what I was treating."

"I really couldn't say, sir." The optio's tone was repressive.

"How about a hint?" Postumus felt his irritation growing and squelched it. "Come on, man, it does make a difference if I'm going to pull a tooth or take someone's leg off, and if the governor wants it kept quiet, I can hardly come traipsing back here for what I need."

"I believe, sir, that you are to treat an infection." The optio resumed his parade stance and it was evident that no further information would be forthcoming.

"Very well." Postumus gathered everything that could conceivably be needed to treat anything from a hangnail to gangrene, stuffed it in a spare kit, collected his cloak, and doused the lamp.

"We'll go by the back way, sir, if you don't mind." The optio beckoned and Postumus shrugged and followed him.

There was just enough moon to see by as they slunk from the back of the hospital to the back entrance of the Principia, where a disinterested sentry passed them through on the optio's word, and then down an ill-lit corridor to the commandant's office. Centurion Frontinus sat within, his hands wrapped around a cup of hot wine and his scarred face illuminated by the fitful light of a single lamp. He nodded to Postumus and gestured to the doorway beyond.

Inside, Postumus found the small chamber that Frontinus used as a secondary quarters also lit only by a single lamp, and inhabited by Lollius Urbicus, a plain cloak of gray wool about his shoulders and his feet stretched out to the brazier whose coals glowed red in the gloom. He was a tall man, angular and heavily muscled, with dark skin, short curls of iron-gray hair cropped in a military cut, and a beard in the style of the late Emperor Hadrian. Behind him, on a camp bed, was a slight figure muffled in a dark-and-white checkered cloak that left very little to be seen but a pair of long dark braids. They were tied at the ends with enameled metal balls, a wholly feminine fashion even among the Britons.

At the sound of Postumus's footsteps, the figure stirred and sat up, pushing the straying tendrils of hair back from her eyes. Her face was devoid of the elegant makeup she had worn when he last saw her, and the ruby ring he remembered was also gone, but it was unmistakably Claudia Silva. The skin on his neck prickled when he saw that her upper arms were crisscrossed with fresh scars rubbed in with blue woad. His first thought was that it must have hurt like Hades at her age, and his second was that the Picts also tattooed their women.

Lollius Urbicus nodded at the optio, who disappeared, returned with a second chair, and obediently disappeared again. "This is Senior Surgeon Corvus, of the Sixth," the governor informed Claudia. He rubbed his fingers over each other as he spoke – a touch of arthritis, Postumus thought, momentarily distracted.

"Thank you, Your Excellency, we have met before," Claudia said. "And how is the soldier from the arena?" she asked Postumus.

"Ducked it," Postumus said. "I was afraid he might."

"I'm sorry."

"If you could spare a moment," Lollius Urbicus murmured and Postumus flushed. "I want you to look at this damned fancy-work." He nodded at Claudia, and Postumus saw that both her arms were badly inflamed.

He pulled the bronze lamp stand closer to the bed. "How long since this was done?"

"Some two weeks ago," Claudia said.

"And by some witch woman out of the hills, I expect," Postumus said. "It's a wonder you don't have gangrene."

"I daresay," Claudia said tartly, "but I had no opportunity to have it attended to earlier."

She couldn't show anyone those scars, he realized, while they were still raw. He lowered his voice. "You realize these are permanent, you fool?"

Claudia leaned back against the pillows. "Yes. I'm not as big a fool as you think," she said tiredly. He saw that her blue-green eyes were bright and her face was flushed and hot to the touch where he put his hand to it. He began to sort out what was wanted from his kit.

Lollius Urbicus withdrew to confer with Centurion Frontinus, remarking as he did so that he expected he did not have to tell Surgeon Corvus that after tonight he was to forget that any of them had been there.

"Indeed, sir, no, sir, and I'm not the fool he takes *me* for either," Postumus said when he had gone, "so we are even."

Claudia laughed softly and bit her lip as Postumus dabbed the woad-pricked patterns with vinegar and began rubbing salve into them. When he had finished, he looked around and found a flagon of watered wine and a cup on the three-legged table by the bed. He mixed a decoction of willow into it and handed it to her, watching as she took her first sip. "This will help."

She took another sip and gagged. "That's vile."

Postumus retrieved the cup and set it back on the table. "All right," he said, somewhat embarrassed, "how much more of you did they do?"

Claudia's eyes flicked down to her coarse woolen gown. "How did you know?"

"You forget I'm native-born. I know where tribal tattooing goes. Although I'm not sure why you felt the need to be that thorough. Didn't that *hurt*?"

"Of course it hurt. And being thorough is important in these matters."

"It's all going to have to be treated. Mithras knows how dirty those needles were, and woad is an irritant anyway."

Claudia also looked embarrassed but hers was apparently a practical nature. She sat up and without comment dragged the gown off over her head. The tattooing curved down from her collarbone into a pattern that spiraled around each breast to the nipple, and ended in a design like a five-petaled flower on her belly. Her upper thighs were tattooed in the same way as her arms, although they were less inflamed. The blue of the patterns made a bright contrast to her pale skin and the dark smoke of her hair, and Postumus caught himself looking somewhat overlong.

"You're lucky Pictish women don't mark their faces," he said brusquely, and set about soaking another piece of lint in the vinegar. He cleaned the patterns carefully, trying not to notice how the blue spirals accentuated the up-tilted curve of her breasts and the white lines of her thighs.

The vinegar probably hurt enough to distract Claudia from any embarrassment, but when he had finished, she pulled the dark-and-white checked cloak over herself. Postumus pulled it firmly back down again and picked up the salve jar. "This will take out some of the sting."

"What is it? It feels sticky."

"Honey and healing herbs mostly," Postumus said, smearing the concoction along her collarbone. "In a tallow base."

"*Honey?*" Claudia started to laugh. "If anyone had ever told me I'd find myself lying in the governor's office stark naked, letting a man I've only met twice smear me with honey—"

Postumus smiled back, and their constraint dissolved somewhat. "Infection doesn't live in honey. I'd stay away from anthills for a few days, though," he said, rubbing the salve into her breasts, and felt them move under his hands as she chuckled. The Pictish patterns gave her body a wild and beautiful strangeness. He wondered if she had a lover. If she had, he was going to get a surprise the next time he lay with her. This proved to be a dangerous train of thought, and Postumus herded himself back to his task with difficulty.

When he was done, he pushed the stopper into the salve jar and Claudia pulled the gown back over her head.

–

She came to him two days later to say goodbye and to get from him a promised pot of salve; the pricked skin would have to be treated several more times until the infection had subsided. Postumus was at his desk reluctantly coping with the hospital accounts when she came in. The wild blue patterns were covered and she looked much as he remembered her from their last meeting in Corstopitum. (If it had been her in Londinium or Isurium, she wouldn't tell him.) She wore a traveling gown of plain but finely woven wool, and her fine-boned features were accentuated at the eyes and lips by the ladylike use of a paint pot. The dark hair was coiled into a knot at the back of her head, and the ruby ring gleamed on her finger. He saw that she wore a long-sleeved undergown beneath the looser short-sleeved folds of her traveling clothes.

"I am here in my own name as supplies contractor for the new wall," she said quietly as she saw his glance light on her arms. "The woman with the tribal scars isn't me."

But she was there all the same, beneath the multiple layers of clay-brown woolen, in the blue spirals encircling her breasts, and pricked into belly and thighs. "You're insane," Postumus said. "What in Mithras' name do you hope to gain?"

"Knowledge."

Postumus slumped back in his chair.

"And you're not such a fool that you need to ask that," she said. "The Army needs all the knowledge that it can come by."

"Why you? Surely the Army breeds enough spies of its own."

She looked annoyed. "I am native-born also, of a chieftain's house of the Trinovantes on my mother's side, and I speak almost every dialect of Britain. I want more from my life than to spend it selling roof tiles, or as someone's dutiful wife and mother. And the Centuriate, as you have no doubt noticed, does not take women."

He thought of saying that it wouldn't take him or his brother either, but that was beside the point. "For the adventure of it all?" He was skeptical and let it show. "No one with half a brain risks their neck for that."

She glared at him. "You mean no woman does. Every single man in this fort has done exactly that."

"Well, that and for Rome," he said.

"Precisely. I am good at being unnoticed, and I listen carefully."

"The wind in the heather," Postumus said. "Where did you spend last summer?"

"Exactly where you think," she said, looking him in the eye, "so you needn't ask."

Her eyes, he noticed, had a tendency to shift their color, and now they were the deep shadowed green of well water. Brendan of the Selgovae might have seen her eyes when they were that color, he thought, and not known what he saw.

"May I sit down?" she asked quietly. "Or are you going to throw me through the window?"

"Because you betrayed Brendan? It saved our hides, so don't be an ass." And how was that different from his own excursions? "And yes, of course, sit down. It's the governor I'd like to throw through the window."

"For sending me to Brendan?" she inquired, settling herself in the visitor's chair with one foot drawn up beneath her. "Postumus, listen to me."

It was the first time she had used his first name and, startled, he paid attention, as he had with Galt.

"When I was nineteen, I was married to a man more than three times my age, who had a certain amount of political clout and the ability to haul my family out of a financial bog. I think I told you he wasn't a bad man, and he wasn't, but his shade would be rising from his grave right now if he knew I was running the business by myself. His position was that my job was to come to bed when he wanted me to, look pretty, be his secretary, and have babies. Of this delightful list, I escaped only the babies, the one thing I wouldn't have minded. But he was old and he drank too much and it never happened. That was the sum total of my life for the seven years I was married to him. If he hadn't died, I would have gone mad."

Postumus was listening intently now. He reached a hand up to the shelf behind him for the green glass cups and took an earthen jug of wine from the chest at his feet. The green glass cups and the jug of wine were a practiced social ritual with Valerian and Frontinus and certain others of his cronies, but he had never brought them out for a woman. Nor, he realized, had he ever considered what women's lives were like.

Claudia accepted the wine and sat staring into it, as if the Oracle of All Answers lay somewhere in its depths. "I spent the year after he died fighting the Lindum magistrates for the right to administer my own inheritance, and then every man in my husband's company for three minutes of his complete attention. Once I had that" – she smiled grimly – "and things were running smoothly, there was very little else for me to do. And a war had started. I have spent the last three years as Lollius Urbicus's eyes and ears, and I find that my life has some shape to it now. I will be glad when peace comes and I can go back to knowing where I will sleep next, and no dreams of a knife in the dark. But for now, I am needed, and I serve. As you do."

She took a swallow of wine and leaned back in her chair, eyes open to his and candid, and Postumus realized where he had seen that look before. It was Justin's look, or Valerian's, pragmatic and dangerous.

"Is it lonely?" he asked, curiosity getting the better of his tact.

"No more than you are, I suppose, or any of us," she said, seeming not to be offended. "I can't marry again so long as I serve the governor, but then I've never wanted to. I am better off as I am, most likely."

"All men aren't like your husband," Postumus said, feeling somehow vaguely insulted.

She gave a little laugh. "So I am told, but I have yet to have one show me the difference."

I could, he thought suddenly, and nearly rose from his chair before he caught himself. Clearly he was losing his mind. He had the uncanny feeling that she had read the thought, but her eyes were veiled again now, and she stood up, saying pleasantly, "Thank you for the wine, and the salve. I will use it faithfully, I promise you." She held out her hand and he took it in his, slowly.

"The gods go with you," he said gravely, "and the wind blow you safe back again."

She smiled and touched his hand lightly with her other one. "Thank you." It wasn't until she had gone that he realized that he had spoken the old military farewell to an army marching out.

He didn't hear from her again that season, but by the end of summer he found himself with enough and more to occupy his thoughts as the new wall reached the territory commanded by Castra Damnoniorum. It was like a monster being hatched, Postumus thought, standing in the western gate and watching the building crews at work. The deep V of the ditch to the north had already been dug and set about with sharpened stakes and fields of "lilies," and behind it the wall was going up in sections. Each building crew was assigned its own stretch of ground (shorter here than they had been to the east where there were fewer raiding parties loose in the hills) and each section was measured to a finger's breadth to interlock where they met.

The wall would rest on a foundation some fifteen feet across, a base of small stones with boulders laid above them and drainage channels cut through at intervals. Above the stone rose the turf rampart of the wall itself, a towering, straight-sided barrier thirteen feet high, stair-stepped at the top to match the rise and fall of the hills it traversed and to connect with the forts that intersected it. To the northwest, both military road and wall bridged the small river that was the fort's water supply and the riverbed had been made as inhospitable as possible to anyone trying to cross the wall along it. Unlike the southern wall, the wall of

Antoninus possessed no milecastles along its length. Every gate opened from a fully self-contained fort, and those were spaced no more than two miles apart. It would have twice the military strength of its southern counterpart.

The whole of the frontier seemed to be a solid mass of moving men: turf-cutters and carriers with wicker baskets on their backs, stonecutters who shaped the heavy river stones used for the foundation, and lines of sweating legionaries who passed them hand to hand to the builders. Surveyors with weights and tripods were everywhere, measuring and remeasuring and stretching lines to trip the unwary. At intervals, officers of the engineers paced along the perimeter, inspecting the work in progress and consulting with the centurions in charge over sheaves of papyrus plans. And above it all, the new wall rose, solid and impenetrable, a breaker of men and chariots that would toss an invading army back like a giant hand and leave them tumbled among the sharpened stakes of the ditch. To the Britons watching it rise from the villages along its length, it must have looked like a raw wound cut clean across their land.

The military road that paralleled it to the south had been laid in Agricola's day, and repaired at the start of this new campaign. Now it was crowded with wagonloads of stone and rubble, with surveying equipment, and carts with rations for the building camps whose cookfires rose on the far side of the road. Beyond the raw scar of wall and ditch, Postumus could see the dust of the cavalry patrols crisscrossing the land to the north like the shuttles of a monstrous, deadly loom. The Agricolan forts lying north of the eastern part of the wall had been re-garrisoned as frontier posts, but here in the west heavily armed patrols formed the only buffer along the edge of Pict country.

Of Claudia and her supply wagons there was no sign, but Postumus caught himself staring occasionally at the bleak hills to the north.

As the eastern section was completed, the main army moved west with the building camps and for the second time since his posting to the Sixth Victrix, Postumus found himself actually serving in the same place as his legion. The Victrix was the best of its kind, as Licinius had said, a legion to build a loyalty to, and Postumus soon renewed acquaintance with most of the officers posted near Castra Damnoniorum, including the now happily landlocked Appius Paulinus. Detachments from the Second Augusta and the Twentieth Valeria Victrix were also at work on the wall and they too were quartered in the western forts, while the auxiliary garrisons were sent to permanent postings along the completed stretch of the frontier. Frontinus, however, stayed. Aelius Silanus had lost the senior centurion of his Fifth Cohort in a skirmish with the Picts, and had formed a favorable opinion of the Damnoniorum camp commander. Applying cajolery and a hoarded amphora of Falernian wine in his arguments with the governor, he had managed to hang on to Centurion Frontinus as a replacement.

Postumus, Lucian, and the new Fifth Cohort commander held a small celebration that night in Frontinus's new quarters. His old rooms in the Praetorium were now occupied by the legate, but as Frontinus said cheerfully, it was a fair enough exchange. Posting to a legionary cohort meant promotion and more pay, and a better stab at further advancement.

"Not that there'll be much chance for anyone to cover himself with glory this year." He rubbed the scar on his cheek. "It's going to snow soon. I don't like the looks of this winter. We'll just get the damned wall up in time."

—

It was Samhain again, the leaves turning gold and copper and then fluttering away on the wicked little wind that cut through all the chinks in the walls. In the High King's hold, the hearth fires were cold and the cattle had been driven down from the summer pastures before nightfall. The need-fire lay ready to light with the first spark of the fire drill. Everyone of the High King's clan would be gathered within the walls by dusk, against whatever rode a Samhain wind. Galt leaned, arms crossed, in the doorway of the Great Hall in the upper courtyard, under the row of skulls that adorned the lintel, with the blood of the Sacrifice splashed across the stones under his feet. He had long ago given up hoping for the old king to come back on that wind, but it was a habit all the same, to watch the New Fire lit and see the sparks rush up into the black sky like a message.

In the falling dusk, a chariot came whipping up the switchbacked road and through the triple gates. Rider and driver dropped down near the unlit fire as a slave came up to take the ponies' reins.

"Phah! A bad night to be late!" Dawid stamped his feet in the gray cold. "Are the rest here?"

"Rhodri and Duncan came in this morning," Galt said. "Conor was just before you."

"And the Pict?"

"He's here."

The open courtyard was dressed with evergreen and bundles of corn from the last cutting and the air was thick with the smell of roasting meat, turned on spits all day before the fires were doused. Men and women both wore their best, the bright thick woolens of native weaving and the thin silks dyed with foreign dyes from Rome that were a mark of wealth, gold or bronze or enameled torques and rings on their necks and arms. Even slaves were given new clothes this night, at the start of the new year.

The High King came from the dark hall with his Council behind him, and everyone turned to stare at the stranger who walked beside the Council lords. He was tall and red-haired and thickly tattooed across his face and whatever else of him could be seen beyond his checkered breeches and cloak of wolfskins.

Galt and Dawid fell into step beside them as dusk deepened into blackness and six of the Council lords' households approached the great fire drill, with Talhaiere at their head, a small green branch of yew stuck through his belt. They wore their hair loose and were weaponless. Iron would cut across the magic of a need-fire and douse it before it could begin. Talhaiere raised his staff to the sky, and the six took it in pairs, spinning the drill on its base, wood on wood, raising fire by friction. The clan held its breath. Here in the Brigantian Hills it was ink black, almost too dark to see each other, with only the great river of stars and a sliver of bronze moon over the horizon, no braziers or hearth fires left to keep old men warm or the stew hot. The fire drill's first pair handed off to the next, sweating even in the cold air. A wisp of smoke rose and the smallest household hounds knelt beside it to feed it wisps of tinder, as the next team took the drill seamlessly from the first. The need-fire was a task for free men, not slaves, and an honor if you brought the first spark. A third pair stepped up as the second gave over, Rhys and Dawid's small Colin, proudly taking his first turn since graduating from hound status to warrior at Beltane. A spark glowed in the tinder suddenly and they spun the drill faster. A tiny flame flowered, wavering in the wind. The hounds carefully fed it more dry grass, and then small twigs and soon it lengthened and leapt up, and there was enough for a torch to light the bonfire. When it was blazing, the oldest child from each house fed their own torches at it and ran through the night to rekindle the hearths.

Galt gave a sigh of relief. For the New Fire to fail at the first try was always a bad omen, but worse when the Pictish emissary was there to see it.

A slave broached a barrel of beer in the courtyard beside the fire and small boys passed wooden cups, filled at the hinge of the year to drink the new one in.

Bran led the Council and the Pictish lord back into the Great Hall where meat carved from the sheep and cattle sacrificed on the king's sill at midday was piled on silver platters, dressed with herbs and sauce and quartered apples. The length of the table was laden with bowls of late summer fruit, berries, apples, breads, and pastries, and slaves circulated with flagons of beer and cups of silver or Roman glass or polished oak banded with gold. The High King's wealth shone in the gold on his head and neck and arms and on the riches of his table.

Talhaiere said something softly to Bran and the High King shook his head angrily and lifted his cup. Rhys had gone to Talhaiere to make penance after a week of evil dreams. The king had not and it was clear that he was not going to, not even now at Samhain. *If I told the Pict that, he would leave*, Galt thought. He shook his head. It would happen as it happened. A bout of coughing shook him. The winter cold had settled in his lungs through the summer.

Bran took a long swallow from his cup, a deep two-handled vessel of gold embossed with a human figure bearing stag's antlers. The Horned One was an old god and the cup had been the old king's, and it was perhaps an ill choice too, Galt thought, and then, *Pah! I see omens in every shadow.*

Bran glared at Talhaiere. "Let us sit, and we will hear what words the envoy of the Caledones has to speak."

They took seats around the feast table, with the Pict, who was called Aedan, beside the king. Galt sat at Bran's other side, and Dawid, Conor, Rhodri, and Duncan across. The clan chiefs' hounds squabbled with the king's dogs underneath until a slave with a pitcher of beer kicked them into silence as she passed.

"From Dergdian, king of the Caledones, his greeting." Aedan's accent was odd to their ears but understandable. He was the son of the king's sister, and because kingship among the Picts passed in the mother's line, Dergdian's likely heir. Thus he carried more authority than Brendan's envoy had done. Under his wolfskin cloak he wore a shirt of finely dyed scarlet and breeches checkered brown and green. A heavy torque of twisted gold wire marked him as a lord of standing in his tribe, and a double spiral of red gold clasped his russet hair.

"What does Dergdian send beside greetings?" Duncan inquired. He stabbed a piece of meat with his knife.

The Pict gave him a level look. "He sends me to ask if the Brigantes will pull carts under the yoke of Rome again, or fight like men."

Bran stiffened, but Galt said quietly, "It is an ill idea to insult a king in his hall, Aedan."

Aedan shrugged. "No insult is meant." He drank from his cup, of Roman glass filigreed with gold. "The king of the Brigantes will do as he thinks best for his clans. In the highlands, we are averse to stone roads cutting our fields in half and to foragers reaping our grain and driving our cattle off, and to young men taken across the water to fight Rome's battles."

"When we last made peace with Rome," Galt said, carefully selecting a piece of sauced mutton as he spoke, "Dergdian's men left the council hall and took the legion's gold Eagle with them. That did not sweeten Rome's terms."

Aedan shrugged. The hearth fire snapped and gave off a gout of smoke. Galt coughed, his lungs burning. He put his mouth to his sleeve and when it came away there was blood on the cloth.

Aedan's expression was more speculative than solicitous. "The king's harper is not well?"

"I am well enough," Galt snapped.

"Where is the Roman Eagle now?" Rhodri asked.

Aedan shrugged. "Perhaps in the king's hall." And perhaps not. Things like that carried powerful magic. Dergdian would not part with it for some Brigante lord's asking.

"Were we to ride, what surety can the Caledones give that they will have our backs?" Conor asked.

"If we did not ride when Brendan called, for what reason would we ride now?" Dawid asked.

"They will have almost all their soldiers on that wall," Rhodri said. "If Dergdian pins them there..."

"If? Again, what is our surety?" Conor leaned across the table.

Bran watched them, his head turning slightly toward each voice. Galt could see his fingers clenched on his cup. He had been in a vile temper all day, fighting with Talhaiere and blaming Galt. The cup was empty again and he held it out to the slave to fill.

"The Eagle," Rhodri said again. The Brigantes, living in the shadow of a legion, knew what an Eagle meant. It was the soul of a legion, its loss a disgrace. The Romans thought it could turn the tide of a battle. It would be a most useful thing.

"The last lord of the Brigantes let the Eagle slip from his fingers," Aedan said. "We would not be giving it to an untried pup."

The insult in his tone was calculated, and Duncan and Conor both rose from their chairs in a fury, scattering small dishes and salt cellars.

Bran rose too and slammed his chair back so that it rocked on its legs and nearly toppled. Aedan's cup tipped over, its dregs of beer spreading on the table. "Let Lugh Shining Spear hear me! There will be no talk of pups from the Caledones' lackey! The Brigantes will march!" He picked up the spilled cup and smashed it on the table so that the shards fanned out like spread fingers.

Afterward, the Council tried to make something of that besides the obvious while Aedan watched, uninterested. They would do what they would do. If he had provoked the Brigantes' king to war, that was good, whether they allied with the Caledones or not.

XIII. Beann Caledon

Dergdian watched the woman unpack her cures with some suspicion and the ever-present hope of a man with a chronic condition. His fiery hair was streaked with gray, bound at his forehead with a gold fillet. Gold bands set with carnelian encircled his arms and over his shirt and breeches of fine ocher wool he wore a fur-lined cloak against the damp cold of the stone-built fortress that hugged the slopes of Beann Caledon. None of which did anything for the itching sore in his eye. He scratched at it as she knelt in the strewn rushes on the floor, unpacking her goods.

She took note of the eye, set in a long impassive face that made her think of masks from the midsummer Horse Dance, and offered him a disk of ointment in a clay pot, with a respectful gesture. "For soreness of the eye, this treatment dissolved in water with a few drops of wine is most efficient."

Dergdian's slaves and household had gathered while she spread the rest of her goods on the rug in which they had been rolled. A small child peered at her from behind his mother's skirts. Visitors, even traders and cure-sellers, were rare. A slave took her wet cloak and hung it on a hook by the hearth and she nodded at him gratefully. It had been raining all day, all week in fact, and a sodden journey through the highlands had left her chilled to the bone. She was dressed in a plain brown woolen gown with fur boots beneath. Her brown hair hung in braids tipped with little enameled balls but otherwise she was without adornment save for the flower that bloomed just under her collarbone and the spiral patterns encircling her arms.

Dergdian inspected the cake of ointment, stamped with an oculist's mark that spoke of a journey from the south. "What are you called?"

"Aifa," she said, spreading out her other wares.

"You have come from the south? Through the Eagles' new wall?"

"The Eagles pay little attention to such as me," Aifa said. "I was born in the north islands of Orkney, and I have been as far south as the Silure lands where the traders' boats come in at Sabrina Mouth, and to the great palace in Londinium, just to bring these cures to you."

A gray-bearded priest in a white robe folded his arms and glared at her. A gold sun disk two handspans wide hung across his chest. She would need to tread warily with him.

"And they let you through their gate?" Dergdian said thoughtfully. "Marked as you are?" He nodded at her arms, the blue patterns showing where she had pushed back her sleeves.

"These are Cornovi marks, not Caledone." It had been thought best to choose a tribe she was unlikely to actually encounter. The Cornovi inhabited the wild islands off the farthest northern shore and were all reputed to be witches and half-seal.

"My grandmother was a Cornovi woman," Dergdian said. "What house do you come from?"

"None," she said shortly, cursing Dergdian's grandmother. "My mother was a Cornovi woman. I don't know about my father. Perhaps he was a gray seal, as she said once when I asked. At any rate she took me to the priests for my initiation and they allowed it, so that is all I know."

Dergdian seemed satisfied. If she was rumored to be a seal child, it was clear why she hadn't stayed among her people. Any prospective husband would be waiting for her to disappear into the sea some night. It had been rumored that his own grandfather had hidden his wife's sealskin in a chest to keep her with him.

"And you are recently come past the Romans' camps?" the priest inquired. "What are they doing there now?"

"Building things," she said. "Granaries and temples to their gods and bathing houses. And wall. Mostly wall."

"Their wall is cursed," the priest said flatly. "They will see."

"No doubt." She continued to arrange her wares. "For pain in the ear. And for toothache." She set a stoppered green glass flask of oil and a bronze pot of unguent on the rug. "And quicksilver for troubles in the generative parts." This was bottled in an iron flask since the cure tended to dissolve other metals. "And for cough and to sweeten the breath, frankincense from the Incense Route in the vastness of the East."

She wrapped the cake of eye ointment in its silk bag again and added a substantial piece of frankincense, the most valuable of her wares. "A hearth gift for the lord of the Caledones," she said, presenting it to Dergdian.

He nodded and took the bag, formalities achieved. "You are wet and tired, which is no way to welcome a stranger among us. Rest and eat and there will be time in the morning to show your wares to the house."

"The lord of the Caledones is kind. I am weary, as he says. In the morning I will be most happy to see any in the lord's hold who seek a cure."

They gave her a chamber in the upper levels of the hold, a straw mattress with a blue rug over it, and a meal of mutton and beer with the king's household, where the priest studied her with a suspicious eye. A pile of great gray hounds lay under the long table, occasionally squabbling halfheartedly over whatever was dropped, but mainly sleeping. Her own sleeping chamber was plain, but someone had warmed the bed for her and there was a fire banked on the hearth. The girl who showed her to it assured her that the slave who minded her pack ponies had been fed and bedded down with the king's people, and the ponies stabled out of the rain. Probably into a better space than Brys, she thought, yawning. Poor Brys.

In the morning she saw such patients as suffered from the afflictions whose cures she peddled, in an unused chamber in the west of the lower court, furnished for private consultations with two rough chairs and a table. Unlike the chamber she had slept in, it was a dismal room, dank and windowless, lit by tallow lamps, with water leaking from the walls.

A slave with matted hair and a worn gown brought her a cushion for her chair and a breakfast of porridge and beer. "Maon High Priest says I'm to see to you, Lady. I am Teasag if you need anything more."

Aifa cocked her head to the small stream running down the wall. The floor was packed earth and the water sank in quickly but it left a pattern like a river delta. "Does this chamber always leak like that?"

"Often enough when it's been raining," the girl said. "That's why it isn't used. This is more than usual, but it will stop when the sky clears."

Aifa gave the wall a long look. There was substantial water in there, she thought, maybe enough to bring the western wing down one day if it was built over one of the limestone caves that pocked the ground here. Claudia Silva would know that. But Aifa wouldn't, and needed no discussion of the source of her knowledge. "Thank you, Teasag," she said. "If there are people to see me, send them in one by one."

"Would the lady be willing to look at me?" Teasag looked miserable. "I can't pay but I have this." She held out a small bit of amber on a grubby thong. "It hurts all the time."

"Let me see."

Teasag pulled one reddened breast from her gown and grimaced.

"You have an infection in the nipple." And why hadn't anyone treated that by now?

"Maon the High Priest says it is because my womb wanders, and not to make a fuss."

"Maon the High Priest hasn't got a womb, or tits, so how would he know?" she muttered. Druids were famous for only thinking about the stars. "Rub this on it and try to keep it clean. If you can find a bit of honey, that will help too." She gave her a salve of the expensive frankincense in verdigris and tallow and told her to keep her bit of amber. It was probably the only treasure she owned. "Perhaps you don't want to show this to Maon," she suggested and Teasag nodded and hid the little jar in the folds of her gown. And if Maon had sent her to spy, she wasn't likely to do so now.

"Now go and see who is waiting."

Most who came to her had already tried most of Maon's treatments, to some degree of success, or not, and what Aifa had to offer was similar, but bore the enticement of the exotic. She glimpsed him in the passage now and then, an irritable and suspicious wind blowing down the stone hallway. The priests of the Britons were a formidable force and their knowledge was vast and old, particularly among the Druids, who were banned in the south because rebellion sprang out of the ground like weeds wherever they were. Maon would not be someone to cross more than she could help.

She offered wild leek in goose grease and olive oil for earache, cakes of soluble ointment for sties, plantain for toothache, and garlic and powdered cow horn in quicksilver for the miserable tribesman who had ridden with Dergdian's envoy to the Brigantes, he told her proudly, and had apparently visited a brothel somewhere on their travels.

"So you will fire the heather between you and catch the Roman in the middle?" she asked, distracting him from the embarrassment of a personal inspection of his troubles. "I shall go south to Calleva and wait that out, I think."

"Maybe. If the king of the Brigantes honors his word, drunken though it was spoken. They are an unreliable people. Ow!"

"So I have heard. There. Use this as I showed you and it will help." Probably. It often did. Or not.

"Thank you." He regained his dignity with his breeches and said seriously, "I would go south, Lady, truly. South of the old wall. When we have stripped this country of the Roman kind then it will be the time to come north again."

"I had thought as much," she said. "And so thought to come this way now while I can. No one profits in a war but the winner and the ravens. I'll visit Lord Dergdian's clan lords and perhaps the Epidii on my path south again, and winter in comfort elsewhere."

In the morning she was on the track to the next holding in Dergdian's mountainous kingdom. The pack ponies were saddled and re-loaded with her wares, her own mount dancing in the leaf-strewn wind. The rain had stopped but the ground was sodden and water dripped from eaves and thatch. Woodsmoke rose above the soaking roofs and a disheveled rooster, late to his job, crowed from the top of the gate. She saw Maon watching from the wall of the upper level while Dergdian's household went about its morning business.

"Faugh! That is an evil place!" Brys tightened the strap on the spotted pony, the one who always blew his belly up. He kneed him sharply and the pony exhaled. "I heard voices all night, like something come up from Annwn."

"What kind of voices?" Brys wasn't usually hysterical.

"Whispers and gibbers and squeaking. The kitchen slaves say it's the shades of the dead come to speak to the living. They come when it rains."

"You were supposed to be quartered with Dergdian's slaves. Where were you?"

"In the storehouse, in the hillside there." Brys jerked a thumb over his shoulder past the stone walls of the chamber where Aifa had seen her patients. "It's a cave, really, but they use it for grain. I hate caves anyway. I asked why they'd put me there then and they said because they wouldn't sleep in it." He spat. "And I won't either, not again."

Teasag hurried into the courtyard, stopping once to look over her shoulder. She held out a wrapped bundle from her apron: boiled eggs and bannock.

"For the road, Lady."

"Thank you, Teasag." Aifa stowed it in a pack saddle and paused. "Teasag, that chamber I was given to show my wares in…"

"Yes, Lady?"

"Don't sleep in that tower, or in the cave where your people put my slave."

Teasag looked puzzled but she nodded. She looked up and caught sight of Maon on the wall. "I must go. Safe journey, Lady." She fled into the keep.

"None of them will go in that cave anyway," Brys said. "I told you. They put me there to be funny." He spat.

She mounted her horse and took the spotted pony's lead. "Best we're on the road," she said. "Now, I think."

She looked across the narrow valley dotted with the dark shapes of horses to the crest opposite, already snow-covered. With luck, the tower would hold until they were well out of Pict country. She wondered if that was why Maon had put her there, for a witch to blame when that cave collapsed.

–

To the south along the new wall, it was turning colder each day and they could see white draping the mountains of the far north. Governor Urbicus was far from satisfied with the Pictish situation and had no intention of moving his legions out until he was. The Army would winter on the frontier again.

In the meantime, with the threat of winter, the tempo of life in Castra Damnoniorum redoubled. Every available man was put to work to close the gaps. The Picts, too, seeing their last chance to smash the wall before it could be completed, came down out of their northern mountains to harry the monster that Rome had created out of their own turf and stone. It was becoming evident that there were also more of the rebels from Valentia unaccounted for than had been thought.

"Like trying to kill off an anthill," Frontinus said. "You can't. You just try to keep 'em out of the kitchen," an oddly domestic analogy that summed up life on the frontier. "Somebody's been cutting up our patrols and stealing horses and putting dead sheep in the water, and generally being a nuisance," Frontinus said disgustedly, "and if it isn't the fay, I rather expect it's the Picts."

The building crews worked jumpily into the fall, while the main army, including Valerian's Dacian cavalry wing, were held at the ready to meet whatever was coming out of the hills.

And then, with the Picts and the die-hard rebels of the Selgovae gathering like a dark cloud to the north, and the Army grimly affixing new points to its pilums, winter dropped on them without warning, in a raging blizzard that toppled trees and howled like the Wild Hunt up and down the hills.

"What in the name of the Mother is this? The sun was out this morning!" Valerian staggered through the door of the Principia and slammed it behind him against the raging white storm outside. "We barely got our horses inside before that thing buried 'em!"

"This, Wing Commander, is the Fates," a voice drawled from the opposite side of the room. "Making themselves a pest."

Valerian shook the snow off and saluted. "My apologies, sir, I didn't see you." He joined the other officers gathered around the commander's desk.

"Quite understandable, in the circumstances." Lollius Urbicus looked grimly at the shuttered windows, and then turned back to the two Frontier Scouts who stood steaming damply before the brazier. "Is this going to let up, or are we stuck here till spring?"

"I'd say we're stuck till spring, Governor," one of them said. "This is wolf winter, not normal weather for this country, so I wouldn't trust it. It'll let up for a while, of course, but then it may come down again and trap you the gods know where. And those painted demons in the north will have all the advantage. They know the country. I've heard their Druids can control the weather. Maybe it's that."

Lollius Urbicus turned to study the windows again, which were leaking icy wind despite the shutters, hands rubbing the cold from his fingers and apparently much in thought. He was dressed in riding uniform and the purple folds of his cloak were of heavy wool lined with fur. He wore fur-lined boots and the scarlet brush of his helmet crest was somewhat the worse for the snowstorm. He turned his head finally, the gilded figures on his breastplate shining palely in the lamplight. It was nearly pitch dark outside in the center of the storm. He looked at the commander of the Victrix. "What are your feelings in this matter, Silanus, Druids notwithstanding?"

The legate leaned back in his chair and tapped his fingers on his thigh. "I think," he said after a moment, "that we would now be unwise to go out to meet them. But I think also that they may come to us, with the first break in the weather. As has been pointed out, *they* know their way home."

Lollius Urbicus nodded. "It seems we are in agreement. We will hold where we are and go after them in force with the thaw." He looked around the room. "But that doesn't mean we leave anything else till the thaw. I want every one of those gaps in the wall closed up if you have to tie the men to each other and tie the end to the Praetorian Gate. If we don't close those gaps before the weather clears, we'll have a lap full of Picts when it does. And you'll have Typhon's own time keeping them out with a nice half-mile hole in the wall every two miles." He nodded at the officers gathered around him. "Dismissed."

–

It stormed for three days, a suffocating white blanket that fell on the frontier and kept falling. Postumus, Lucian, and Flavian were faced with a succession of frostbitten toes and ears, and the veterinarians coped with an outbreak of thrush among the cavalry horses as the stables grew progressively wetter. On the fourth day, the storm lightened to drifting whorls of snow and every man in the Army went out with shovels to clear the road, with the building crews behind them. They worked furiously, one eye on the blackened sky, and they had closed another three hundred feet of wall before the wind came up again, driving the storm before it. They made it back to camp a scant minute before the outside world vanished behind a howling wall of snow.

After that they worked when they could, wet, cold, and miserable, as the icy hand of winter took an ever stronger grip on the frontier. Great white frozen drifts stretched as far as a man could see, blanketing hills, masking the riverbeds, and even covering trees where the relentless wind piled the snow higher than their topmost branches. Only the frontier road showed clearly, scraped and shoveled each day that the weather held, by the sneezing, miserable soldiers whose forts it linked. The storm couldn't hold forever and they worked desperately on the wall in each slight break in the weather, knowing that this might be their last, and on the next they might find the Picts there before them. That winter everyone served on the wall – cavalry, cooks, and legionaries, scribes and tribunes, and Postumus and his medical staff – digging the channel for the rubble fill at the base, and heaving the heavy stones into place above it. The snow had to be cleared now before the turf could be cut, and the mere cutting was almost impossible when the ground had frozen. They burned a line of bonfires from end to end of each unfinished section, but as soon as the storm came up again, they went out and it was all to do over.

Postumus, on top of the rampart, was wearily stacking turf in overlapping lines like brick, as the wall rose beneath him, while Lucian sent empty baskets down the pulley line and raised the filled ones to the top. Beyond them, on a completed stretch, a second crew was building the parapet that would guard the outer edge. The bitter wind bit clean through cloak and leggings to the bone and the air was like broken glass. Postumus, coughing, thought that he would have more chest colds than his own to dose that night. Below him he could see Valerian, his Wing Commander's uniform exchanged for a rough leather tunic, making part of the line that passed the heavy foundation stones from their pyramided stacks by the road up to their beds on the rubble fill. By evening he was exhausted, every muscle aching and his fingers scarred and split open from handling the frozen turf. Like everyone else on the frontier that winter, he fell into bed like a corpse and slept until there was enough pre-dawn light to see whether they could work again that day.

Once when the weather held for three days, a supply train got through, bringing with it the few small luxuries that made that winter bearable – wine, olives, cases of earthen honey jars, and a load of apples from the south – with a note that said, "To the men of the frontier at Saturnalia, from Lollius Urbicus."

They cheered him that night, a cheer that rang the length of the wall. He was still in camp, of course, pacing up and down his wall, encouraging the diligent, bestirring the idle, and stacking turf himself. He must have sent a courier south with his orders when the first storm broke.

Postumus, bandaging a legionary's swollen fingers with his own bandaged hands, looked up as a shadow fell across his light. It was Tertius, in the uniform of a Medical Corps orderly.

"I'll do that, if you'll show me how," Tertius said, taking in Postumus's haggard face and bandaged hands. "I may as well start learning."

Postumus blinked. For some reason he seemed to encounter Tertius only in circumstances that already had an otherworldly feel to them: on his first day in Licinius's old hospital; in the arena; or when he was half awake; and now here, snowbound on the far edge of the world, racing a snowstorm to finish a wall.

Tertius took a step forward. "Are you all right? You don't look so good." His wolf-toothed face was unaccountably concerned. "I wasn't sure you'd have me now, but it looks like it was maybe a good thing I came."

"Where in Hades have you been?" Postumus managed to ask.

"I won some money, you see." Tertius looked embarrassed. "I'd been to see the lady you sent me to, but then I won on the races, so I didn't go back."

Postumus noted that Claudia hadn't mentioned that.

"It kept me drunk a good long while, so I didn't have to think about things, like. When that ran out, I was afraid to come round the legion. After signing up and then not showing, I thought I might be listed Unlawful Absent, so I took another job, sort of, but I couldn't stick it. Then when we heard there was still trouble in the north, well, it seemed like maybe better to be with the legion somehow than not at all. So I went down to Luguvallium, knowing you were at the western end, and then I found out I'd missed a supply train out of Corstopitum by two days, and the last one out of Luguvallium by one. I'd about decided to try to catch up with it on my own when the governor's wagons came through. You'd better let me do that, sir," he added.

Postumus made room for him beside his patient's chair. "I, uh... did think you were long gone. In fact, I had your re-enlistment scratched, so you needn't worry about that. But Aesculapius knows I'm glad to see you." His calf and thigh muscles felt like hot irons had been run through them and the room was beginning to take on a vague, misty quality. He could leave Tertius in the hospital in the day while they worked, and then there wouldn't be so much to do at night... "You... spread the salve over the whole hand and wrap the bandages lightly, just enough to keep the dirt out. He'll have to take them off in the morning and get gloves on." He staggered slightly as he spoke.

Tertius began to gently wrap the legionary's hands. "Is he fit for work, sir?" he asked, seeing the raw cracks along the fingers and the swollen knuckles.

"No," the legionary said tiredly, "but neither is anyone else. You picked a wonderful time to join up."

Postumus was still standing in the middle of the surgery, as if wondering what he should be doing.

"I saw that lady again," Tertius said. "The one who would have given me a job if I hadn't gone off drunk. She didn't seem mad about it. She was in a camp on the Clota not so far from here. I thanked her for wanting to help me and when I said where I was going, she said to thank you for the good wishes and to tell you that the wind blew somewhat chancy at the moment. Said you'd know what she meant."

Claudia? What in Hades was she doing camped on the Clota in this weather? And had she come out of Pict country with news or with a vengeful tribe on her tail? Only desperation could have driven her out in this white death. He tried to concentrate on that, but the question kept slipping away from him. Flavian was bandaging the last patient. Postumus pointed at him. "See him for quarters and be here in the morning," he told Tertius. He got as far as an empty bed in the nearest ward and collapsed.

In the morning he was back to work on the wall again.

XIV. Wolf Winter

All that long winter they worked on the wall, until for Postumus life became a succession of frozen, pain-filled days, evenings spent on an endless sick parade of broken, lacerated hands and lung disease, eased somewhat by the advent of Tertius, and nights of exhausted sleep too deep for dreams. He had little time to wonder further about Claudia. There was only the endlessly falling snow and the wall.

For the men of the frontier it had become almost a living thing, and the focus of their existence. They slept in its shadow and spent their days along its snow-shrouded length. They died atop it, frozen, sick, and hopeless.

In the space of one week, Postumus lost six men to lung fever, men too weary to even cough up the phlegm that choked them. And two more died when the storm came down and hid the lights of the fort before they could reach it. They found them the next day not a hundred feet from the gate – on the wrong side of the wall. They had tried to follow it back to the fort and blundered instead through one of the remaining gaps, into an endless, sightless void where the very ground rose up and covered them.

But slowly, some days only a few feet at a time, the gaps closed up. Lollius Urbicus and Aelius Silanus were every-where, like a pair of graying wolves, pacing, inspecting, working until they were ready to drop, and then sitting until dawn over the few intelligence reports that still came through. They rode the length of the western wall and back, quartering each night in a different fort, and these days the tribune assigned to the Sixth was much in awe of his commander.

Postumus approached Lollius Urbicus at the first unobtrusive moment he found, and relayed Tertius's message to him, but the governor merely nodded and said, "Thank you, Surgeon Corvus, I was aware of it," and offered no further information. As Postumus saluted and turned to go, he added quietly, "A word to the wise, Corvus – don't form an attachment there. Those who travel that road can't afford them; and it almost always ends with someone being stupid and a danger to himself and the Army."

"Yes, sir." Postumus held himself at attention, seething.

The governor continued, not unkindly, "She is, to the best of my knowledge, still alive, although the Picts have a long reach. The situation we suspected has been confirmed. And that is more than you have any business knowing, so let it rest at that." He rubbed his stiffening fingers together to warm them, his angular face dark and preoccupied.

Of necessity, Postumus forced himself to be content with that, while the wall crept on, until on the last bleak day in February, the last block of turf was dropped into place and the last sharpened stake driven into the palisade. And then, as if the Fates had granted them so long and no longer, the leaden skies drew back from the pale sun, and the enemy in the north came howling down out of the hills on a wind that blew straight across the Styx.

The top layer of snow had frozen to a solid crust and they streamed along it like the crest of a tidal wave, half-naked even in the frozen air, the blue of their war paint and the scarlet of the feathers on their spears brighter than any colors Postumus had ever seen, while the signal fires burned along the wall. The Picts concentrated their attack where the frozen river cut the wall above Castra Damnoniorum and the cohorts of the westernmost forts came stumbling along the frozen road to join with the Damnoniorum garrison. The snow had filled and frozen in the ditch outside the wall, and the legion had been unable to clear it in time. The Picts and a handful of pale-haired warriors of the Selgovae came across it to hurl themselves against the ramparts of the wall and the frozen, wretched army that guarded it.

The legion fell out to the rampart stairs and through the gates, wracked and coughing, their feet swathed in bandages and leggings, and the wrecks of their hands closed painfully around pilum shaft and bow. And then, as the first blue-stained figure flung itself at the defending army, a madness seemed to seize them that was more deadly than all the centuries of Roman discipline that stretched across the years behind them. This was *their* wall. They had fought for it and died by the hundreds for it, and it was theirs!

They were up on the ramparts before the trumpets could sing out, gaunt and snarling as winter wolves, and their pilums took down the first line of the enemy in a red rain of death before the wall. Where the Picts had slipped through the river gap, they stumbled through the snow to meet them, first with flung pilums and then with swords.

"Hold them! Steady and hold them!" Aelius Silanus shouted, but they were lost to him, their haggard, unshaven faces turned to the men who would rob them of their wall.

Appius Paulinus, below the wall at the head of his cohort, felt them dissolve around him, rushing the enemy like berserkers, while he shouted at them to re-form. His standard-bearer dropped the cohort standard and took a Pict by the hair, slicing his dagger across the man's throat. Then he picked it up again and swung it like a club at the next man who came at him.

On the ramparts they took the Picts in the throat or the chest with reddened swords as they rose above the parapet, or flung them with bare hands down into the scarlet snow below, and their madness seemed to rise with the heavy smell of blood that clung to the cold air.

"Mithras God," Aelius Silanus whispered. He signaled to the trumpeter beside him, but the notes of the trumpet call went unheeded as his army fought and clawed like demons with the enemy. He seized the trumpet from the awestruck soldier beside him.

"No! Let them be!" Lollius Urbicus scrambled up the rampart stair behind them.

"If they break—"

"It is only the madness that keeps them going," Urbicus panted. "Break that, and they *will* break. They built it, let them hold it their own way."

Dumbly, Silanus let the trumpet fall, and together they watched the battle for the wall they had laid down across the edge of the world.

The Picts gathered for a final charge and with one last scream of fury, the gaunt and bandaged army threw itself against them and hurled them out and down. Half the Pictish front line went down into the carnage in the frozen ditch.

And then they were gone, and the bandaged soldiers along the wall stood shaking and bewildered as the bright unaccustomed sun lit the blood-stained snow.

Numbly, like men coming out from under a drug, they gathered their dead and their wounded. Lollius Urbicus leaned on his general's staff in the trampled snow and looked up at his wall, and the billowing black cloud that rose beyond it where they were burning the Pictish dead. After a moment, Silanus joined him, his helmet under one arm, and his gray hair plastered against his forehead. Their breath made little clouds of steam in the cold air.

Silanus drew his cloak more closely about his shoulders. To his last breath, he would carry the memory of the Sixth as he had seen them that day.

"The Sixth is a good legion," Urbicus said softly. "One of the best – they proved it today. You mustn't blame them for what happened. They have been pushed past the point of breaking most armies. And in any case," he added, "they put Ahriman's own terror into the Pict."

To the east outside the fortress walls another cloud of smoke began to rise, the funeral pyre of the dead of Rome, accompanied on their journey by the prayers and sacrifices which the Pictish dead had burned without.

–

"You are to be commended for the zeal with which you have defended this wall, which was built at what cost no men know better than you." Aelius Silanus paced up and down before the paraded Sixth Victrix the next morning. "*I* commend you, as does Governor Urbicus." He took a wreath of dried winter grasses from the governor's hand and presented it to the standard-bearer of the Sixth. "It will be exchanged for one of gold when gold is more easily come by," he said, and then they understood him, and raised a cheer that rang exultantly across the empty reaches of snow, as the standard-bearer hung the wreath around the Eagle's wings.

"*However*," Silanus said, his voice pitched to sound above the cheering, and they fell silent. "There must never – *never* – be another day that your commander speaks and you do not heed him. The Fates looked on you gently yesterday. An army too far gone in fury to take commands generally reaps bare bones in the heather instead of wreaths of honor. The next man who disobeys me in battle for whatever cause will not live to learn whether the battle is won or lost." He fingered the hilt of his sword. "I trust I make myself plain."

They kept silence in parade formation, eyes front and beginning to look ashamed.

"Your performance yesterday was as foolhardy as it was brave, and the foolhardy soldier gets little comfort from glory when he is dead of his own stupidity. There is no place for that man in the Eagles." He paused again, eyeing the assembled legion, barely recognizable with bandaged hands and feet, and faces winter-thin. "But never think that I am not proud of you," he added softly. "You are dismissed."

–

"Wily old bastard," Valerian said afterward in the hospital while Postumus was re-dressing his sword-cut leg, always the hazard of the cavalryman. "They almost cheered him for chewing them out. That man knows how to command. Him and old Foxy Urbicus." He gritted his teeth as Postumus dabbed on more salve.

"I am not sure which army I was most afraid of," Appius Paulinus said. His pale hair was shaved on one side where Flavian had treated a gash from a spearpoint that had gone up inside his helmet.

Valerian shook his head. Even his beloved ala had got loose from him, chasing the retreating Picts until the horses were floundering in snow and they had no choice but to stop. "We have the winter to see that that never happens again," he said. "They'll be back come spring. They were just trying it out, to see how far we'd gotten."

Back come spring. The specter of a war host massing in the hills for an attack on the weaker western end of the wall was uppermost in everyone's mind now that the shock of the battle had worn off, leaving them no longer numb, but determined and infinitely wary. They all knew that news of that winter battle, and the state of the wall garrisons, was spreading like a ripple through the north.

Valerian swung his legs off the table and tested his weight on them gingerly. "The governor's called a commanders' council," he said. "It wouldn't do to faint in his lap." He put some more weight on the bad leg and nodded. "I think I'll do."

"You will if you keep off it," Postumus said, "and don't show off."

Valerian grinned and gave him a rude salute, exiting with as much swagger as his stitches would allow. Postumus turned to his next patient, a legionary with a bellyache that so far had responded to none of the potions hopefully poured down him. He winced as he flexed his hands. They were beginning to heal, but in truth the surgery staff wasn't in much better shape than the rest of the legion. It would be a long time before the army of the wall was fit again.

He mixed yet another potion and stood by while the legionary with the bellyache drank it down. The man's face was flushed and hot to the touch and he seemed to be in much pain. Postumus was beginning to get worried. There was no sign of the flux, only the constant twist of pain in the belly, accompanied by nausea and vomiting. He had eaten nothing suspicious that Postumus could discover. Nor could he find any sign of tumor. There had been another man, in Syria, another surgeon's patient... Vainly he wracked his memory, but nothing more came forward. He had heard of him only secondhand, and all he knew was that there had been a man with a bellyache, and in the end, it had killed him. But how? And what? Aesculapius let that potion work. But he knew, in truth, that it was far too low in the belly to be an ulcer.

He signaled to Tertius to take the man and put him to bed in the ward next to the surgery. "I want him where I can watch him," he said. He went to the hospital office and began pulling his library from the shelves. What he wanted apparently didn't exist, and in any case, interruption in the form of an optio cut short his search.

"The commander's compliments, sir, and you're wanted in the Principia."

Now what? Postumus thought in exasperation, pulling a comb from a compartment in his desk and running it through his hair. He pulled his surgeon's apron off, checked his tunic for stains, and followed the optio, by the direct route this time, to the Principia.

In the commander's office, a serious-faced gathering warmed its hands around a brazier: Lollius Urbicus, his weathered face sharp-featured and thoughtful; Aelius Silanus, fingers drumming on the red leather skirt of his harness and his eyes intent; Claudius Charax, the legate of the Second Augusta at Isca Silurum, most of which was now attached to the northern army; the commander of the detachment of the Twentieth Valeria Victrix from Deva; a smattering of tribunes assigned to the three legions, earnestly absorbing strategy at the old generals' knees; and Valerian – one flyaway eyebrow still quirked in surprise – handed the cavalry command of the army, with a sardonic comment from the governor that he hoped Valerian could hang onto this honor longer than his predecessor had. Since the man in question would now be remembered only by a gravestone set into the northern wall, Valerian had said that he hoped so too.

At the governor's invitation, Postumus drew up a stool by the brazier, and they shifted a little to make room for him. Lollius Urbicus rubbed his hands above the fire, his signet ring glowing orange in the flame. "One of these days they'll stiffen up on me and stay that way," he said, curling and uncurling his fingers; businesslike hands with large knuckles and neatly trimmed nails. He turned to Postumus and said abruptly, "Very well, Corvus, what kind of shape is this army in?"

"Frankly, sir, they got by on nothing more than sheer temper," Postumus said. "I don't think they can do it again."

Urbicus nodded. "How long?"

"To get them fit? By the thaw, I think, if we can keep them decently fed. They need rest more than anything – time to mend."

"And a quiet back gate," Silanus said. "Corvus, I'd like you to repeat your opinions of the Brigantes, so that the rest of the command may have it firsthand."

The Brigantes. That whole late summer passage and the conversation in Isurium had faded before the snowbound reality of the wall, and Postumus brought it back with difficulty at first. But slowly the images grew brighter in the fire's glow as he called them from memory: Bran, an implacable, unimaginative enemy with a possibly dangerous blind side; Galt, more clever than his king, and with a clearer view of things-as-they-are; Dawid, unquestioning and faithful, but warily friendly.

Britain's generals listened intently while he spoke, and afterward there was no sound but the crackle and hiss of the brazier, and the soft creak of a breastplate as someone shifted in his seat.

"And what is your overall opinion of their stability?" the commander of the Victrix detachment asked finally. The firelight glinted on his burnished armor and the gold-bordered scarlet of a First Centurion's cloak.

Postumus hesitated, wishing he could find some other answer than the one he had first given Aelius Silanus. "Galt has a good deal of influence, but it's not endless," he said at last. "There's no love lost there, I think. The High King will make a war if he sees the chance that the rest will follow him."

"The High King would do well to remember that the Victrix is not the Ninth Hispana," Aelius Silanus said shortly, and Postumus flinched, but the rest seemed not to notice it.

"It was the war with the Hispana that killed his father," Postumus said, carefully noncommittal. "He has no love for any legion that garrisons Eburacum."

"Talk of a dead legion is an ill omen for a new war," the legate of the Second said, and there was an uncomfortable silence.

"It is my fortress their souls are caught in," Silanus retorted, his words hanging like an echo in the still room.

"My fortress and these hills, perhaps. Or did you notice nothing when you re-garrisoned Castra Pinnata?"

"The signs of an old burning, no more," Urbicus said. "I am a practical man and raise no ghosts." He leaned closer to the fire. "We must see to it that the Britons leave theirs to lie as well."

"Catapults are always persuasive," Valerian murmured, and a chuckle went around the room. The tension dissolved and Postumus eyed his friend admiringly. Valerian would have a yet higher command someday, if he lived, that was plain. Postumus wouldn't have been surprised if he did end up emperor. Valerian would wear the purple better than many a sword-made Caesar.

After that, talk turned to the immediate goal of final pacification of Valentia, and containment of the troublesome Brigantes in the south. There was neither the manpower nor the desire to conquer the highlands, but they were going to have to, somehow, put a dent in them, for the peace of the frontier.

"With the thaw comes the Pict," Urbicus said. "If we can't demonstrate the error of his ways then, we may spend years trying to do it, and the price will come high. I would like to hear your suggestions, gentlemen, before I reach a decision."

"Send a strike force north and kill him where he lairs."

"If you can find him. The Pict is the man who isn't there, even when he is."

"Let him come to us. Burn him *south* of the wall, for a lesson."

"And maybe have the Selgovae come rustling out of their holes and help him? We must take them first."

"Find them first, you mean. The better part of them are lairing with the Picts already. The rest are skirmishers, left for our annoyance. Turning out a legion after them is like hunting rats with a catapult."

"And what of the Brigantes? Half the forts in their hills are unmanned now."

"They are under treaty."

"They're going to break it."

"If we break it before they do, we'll push them into rebellion. We can't afford that until Valentia is nailed down."

"We've still a strong base in the south, and the Twentieth can move up fast enough if they look like trouble."

Urbicus sat quietly and let them gnaw on the problem. When each of the commanders had had his say, he folded his arms and stared thoughtfully into the coals for a moment. "This wall is more than a barrier," he said when he looked up. "It is a force in itself. Its purpose is to guarantee absolute peace below it and excellent behavior above. We cannot do that by holding it as a defensive line. So our first priority becomes the Picts – and to drag a net through Valentia for the Selgovae skirmishers that we missed last fall. With the wall closed up, there are only two ways those can slip north around us. See here." He pulled a sheaf of maps from a drawer in the legate's desk and spread them on the map table.

"We are at the narrowest neck of Britain, and the wall cuts clean across it. To get past us, the enemy must break the wall or cross water. Here, at the Bodotria, or here, across the Clota." He indicated the wide river mouths at either end of the wall. "It is a narrow stretch on either side, but dangerous for a man who doesn't know those waters. They can take only a few across at a time, that close to the wall – our farthest forts sit right on the bank at the only fords. To move an entire army across either water unseen would take months and our scouts would spot them long before that. And the farther out from our forts, the wider the water and the greater the danger. They have the ships to do it, but we have fleets in harbor at both ends. In the east we have reoccupied the forts north of the wall as far as Castra Pinnata. So. For the Pict in the north, the only way is *through* the wall." He unrolled another map and laid it half across the first, pinning the edges with a set of bronze weights. "And first they have to get past the forts above the wall. These block the glens that are the Picts' roads south. The garrisons there couldn't stop a massed army but they can reduce their numbers and give us warning before they have to let them through.

"And for Brendan's skirmishers, the only way north is across the Bodotria in the east or the Clota in the west. They have no boats left, we saw to that. If you, Commander," he nodded at Valerian, "take a cavalry sweep from the southern wall north to us here" – he fanned his hand across the top of the first map – "you will drive the Selgovae before you to either end of the wall, and with luck you may split them. If not, in my thinking, they will make for the west and the mouth of the Clota.

"In the east, we have two forts garrisoned along the coast and outposts beyond the wall to stand between them and the main army of the Picts. And also ships of the Fleet, patrolling from Horrea Classis." He shifted maps again to show the naval station at the newly reopened warehouses above the northern forts. "And while the Votadini south of the wall in the east do not love us, they cast their lot with us a long time ago and are afraid of us enough to be reluctant to shelter fugitives under Rome's nose.

"In the west, they will have to go through the territory of the Damnonii, with whom we are at peace but who might be persuaded to give them boats anyway, if they thought we wouldn't find out, to make a safer crossing into the country of the Epidii." He tapped the map. "The Epidii are a small tribe and much under the Caledones' thumb. Moreover, we have no forts among those hills, and only one small post at the southern edge of Clota-Mouth. They could even" – he drew his hand parallel to the wall and westward beyond it – "cross here, where the Epidii lands jut south into the Hibernian Channel, and work their way north with the Epidii to guide them. You must remember that there are more tribes of the Picts than the Caledones, but the Caledones are the strongest. How many march against us depends on how many Dergdian of the Caledones can draw under his banner."

"So we harry the Selgovae north to their brother wolves," Valerian said, studying the maps. "And you wait for them – where?"

"Here above Bodotria with the Fleet." Lollius Urbicus tapped his finger on the eastern coast. "But mainly here, before they can cross, west and south along Clota–Mouth, in small units well linked by courier. I intend to pull in the Frontier Scouts for that. I want no beacon fires or obvious patrols to give them suspicions."

Charax, the legate of the Second, studied the maps. "Can you be sure that the Selgovae won't simply go underground again and wait it out?"

"Not according to the latest information," Urbicus said. "And the source has so far proven true. If Brendan's wolves can't run at will to harry our backs, they will head north to join the main war host. And here is where we will catch them." He drew his hand again across the northwestern edge of Valentia.

"Will they fight while we hold Brendan for their good behavior?"

"If it comes to that, they will let Brendan die, on Brendan's orders," Urbicus said. "By information from the same source."

Postumus, watching this war council, remembered Hilarion depicting Julius Caesar's Gallic campaigns for an enraptured audience of himself, Justin, Marcus, and Constantia with the aid of two toy soldiers and a clay horse on the nursery floor. It had all looked very simple, as it did now, when one could compress an entire army into one clay horse and maneuver it at will. Only now Postumus knew the odds, and the number of other clay horses that might be waiting beyond the next line of hills. He hoped that the governor's source of information knew as much as it said it did.

"And how good is your source?" the legate of the Second asked, unconsciously echoing Postumus's thought, and the commander of the Valeria Victrix detachment leaned forward. It was plain that that question was in his mind also.

Lollius Urbicus considered the fire for a moment. "The source is excellent if somewhat unorthodox," he said. "How long it will last, I cannot say. I suggest we use it while we can – and shut up."

Valerian, Postumus noted, was looking intrigued, his relentless curiosity piqued by the governor's reticence. Aelius Silanus, on the other hand, maintained an expression of blank composure. After another brief discussion of logistics and provisioning, Urbicus dismissed them, saying only, "Corvus, you stay."

Postumus halted, anxious to get back to the belly case.

"Are the rest of the wall garrisons likely in the same shape as this one?" Urbicus asked. "I need your assessment and I didn't want to push it in front of the commanders. Commanders always insist that their men are prepared to fight Carthaginians on elephants."

"I expect so," Postumus said. "Of course, Chief Surgeon Aquila will want to make his own assessment."

"Chief Surgeon Aquila has a bad hip and is too old for this kind of goings-on," Urbicus said, "whatever he thinks. You're in charge of any assessment that needs to be made out here."

"Well then yes, sir, they're a mess. Am I to report that to Chief Surgeon Aquila as well? Frankly, he terrifies me."

"He was the ranking senior surgeon when I was in Judaea with the Tenth Fretensis," Urbicus said, grinning. "When you see him, ask him if he remembers killing the cook's cow."

"Killing the—"

"The legate's cook wangled a cow somehow from one of the locals, and he used the cream to whip up elegant little trifles for the legate's table," Urbicus said. "The cow was no spring chicken and she'd been leading rather a full life on open pasture before she joined the Army. She kicked down the door of her stall one day and went looking for something to do and found a whole crate full of melons. The next thing anybody knew, the legate's melons were inside the legate's cow and the cow was bellowing the place down with bloat." Urbicus smiled reminiscently. "It's a simple enough procedure. You make a little nick in the belly and the gas comes shooting out and the cow goes on her way looking much relieved. Almost any farmer can do it. I can do it. But it doesn't work on horses and the cavalry vet wasn't farm-bred. So

Aquila stepped in and offered to do the honors." Urbicus chuckled. "Turned out he'd never done it before, just watched his dad's old cowman a couple of times. Anyhow, he either jabbed too deep, or he jabbed in the wrong place, because the cow's eyes glazed over and she went down with a crash right on his foot, dead as a stone. It gave poor Aquila the shock of his life. He worried for about six months after that that he might be fallible."

"He's gotten over the notion, I assure you," Postumus said. "I know two senior surgeons who'd give a month's pay for that story."

"Just moo at him if he chews you out. Dismissed, Surgeon."

Postumus strolled back to the hospital, savoring the tale, and found Valerian waiting for him. It was snowing lightly, a lazy drift of flakes fluttering in the lantern light, and to the north a pair of hunting wolves called to each other.

Valerian shivered, twitching his skin like one of his troop horses. "A fine night to sit by the fire with a game-board. Providing, of course, that I don't have to play with young Lucian. That lad could make his fortune in a place like Corinth or Alexandria."

Postumus chuckled. "He keeps the patients amused, and lets them win enough to feel encouraged." He was about to retire to his office with his friend and the small store of good wine, which he kept hidden from the depre-dations of his patients in a locked records chest, when Tertius hustled into the surgery and saluted.

"We were just wondering whether to send for you, sir. Trebonius is worse. Lucian's with him now, but he'd like it if you'd look in, sir."

236

Postumus hurried after him, with Valerian following somewhat dubiously behind. Like many of his kind, hospitals, when fulfilling their prescribed function, made Valerian nervous. You could, as he had once said to Postumus, tell yourself all you wanted to that spear wounds were not contagious, but there remained a feeling of ill luck all the same, and that might be just as dangerous the next time you had to fight someone.

Trebonius had been isolated in a four-bed ward, one of a series of identical rooms that ran the length of the corridor. He lay doubled up on his cot, his hands to his belly and his skin fiery to the touch. Lucian was with him, helplessly trying to do something, anything, and looking unnerved. He welcomed Postumus with relief. "I was getting ready to send for you, sir," he said. "Nothing's done any good and I think that last potion made him worse."

Postumus ran his hands over Trebonius's abdomen. The soldier's eyes were becoming glazed, but he gritted his teeth and tried to answer the surgeon's questions. The pain, agonizing now, seemed to have centered itself on his lower right side.

Postumus stood up. This man was going to die. He looked again, helplessly, at Trebonius's belly. Something in there was wrong, horribly wrong, and he didn't know what. And because of that, Trebonius was going to die.

He beckoned to Lucian. "Give him some opium," he said softly. "And henbane. Enough to kill the pain."

Lucian started to protest, then closed his mouth again. He went to fetch the drugs stored in a locked cabinet in the dispensary.

Postumus touched Trebonius's forehead gently with his hand and turned from the room. Valerian looked appalled.

Opium mixed with henbane would knock Trebonius cold, and he might not wake up. Even the cavalry commander knew that much.

Postumus turned a weary face toward him. "He's going to die anyway. At least let him have some sort of peace."

Two days later Trebonius died. Postumus tried vainly every remedy he could think of, but he knew from the start that none of them were going to work. Under Tertius's horrified gaze, and Lucian's sympathetic one, he administered whatever it took to still the agony, and Trebonius spent those days in a dream-filled trance, murmuring of strange visions and unknown creatures that frightened the life out of the orderlies.

Postumus also felt that he himself traveled in a strange country where all his knowledge and his skill were as nothing in the fearsome face of the unknown. Trebonius died at the eighth hour of the night. Postumus saw him bathed and wrapped in a winding sheet by the orderlies, and then sat beside his bier in the mortuary.

XV. The Horned God

A single lamp made one pale splash of light over Trebonius's cold belly, just below where Postumus had pulled the winding sheet back. He wasn't sure he could do this, or if he wanted to do this. The ivory statue of Aesculapius that he kept in his kit stood on the table beside him where he had affixed it with a glob of wax.

"What do I do? Tell me, Lord." Aesculapius said nothing. The shade of Trebonius, if it was actually there, said nothing either. They would come for him at dawn to light his pyre.

"Have you lost your mind? Sir." Lucian, in the doorway, took in the scalpel on the table beside the lamp.

"I don't know," Postumus said. "What are you doing here?"

"Tertius said you didn't look well."

"Tertius should mind his own business."

Lucian looked cautious but determined. "Tertius said you locked yourself in the mortuary. You've lost your mind. You're about to commit sacrilege and I'm not going to let you. Sir." He snatched the scalpel away, and hid it behind his back, as if it was the only one available.

"Don't you want to know?" Postumus asked him.

"Not like that," Lucian said, horrified.

"How do we *learn*, then?"

"I've sent for Commander Valerian," Lucian said.

"What in Death's name for? He doesn't know and I don't want him here. I don't want you either."

"To make you see sense. You haven't slept."

Valerian, in an undertunic, cloak, and boots, strode briskly across the mortuary floor and yanked the sheet back up. "Is this why you sent an orderly to roust me out of bed?" He put his hands on Postumus's shoulders and made him look at him. "You'll get cashiered. Or worse. I don't know what they do to people for this."

"You heard the governor," Postumus said. "He doesn't believe in ghosts. Neither do you. You told me."

"That doesn't mean everyone else doesn't. If you do this and it becomes known, the troops will all think we're cursed. *Then* you'll have trouble."

"*I* believe in ghosts," Lucian said firmly. "What if you do cut him open, and you find out what was wrong? And let's just say that no one notices it when they burn him, which is not possible, but we'll assume it."

"Then maybe we save the next life," Postumus said, but he knew that was unlikely too. It was just the not knowing that drove him mad, possibly quite literally, according to Lucian.

"How many men survive a wound that goes clean through the guts?" Lucian demanded.

"Almost none. None, really." Postumus's head was beginning to ache.

"So no one is going to survive surgery for whatever this was either," Lucian said.

"I can't think clearly," Postumus said. "Go away."

"And leave you here with a scalpel?" Valerian inquired. "You have battle nerves. It doesn't matter that you haven't been fighting. I've seen this in my men. Go to bed. You can't do this now anyway because Lucian and I know about it, and we'll be guilty too, and I'm not planning to get stoned to death or whatever the punishment for sacrilege is, which I don't want to find out."

Postumus rubbed his temples. Maybe he had a fever himself. Valerian took him by the arm and nudged him away from Trebonius. "I'll see him back to quarters," he said to Lucian.

"I'll just wait here till morning," Lucian said. "Outside the door, maybe."

—

When Postumus woke up, the sun was low in the winter sky, almost sunk beneath the hills to the west. His head ached and his mouth felt as if he had been drunk. His hands, when he tried to pour water from the jug on the table, shook. He lay back down, looking at the ceiling. A chair scraping in the next room informed him that he wasn't alone.

"You ought to buy a housekeeper," Tertius informed him. "The commander told me to keep an eye on you till you were awake, so I tidied up a bit."

"I haven't had time," Postumus said. "And I don't want a housekeeper." He sat up again.

"I'll tell the commander you're awake."

"Don't." Tertius went anyway, and Valerian appeared with a bowl and spoon, and a jug.

"Here. I brought you some food. Tertius is right. You need a housekeeper. Or a cook. What have you been eating? There's nothing here."

"I've been busy. You're not my nursemaid."

"They burned Trebonius this morning," Valerian said.

Postumus sighed and rubbed his hands over his forehead. "I wasn't going to go back. I don't know what I was thinking. Just that we've lost so many and we don't *know* anything. I'm sorry." He stuck the spoon in the bowl and ate. "I know better. I would have pulled any man in my state off the line."

Valerian nodded. "It's been calm enough today. Lucian says to tell you that he and Flavian can deal with anything that comes up and please to sleep and then go do something to amuse yourself besides beating your head against the wall."

"Is that a direct quote?"

"It is."

Postumus finished the stew in the bowl and the watered wine in the jug. "Very well, then. I'm going to go and make sacrifice for Trebonius's shade, since we're all so convinced he has one. I owe him that."

Valerian nodded. He paused in the doorway. "Don't think I don't understand. Trebonius might even have appreciated it, for all we know."

Postumus wondered if that was true. Would your shade want to know why it had died? He expected it would. Something to tell the boatman. However, he was beginning to feel more of this world after sleep and food, and the urge to risk his career had faded. And in any case, as Valerian said, they had burned the body. He found a clean tunic while deciding that Tertius was right. He didn't want a housekeeper, but he needed to clean the mess. He ferreted through the worst of it, tossing clean and dirty clothes at the appropriate containers, and taking the bowl and jug to the water barrel to wash them. He set out for the fort baths in the dusk, and then, clean, by lantern light to the graveyard outside the walls.

By now a faint glow of night lanterns illuminated the sentry walk and the graveyard was in shadow. He left the fort by the Dexter Gate and skirted the ditches that over-laid the remains of an elaborate bathhouse from Agricola's day. Rumor said that it had been the general's own. A stray tile with a cat's toes clearly printed in it caught his eye. Castra Damnoniorum had been a frontier post with the beginnings of a civil colony then. Now that the wall was built, the civilians would come back – at first the tarts and tinkers, and later, if the wall held, wives and honest shopkeepers with cats; the solid, settled folk of civilization.

For now, there was only a little biting wind whistling through the stones and ditch. The graveyard lay just past Agricola's bathhouse. A fresh wooden marker identified the place where Trebonius's ashes had been interred. DIS MANIBUS, to the shades... SEXTUS TREBONIUS SEJANUS, OF THE SIXTH LEGION VICTRIX, OF EIGHTEEN YEARS' SERVICE, LIES HERE. Beside him the fresh grave of the dead of the last battle had only a single marker with their names and years of service. Later, friends and wives might pay for stones.

Postumus brought out the flask of wine he had carried under his cloak and poured it over the grave while an owl hoo-hooed from the woods to the south. The wine made a dark splash on the cold earth. He broke the clay flask over the wooden marker.

"Who are you mourning?" a quiet voice said behind him and he jumped, scattering the shards on the grave.

The figure in the shadows leaned on a spear, muffled in a heavy cloak and woolen trousers, with thick wolfskin boots. The voice, however, was Claudia's.

"What are you doing here?" he demanded. "How long have you been watching me?" And why did everyone he knew seem to think that he needed watching, as if he might be doing something foolhardy, particularly Claudia, who was almost bound to be doing something foolhardy, dressed in breeches?

"Long enough to see it was you and give Fortuna thanks for it. We are camped to the south there." She pointed through the woods behind her. "We've been watching the paths between us and the fort to make contact with the governor when we could. You are fortuitous."

"What do you need?"

"I have something I want you to take to the governor."

"Which you cannot take yourself?"

"Not just now, no. Will anyone miss you if you don't go back to the fort tonight?"

"As it happens, no. They'll miss me if you get me killed, though," he added.

She gave a small low laugh that was not entirely reassuring, and beckoned him to follow her into the shadow of the woods, where a pony stood stamping its feet in the icy air. He did, and she swung herself up on its back and motioned for him to get up behind her. Lucian had said to go do something besides bang his head against the wall, he thought. This appeared to be something.

When he had mounted, Claudia turned the pony's head to the south and it stepped out surely on some track that only it could see. After an hour it began to snow, and he wrapped his cloak more tightly about him, envying Claudia's wolfskin boots. His own boots and leather leggings were sodden and the dismal scraps of fur clinging to them looked as if they might have been made of Theodore's dormice.

The woods were silent and Claudia seemed disinclined to talk. She looked over her shoulder once to see, he thought, how quickly the snow was filling in the pony's tracks. The moon was up, making black and white shadows of their prints.

"Is something following us?" he whispered in her ear. He thought it was. He had the same feeling he'd had in the guest chamber in Dawid's hold. And if so, where was it following her from? Or to? And what was he doing riding behind her without his lorica on and nothing but a belt knife?

"I think so." She put her heels to the pony's flanks, not trying to be silent now. "There are three of them, or there were, and a dog. They must have just picked up my trail again. They don't dare go too close to the forts."

"Three of what?" he asked as they flew under an overhanging branch, snow spurting from the pony's hooves.

"Dergdian's men. They started on our trail just as we were coming out of the highlands. We've been playing catch-me-not with them ever since."

He could hear the sound of hooves not far behind them. Whatever it was wasn't trying to be silent now either. Claudia's pony, laboring under the double weight, staggered and scrabbled in the dark up a steep track of snow-covered scree. The moon turned the snow and bare black trees to a nightmare landscape until he could easily image the Wild Hunt on their trail and no mortal pursuers.

The pony slid and slithered down the far side of the ridge they had just climbed and they could hear the hunt closer now, and the baying of the dog.

"Not far!" Claudia said, leaning forward to urge the pony on. "If I get you killed, I am sorry."

They came at a gallop past the wooded overhang of a low hill, and Claudia dropped the reins and put her fingers to her mouth, making a screech that reverberated over the silvered landscape. She drew rein and they slid from the saddle as the hunt came on them, three horsemen, as she had said, and a dog, a lean gray hound that bayed at the sight of its quarry. Claudia leveled her spear at them, fox-haired men with tribal marks across their faces, clothed in brown and white that melted into the snowy landscape. As they came, Postumus pulled out his belt knife, for what use that would be.

The scrub at the base of the hill shuddered and a flung spear from behind Postumus's back took the nearest of the hunters in the shoulder. The other two drew rein, cursing. Someone put another spear in Postumus's hand, and he saw a burly blond man in a rough leather shirt and a smaller one with a braid of black hair down his back, spear-armed and circling the hunters. They danced, feinting until one of Claudia's men closed and took the leader in the groin with his spearpoint and the black-haired one came at him with a sword as he fell from his pony, nearly taking his head from his shoulders while the first pulled his spear back and blood poured onto the snow.

The first of the pursuers was dismounted now, yanking the spearpoint from his flesh in a spray of blood, and Postumus lunged at him. The ground underfoot was icy scree, and he stumbled more than once trying to balance the unfamiliar spear, heavier than a hunting spear and lighter than a pilum, its unaccustomed weight throwing his arm off. The Pict faltered, blood dripping, and Postumus prayed the spear in his shoulder had hit a vein. By reflex he ticked over what you would do to stop the blood and then reversed it, seeing what would make it worse. He feinted with the spear, jabbing to his left so that the Pict would have to use that arm. Each time the Pict parried, he was a fraction slower.

Claudia had lost her spear in her fight with the third man, also dismounted now, and her arm was bleeding. More red splotches on the white snow. Her men turned their attention that way as the Pict dropped his spear to grab Claudia by the wrist, knife in hand. Her men would kill him easily now, but it was clear that his whole goal was to kill her first.

Postumus's adversary staggered, the blood loss finally telling, and dropped, not dead but no longer fighting. Postumus spun to drive his spear into the back of the last man as Claudia struggled in his grip. She had her own knife out now, and plunged it into the man's face, deep in the eye socket so that he fell back howling on the spear and Postumus put his belt knife through his throat. He looked up to see the blond man now cutting the third Pict's throat for good measure. It was clear that no one was interested in prisoners.

"Mother of All, that was close." Claudia put her bloody hands to her forehead. "And you, I am sorry." She turned to Postumus. "I truly thought we had shed them. Brys, take these and bury them, please."

Brys looked disinclined to bury people in the snow in the middle of the night.

"I don't want the wolves scattering their bones for anyone to find. Alan, you help him. And catch the ponies."

"What about that?" Brys jerked his thumb at the hound, sitting in the snow beside the dead.

The dog appeared perplexed but not overly unhappy. Postumus took a step toward him and he didn't growl. Postumus whistled experimentally and snapped his fingers and the hound trotted to his side, looking relieved that someone was telling him what to do.

The dark-haired man shook his head disapprovingly but Brys said, "He didn't go after us, now did he? He's a tracker, that's all." A dog was a dog and he was just as glad not to have to kill one.

They disappeared into the curtain of winter-torn scrub at the base of the overhang and reappeared with shovels. Postumus wondered what else was in there. The night had taken on a dreamlike quality somewhere between hallucination and ancient myth that might reveal anything – the Isle of Apples or a portal to the Minotaur's labyrinth. He looked at the dog, which had sat down on his foot.

"Come." Claudia beckoned to him. "Bring the hound if you will." She pushed the undergrowth back and stood away for him to enter what proved to be a portal not to the Otherworld but to a deep cave. Its damp, rocky chamber stretched back into a dim distance behind the glow of the campfire at its mouth. In it, Claudia and her drivers had pitched their tents and used its bramble-choked entrance to guard them from both the bitter wind and from human sight.

Farther into the shadows, Postumus could see the bulk of loaded wagons, and hear the stamp of tethered ponies. He crouched by the fire, grateful for the warmth. Outside, the snow had begun to fall thicker and presumably Brys and Alan were digging a grave.

"You are soaked." Claudia pointed him toward a tent, a sturdy affair of tanned leather with piles of native blankets on beds of straw. An oil lamp burned on a small folding table, and a pack saddle in the corner apparently served as a clothes press. Of the trappings of a prosperous contractor, Postumus could see no evidence. Those would be stowed in the wagons. Claudia had nothing in use now that could not be packed in a hurry. She had obviously meant it when she had told Tertius that the winds blew somewhat chancy.

She pulled a bundle from the pack saddle, breeches and shirt and cloak, and wolfskin boots like her own but considerably larger. Postumus wondered which of her drivers she was robbing for him.

"Get into these. And if you'll give me your wet ones, I'll hang them by the fire."

She dropped the tent flap and waited tactfully outside while he stripped off his sodden tunic and leggings and handed them out to her. The new clothes were probably Brys's, several sizes too big, but clean and blessedly dry. The hound, which had followed him in, leapt onto one of the beds, turned around three times and lay down. He took up most of it. Postumus was lacing the breeches when Claudia reappeared.

"Here." She handed him a cup of hot wine and a bowl of stew and motioned to him to sit and eat.

"They wanted to kill you," he said, while the hound watched him hopefully, thumping his gray feathered tail on the blanket. "They were willing to die to do it."

"Yes, and before I could get to the governor. After, it would have been vengeance only, although I am sure they would have taken it."

He couldn't think of anything useful to say to that, other than to hope there were no more of them.

"Who were you mourning in the graveyard?" she asked him again after a silence. "The battle dead? Do you always do that?"

"No."

"A friend? If so, I am sorry."

"A man I couldn't save," he said. And then, because he knew her secret, he told her his. "He had a bellyache that

249

nothing would cure, and I tried everything I know. But we know so little. He died screaming anyway, or would have if I hadn't drowned the pain in opium and henbane. When he finally did die, I wanted to cut him open to find out why. Fortunately, my friends have more sense and they stopped me."

Claudia looked honestly horrified.

"Are you shocked?" he asked.

"I'm thinking the gods might have asked a high price for that knowledge, if you had done it."

"You stood to pay a high price for your own knowledge," he pointed out.

"There is something I want to show you." She took the oil lamp from the table.

He followed her past the fire at the cave mouth, and the dog accompanied them into the shadows beyond the wagons. The cave was high-ceilinged and deep, and at the back it had been enlarged by the hand of man – a hand that had wielded a rough stone chisel. The rear of the cave had been cut out to form an altar, knee-height from the main floor, and on the stone wall behind it in the flickering light danced a painted form whose antlered crown reached into the shadows. Postumus felt the back of his neck prickle again.

"The tribes know him as Cernunnos," Claudia said. "But the Horned One is older than that, and this place is older. Older than us or the Selgovae or the Brigantes. Older than the ancestors of the Painted People. Maybe it was the old dark people's once, but even what's left of them don't remember. And yet it was once the meeting hall of a great people – kings in the land."

Postumus stared at the naked dancer with the deer's mask. There was an unsettling power in that form, as if the god was still in it but the people he had danced for, his own people, were no more.

"If we do not hold this country," Claudia said, "we and the tribes both will be like the Deer Men. Gone, with nothing but paint in a cave to show where our altars were. If you do not believe me, ask the Fleet about the pirates in the Channel, or the coastwise farmers about the sea raiders."

Postumus nodded. He had heard his mother say the same, and Hilarion, and Licinius, and any of Britain's adopted or native-born who could see how the wind would blow here if Rome was gone.

Claudia moved away from the dancing figure to lean against a wagon wheel. "We left these here when we went north," she said, patting the wheel rim, "for a hiding place and provisions to fall back on. It was as well."

Postumus leaned against a wagon opposite and they faced each other in the oil lamp's dim light, with the Horned God at their back. "How was the hunting?"

"None so ill at first," she said. "I traveled as a witch woman, a dealer in eye ointments and small cures. They were genuine, too, in case you are wondering. I do have some small knowledge. I took Brys with me, and left Octavius here with the wagons."

"That sounds something more than foolhardy," Postumus said.

"I carry a long knife." She smiled. "And I am not so brave as that sounds. There are few among the Painted Ones who will cross a witch."

"What were you going to do if you were found out?"

"I was," she said flatly. "Or at least there was a priest who had his suspicions. Myself, I think he merely did not care for the competition, but he may have had more powers than I think. Also, Dergdian's hold is somewhat the worse for wear but I didn't do that. There was a leak in his walls and a cave underneath and the expected thing happened just after I left. I heard it in the last hold that I visited and left in a hurry. I had thought about warning him, but I was afraid he would think I did it. He probably does anyway. At all events, it became known in the hills that I was not what I seemed, and they began to trail me. I am little use to the governor now beyond the frontier."

"I said you were a fool," Postumus said, still leaning, arms crossed, against the wagon wheel. "You've scarred yourself for life, and for what? To nearly lose your hide and learn nothing."

"You're wrong," Claudia said. She crossed her own arms and stared back at him, stubborn-eyed. "I know how many horses the Painted One has, and where they are pastured. I know where his brood mares graze, and where his king's hall is, and how many warriors can take a war trail at the thaw. My scars have been bought with a fair price."

"Perhaps. But you haven't taken this to the governor yet?"

"No. We knew we were followed. Arriving at the wall in midwinter when no one has a right to be traveling is conspicuous, and I do have some concern for my own skin left. That and the fact that if I'm seen in the fort, I won't be much use south of the wall again either. I came tonight to see what I might do, but I was beginning to worry."

"You want me to carry your tallies to Urbicus, I take it."

"Those and a letter from me. Some of the knowledge gained is more, shall we say, nuanced than will fit on a tally stick."

"I am, apparently, at the governor's service." Postumus touched his fist to his chest. As they made their way to the mouth of the cave, he turned to look again at the horned figure on the wall. It moved, he thought, in the last glow of the oil lamp's dim light, but only from that. Probably.

At the cave mouth, her drivers were now stamping the snow from their boots, shovels propped against the rock wall. She gave them some low-voiced orders and they nodded. They settled around the fire and dipped bowls into the stew pot. A pan rested in the coals of the banked fire and Claudia gingerly pulled out a few pieces of barley cake. An earthen jug and cup sat on the floor beside it and she picked those up also and turned to the tent where Postumus had changed his wet clothes for the driver's dry ones. He suspected that the two drivers had been evicted from it for his sake. The dog stayed beside the fire, where Brys had given him a bowl of stew.

Claudia put two of the barley cakes into Postumus's hand and motioned for him to sit again on the piled rugs and straw. She curled herself up catwise across from him, her feet tucked under her, and poured two full measures of wine from the jug. She handed him back his cup and raised the other to him.

"To the pursuit of knowledge."

"Wisely or otherwise," he said but he drank. He took a bite of the barley cake and stretched himself full-length on the straw. It was soft and smelled faintly but not unpleas- antly of horse. Tomorrow, presumably, she would send him back to the fort to deliver her package to Governor Urbicus and the gods knew how that would be received, considering that Urbicus had explicitly told him to stay away from her. But tonight, he had food and wine and straw to lie on, and he was suddenly content. The oil lamp glowed between them and threw magic and shadows across the tent walls.

Claudia stretched out on the second bed and propped herself on one elbow, her wine cup in the other hand. She had taken off her cloak and her dark braids tumbled over her shoulders. He thought she was beautiful as a wild briar, and of the patterns that coiled along her breasts and thighs, underneath the rough woolen shirt.

"Have you healed?" he asked.

She seemed to think for a moment, and then she said, "Come and see." She pushed up the long sleeves of her shirt.

He rose and crossed the tent to sit at her side. The patterns were still bright, but the skin was clear. "And the rest?" he asked her.

She tilted her head at him. "If you want to see those too, you should close the tent flap," she said.

He did, before she could change her mind, or he could regain his. When he sat back down, instead she pulled the thongs from her braids, shaking the long hair free. He wrapped his hands in it. It spilled about them like dark smoke and the blue-green eyes caught his and held them like a green sea-tide. He thought of a nursery tale of the man who had gone into the hollow hills with a woman out of a sidhe.

"Are you real?" he whispered. "If I lie with you in this cave tonight, will I wake up to find a hundred years gone by?"

Her voice was husky. "I don't know. Try it and see."

He slipped his hands over the rough woolen shirt and felt her breasts upturned beneath them. She shivered as he drew the laces free, and held up her arms for him to pull the shirt over her head, whispering something he couldn't hear as he traced the fragile spirals at the tips, healed now and as if they had been a part of her always. Her skin was very white against the dark blue lines of the tribal markings, white as the White Horse of the south downs and he could almost imagine her as one of the Old Ones, British entirely, the Horned God's people, maybe, who had first cut that into the chalk hill and set the standing stones that dotted Britain. The motion of the world slowed as he slipped open the buckle of her belt, and pulled apart the thongs that laced her breeches close on her hips. He slipped those free too, holding one small blue-veined foot in his hand for a moment while she lay naked before him. Slowly, he saw desire outweigh uncertainty in her eyes.

He stood and stripped off his borrowed clothes then and stood, naked himself, above her. She lay with one knee drawn up as if in acquiescence, and one arm flung out across the straw. Then she held out the other hand to him. He knelt over her and felt her shiver again under his hands as he traced the tattooed patterns on her thighs. He put his arms around her and felt her hands come up to tangle themselves in his hair as she wrapped her legs around him.

Postumus woke in the morning as the faint dawn light that penetrated the cavern mouth softened the dark air outside the tent. Claudia was still curled in the crook of his arm. Her hair was tangled and knotted with straw and she was still naked under the cloaks that he vaguely remembered having pulled over them. He lay still, now wondering what evil genius had prompted last night's adventures, telling over in his mind the possible consequences, not the least of which was what they were going to do if he proved more potent than her husband and she found herself with child. There were ways around that, of course, but he had always done as most men did and assumed that the woman in question had taken care to deal with the problem. But Claudia was no tart. A point, he now thought, that should have occurred to him last night.

Claudia stirred and opened her eyes. She lay comfortably against his arm, but didn't look at him. Instead she seemed to gaze into the darkness at the far wall.

"Wondering how we could have been so stupid?" he said at last, gently.

At that, she turned toward him. "No," she said frankly. "Only why no one ever told me it was supposed to be like that."

Postumus watched as she sat up and rummaged in the darkness for her clothes. "I'm flattered, but your husband must have been a fool," he observed. And was he her first lover since then? That gave somehow even more weight to his worries. And then, thinking again of that, he said bluntly, "What if you are with child?"

"It seems to me unlikely," she said, lacing the thongs of her breeches, "or I wouldn't have done it."

It was all the answer he could reasonably expect, but he said, "Will you at least let me know if I've done anything irreparable?"

"I will," she said, picking the straw from her hair.

What they would do then, he had no idea. "And what will you do now? When I have taken your tallies to Urbicus?"

"Go south for the winter, or what's left of it, like the gray goose."

Leaving him with only a feather by his bed to mark her presence in it, he thought.

"Do you become respectable again then?"

"For this war, at least. I have given the legions all I could learn. It is their turn to make use of it. I shall go home and tend to my roses."

And he had a hospital, likely soon to be overflowing with men sent to act on that hard-earned information.

She rose in the dim light, motioning for him to stay, and returned in a moment with his uniform tunic and leggings, with the dog at her heels. She lit the guttered oil lamp and the dog hopped onto the bed beside him. "Brys and Octavius were still snoring," she said. "I have kicked them awake somewhat rudely but it is just as well. I have no wish to be a scandal to my honest drivers. I think this is your dog," she added.

Postumus stood up, shoving the dog aside. "I don't recall asking for you," he told it. He pulled the white linen folds of his undertunic over his head, and then the scarlet uniform tunic, and drew on the close-fitting woolen breeches that ended just below the knee. "I hate these things," he said, cross-lacing the stiffened leggings over his calves. "They are completely inadequate."

"I asked Lollius Urbicus why the Army doesn't adopt British dress for British winters," Claudia said, "and he told me it was a matter of national pride."

"And so it is," Postumus said. "It's hard to think yourself better than the other fellow when you look just like him.

Trousers are for barbarians. Romans wear tunics. Even if they have to wear leggings under them."

"And so we preserve our national superiority," Claudia said. "With tunics over our trousers."

"Exactly." He fastened his belt, with the double caduceus insignia of his trade, and they emerged from the tent into the drafty hall of the cavern where Brys was burning oat cakes over the fire. Two saddled ponies were tethered by the cavern mouth. It appeared to be the next morning, and not a hundred years gone.

XVI. Galt Again

Still, when she had bidden him goodbye and put the leather-wrapped parcel for the governor in his hands, and Octavius had guided him back though the dawn mist to the edge of the wood below the fort, he felt a certain unreasonable relief to see Castra Damnoniorum apparently as he had left it.

Wrapped in mist, the fort walls and the remains of Agricola's bathhouse appeared unchanged. Trebonius's grave, as he passed it with a small salute, was still fresh, although snow-covered now. The sentry who passed him in through the Dexter Gate, with the dog at his heels, appeared to still know him. All he had acquired from a night with the fay was a dog. His relief at that amused him although it left him still inclined to question his sanity. He made for the governor's office before anyone could ask him where he had been.

"Sit," he said experimentally to the dog, outside the Principia. The dog cocked an ear at the strange word. Postumus tried British and it hesitated a moment and then sat. "You'll have to get used to the accent," Postumus told him and he thumped his tail. What in Diana's name was he doing with a dog? He didn't have time to hunt, which appeared to be what it was trained for.

The governor's optio also passed him in without question. Postumus had thought it a fortunate coincidence that the governor was still in residence, but it occurred to him now that the governor had more likely been waiting for his spy's report.

Lollius Urbicus looked up from a breakfast of olives and boiled eggs when Postumus entered. Postumus saluted and the governor raised an eyebrow and waited.

Postumus handed over the leather-wrapped parcel from Claudia and Urbicus raised the eyebrow higher. "I do seem to remember telling you to stay away from a certain person," he remarked, cracking an egg.

"The certain person came to me," Postumus said, wondering uncomfortably if Urbicus somehow knew what else he had done with the person. The governor's staff generally considered him to have the second sight.

Urbicus unwrapped the leather bindings. The tally sticks fell out in his hand, and a stack of wax tablets with them. He didn't tell Postumus to go away, so Postumus waited as he read the sticks, and then the tablets, and watched him scrape the wax carefully clean with a stylus when he was through. "Perhaps you are fortuitous," he commented.

Postumus stayed at parade rest and waited to see what that meant. It was the same thing that Claudia had said.

Urbicus arranged the tally sticks in a neat row on his desk, pushing his breakfast dishes out of the way. "Men, stores, horses. More than I hoped. Not so many as I feared. The situation is promising if the Brigantes stay clear."

Postumus nodded, wondering if that was more uncertain than it had been.

"What I am telling you will not leave this room, Surgeon. Do I make myself clear?"

"Of course, sir," Postumus said, also beginning to wonder uneasily why he was telling him in the first place.

"Sit down, Surgeon. You make me twitch standing like that."

"Yes, sir." Postumus sat in the visitor's chair opposite the governor's desk.

"It appears from this person's information that the Picts do not trust the High King of the Brigantes. This is not news, exactly. None of them trust each other. But – Bran has apparently made a drunken vow, while the Pictish emissary was in his court, to fight the Roman occupation to the death. His and everyone else's, of course. Does that sound likely to you, Surgeon? You met him."

"I'm afraid it does, sir." An image of Bran, simmering with fury at practically everything, crossed his mind. Anger seemed to be his natural state.

"According to this report, the Brigantian council lords were resistant, but there was the sentiment among the Pictish lords that that might change, in the absence of Lord Galt. And it appears that he has been ill."

"He was coughing when I saw him by chance in Isurium at Beltane," Postumus said. "I put it down to a cold, and so did he, but…"

"It isn't. He was spitting blood."

Postumus closed his eyes briefly, grieving. That would kill him. He didn't know why; only that it would. He thought of Trebonius and wanted to scream.

"You are distressed," Urbicus said, not unkindly.

Postumus looked up. "I liked him. And he has held Bran in check."

"I've never met him and I like him for that reason," Urbicus commented. "We need to know how long he is likely to live."

"I can't tell you that," Postumus said. "Lung disease has a lot of variables. He was only coughing when I saw him."

"You will contrive to renew the acquaintance."

Postumus balked. "I am needed here, sir."

"I am aware that if you wanted to be a spy, you would have joined the Frontier Scouts," Urbicus said.

"I would, sir." The thought of repeating the dismal experience of watching Trebonius die left him feeling rebellious.

"You are native-born, aren't you?" the governor said. "Like her." He waved his hand at the tally sticks. "Your world won't endure without Rome, Surgeon. Not unless Rome continues to settle in, marry in, breed in, produce more families like yours and hers, several generations down."

"I had the same conversation with her last night," Postumus admitted.

The governor gave him an irritated look. "I shan't inquire what other conversations you had last night. But you take my point. We must deal with the Picts in the spring and we'll have to pull nearly every man out of the Brigantian forts to garrison the wall. I must be sure we aren't leaving a nest of adders behind us. The Picts will lick their wounds for a while, but come spring they'll have a go at pulling it down. We'll have to be quite sure there's no one behind us pushing while they're pulling. And their High Priest is apparently a Druid." Urbicus looked exasperated. Druids were forbidden and were executed anywhere that Rome could find them because they fomented rebellion, and not even a king would go against their word.

Urbicus shoved the tally sticks into his desk drawer. "As soon as the weather clears, I expect you to contrive a way to visit Lord Galt."

That was apparently the end of the interview. Postumus rose and saluted, collected the dog, which was waiting for him outside the Principia, and made his way across the fort to the hospital. Someone had drawn a buck-toothed caricature of his centurion, identifiable by the transverse crest on his helmet and the vine staff in his hand, on the outer wall and Postumus expected that someone would also be out there shortly with a brush and bucket, afterward to use them on the latrines as well, but it was good to see they had enough energy to be troublesome.

His staff greeted him cheerfully, apparently under the impression that he had spent the night innocently sulking in his quarters.

"You've got a dog with you," Tertius said.

"It was supposed to be a goat, but they cheated me," Postumus told him. "Get to work."

Sick parade presented him with several cases of healing frostbite to be re-checked, one bad cough which worried him and made him think unhappily of Galt, a broken nose and split knuckles on the respective combatants of a drunken disagreement, and one case of outright malingering with which he could thoroughly sympathize.

The men were only beginning to recover from the battle with the Picts and the exhaustion of the push to close the last gap in the wall. When the weather held, their officers took them out for slowly lengthening drills, to keep them out of trouble as much as get them back in shape, and Valerian's cavalry conducted sweeps up and down the wall. Now that it was complete, dedications began to be installed along its length, commissioned by the troops who had bought it dearly. At Castra Damnoniorum, a brightly painted relief of Roman soldiers with bound captives on one side and the governor conducting a pre-campaign sacrifice on the other flanked an inscription declaring that for the Emperor Caesar Titus Aelius Hadrianus Antoninus Augustus Pius, Father of his Country, the Seventh Cohort of the Sixth Legion Victrix had built 4793 paces of the wall.

When the governor, making ready to conduct his inspection of the frontier forts, informed Postumus that a supply train now making its deliveries to the wall would be going south again toward Eburacum the next day, and that its hospital and those in the Brigantian Hills were due for inspection by a senior surgeon, it was clear what he meant: Go with it and find Lord Galt.

And see if you think he's going to die, Postumus thought miserably. On the other hand, maybe the intelligence was wrong. It was thirdhand, from Claudia from a Pictish lord who had seen Galt in the winter, with probably someone else in between as well. He packed the gold and blue enamel arm ring that had been Galt's gift to him into his kit. Show it to a man of the Brigantes, Galt had said, if he should ever need to. He doubted that Galt had meant for him to use it to spy on him, but perhaps he had. Postumus thought that Galt would do a good deal to stop a war. Galt had no love for Rome, but he was a man who could see farther into a millstone than most. Certainly farther than Bran.

He handed off to Lucian and Flavian, mounted Boreas and fell in beside the wagons heading south. The dog seemed determined to come with him, so he let it.

"Do you have a name?" he inquired. When it didn't answer, he thought it over and settled on Finn. There had been a similar great gray dog in his babyhood with that name and it seemed comfortably familiar.

It was cold, with a little spit of snow still on the wind, and he thought wistfully of the straw bed and the fire in Claudia's cave, and of Claudia herself for that matter, naked and warm under the blankets. At night he slept in a wagon bed, in the company of Finn's bulk and a large and hairy driver, both of whom snored, and it was not the same at all.

At the old wall, he parted with the supply train and made an inspection of the hill fort hospitals at Longovicium and Vinovia for verisimilitude. Was it true the governor was going to pull all the troops from the hill forts and send them north, the junior surgeons in charge wanted to know, and all Postumus could say was that no one knew what was in the governor's head, even when they thought they did.

None of the Brigante lords were likely to be in Isurium until the Beltane council more than a month away, but there were families of the Brigantes who had settled into town life. Someone would know someone who could reach Galt. Postumus took his dinner at an inn called the White Mare and made friends with the serving girl, not a slave but the daughter of the household, over lamb stew.

"Well, I don't know," she said, turning the arm ring in her hand and widening her eyes a bit at the pattern of running horses. Postumus had not seen it elsewhere and it dawned on him that it was probably Galt's family mark. "But my brother, he trades in the hills often, pony trappings and copper pots and glass, and cloak pins and fairings, the sort of thing that people are happy to see after a nasty winter. He's going out tomorrow. I could send it with him. Anyone up there will recognize that" – she clearly did – "and send it along the way."

"Thank you," Postumus said, handing over a silver denarius for encouragement, although he doubted now that anyone would steal that arm ring. "The message that goes with it is that Surgeon Corvus of the Eagles would like to visit with Lord Galt and see how that healed leg of his is doing."

She nodded. "We heard that a surgeon of the legions had done him a kindness. He is much loved. I'll give this to my brother. Will you be staying in Isurium to hear an answer?"

"I'll be at Eburacum Fortress," Postumus said. "Earning my pay." He smiled at her and left another coin on the table above the cost of his meal. "Thank you."

–

Find Galt, Postumus thought as he rode south toward Eburacum. *Oh certainly, that will be easy. Perhaps you'd me like to rediscover Atlantis while I'm at it? It's bound to be around here somewhere.* He arrived, grumpily, at Eburacum, his expression unnerving the junior surgeon in charge until he realized that the senior surgeon had not come down from the new wall just to tell him that he was Doing It Wrong. In fact, Gemellus appeared to have improved his skills considerably.

When he arrived, Gemellus was taping the ribs of a cavalryman who had been kicked by an ungrateful troop horse, and lecturing him on the subject: "If I find you've been beating that horse again, I'll prescribe a course of purge and see that you're made to take it. They're living beings, these animals, not some practice dummy you can pound on. Treat them kindly and they won't kick you, you fool. Go on as you're going and you'll see the error of

266

your ways the first time you take that horse into a fight. I'm writing a report for your commander."

He jumped when he saw Postumus in the doorway as the trooper departed and Postumus rearranged his face to look less like a man about to bite someone. "I hadn't thought of threatening them with purge," he said, grinning. "I'll file that one away."

Gemellus relaxed. "I was farm-raised, sir. I don't like to see the animals abused. We rob them of enough as it is."

Postumus was liking Gemellus better by the minute. "I'll have a word with his commander too, to back you up. I've left my horse in the stables, so I'll be about there soon enough, I hope. I'm just waiting for a message to come through."

Gemellus looked curious but also knew enough not to ask, and Postumus settled himself into his old quarters, blowing the dust off the furniture, to wait and see what happened.

He set about making himself useful in the surgery in the meantime and shortly discovered that the reason for his junior surgeon's new skills was that Chief Surgeon Aquila was in residence and seemed to have taken Gemellus under his rather frightening wing. He had appropriated the senior surgeon's office too, as Postumus discovered the next morning when he went to use it himself.

"I wondered when you'd take the time to look in on your own hospital," Aquila said.

"First chance I've had," Postumus said. "I'm glad to see you here, sir." He was relieved that Aquila hadn't appropriated his quarters as well. He was probably sleeping in the legate's bed in the Praetorium.

Aquila shifted uncomfortably in his chair. "Arthritis in my hip. I can't ride anymore, much less walk more than a bit. It must be someone's fault, but I can't figure whose. You left that idiot in charge here, so I've been teaching him."

Postumus blanched. Gemellus would probably fall on his own scalpel in a week.

"I don't know how they trained him. It must have gone in one ear and out the other. But he's shaping up." Aquila stood and Postumus could see how bad his hip had gotten. "Go make yourself useful and send him to me. We're going to go over the herbal again before he poisons someone."

Postumus passed on the message, somewhat edited, and waited for Gemellus to flinch, but he didn't. He pulled his apron off and washed his hands at the surgery basin. "He'll look at them and if they aren't still damp, I'll hear about it," he said cheerfully.

Maybe the old demon was mellowing in his dotage, Postumus thought. Before he left, though, he'd tell Gemellus the story of the cow, just in case.

To his surprise, it didn't take more than a few days. Clearly the arm ring carried the power that Galt had said it did. A sandy-haired boy who looked barely past his warrior initiation arrived to announce himself to be Colin of Lord Dawid's house, here to take the surgeon to Lord Galt.

"Thank you. He's with Lord Dawid, then?"

"This winter past."

Galt had his own holding, but it seemed he was seldom in residence. As the High King's war leader, he would sleep in the king's hall. And when on outs with the king, apparently with his fosterling Dawid.

Postumus buckled himself into lorica and helmet, strapped on greaves and sword belt, picked up his packed kit, and whistled for Finn. He hustled Colin to the cavalry stables and back out of the fortress as quickly as possible lest he note the bareness of its streets, although that must be common knowledge. If the Brigantes didn't know that already, they were asleep. Colin had tied a small yew branch to his spear (tactfully left outside the gates) and he handed another to Postumus to hang from his saddle horns, a sign of peaceful intent to whoever was watching, and Postumus knew that someone would be.

It had been summer when he had come last to Dawid's hold, the hillside purple with heather. Now it was brown and splotched with snow and at dusk a white hare shot across their path ahead of the silent shadow of an owl.

"How has Lord Galt's leg held up?" Postumus asked as they rode through the bare woods with Finn at their heels. "I am hoping that I have done him lasting good."

"His leg is well enough," Colin said. There seemed to be more and Postumus waited for it, but it didn't come. Colin was not the chatterer that young Evan had been. He seemed to talk to the trees, however, or to something in them, short soft hoots and whistles that Postumus didn't comment on. By the time they neared the hillside track to Dawid's hold on the second day, there were at least five watchers behind them that Postumus had spotted and no doubt more that he hadn't.

As they rode through the gates, two men in the farm-yard cast him a sidelong glance, and four girls bringing washing up from the river stopped to stare at him as a slave in an iron collar came out to take the horses, but no one made the Sign of Horns at him this time.

The skull set into the lintel above Dawid's door greeted him with a fierce grin and Postumus resisted the urge to salute it, thinking madly that it much resembled Lollius Urbicus in a similar mood.

The woman who ushered him in, whom he remembered as Dawid's wife Brica, seemed rather more welcoming than she had when the king had been in residence. He wondered how Bran's drunken vow, assuming that information was accurate, had split the households of his tribe.

"May the sun shine on your path, Lady," he told her in British, heavily accented and with his mother's voice and the dialect of the south, and she greeted him with a small smile.

"And on yours, Surgeon. Lord Galt is pleased that you have come. Colin, take the surgeon to him, please, and see to it that they have food and drink. And something for the dog."

At the door of Galt's chamber, Postumus knew that something was wrong, that it was bad, and that he couldn't undo it. He said none of that but went to the man propped on the wolfskins on the bed, and sat in the chair beside him.

"Surgeon Corvus," Galt said, and waited for Postumus to tell him why he was there. He was wretchedly thin, and his chamber was so tidy that Postumus knew that someone else was straightening it for him because he didn't have the strength to do it himself. And the smell that Postumus had inhaled at the door was like a cloak around his shoulders, the scent that the deathly ill give off no matter how clean their flesh.

"Lord Galt." Before he could say more, Galt began to cough, reaching for a cloth lying on the floor and pressing it to his mouth. The coughing wracked his body and when he put the cloth down, Postumus saw the blood on it.

"It was… not a winter cold," Galt said, taking a ragged breath. "As you can see. Is that why you are here?"

"The wind in the heather said you were unwell," Postumus admitted.

Galt didn't ask where the wind blew from. It didn't matter. "I find that I am glad to see you," he observed as if the notion surprised him. "I see you have acquired a dog."

"And I you. The dog was accidental. And I am most sorry that the rumors seem true. Does it pain you greatly?"

"Did you think you would work some cure?" Galt inquired. "Or just tell your governor when I am like to die?"

"If I had a cure, I would have brought it." There was no point in mincing words. Clearly, Galt knew. "And the governor's concerns and mine are not necessarily the same ones," Postumus said. "But yes, we would both like to avert the war that your High King seems determined to start."

Galt muttered something under his breath that Postumus took to be a curse, and not one aimed at him. As he shifted position in the piled skins, Postumus saw that he was wearing the arm ring. It sat loosely around his wasted arm. "I have some weight in the Council yet. And there are elders who remember the last war."

"And the High King?"

Galt sighed, a long, irritated breath. "The king has a need for vengeance and a stiff pride. He is not one who can look very far down a road, or change a path as his father could." Galt's face as he spoke of the old king made Postumus remember what Galt had said that Beltane night. *He was the other half of my soul.*

"If his father had lived, would it have been different then?" he asked.

"If he hadn't died when we destroyed your legion, Rome would have seen fit to kill him, I expect." Galt stopped to cough into the bloody rag. When he had his breath again, he said, "But if not, if they had left him his kingdom – yes, I think it would have been."

The door opened and young Colin appeared with a tray of meat and a small round cheese, accompanied by a pitcher of beer. He set them on a table and drew it near the bed. Galt smiled at him gratefully.

"Lord Dawid says to see if there is anything else you will need," Colin told him. He set a bowl of porridge and scraps of meat on the floor.

Postumus smiled at him. "The household is most hospitable."

"If you would make up a chamber for the surgeon," Galt said. "There is not much he can do for me, but we may talk a while."

When Colin had left, Galt motioned at the tray. "Eat. I find I can't keep much down these days, but the beer does me good. Will you stay a day or so? How anxious is your governor to know the state of my health?"

Extremely anxious, Postumus knew, but he said, "I will stay." A day or two would make little difference, as long as Galt lived.

He left Galt to rest, and slept himself, and the next day they slipped into the kind of conversation they had exchanged when Galt's leg was healing. Postumus had shed his lorica and helmet and gratefully accepted a pair of trousers better suited to the smoky chill of Dawid's hold than his own military tunic and short breeches, thinking with amusement of Claudia's conversation with the governor. Dawid sat with them occasionally and Brica came and fussed about Galt, changing bedclothes and brushing his hair, but mainly they left the two of them alone.

"It does him good to talk to you," Dawid said when they passed each other in the doorway. "I don't know why, but it does." Postumus wondered what way Dawid would go, if the king began a war. He would follow, no doubt, as Galt would have, if it came to it.

"And have you settled, yourself," Galt asked him when Postumus slid close to asking that, "on whether you are a Briton or a Roman?"

"There is always dual loyalty for the native-born," Postumus admitted, "but it's to the land of Britain and the government of Rome, not the other way around. When I was small, I simply thought of myself as a Roman whose home was Britain. When I found out what happened to my father's legion and how Rome treated the ones who survived, I felt betrayed. But the Medical Service and the Army have taken the edge off that somewhat. I've seen enough of the calculations involved in holding an empire to see that we have tried to hold too much, and yet we have it, and if we abandon it, we abandon the citizens we have settled there."

"That has always been the push and pull, has it not?" Galt said. "When we saw fit to fight Rome last, it was because the emperor had left your forts too lightly guarded."

"Fortunately, neither the last emperor nor this new one have been so minded," Postumus said, hoping it was true.

"I understand that he has added 'Pius' to his name," Galt said with a small smile. "For what is he known to be so dutiful?"

That Galt understood Latin well enough to grasp the subtleties of the term was not lost on Postumus. It was said that the designation came from having compelled the Senate to deify the deceased Hadrian over its own objections. Or for Antoninus's refusal to execute the senators whom Hadrian, in the bad temper of the ill, had condemned to death. "Since the Senate awarded him that title, I rather think it's for being dutiful to them," Postumus said.

"I had hoped," Galt said, "when the king was of age and I was less needed, to see that empire that Rome has made us a part of." He smiled. "See if the tales the traders tell are true."

"Probably not," Postumus said.

"No cities made of marble, with streets of gold?"

"Marble, yes. Rome is largely built of it. Golden streets, no."

"Have you been to Rome?"

"No. You would be surprised by how many of us haven't."

Galt took a careful sip of the beer in his cup, and lay back against the piled skins on the bed. "Tell me where you have been."

"In Syria most recently, before this posting."

"What is it like?"

"Most unlike Britain. Very hot and dry, with palm trees. And scorpions."

"I have seen a painting of palm trees," Galt said. "But not of scorpions."

"They're rather like a cross between a spider and a cricket," Postumus said. "Or a thumb-size lobster. With a stinger on the end of the tail. Very nasty."

Galt looked dubious and Postumus got out of his chair and knelt by the hearth. He drew one in the ash with his fingertip. Galt leaned on one elbow to inspect it.

"They get in your bedding and your boots and into the roof thatch and drop on your head," Postumus said. "I had a commander who slept with a parasol over his head."

Galt laughed. "So should I. Tell me more."

Postumus considered what to tell him of the things that he would never see now. Galt was the first Briton he had known who had shown any interest in the outside world.

"There is Petra, that's in Arabia, to the south. I went there once with a tribune's family doing the grand tour. They wanted a medical man along for the mother-in-law, which really meant someone to play Tabula with her when she got bored, so my senior surgeon lent me to them. But Petra was worth it. A whole red sandstone city carved out of living rock – temples, houses, cisterns, offices, baths. When the sun hits it, it glows."

Galt raised his eyebrows. "My people would think twice about investigating a hollow mountain."

"There are no tales of ban-sidhe that I know of, although they do carve their tombs into the rock. The tribune's family had money enough to be wasteful and the mother-in-law would take sheaves of papyrus and sit by the public fountain and draw the monuments and the temples. We paid camel drivers to stop and hold their animals still so she could sketch them. I carried her paint pots."

"An arduous posting to be sure," Galt said.

"It didn't last long. I was back to chasing the scorpions out of the hospital dispensary soon enough. But I was glad to have seen Petra."

"What other wonders does your empire hold?"

"The Great Pyramid at Giza and the Pharos at Alexandria are accounted to be among the requirements for any grand tour, but I haven't seen them. My Uncle Licinius saw the pharos and described it as 'large.' I've been to Helike, though. You'd like that. A whole city under the sea – it sank in a tidal wave five hundred years ago, off the coast of Achaea. You take a boat ride out and you can look down on the temples and statues and such. They used to be more spectacular than they are now, but the ocean is slowly eating them away."

Galt lay back down. "I am tired now. Perhaps I shall dream of sunken cities." His eyes closed.

–

In the morning, Postumus folded the borrowed breeches and tunic neatly on the also neatly folded blankets of his bed, like a well brought up houseguest. Then he took the vial of eastern poppy from his kit and slipped it into the pouch at his belt.

Galt sat halfway up, taking in Postumus's lorica and military cloak, and the helmet under his arm. "You are leaving." Postumus remembered the same words spoken two years ago while they walked the ponies up a hillside track.

"I must," he said as he had said then. He fingered the callused spot under his chin, left by years of a helmet strap rubbing there. Not as thick as the ones the soldiers bore, of course – you didn't wear a helmet in the hospital – but there nonetheless, mark of a loyalty to something besides just the idea of Rome.

"I am glad that you came, for whatever reason," Galt said.

Postumus took the small cloth-wrapped bundle from his belt. "I imagine your healers have done all they can, and will. This is for pain; you can use it if it gets too bad. It's all that I know to give you. A few drops in a cup of beer." He didn't say, *Be careful, you can also kill yourself with it*. Galt knew that, although Postumus doubted that he would.

Galt took the bundle and laid it on the table. His hand and arm seemed even thinner and paler than two days before. He pushed the blanket away to show the blue enamel arm ring with its circle of leaping horses. "Travel safely." He paused. "If this comes back to you again, you will know that I am gone."

Postumus nodded. Dawid and Brica were waiting in the doorway to show him out. Boreas was tethered outside, saddled and hung conspicuously with green branches on both flanks. He thanked Dawid and Brica for their hospitality and rode away with Finn at his heels, down the hillside track into his own world.

XVII. Dis Manibus

The trees leafed out and the slow dance of spring spread across the countryside, and Postumus rejoined his legion with the firm intent to stay there. This was his job, his place to be. Moodily collecting his pay and grumbling at the stoppages (for his retirement account; for rations; for winter boots), he found a letter from Justin waiting. As a rule, Justin's missives were short, cheerful accounts of his doings, but this time, aside from the usual felicitations, there was an exasperated tinge to his brother's voice.

> *I must envy you your post with a unit that is up to strength. Certain elements in Dacia Inferior and Germania are being troublesome and we are being shuttled about to patch holes while we build new fortifications in the Agri Decumates. We are to shove the Limes Germanicus fifteen miles forward, it seems. At the same time, we hear that Judea and Egypt are restless and need looking to. Presumably with yet another detachment of my troops, which I can't spare. On the bright side, I have leave coming up and am going home to kiss the family.*

Postumus folded the letter up again, regretting that he had used all his own leave carousing in Londinium with Valerian. On the other hand, he was unlikely to be granted any just now anyway. He put his hospital to rights, played latrunculi (and lost) with Lucian, taught Finn Latin, and polished his armor. Lorica, helmet, and greaves restored to a suitable shine, he wrote back to Justin, to Constantia, and his parents, cheerful chatty letters that didn't mention anything he had actually been doing beyond these harmless occupations.

–

Valerian, with a highly mobile army of cavalry, made another sweep of the south. He let it be known in each village that the house found to be harboring a fugitive would be burned, and worse happen to its inhabitants.

"And what would there be here for them to stay?" a woman asked him. The basket over her arm held a few scrawny turnips, the remnants of her kitchen garden. The corn in the fields had all gone to feed the army, first Brendan's and then the Romans'. She spat at him and walked away.

By late spring it was becoming clear that Lollius Urbicus's tactics had resulted in the remnants of the Selgovae massing south of Clota-Mouth, according to the scouts. They had been harried steadily northwest, any diversion hindered by the unwillingness of tribes south of the new wall to shelter fugitives who had Rome on their tail. Word was that the Caledones and an unknown number of the Eastern Pictish tribes were massing in the north, presumably to meet them. The Picts were, just now, two separate bands and it would take them time to join. The mountainous river-laden country in the west made travel directly to the east difficult for a war band. If they rode south toward the Epidii lands, a substantial auxiliary detachment blocked their path. The eastern tribes would have to move south through the glens that led to the lowlands near Castra Pinnata and the naval station at Horrea, where they could be stalled by the glen-mouth forts. Urbicus intended to rid himself of the intractable Selgovae completely and then, if the Picts were still interested, he would be happy to settle their ambitions for the next two generations.

The morning that the governor gathered his forces from their scattered and hidden encampments below Clota-Mouth, the air was still with the wary silence that an alien presence makes among the sky and forest creatures. They waited on a ridge above a valley cut through by a small tributary of the Clota, well back in the trees, like a hawk, Postumus thought, waiting for lunch.

The Selgovae band came up the valley on the near side of the river, a cluster of chariots and horsemen and men on foot, loaded wagons trailing them. They looked to Postumus desperately weary, like hunted creatures stumbling up the uneven ground.

Urbicus and his generals conferred, the sacrifices for victory were made, and the first and then the second trumpets sounded. The Selgovae could hear them if they wished, because it was too late.

Besides the bulk of the Victrix, there were six cohorts of the Second Augusta and nearly half of the Twentieth, supplemented by auxiliary units of archers and horse. Valerian's main cavalry units were behind the Selgovae on their path north, pushing them toward the waiting legions. There would be no prisoners, no treaties this time. Brendan had already been executed when his tribesmen's ragtag army had re-formed to overthrow the last treaty.

Postumus, watching the Britons streaming through the valley, thought that they must know by now, but there was no way to turn back at this point, driven before Valerian's cavalry. With Lucian and Flavian and the surgeon of the Twentieth, he made a last inspection of the hospital tents. Most of the medical staff, including Postumus and his juniors, had been pulled from the wall forts to join Urbicus in the field. Postumus had tried to leave Finn with the garrison at Castra Damnoniorum but Finn wasn't having it, and when Postumus had chased him back twice, he had given up. He could only imagine what Calpurnius Aquila would have to say about that, but Calpurnius Aquila's bad hip had forced him into retirement. The other two legionary detachments had their own surgeons and hospitals, combined for the campaign into a single unit, and they amicably sorted out duties between them.

"We're all glad not to have old Aquila breathing down our necks," Lucian said. "I've never been so terrified of anyone in my life."

"You will be," Tertius informed him. "What I saw of the Picts the last time was enough to last me the rest of my life."

"I was there," Lucian said tartly. "I remember." Tertius had a habit of regaling the surgical staff with gory reminiscences of his days as a fighting man. "And I expect I've seen more blood than you have."

"Settle," Postumus said.

Tertius regarded Lucian's ability to beat nearly anyone at any game as sinister, and Lucian's mathematical explanations made his head swim. He invariably countered with the thing that he knew best, which was how to kill people.

The third trumpet, the Order to March, cut the morning air and the massed army shook itself like a hound turning to the hunt.

The battle was short and bloody. The last of the Selgovae, on foot or horseback but with few chariots among them, and with the cavalry at their rear, hurled themselves furiously at the Roman auxiliaries as they streamed down the ridge. The auxiliaries responded with a rain of pilums and arrows and then raised their shields, moving back slowly, until the momentum of the Selgovae charge broke. The trumpets sounded again and the legionary troops moved out of the trees from either side before they could regroup, and clicked shut around them like a lock. Brendan had freed his people of Rome only in the sense that the dead are free.

–

"Are there no prisoners?" Flavian asked, pushing his bloody hair out of his eyes. The casualties on the Roman side had been minimal and when that was the case, there were generally prisoners brought in to be seen to.

"No," Postumus said.

"None?" Lucian looked surprised.

"None." Not for the slave market or for a treaty exchange. Urbicus's orders.

"They've been allowed to take their own wounded off, then?"

"No."

"Use your heads," Tertius said. "If they weren't dead when they fell, they are now. Old Urbicus isn't bothering with anyone who's not in one piece, and they're bound to wish they weren't."

"Clean up and then eat," Postumus said shortly. The governor's tactic might give any other rebellious tribe a thing to think about. Or not.

They made camp for the night when the scouts had found a spot that met the governor's requirements, which were many, beginning with a water supply that could not be easily tampered with, and awoke in the full expectation that having dealt with a mosquito, they were about to engage a hornets' nest.

Instead scouts reported that the Pictish war bands which had been riding to join forces above the wall had both pulled back. Couriers from the northern forts confirmed it, and the governor took the counsel of his generals over breakfast.

"They're hoping we'll chase them up into their glens where every hillock looks the same and they can come round behind us," Valerian said, peeling a peach. A military governor's tent was palatial and included a wooden floor and three of his personal slaves who passed bowls of porridge, fruit and olives, and filled the general's silver cups with watered wine. Valerian mimed a circle with his knife blade.

Claudius Charax, the legate of the Second, snorted. "We're not such fools, I trust."

"Julius Agricola was," Urbicus said, "and he got everything short of an actual triumph for it." (Triumphs went only to emperors, no matter who had done the fighting.) He waited while they absorbed that idea. No one who had reached their rank was without further ambition. "*However*, Agricola went up by sea, thumped them and took hostages, and stopped trying to hold the highlands afterward. My opinion is that it can't be held, and I have no intention of trying."

"The whole point of the new wall is to guarantee good behavior below it, and to keep anyone above it where they belong," Aelius Silanus said. He ate an olive and looked unappreciatively at the porridge. "That seems to be what they're doing, for the moment."

"Will they stay clear?" the commander of the Twentieth detachment asked.

"Do fish have wings?" Urbicus shook his head. "But they'll see if they can't tease us into chasing them first. Without Brendan's warriors, they don't have an ally. They'll be back talking to the Brigantes again, I'm thinking." He nodded at Silanus. "In your back garden."

–

"And so we're to do a tour of the northern glen-mouth forts and Castra Pinnata," Valerian said when he stopped by Postumus's tent to offer his assessment while Postumus polished his armor. "To reinforce those garrisons and make sure we'll know about any force that's on the march out of the highlands before it gets here." Scouts and couriers had been coming and going all morning and rumors were flying: The Picts were on the march and had fired a fort of the wall. The Picts had come up the Clota by ship and were at their backs. The Picts had called down a fog by Druid magic and retreated under its cover.

Postumus scrubbed at the cheek piece of his helmet. A large part of a soldier's life involved polishing armor, which rusted again immediately if not attended to. He was accounted mad by most other officers for not having a slave to do it. He had found, though, that a number of surgeons shared his aversion to having another responsibility to see to. There were enough of them on the operating table.

"Castra Pinnata," he repeated after a moment.

Valerian nodded.

"Do you know who he's taking?"

"Three cohort detachments from the Second and the Twentieth. Two from the Sixth because he wants most of them back in Eburacum to keep an eye on the Brigantes. Half the attached legionary cavalry – most of the auxiliaries are going into garrisons on the wall. And you."

Postumus held the cheek piece to the light, concentrating on it as if to see if he'd got it clean.

"It mightn't be a bad thing," Valerian said gently. "Sacrifice to the shades and clear them out of your head."

"I'm that transparent?" Postumus put the helmet down and scratched Finn's ears.

"You'll get your orders in an hour or two, I expect," Valerian said. "When I left, he was madly making lists. I suppose I should go and do the same." An army on the march was made of lists: lists of Fit for Duty, lists of horses in reserve, lists of numbered catapult parts, of extra pilum points, harnesses, spare cart wheels, and tent pegs.

Postumus occupied his mind with lists of bandages and cots, painkillers, wound dressings, bone saws, spoons, and forceps, and thus avoided making a list of reasons a perfectly healthy surgeon should not ride north with the governor.

Otherwise left to make his own choices, Postumus sent Lucian back to Eburacum with the assurance that Calpurnius Aquila was now safely installed on his farm in Gallia Narbonensis. Lucian was accompanied by Flavian, Quintus, and a protesting Tertius, and Postumus took Cinnamus north with him. With a little more practice, Cinnamus would be ready for a junior surgeon's posting and it wouldn't hurt to get him under the governor's eye as a likely young officer.

In the morning they were on the march, Postumus on Boreas with Finn at his heels, east on the military road along the wall to where the old Agricolan road led north to Camelon and the glen-mouth forts. Governor Urbicus had sent Aelius Silanus and Charax of the Twentieth back to their respective fortresses to make their presence felt, and rode with the senior centurions of the legionary detachments, and with Valerian, in command of the cavalry. When they left the wall on the second day, the detachment from the Augusta, which had been posted to the Bodotria Estuary, joined them and the detachments re-formed in hostile-country marching order, despite continuing reports that the Picts had retreated to their highland fastnesses. North of Camelon, they passed a few small farms in the lowland river valleys, neat steadings with hayricks and ponds and geese in the yard, but no one seemed inclined to take notice of them. These were still mainly villages of the Damnoni and they were disinclined to trouble either the Romans or the highland Picts. Once they stopped to sacrifice at a roadside shrine to Epona, the Gallic-British horse goddess who carried the souls of the native dead and was patron to most of the Empire's cavalry. The road was recently repaired, with fresh stones set where the old had been uprooted by weather or by some farmer for his cow byre. Urbicus, at the center of the march, in consultation with his scouts and with a watchful eye for signal fires from the north, kept to a standard pace, and pitched camp at midday on a tributary of the Bodotria.

The next day they made their way up the valley to ford the Bodotria itself. Cavalry stationed themselves in the relatively shallow water on either side of the ford to break the current above and rescue anything that fell in the water below, and the main army crossed in between. Finn happily swam at Boreas's flank and shook himself off on the other side in a shower of muddy water. The riders downstream retrieved floating pilums, packs, baskets, cookpots, and a helmet. These items being restored to their owners, the column marched on, singing insults to the Picts now that the governor had relaxed his order for silence.

Oh the Briton's all tattoos,
He paints his nether regions blue!

Valerian's voice carried nearly the length of the column and the song was infectious. Postumus found himself singing along under an accommodatingly sunny sky, carefully *not* imagining the Ninth Legion on this road and almost succeeding. At midday they camped outside the walls of the southernmost of the highland forts at Alauna Septentrionalis. Garrisoned by a cohort of Batavian infantry, Alauna had a small but extremely serviceable hospital with a surgeon named Domitius in charge. Domitius was young and, like the governor, he was from Libya. It was how Rome built its Empire, scattering its offspring from one side of the world to the other. He promptly invited Postumus and Cinnamus to hunt deer the next day.

"The commander says you're to stay two days," he told Postumus, "and that dog of yours looks like a deerhound."

Postumus had no idea whether he was or not, but they set out in the morning, with the governor's permission and borrowed hunting spears, from the Alauna garrison. Domitius led them up a steep track into the hills to the east, pointing over his shoulder at the Alauna watchtower. "Just keep that in your sight if we get separated and you won't get lost."

Valerian, drilling the cavalry below, watched them with a wistful eye.

The hills were threaded through with little glens carved by the mountain streams that bubbled over rocky escarpments and wooded slopes to feed small villages along their downstream banks. Finn demonstrated his ability to catch a hare if not a deer and Postumus took it from him, gutted it, and hung it on his saddle horns in case a deer was not forthcoming. At midday, they stopped at a spring to water the horses and to eat a meal of dried fruit and the ubiquitous military biscuit.

"What's this?" Cinnamus knelt down, pointing. Where the spring bubbled out of the earth was a little bowl cut from living rock over which the water flowed into a natural basin below before trickling away downhill to join whatever tributaries led, smaller and then larger, through the network of waters to the Bodotria and the North Sea.

Inside the little bowl someone had left a white stone, a silver coin, and bronze figure the size of a nut.

"I'd as soon eat somewhere else," Domitius said. "This place has a dark feel to it."

Postumus could sense some power there, but it didn't feel sinister. Just something not his, to leave alone. He whistled Finn away from it as soon as he had had a drink, although he thought a dog would probably be welcome.

"It belongs to the Mother," Postumus said. "The Picts give their first worship to the Goddess, and this is one of her shrines."

"One of our men found one of these in an oak grove once," Domitius said, "and came back with a suppuration on his hand that still won't heal. It cracks open again just when I think it's gone, and oozes pus."

"If he stole from it, he got off lucky with just a blistering rash," Postumus told him. He shed his lorica, helmet, and greaves, and laid his sword and dagger beside them, well away from the spring, before he pulled a coin from the purse at his belt and left it beside the other things in the bowl. He touched his hand to his forehead. "In thanks for your woods, your hills, your creatures, Lady," he said in British, "the hooved and the footed who belong to you."

Domitius observed him admiringly. "You might be a native," he said.

Postumus grinned at him, once he was away from the spring. "I am. I'll do something about your soldier with the rash if you like. If anyone had seen him, he'd have had the whole local populace down around your ears."

Domitius winced. "Tell your Goddess that we'd appreciate it if that didn't happen," he said.

Finn proved to be an admirable deerhound, although once they brought it to bay, he sat down and wagged his tail. He apparently just liked to track things. Postumus thought of him sitting in the snow outside Claudia's cave, waiting for someone to tell him what scent to follow now.

Before they gutted the deer, Postumus said another prayer to the Mother and to the Horned God too, because all horned creatures belonged to both. At Alauna, while Domitius and Cinnamus put the deer on a spit, Postumus looked at the hand of the auxiliaryman who had trespassed in a grove, and treated it with the same salve that Domitius had no doubt used.

"What did you steal from it?" he asked.

"Nothing."

"I don't believe you and it doesn't look like the Goddess does either."

"Nothing!"

"What else did you do then? You'd better tell me."

The infantryman looked sullen. "Pissed in it," he muttered.

"How long have you been in Britain that you don't know better than that?" Postumus gave him a disgusted look. "You're lucky this is all you got. And that it's on your hand."

"How was I to know it was sacred? There ought to be a sign, like." The man was beginning to look frightened. "What do I do? Domitius says he'll invalid me out if this doesn't heal."

"Go back to the grove and make sacrifice. Give the Goddess a gift – some silver, something valuable, a flask of wine. And take your armor and your knife off. Don't take iron in." He paused. "And don't go hunting there, particularly not for anything with horns."

Afterward he told Valerian, who looked honestly horrified. "What you absolutely do not want to do is get the natives in a taking over their gods. I'll just have a word with his commander."

When they rode out the next day, Postumus observed the infantryman cajoling his horrified commander into letting him go back into the hills. The hand might or might not heal, but none of the garrison would defile a shrine again.

The villages thinned out as they marched north, and the skies ahead stayed clear of signal fires. The governor, in a jolly mood, let them sing again as they went.

Oh fare you well, my darling, we're off in the morning
And we may not be back when it's over...

They sounded much more cheerful than their song. It was another day's march to the first fort on the highland line, and then to Tamia, halfway up the Tava to Castra Pinnata. They would come back by way of the western glen-mouth forts and so south again to the wall. Each morning they were a little closer to Castra Pinnata, Postumus a little more jumpy and withdrawn until Valerian dragged him to his own tent, the night before the last march north, and got him as drunk as possible. In the morning, they followed the river to Castra Pinnata, Postumus nursing a headache under his helmet but grateful all the same.

Castra Pinnata had been built to house a legion, and the outlines of its walls still stood in tumbled stone. The rest had been burnt, not once but twice. The ditch and ramparts, re-dug and rebuilt to a smaller circumference, enclosed only a scattering of new timber buildings at the center, where blackened stones marked the old outlines of Principia and hospital.

The encroaching weeds and briars had been uprooted and the streets laid out again in their old pattern with military efficiency. The forest creatures who had moved in each time that man had left were only recently evicted, still lairing among the rubble of the outer walls. A fox scurried out of sight as the governor's cavalcade passed through the remains of the old Praetorian Gate.

The sun glinted on the gilded standard of the garrison, a detachment of the Aelia Dacorum, as they halted before the Principia for an official reception, and Postumus wondered what the foxes thought of it all.

Built by the Twentieth Valeria Victrix in Agricola's day on the banks of a navigable stretch of the Tava, Castra Pinnata was to have been the lynchpin of his short-lived occupation of the highlands, until revolts elsewhere pulled troops from Britain. It was abandoned then and burned to keep the Picts from using it, and then burned again when the Ninth Legion died in it. Each time the foxes would have moved back in, and the deer and the badgers and the owls and the mice. The only men left until Governor Urbicus had sent the Aelia Dacorum here were under the ground somewhere.

Postumus picketed Boreas with the troop horses and toured the hospital, reassuring its resident surgeon that he wasn't Calpurnius Aquila, while the governor's entourage put up their camp outside the garrison's new walls but inside the old perimeter. Formalities achieved, Postumus dragged his own tent, the red leather of an officer's abode, from the baggage wagon and erected it, a task which generally involved much cursing, and thought again about buying a slave. The notion only occurred to him when he was at a task he didn't care for, so it probably wasn't a great idea. If he married and had a household to see to, that would be time enough. When he had finished, he looked out over the tumbled rubble to the meadows and river beyond, and whistled Finn to heel. The graveyard was going to be here somewhere, outside the walls, and he might as well get it over with.

He had gone nearly round the old perimeter when he found it in a meadow below the Sinister Gate. The ground was overgrown with scrub and briars and a hare erupted from the thicket as he approached. There was only one stone, tilted now, and sinking on the right side into the turf.

DIS MANIBUS
LEGIONARII IX HISPANA

Nothing more, just the two lines.

They would have burned all the bodies, of course, a ghastly task in summer when they had lain rotting for days. Postumus closed his eyes. There would have been rain, and ashes, and mud, and carrion birds that had got there first. The Britons would have taken their own dead away, along with any loot they found, and the legion's Eagle, still a disgrace, a lost Eagle; that was still here somewhere in the mountains to the north but Rome would never see it again unless they occupied the highlands entirely, and that was not an investment that Rome would make even for a lost Eagle, particularly not that of a disgraced legion.

Postumus pulled his belt knife from its sheath and pricked his forefinger with it. He rubbed the drop of blood on the stone. A prayer, an offering, he wasn't sure what. They were the same really, weren't they? "Dis manibus…" It seemed important to give something of himself, some connection to the scattered ash mixed with earth below the turf. What was left of a legion, and his father somewhere in it.

Governor Urbicus, riding the perimeter with his staff officers, caught sight of the silent figure in the meadow, motionless, head bowed over the old stone with the dog at his heels. He drew rein and watched, and Valerian leaned over and whispered in his ear. The governor nodded and they rode on, but when he made sacrifice that evening at the Shrine of the Standards, he added a prayer for the last men who had tried to hold this fortress.

—

"This is good broth. Drink it now."

Brica knelt beside the bed and Galt smiled at her, but he shook his head.

"Just a little."

He sighed and held out a thin arm from under the furs that covered him. He was always cold now. He struggled up on one elbow and she held the cup to his mouth.

He managed a sip without choking. "There." His voice was hoarse. He pointed at the small bundle that Postumus had left him and she nodded and stirred a bit into the broth. It took the edge off the pain so that he thought he could bear not to drink the whole vial.

"Dawid is here to see you," Brica said. "He has been in the high pastures with the herdsmen, looking at new foals."

"Not at Council?" Galt looked surprised.

"So far there hasn't been one." Dawid pulled a chair next to the bed. Brica took the broth and untouched food away and began to tidy the room.

"I am a stone in the king's shoe," Galt said.

Dawid smiled. "You are." Those who stood between the worlds held power, and because Galt had also been regent and the king's foster father, the Council wouldn't vote for war against his advice. Not now. Nor would the king risk Talhaiere's anger and cross him further.

Galt lay back against the furs as the drug began to work. There was a space between the pain and the sleep when he could feel as he used to, or something like it. It never lasted long. "And what of the day when he can shake the stone out?" he asked.

Dawid looked away, at the saffron glow of the embers in the hearth. He took off his cloak. The room was stiflingly hot. "The king is my foster brother," he said slowly. "I will counsel against war, you know that."

"And if he sends the call anyway?" Galt asked.

"I will follow," Dawid said. "You know that too."

Brica slammed the dishes down on the clothes chest and spun around. She didn't say anything, but her lips were pressed together in a thin line.

Dawid stood. "When it is time, I will send that arm ring to the surgeon of the Eagles for you, as you promised him. I can't do any more."

Galt touched the enameled band. Dawid knew that a warning to the Eagles might cut off the possibility of war. And also that it might only mean another loss if Bran was determined. "You were a hound the last time we fought," Galt told him. "And the king an infant. The world changes."

Dawid didn't answer and Brica followed him out. Her shoes made an angry rustle in the straw on the floor. They would quarrel over this, Galt knew. But what else was there to say? Even in the grip of the drug, maybe more so then, he could remember how Bran's father and the surgeon's father had fought each other to the death while he watched. He had never told either of them that, why should he tell Dawid now?

Sometimes he resisted the drug for the dreams it gave him, sometimes he welcomed them, thought of taking more and slipping entirely into that next world, wherever it was.

–

It was dark and he sat naked with seven other boys around a dead fire, shivering, on the night of their initiation into manhood. Vortrix was next to him, his corn-colored hair catching the moonlight that filtered into the hut, each stifling his fear for the sake of the other. "I will be your hound now, and not the king's," Galt told him.

The Beltane fires were dying to embers as Vortrix and Branwen, old Cathuil's daughter, leapt them hand in hand. He was king now and needed an heir.

They were washing away the dirt of a hunt where the river pooled into a swimming hole, diving like fish into the depths, rising to splash each other or throw handfuls of river moss. Vortrix's hair was dark with river water, slicked back like a seal and plastered down his back. He dived, grabbed Galt by the ankles, and tumbled them both laughing into the shallows.

The roan chariot ponies thundered down the slope into the Roman line. The chariot was a live thing under his feet, the ponies' reins an extension of his hands, and Vortrix was beside him, war spear in hand, bare chest painted the blue of his war shield and the King Mark tattooed on his brow.

The fire of their torches ate away at everything the Romans had rebuilt at Inchtuthil, that they called Castra Pinnata. Fading sunlight through the burned roofbeams washed the still body as Galt whispered his last oath. "So I swear, who am the Hound of the Father." There was blood in Vortrix's pale hair and soaking his arm and thigh.

The dreams came and went, but it was always Vortrix at the heart of them. Sometimes Galt thought he was real, felt his hand touch his own. Vortrix had died because that was his right. Maimed, he could not have held the kingship, nor could a regent have ruled effectively with him hovering like a ghost in the background. He had died to secure the kingship for his cub, to stop another inter-tribal war. Kings had died thus before. Had anyone instead lived beyond his wishes for the same cause?

Galt turned restlessly in the bed.

"He talks to someone," Brica whispered, peering through the door again.

"The old king," Dawid said. "He comes to him when he dreams."

Brica looked uneasy. "From the Otherworld? Or just a fever dream?" Wandering spirits were dangerous, particularly those of powerful people.

"Both, maybe. It doesn't matter. He only comes to Galt."

XVIII. Epona's Mare

It was fall when the governor's detachment rode south again through a scurry of wind-driven leaves and intermittent rain. As they neared the new wall, the sun came out, flinging scraps of rainbow into the sky over the half-built temple that was rising to mark the governor's conquest.

They made camp in sight of it and one of the governor's junior staff fetched Postumus from his armor-polishing. "Governor Urbicus wants a word." He shook his head at the polishing rag. "You need a slave. It's not dignified."

"So I've been told." Postumus put the rag down and followed the messenger to the governor's tent, somewhat warily. Any time the governor had sent for him before, the results had been unsettling.

This time the governor waved him to a seat beside his camp table and handed him a cup of wine. "Have a drink and a bite to eat and then we're going to go look at my temple." It was a pleasant day, the tent flaps rolled up to catch the breeze. The governor pushed a plate of olives, eggs, and cheese toward Postumus. He was in field armor, his scarlet sash knotted around a serviceable cuirass.

Postumus suppressed the various questions he could have asked, which mainly boiled down to "Why me?" and drank the wine, which was excellent.

The governor didn't elaborate. He fed an egg to Finn, who had crept into the tent at Postumus's heels, and remarked that he needed a dog himself.

"His loyalties are suspect," Postumus said. "He switched sides for a bowl of stew."

"And perhaps you are a better master," Urbicus observed. "I doubt that he would part from you for stew. Dogs know things, I have found." He stood. "Come along. I sent for your horse and mine. We'll ride across and see the progress."

The circular temple was cut into the hill above one of the many tributaries that flowed east into Bodotria Estuary. The governor had designed it himself in the style of his homeland. Three cavalry troopers accompanied them, and Postumus was certain that others had gone ahead. Urbicus wouldn't ride unprotected even this close to his wall. But he seemed to wish for privacy and the troopers hung well back as they rode, and halted at the short rough-cut road that led to the site.

Boreas and the governor's horse picked their way up the temporary track, still dirt but graded to allow drays of dressed stone to make their way up. A legionary crew was at work and saluted as the governor arrived.

Urbicus nodded at them. "Very satisfactory. We wish to go inside. Please take a rest and don't drop anything on our heads." He led the way into the temple while Finn nosed at the foundation stones and peed on one. Postumus pretended not to notice. He assumed the gods made exceptions for dogs.

Inside, the floor was still rough, lacking the mosaic that would adorn it later, and the roof still open above the scaffolding, the dome unfinished. Inscriptions dedicating it to Victory would be set into the plinth below her winged figure, and commemorate the emperor and the governor who had built it and reconquered the North. It was a message to the Picts as well: We are here to stay.

"You are right about young Cinnamus," Urbicus said when they had admired the progress and the marble plinth where Victory's gilded bronze statue would stand. "The Twentieth has lost a junior surgeon – to promotion, I'm glad to say – and I think I shall send him there. He's going to be good, as you say, and I don't want another province snatching him just now."

"Thank you, Governor. I take it you are of the opinion that we will continue to require good surgeons?" And the governor had not brought him out here to tell him about Cinnamus.

"I am always of that opinion. Monuments notwithstanding. I have a question I must ask you, and I fear it is insensitive, but since I am not known for my sensitivity, I shall ask it anyway."

Postumus pondered which thoroughly embarrassing question regarding the governor's personal spy might be coming, until Urbicus said, "Did you lay your ghosts to rest at Castra Pinnata?"

Postumus tried to switch horses and found no ready answer.

"General Valerian told me," Urbicus said. "I was grateful to him. I would not knowingly have put a good officer in an untenable situation."

"Untenable, no," Postumus said. "Painful, yes, but I think I am glad we went there. And if you had known, you might not have taken me."

"I wouldn't," Urbicus said flatly. He fingered the small stone fish that hung around his neck, a talisman of some kind. Even a governor needed luck. "Which goes to show that I am not infallible, but don't let that go to your head."

"Certainly not, sir."

Urbicus nodded. "Very well then. I am under no illusions that the Picts' ambitions have been curtailed. They are waiting for something. Possibly the Brigantes, which is why the Sixth is going back to Eburacum in full force. And also why I want a Chief Field Surgeon in place before I have a need for one. If we should march north again, if we should end up fighting the Picts at Castra Pinnata again, if you should be the Chief Surgeon, would the ghosts there keep you from your job?"

So not about Claudia at all. Claudia might have been easier. But he had an answer now, now that he had been to Castra Pinnata. "My family has generations of service in the Eagles. I will serve and my ghosts can talk to me about it afterward."

Urbicus smiled. "A straightforward answer. I would have worried if you had denied the ghosts. Very well, if we campaign next spring, you will take Aquila's place. He recommended you, by the way."

"I'm grateful. Or appalled. Or both," Postumus said. "Before he left Eburacum he terrified my third junior surgeon into competence."

"He has that capacity. Just remember the cow and don't get a big head." Urbicus nodded again and strode out, indicating the completion of whatever it was they had been doing.

—

With the new wall fully garrisoned by auxiliary units, many of them pulled from the Brigantian Hills, the

Sixth Victrix settled into its home fortress for the winter, patrolling the hills as weather permitted. The streets and drill fields echoed with the noise of five thousand men whose officers were trying to keep them in shape over the winter, while the civilian town along the riverbanks did a brisk business among the returning troops and their accumulated back pay. Postumus's morning sick parade returned to patients with coughs, legionaries who had injured themselves with their own weapons, and sudden unexplained rashes that appeared after visits to Rusonia's House of Fine Dining, With Extras.

Valerian's Dacian wing, to which he was currently returned, was mainly assigned to the wall, but he rode into Eburacum on the first day of Saturnalia for a visit with the governor and the legate of the Sixth and went afterward to the hospital to find Postumus.

It had snowed the day before, but the sky cleared afterward and half the garrison was engaged in pelting each other with snowballs in the streets. Because the previous winter had been miserably spent building a wall in a blizzard, the legate and the governor had declared this Saturnalia a rest from most duties, and had provided five days' worth of wine and figs and dates and various other imported delicacies shipped up the river from the south.

Postumus was in an empty surgery, ceremoniously serving dinner to the orderlies on the surgery tables, with the assistance of his junior surgeons and Quintus. The surgery lamps and cabinets were decorated with bunting made of bandage linen and evergreens, and Postumus himself wore a crown of bronze catheters and ivy. Valerian watched in amusement, snow melting from his boots onto the stone floor, until they saw him in the doorway and hailed him in.

"Io Saturnalia, Valerian!" Lucian beckoned him to the table. "Have a sausage."

"Thank you." Valerian drew a chair to an empty spot at the second table, tactfully draped in white linen to obscure whatever bloodstains might be left from its usual use.

"We're just drawing for Princeps," Lucian said. "Here." He held out a wooden instrument case filled with small clay beads.

Valerian reached in, feeling them carefully so as not to get the one with the 'X' incised into it. The Saturnalia Princeps was supposed to be a slave or servant, or in this case, one of the orderlies. It wasn't done for an officer to win the role.

The box went around and Tertius extracted the winning bead, grinning. He declined to annoy Postumus, but Lucian, Flavian, and Gemellus were fair game.

"I brought you something," Valerian said to Postumus while Tertius directed the junior surgeons in a dance that he was making up on the spot. Valerian held out a small leather bag and Postumus emptied it into his hand. It was a sigillaria, one of the small figurines traditionally given as Saturnalia gifts. This one was a bronze mouse about half a finger length long.

"For toothache," Valerian observed, and Postumus laughed.

"Wait here." Postumus departed for the hospital office and came back with a similar bag. "I've been keeping this in the hope that you'd show."

Valerian shook out a small dragon, very much in the mode of a cavalry draco banner. He smiled. "Io Saturnalia."

Around them, the junior surgeons were marching in a complicated field drill, directed by Tertius. Like Postumus, they were all supposed to keep up their training with periodic drills and marches, and like Postumus, they evaded it when possible, so none of them were surefooted. They were also mostly drunk. The orderlies applauded when Flavian fell into a table and knocked a sausage on the floor. Finn collected it and disappeared down the corridor.

"After him!" Tertius pointed a finger at Quintus, who had been trying to be inconspicuous. "Rescue our sausage!"

"He's a dog. Do you think he's going to hold it for ransom?" Quintus said. "It'll be gone by now, and anyway, it was my sausage."

Tertius seemed to see some wisdom in this and settled for making them all sing a song in his praise, with many verses.

Postumus beckoned Valerian out of the surgery and they settled in his office while the festivities went on. "I put up pretty much anything they could break," he said, removing his crown. "As long as they don't overset the lamps, we'll be fine. Just keep your nose open for the smell of smoke."

"My grandfather disapproved of Roman ways in general," Valerian said, "but he took to Saturnalia like an Italian. He once got so drunk at the feast that he fell into the hearth when there was a fire going. My grandmother pulled him away and my mother rolled him up in a rug and put him out. I was four. It was the high point of the holiday for me."

Postumus got down the green glass cups, which he had had no intention of exposing to the festivities in the surgery. He poured them each a modest amount. "I have to thank you for telling old Urbicus my tale. I don't think I could have managed to."

"I was afraid you might not appreciate that."

"I did, though. He asked me if I could deal with the ghosts if we ended up at Castra Pinnata again, when the Picts do whatever it is they're going to do."

"We all know perfectly well what they're going to do," Valerian said. "It's the particulars that are uncertain."

"Anyway, I had to think about that. I suppose I gave him a reassuring answer. He's made me Chief Field Surgeon, when the Picts, et cetera."

"He told me." Valerian raised his cup. "Io Saturnalia."

–

After the festival's end, the officers of the Sixth were occupied in collecting their charges from various ditches and from the comfortable rooms at Rusonia's, but it was generally agreed that the holiday had been good for morale. When the legate decided that matters were sufficiently in hand, he allowed pay, which had been prudently held back until after Saturnalia, to be dispensed.

Postumus traded pleasantries with Appius Paulinus and Frontinus in the offices of the Aquilifer, the bearer of the Eagle who also served as legionary banker, while the officers' pay was brought up from the strong room under the floor of the Shrine of the Standards. The imperial post, also delivered to the pay office, produced a pair of letters addressed to him as well.

The first was from Constantia, who could generally charm the optios at Isca Fortress, who remembered Hilarion, into letting her slip letters into their mail bag. Unlike his mother, Constantia had mastered a lovely, readable script. Gwytha's letters often took deciphering and intuitive leaps of faith.

I write for all of us to wish you a happy if belated Saturnalia, which will be over by the time you get this. This year the youngest herd boy got the cake with the coin in it for Princeps Saturnalia and made us all walk in a circle in the courtyard, baaing like sheep. Mother gave everyone new clothes and we had a fine time. My hedgehog has apparently met another hedgehog because there were baby hedgehogs in the pantry this summer. Just now they are all hibernating among the turnips. Cook was very unhappy about it and threatened to go to Papa and buy herself and go open a restaurant in Calleva, but I talked her around and gave her my silver bangle with the moonstones.

Which is a good thing because the biggest news is that Justin has apparently removed his head from whatever treatise on strategy he has been reading, and has finally noticed Aurelia. They will be married on the day before August Kalends and we all hope that you can be here. June is supposed to be luckier, but late July is when Justin can get leave again. He gave her a ring before he left and Papa and Uncle Licinius are consulting lawyers and drawing up the contract. They tend to bog down over minutiae, but I think they're enjoying themselves. Mother and Aunt Felicia are occupied with the guest list and extensive lists of Things That Must Be Done to both houses, since he'll have to take her home to our house. She can't go all the way to the Rhenus on her wedding night. I'm very pleased. I really like Aurelia and she will make a fine Army wife. She's prepared to follow him wherever he's posted, which I should hate, but she seems perfectly cheerful about it. Justin's had another promotion, in case he didn't write to you, and should be able to afford decent quarters and staff to look after them.

Postumus tucked the letter into his tunic.

"Good news, I trust?" Paulinus said, trying to read his expression. Winter quarters were dull; anyone's news was interesting. "Or not? Sorry. I shouldn't pry."

"Excellent news. My brother is getting married at the end of July. They hope I can be there. That's the debatable part."

"Soldier's dice," Frontinus said. "A constantly rolling variable."

Neither of them had any mail and they looked wistfully at the second letter but Postumus slid it into his tunic with Constantia's.

In his quarters, he contemplated the outside of the wooden tablet. It had come from Lindum and he only knew one person who lived in Lindum. Or who could also get her mail into the imperial post. He broke the tablet's seal with his thumbnail.

Postumus my friend,
I never thanked you properly for the help you gave me last winter and thought to let you know that I am back in Lindum, tidying up various business messes made in my absence and tending my roses. An elderly rose collector of my acquaintance has given me some specialty cuttings, and I have sent a few to your Aunt Felicia to try in her garden. I understand that you have been to Castra Pinnata, and apologize if I have been told things

that are private to you, but I hope that it eased
your mind all the same. As someone of our mutual
acquaintance said, those of us who are native-born
often walk a troublesome road. Do you still have
the dog? You and he would be most welcome should
you have the opportunity to visit Lindum.
      Claudia Silva

He was pleased to know that she was in Lindum and not
risking her tattooed hide among the Caledones. And also
suspicious of the fact that she was clearly still in touch
with Lollius Urbicus. And asking about him, it seemed.
Or perhaps Urbicus had asked her about him and her
assessment of his stability. Postumus felt mildly annoyed by
that, but Urbicus's priorities had no room for his surgeon's
sensibilities. He found after a moment that he didn't mind
her knowing, but he wondered what else she knew. She
would be risking her life trying the spy game on the
Brigantes with those tattoos. Claudia had sold her usefulness for one valuable trove of information. He hoped she
remembered that.

–

"All that can be done has been done." In Dawid's hold,
Talhaiere bent over the sleeping man while sleet came
down outside. His staff, surmounted by the gold disk of
the Sun, stood above the bed. "He travels in some other
world now, with other company."

Galt stirred and held out a hand, now bone thin, to
someone no one else could see, and murmured something.

It was the gray hour before dawn, the sun just cutting over the green trees along the ridge to light the gold diadem in the High King's corn-colored hair, and the gold torque at his throat. His shield hung at his horse's side, and the gray stone walls beside them were deserted, grown with moss and wild grasses. A curlew wheeled in the air overhead but it made no sound. Vortrix held his hand out and Galt leapt onto the horse's back behind him. A stag grazing among the trees raised his antlered crown to watch as they rode away westward, the sun on their backs, before he lowered his head to the grass.

–

Brica watched the body go still and began to weep.

Dawid put his arm around her. "We knew death was coming, and he has endured much."

"I weep for all of us," she said, "and for men's stupid pride." She glared at them both. "Go and tell the king his foster father is dead."

Dawid waited until Talhaiere had stumped out of the room. That would be the High Priest's chore, and he didn't envy it. He pulled the enameled band from Galt's arm and weighed it in his hand while the sleet made a metallic whisper on the roof outside.

Brica caught her breath. "The king would call that betrayal."

"It may be," Dawid said. "I don't know. But I swore it. I have to think."

"And then you will ride out with the rest and what good will it all have done?" She began furiously to pull the braids from her hair for mourning.

"I don't know that either," Dawid said. "There is some circle to be closed here but I don't know what it is."

–

Talhaiere stepped from the chariot by which Dawid's driver had delivered him to the king's hall. He hitched his green robe above the puddles of freezing rain in the courtyard, leaning on his staff, hood pulled over his white hair.

"Where is the king?"

The small hound who had come to take the horses bowed hastily and pointed. "In the Council Hall, Lord. With Lord Duncan."

Talhaiere stood in the Council Hall doorway until they noticed him. "I have need to speak with the king alone."

Duncan rose, leaving a half-eaten meal. There was one reason Talhaiere would be here, and a test of wills between the High Priest and the king was not something a man in his right mind would wish to be part of. There was too much power loose there, worldly and unearthly. The air crackled with it.

"He is dead," Bran said flatly.

"Yes." Talhaiere pushed his hood back and shook the rain from his hair and beard. "You will come to Dawid's hold and mourn him. And then you will make penance for trying to kill that Roman in Dawid's hall. Before anything else."

Bran stood, knocking his cup aside so that the dregs ran down the table and dripped in the rushes on the floor. The King Mark on his forehead stood out against his reddening face. "I have told you no! I will mourn Galt, for the shortest time necessary, and then we will move!"

Talhaiere glowered at him. Bran was shouting. Talhaiere pitched his voice so low that the king was forced into silence in order to hear him. "It is not given us to know how any course we set will end; our fates are not foreordained. But some things are inevitable, and men's actions have consequences in the way that roots grow trees."

"Do not come to me spouting Druidical nonsense about roots and trees."

Talhaiere glared back at him. His knuckles were white where they gripped his staff. "The Druids' ways are not ours, but their knowledge is old and deep and we are kin at the bone. You have trifled like a child with dark matters and the longer you wait, the darker they grow. Rhys knew. He came to me after a week of dreams. Have you not had any?" He dared Bran to deny it.

"Dreams are dreams." Bran looked furious and uncomfortable. "It was Rhys who held the knife and Rhys has done penance."

"You ordered it done. Don't argue like a child with me. You have committed sacrilege. Your Council know what you have done. How loyally will they follow you when they see what you risk for the sake of your pride?"

"They follow," Bran said. "They would not go against him while he lived, but now they will follow me."

Talhaiere put both hands on his staff, settling it in front of him so that the sun disk at its top stood above the High King's head. "For yourself, King? These men knew your father, and for that they may follow you. It is you who owe a debt, and something will pay it."

–

The last snow melted and the first muddy grass and shoots of bracken greened the hillsides, and Governor Urbicus made ready to move his forces north to meet the Pictish army that was assembling in the mountain valleys. Scouts had confirmed it, reporting that the Caledones were making their way east to join with the tribes whose lands lay in the central and eastern glens. Urbicus had called out the bulk of the Sixth Victrix, some four thousand men plus their auxiliaries and cavalry, and two-thirds of both the Second and the Twentieth, a force of more than ten thousand. Scouts also reported that the Brigantes remained peaceful, occupied with tending cattle and the spring crop of lambs, and plowing the fields for spring sowing. Those they encountered reacted to the passage of the Roman army through their territory with apparent indifference.

Postumus left Quintus behind to manage as well as he could whatever should ail the small remaining garrison at Eburacum, and took all three of his juniors. He insisted on Tertius driving a hospital wagon, to Tertius's annoyance.

"Shut up. You're no help to me if you drop on the march."

One of Tertius's old century passed with a mock salute, armored and helmeted, sword at his belt, with the regulation pilums, saw, pickaxe, sickle, basket, bucket, chain, and five days' worth of rations on his back. "Hail, Tertius, does the surgeon need another houseboy? Tell him I'm available!"

Tertius made a rude gesture. "Surgeon says I've got the same thing the Emperor Hadrian died of," he informed him proudly.

By the fifth day they were north of the old wall and well into the territory of the Selgovae, a bleak contrast to the tidy farms, fat cattle, and sleek horses of the Brig-antes. Here there were blackened farmsteads, and piles of rubble where anything defensible had been pulled down. Three women digging in a rough garden beside the newly patched walls of a small drystone hut stared as the governor's army passed by in a sea of scarlet and bronze, its wagons laden with catapults and tents and enough food to have fed their village for a year. One raised her hand as if to fling something at them and another pulled her arm down.

Postumus sat down in camp with the surgeons of the other legions, and those assigned to the cavalry and auxiliaries, and set about constructing a protocol for the intake of wounded, remembering the crisp efficiency with which Calpurnius Aquila had ordered his domain. The number of wounded depended on the generals, but the number of survivors on the surgeons. One of them, Galerius of the Second Augusta, was senior to him, and he worried about that, but Galerius seemed unruffled. "I'm due for retirement," was his comment. "You cope with Urbicus."

Postumus had also been pleased to find that Domitius, the surgeon from Alauna, had been promoted to a senior's position in the auxiliaries.

"I've heard that Pictish spears are dipped in whatever nasty thing they can find." Cannius, the surgeon from Valerian's old wing of Dacian Horse, looked around the circle.

"Haven't seen that myself," Domitius said. "In my opinion we're more likely to poison ourselves." He gnawed determinedly at a military biscuit, the evening rations, along with sour wine, olives, and what Postumus considered a dubious cheese. Finn regarded the cheese hopefully.

"I've heard that too," Sabinus, the surgeon of the Twentieth, said. "On the other hand, I've also heard that they have three-inch fangs and their priests can start fires with their eyeballs." He rubbed his chin, the same helmet callus they all bore. It was an almost universal Army habit. "How many men have we got, all staff included?"

"Eight senior surgeons, counting auxiliaries and cavalry," Postumus said. "Plus at least two juniors apiece, probably two apprentices each, and orderlies. Maybe forty all told, plus orderlies, and most of the orderlies can handle basic work."

"That's marginal," Galerius commented. "On the other hand, I've worked with less."

"The first thing we'll get will be the wounded from the chariot charge," Postumus said. "They really do it for effect, to scare the piss out of men who haven't seen it before. It's not sustainable but they make a fine mess while they're at it."

"The ones who've been in Britain long are on to that by now," Domitius said, gesturing at the sea of tents that filled the marching camp. "It's that first time that's so exhilarating." A small amulet carved in the figure of a fish dangled from his wrist, and Postumus remembered a similar one around the governor's neck.

"What is the little fish?" he asked Domitius. "Is it sacred?" Anything that brought luck was welcome.

"Everyone from the Maghreb has one of these," Domitius said. "It's for strength, same as that." He pointed to the small winged phallus that hung from Cannius's neck. "Just more seemly. The Amazigh are a polite people, and we believe in euphemism."

Cannius waggled it at him, then tucked it down his tunic.

"I believe in a sharp scalpel and a bottle of vinegar," Sabinus said. "Decorate it with what you will."

The Watch went by, marking the third hour of the night. They could see Valerian's cavalry riding the perimeter beyond the camp rampart, and the bob of a lantern as an optio from the Victrix came around with the evening's password.

Postumus nodded at the little shrine of Aesculapius set up behind them in his tent. "I believe in anything that works."

XIX. The Carrion Birds

Urbicus's army continued to move steadily north, a seemingly endless stream of infantry and cavalry and wagons, the great gilded Eagles and gold-fringed vexilla of three legions at its heart, and before and behind them the cohort and auxiliary standards and the bright, bronze-headed draco banners of the cavalry that filled with wind to snap back and forth like live dragons. Closer to the new wall, there was opportunity to hunt while the column inched forward, and forage parties had no compunction about raiding local farms, so meals improved. Scouts fanned northward from the main column, and back with such news as they gleaned in the heather. The military post from Eburacum caught up with them there as well.

"Quintus said he thought you'd want this," the courier said to Postumus, handing over a cloth-wrapped package. "So I said I'd bring it along. Don't tell the governor. We're supposed to be military only. He sent you a note with it."

"Thank you." Postumus turned the package over in his hand and unknotted the strings that held the cloth. Inside the cloth was a wooden box, sealed with wax. He pried the seal loose with his thumbnail. Inside the box was a leather bag. Someone had wanted whatever it was well hidden. He almost knew before he shook the thing out into his hand: a gold arm ring, enameled in blue and silver in a pattern of running horses, head to tail, their silver hooves forever above the ground.

–

"He's dead. I don't know how long." Postumus stood in the governor's field tent, the enameled arm ring in his hand. The tent was crowded with the governor's staff. "It came into Eburacum a week ago, by a boy of the Brigantes, Quintus says." He handed the governor the note that had been tied to the package.

Urbicus inspected the tablet and handed it round to the rest.

"If it was Dawid who sent this, I suspect he may have thought about it for a while first," Postumus said. "I don't know how much time we've lost."

"Too much, very likely," Urbicus said.

In a day's time, signal fires from the south and then returning scouts, changing horses at every post, confirmed that. Men of fighting age had been steadily draining out of the Brigantian Hills for a month. The men who had been seen plowing or herding cattle had been women, in men's clothes, breasts bound and even with hair on their faces for good measure.

Urbicus swore at that. "A lovely detail to embellish my report. 'Imperator, I regret to inform you that we have been played for fools by a set of false whiskers from a provincial farce.'" He looked disgusted. His generals and staff remained steadfastly expressionless, although Valerian, standing behind him, put a hand over his face. "The question remains as to where they have gone." Urbicus waved a hand and his optio produced a sheaf of pertinent maps from a trunk. "Thank you. Now then."

Postumus, having set the current emergency in motion, had not been invited to further council, and was in his own tent brooding over the arm ring when Valerian found him later.

"You liked him, didn't you." It wasn't a question.

"Very much. I think he liked me. But we're the invaders here. It makes it hard to gauge that sort of thing."

"What was personal versus what was best for his tribe? I suspect they coincided here." Valerian pointed at the arm ring. "You should wear that," he suggested, turning to the practical. "It might scare the Brigantes when we find them."

"And where does the governor think we'll find them?"

"We're working on that. Most information at this point suggests they went west and then north, possibly by sea. If they sailed far enough out to sea to skirt our forts south of the old wall and then around the coast of the Novantae, they could come ashore in Epidii lands. There are reports – now – of ships going around Monavia Island and north past Novantarum Head. The villagers there 'didn't think we'd want to know about that.' They've now been forcefully informed that we do."

Furthermore, the scouts reported, as soon as the governor's army had passed through Brigante territory, the Brigante women had vanished too, with the children and the mares from the horse herd and anything else that was valuable, into the high mountains where presumably they had some dwelling but not anything that vengeful Romans with questions to ask could find in a hurry.

Certain movements of the Pictish clans now seemed clearer in their purpose, and the consensus was that Dergdian would not back off again, but would close with the Brigante allies from the south and try to envelop the Roman army between them. Urbicus's intent was to repeat his tactics of the previous year, this time taking out the Picts first, before turning on the Brigantes. While Urbicus's scouts were hunting the Brigantes, a Brigante spy was found in the Roman camp by the simple expedient of sounding "To Quarters." Any man not in his tent immediately afterward was an obvious interloper. This particular one, in a Roman tunic and armor that Valerian and Postumus both thought had clearly come from the deserters at Trimontium, gave very little information before he died. They burned his body with the armor and Governor Urbicus made sacrifice for the shade of the man who had worn those charred remains first. When Aelius Silanus asked him why, he said shortly, "He's had twenty-five years of whatever it is the gods inflict on you for betrayal. He was ours once."

—

Teasag crouched on the stony headland behind Maon as he raised his arms to the sky, chanting, and thought evil thoughts at his back. He had beaten her again this morning for no particular reason. She watched as he raised an iron cauldron that was worth more than the king's gold torque, staggering under its weight, and willed him to fall. The cauldron was as large as his torso, adorned around the rim with leaping beasts and gold overlay. Maon braced himself and heaved it out over the cliff edge to plummet into the dark tarn below them. At his side the king untied the braided thongs from a bundle wrapped in a dark hide, and lifted out a great sword. The naked warrior that formed the iron hilt stared out at the sky with round gold eyes. Dergdian lifted the blade above his head and threw it after the cauldron into the water.

Behind them, Dergdian's warriors raised their spears and shields to the gray sky and shouted. Maon turned to face them. "The Mother has taken your sacrifice. Now it is *your* work that her birds may feed on the Roman dead. There must be no thought of turning back or the crows will feast where they will. I have seen this in the sky."

Teasag wondered what the Roman gods thought of that, and what sacrifices were being made to them. And also whether the spy had got free, something she had been wondering since the trackers hadn't come back, and that cave had fallen in as Aifa had predicted. She stopped wondering as Maon kicked her to her feet. While his back was turned, she pulled the thong that held her amber drop over her head and flung it swiftly out into the dark water. Then she picked up his bundles and followed him, stumbling over the rocky ground to where his ponies and driver waited, hitched the bundles onto her back with straps, and fell in line with the rest of the human pack beasts.

–

Urbicus's army fanned into separate columns to pass through the new wall as swiftly as possible, reforming beyond the ditch like a scarlet tide, waves glinting with the silver of polished plate and scale. The wicked little scorpion catapults lifted their heads over the column as it flowed north.

"My brother Justin claims that Hannibal used catapults to heave jars full of live snakes into the Pergamenes," Postumus said as the scorpions rumbled past the hospital wagons, on their second morning past the wall. "Have we thought of that?"

"Poisonous snakes?" Lucian asked.

"What would be the point if they weren't?" Flavian said, tightening his saddle girth.

"According to Justin, poisonous snakes," Postumus said. "But I expect any kind of snakes would do the job. Would *you* stop and check?" The Third Trumpet cut through the conversation. "We're moving!" He swung up on Boreas and fell in beside the other medical officers, grouped with their charges at the center of the column. Ahead he could see Urbicus and his generals on a knoll above them, conferring with a trio of couriers.

From the center of the column it was impossible to tell what was going on ahead. Couriers and optios flew back and forth as it inched north, with orders to shift formation, to halt, to move, to bring the heavy infantry up.

They halted again at mid-morning and the order came abruptly to set the hospital up, and at speed.

The medical staff, from senior surgeons to orderlies, pulled the packs from their wagons and erected the hospital tents with swift, practiced efficiency, one large combined space to house them all. When they had tied the tent poles down and unrolled the canvas floor, they positioned cots and surgery tables, baskets of bandages, and the compartmented cases of pharmacy supplies. They laid out their instruments, each surgeon to his particular liking, tied canvas aprons over their military tunics, and waited itchily for what was coming.

The army had halted on a flat ridge that sloped gently to a valley through which flowed one of the small tributaries of the Bodotria, the ground along its length strewn with tumbled river stone and clumps of trees. In the rear the land sloped downhill again, unevenly, a "stepmother" surface that no soldier ever liked. The Twentieth Legion cohorts, in reserve, dug in a rear guard ditch there. Behind the auxiliaries of the front lines, Claudius Charax and the Second Augusta were at the center, with Aelius Silanus and the Sixth on the right. The left flank was protected by a deep bend of the river, giving breathing space there.

Along the length of the valley on the far side, a faint impression of movement coalesced into a dark cloud and the vibration in the ground of thousands of men and horses on the march. The governor raised his hand and couriers moved from his vantage point to the generals in the line below.

The Caledones and their allies saw the Romans on the ridge and raised a howl, punctuated by the eldritch shriek of Pictish war horns.

Valerian brought his heavy cavalry up, prepared to hit the Pictish flank on the right, and rode for the front of the line, making sure that they could see him, his signifer's draco banner screaming as it filled with air. With the horse archers circling farther out to harry the Caledones' flanks, the auxiliary infantry positioned themselves to take the first brunt of the charge and the legions behind them to move forward on command.

The Picts streaming through the shallow ford in the river were hampered somewhat by the crossing and by the stones that caught at chariot wheels, but there were thousands of them. Over their tattooing they were painted blue and red and ocher like riders out of Annwn, and naked above the waist save for the shields that caught the mid-morning sun like dragon's treasure, heavily embossed with gold and silver. Half a Pictish man's wealth might be on his shield. A man Valerian recognized as the rumored Druid priest by his white robe and gold sun disk rode among the front lines, his driver threading between the other chariots, urging them on. Behind the chariots marched thousands upon thousands of warriors on foot, and they too threw themselves screaming toward the Roman lines.

Scorpion bolts whistled over his head and Valerian said a quick prayer for the accurate calibration of the little monsters as he led his cavalry down the hill into the Pictish flank. A riderless chariot with a broken wheel careened past the cavalry lines, its panicked horses wild-eyed and frantic, the chariot disintegrating as they ran. Valerian paced his horse beside them, leaned down and cut the traces with his dagger before they brought anyone else down. A Caledone warrior dived among the iron-shod cavalry mounts, knife out, and Valerian leaned from his saddle again and caught him across the back of the neck with his sword. They were abandoning the chariots now, having caused what chaos they could with them among the Romans. The Caledone riders ran out along the poles to leap into the fray on foot, pushing into any gap in the Roman lines, while the drivers retreated to the rear.

None of which Postumus knew. In the hospital tent they could only go by the trumpet calls and wait for the wounded to come in to know what was happening. Postumus pushed Galt's bracelet up his arm, out of the way. He wasn't sure why he had worn it, but it felt like a talisman of sorts.

The first casualties were not long in coming, from among the auxiliaries who had taken the first charge. Postumus eased the splinters of the trooper's own shield out of the chest of a decurion of the First Dacians and prodded gently to see whether the horse that had trampled him had broken ribs. Beside him, Lucian was frantically tying the bleeding artery of one of the decurion's men.

Legionary and cavalry casualties followed the auxiliaries; belly wounds, punctured lungs with spears still embedded, an arm nearly severed through, all the ghastly detritus of war. They worked steadily, sorting the worst out first, leaving the lesser wounded to wait, which they did with military patience. As orderlies took each man from the surgery table, another took his place, endlessly. Postumus had learned that you didn't look to see how many were waiting, you kept your focus on the man in front of you, and then the one after him.

He was stitching the thigh wound of one of Valerian's heavy cavalry when a trumpet call too close by to have come from the front startled them all, followed by frantic shouting.

"In the rear!" A bloodied legionary from the Twentieth, which was supposed to be the rear guard reserve, laid a wounded companion on the canvas floor. Another trumpet rang out no more than a quarter of a mile away, the Fall Back and Regroup.

It was difficult to operate while wearing armor plate and most surgeons discarded it in the hospital tent. Now Postumus dived for his lorica and helmet, stacked in the tent corner with his sword and shield, as did every other surgeon and orderly.

"Buckle up! Now!"

To the rear they could hear the sound of furious fighting, a clamor of battle howls mixed with the steady shouts of command from the Roman officers. And how in Typhon's name had the Picts got around behind them?

"Brigantes," the legionary from the Twentieth said as Tertius knelt to assess his condition. "Foot and horsemen." Tertius tied a tourniquet around his thigh. "Out of the fucking sky, so far as we could tell."

Postumus took stock of the hospital tent. All he could see to the rear were the wagons of the baggage train, and the tent was full of wounded from the front. As more wounded began to come in, now from the rear as well, he picked up his sutures again. "Keep at your work until we have orders."

–

The courier worked his way through the press of infantry massed on the right. "The governor's compliments and he wants four cohorts back to reinforce the rear." He saluted Aelius Silanus and rode for the governor's vantage point on the ridge again. Urbicus had seen the Brigantes but too late. They had come out of the trees below the rearguard's posts, from the gods knew where, and now they were no doubt up and over the ditch-and-wall before they could be stopped. They had been ahead, rather than behind as assumed, of the Roman army, with the Epidii and then the Caledones for their guides, and had waited, it appeared, in one of the numerous nameless glens that cut through the Pictish highlands. Now Silanus began the delicate maneuver of detaching half of his legion from the right flank to the rear while the Twentieth Legion tried to hold on, and the Second at the center moved over to fill the gaps he was leaving while the Caledones kept swarming through the ford to swell their front ranks.

The governor's orders to Postumus were to hold. There really wasn't much else that the hospital could do. It couldn't be moved in a hurry. Postumus tried to concentrate on digging out the spear in the patient before him. The soldier had snapped the shaft off himself where it had broken with the blow, and it stuck out a jagged foot beyond the place where it had pushed through the plates of his lorica into his ribcage with the force of a charging horse behind it. It took metal shears to cut away the lorica from around the embedded shaft while the soldier swallowed the poppy tears an orderly brought, and grimaced and tried to hold still.

"Almost there." Postumus eased away the last piece of plate and inspected the wound. Not in the lung, with luck. The plate had blunted its force. He slid the spoon down the shaft's length until he felt it catch the spearpoint. The legionary drew his breath in and bit his lip. Postumus just had it out when shouting from the rear grew louder and he jerked his head up to see a baggage wagon on fire.

"Shields up! Keep them out!" He took a quick look to be sure that blood wasn't pouring out of the spear wound, and snatched up his sword and shield.

Beyond the hospital tent a wavering line of the Twentieth were holding off the attacking Britons, whose obvious intent was to destroy the baggage train and then go through it to the rear of the main army. Flames were already spreading from the first wagon to another and the drivers were pouring out water from the supply barrels on them. A handful of Brigante warriors were already through the defending lines and the main body was pushing hard against the outnumbered Twentieth. If flames caught the hospital tent, it would go up.

"Lock shields and hold them!" Postumus and his handful of forty surgeons and orderlies formed up in a half-circle around the hospital tent, swords out, pushing back against the Brigantes who had got through the Twentieth's line. The wagon drivers had the fire out and it didn't flare up again but the Brigante warriors were streaming through the baggage train, using the wagons for cover. If they got through, they would catch the whole army between their forces and the Caledones.

The Twentieth was falling back in formation, giving ground slowly, waiting for the cohorts of the Sixth. There was no place to carry the wounded – they were fighting nearly on top of the hospital.

Galerius, breathing hard and his mouth set in a grim line, was on one side of Postumus, and Lucian and Flavian on the other. Tertius was the only professional among them, but even he looked to Postumus for orders. That was how the Army worked. Postumus had never commanded a fighting unit, except in mock battle during his training days, but they were all soldiers by training and he was Chief Surgeon. It was up to him. There was no time to think about whether he could do this or not.

They held their shield wall as long as they could and when it finally broke through the sheer weight of the numbers, they fought hand to hand, the battle narrowing to the three feet of space around him, to the blue-painted Briton who dove at him with a long sword and staggered back as Postumus blocked it with his shield, grateful in the moment for the weapons training and drill they had spent so much effort attempting to avoid. The Briton came at him again. Postumus parried the blow and hooked his shield under the edge of the Briton's smaller one and pulled. He raised his own sword, Galt's arm ring still high on his arm. The Briton saw it, hesitated an instant, and went down under Postumus's blow. Maybe Valerian had been right, he thought, turning to face the next one who came at him.

Beside him he saw Lucian, with the same concentrated look he gave to gambling, swing his sword into a Briton's shield arm at the shoulder, and then when the shield dropped, into his collarbone.

The gold and purple vexillum of the Twentieth waved above the melee around the wagons beside the standard of the detachment's Fifth Cohort. The standard disappeared as its signifer fell, the cohort wavered, and then the standard rose again.

"Valeria Victrix!" the man who had raised it shouted and Postumus saw that it was Tertius. The cohort's First Centurion snatched up the wolf's-head hood of the signifer and put it on Tertius's head, shouting at his men to regroup.

"Valeria Victrix!"

Still they were being pushed steadily back, almost into the hospital itself. Postumus saw the cavalry trooper whose leg he had stitched, shieldless, fighting off a pair of Brigante warriors with a long cavalry sword and a pilum he had acquired from somewhere. The Brigantes swarmed everywhere now, into the hospital and through it. They didn't bother to try setting it on fire – whatever torches they had carried had been abandoned – but they cut tent ropes as they went. By now Postumus's makeshift century had attached itself to Tertius and the Twentieth's Fifth Cohort, still falling back in formation, holding the Brigantes as long as they could. A few got through to wreak havoc before the Romans in the rear of what was now a separate battle with its own front cut them down, but mostly the line held, inching backward and thinning with each Fall Back command.

The baggage train was chaos, most of the tethered horses were loose or stolen – Postumus saw a Brigante warrior ride by on what he recognized as the governor's spare mount – and the baggage mules and the oxen that pulled the heavy catapult wagons had kicked their traces loose and scattered, trailing harness behind them. The grain bags had been split open and wine jars broken wherever they sat within reach on the wagons, and the armorers' stores had been overturned amid furious shouting from the Brigante lords to leave the spoils for afterward.

The cohorts of the Twentieth were heavily outnumbered and only the precision of the Roman formation was holding them at all. They had retreated past the hospital now, fighting grimly for every foot, and Postumus watched as the leather sides buckled in when a tent pole went down. Then he was fighting off a screaming warrior with the gold torque of a Brigante lord around his neck. He recognized the man as Rhys in the moment before he slammed the Briton's sword arm with his shield and dug his sword into his ribs. Bran would be somewhere in the thick of it, he supposed, but he couldn't see him. He could only see the chaos in the few feet in front of him as the cohort backed up again.

And then the push slowed. At first it was hard to tell, but the Brigantes' momentum slackened. In a few minutes he was sure of it. A trumpet called the Advance from beyond the wreckage of the baggage train. The battle began to move in the other direction, the Brigantes falling back to meet the reinforcements of the Sixth now at their rear.

—

Dergdian had counted on the surprise of the Brigantes at the Romans' rear, and to some extent it had worked. But the Brigantes had attacked too soon, without waiting for the signal from Dergdian. The High King, as he made plain, took orders from no other lord that he was not to be in the forefront. As a result, Urbicus had been able to pull the cohorts of the Sixth out before the front was sufficiently enmeshed in the chaos of the Pictish charge. Rather than catching the Romans between the Caledones and their allies on one side and the Brigantes on the other, the Brigantes were caught between the Roman rear guard and its advancing reinforcements. And the Picts, with the Roman rear unbroken, were being slowly pressed against the river on the Roman left, where the banks grew increasingly steep and rocky, as the Roman center and right wing slowly encircled them.

And that, Valerian thought, gasping for breath as the Pictish forces began to fall back under the weight of the heavy cavalry, was why Rome won wars. A screaming charge into the enemy's front lines won you honor, but also death. The Romans, solid behind their shield walls and their catapults and the discipline which forbade any soldier to so much as twitch without orders, were a match for far greater forces of undisciplined heroes.

–

The army had taken substantial casualties all the same. British dead far outnumbered Romans but Urbicus had still lost several thousand men, with more wounded. The historian Tacitus had claimed that 11,000 Romans under Agricola had beaten 30,000 Picts at Mons Graupius with only 360 casualties. Postumus, surveying the carnage while the carrion birds gathered overhead, suspected Tacitus of cooking the numbers in Rome's favor.

While the army was still in pursuit of the fleeing enemy, they had put the hospital to rights and begun the process of assessment and treatment over again. Galerius, who had taken a spear wound to the shoulder, had it cleaned and bandaged by Domitius, and went back to work, exchanging his armor for the bloody apron he had been wearing at the start of the battle, with the remark that he was not a lobster. The hospital's only other casualties were Gemellus, who had a deep cut on his sword arm, and Tertius.

The First Centurion of the Valeria Victrix's Fifth Cohort had brought Tertius to the hospital over his own horse in the aftermath.

"He handed off the standard to one of my men and then just dropped," the centurion said. "Right when we had them on the run." Tertius bore no mark on him, and it was clear that his condition had caught up with him at last. But Tertius had died where he wanted to be and under the circumstances, Postumus thought the gods had been kind. "I'm thinking that this should go with him," the centurion said, and gave Postumus the wolf's-head hood.

They camped where they had halted to fight, and it took into the darkness to sort the dead and catch the loose horses and mules. Postumus, relieved, found Boreas cropping grass in a meadow on the near side of the river, plainly waiting for Postumus to come and get him. Finn had fled the hospital when the tent came down and taken refuge under one of the catapult wagons. Postumus found him and whistled him to heel just before dusk as he made his way across the camp to the Headquarters tent, where the governor had requested his assessment of casualties.

The chaos left by the Brigante raid was mostly cleared, and the enemy dead collected for identification. Dergdian was dead, and the Druid High Priest as well. The Druid had been captured to be brought to the governor, but, the governor's tribune said, white-faced, the Druid had said something no one understood, put a hand to his chest and simply died on the spot. Then everyone had been afraid to touch his body and the governor, clearly irritated, had personally put it on the pyre himself. The Army would burn priests and kings lest their bodies hold some power afterward, but the rest would lie where they had been stripped of their weapons and wealth.

Bran was dead, as were most of his ill-fated Council, although Dawid was slumped among the chained prisoners being guarded by the Headquarters sentries. Postumus caught sight of him as he passed and a wave of unexpected despair washed over him. So many dead just because they – the Romans, his people – were here. Not even invading the highlands, just here. Building their wall under their noses. Digging in. Sending down roots. Changing things in ways that would not be undone even if they left.

Having made his report, he whistled again for Finn and found him among the Pictish prisoners, fawning on a Caledone woman, someone's slave by her iron collar and threadbare gown. She was bent over Finn's head, arms around his neck. Postumus whistled again and Finn looked up happily, but he didn't move.

"My dog seems to know you," he said to the woman in the British of the lowlands, and she seemed to understand him. Was she the woman of one of the trackers? He would have even worse news for her than the chain around her ankles if so.

"I gave him scraps," she said, "when he would beg at the kitchen." She ruffled his fur. "He is a great beggar." Her face was bleak but the warmth in her voice for the dog was plain, and almost heartbreaking under the falling light and the sweep of black birds across the sky. The sentries started to cuff her into silence, but Postumus waved them off.

"Who do you belong to?" he asked her.

"Maon High Priest, but he is dead."

"I'm afraid so," he replied gently.

"I asked the Goddess for it," she said. "I gave her my amber drop."

Postumus digested this.

"Will you please tell me if the lady is well?" She dropped her voice with a glance over her shoulder at the other prisoners.

"The lady?" The conversation seemed to have taken an abrupt turn and her highland accent was confusing.

"The spy you sent. It must have been you. The dog was with the trackers they sent after her."

"Why do you wish to know?" he asked warily.

"She was kind to me. Maon turned Dergdian against her after she left and then they hunted her. She gave one of the kitchen slaves some medicine for stopped bowels and I put it all in their porridge that they took with them. To slow them down," she added, as if it might need explaining.

Postumus studied her. "That was enterprising," he said finally. "She is well and she would be grateful to you if she knew that."

"What will your governor do with us now?" she asked him, although she must have known. Conscription or the slave market.

He told her that, and thought a little longer as she sat stoically on the hard ground and stroked Finn. Then he gritted his teeth and went back into the governor's tent.

"I want the Caledone woman," he informed Governor Urbicus, who was conferring with Aelius Silanus over wine and maps. They both raised their eyebrows at him.

"She's hideous," Aelius Silanus said.

"She isn't washed yet," Urbicus pointed out. "You never know."

"Not for that," Postumus said. "She was the Druid's and thinks she killed him. Or at any rate she asked the Goddess to do it. My dog knows her."

"Surgeons are all a little mad," Aelius Silanus informed the governor. "It comes of spending all that time looking at people's insides, in my opinion."

"This one has had a long day," Postumus said, aggravated to the edge of insubordination. "She helped your spy and that may be why the spy managed to stay ahead of the hounds on her trail. She deserves better than the slave market. And you know she's not worth much," he added, reviewing his banked funds.

"What are you going to do with her?" Lollius Urbicus asked and they both cocked their heads at him with curiosity.

"I have no idea," he said, because he didn't. All the same, he emerged with a scrap of papyrus hastily scribbled by the governor and the cheerful comment that at that price he should consider her his share of the spoils. She was still leaning against Finn's shoulder.

"What is your name?" he asked her.

"Teasag, Lord."

"Not lord. Sir."

She repeated it after him, stumbling a bit over the Latin as there was no British equivalent.

"Well, Teasag, I have bought you. I have no idea what to do with you, but you won't go to the slave market.

334

I think the lady would be very angry with me if I let that happen. You can begin by looking after the dog and keeping him out of other people's dinner."

She was silent as he showed the bill of sale to a sentry with a look that advised no impertinent questions and the sentry unlocked the chain. He took her by the arm, not quite sure whether she might run and get herself into further trouble.

A pile of gleanings from the battlefield was being sorted by the governor's staff and cast a jagged shadow in the now lantern lit camp. Shields and chariot adornments, jewelry taken from the enemy dead, all would be handed out at morning parade to the victorious troops. Anything useful from the baggage trains would be adopted by the Army as well, and anything else left to rot with the bodies.

"You understand that there is nowhere for you to go now if you run from me," he told Teasag gently. "I must go and certify my legion's Dead List before our dead are burned. I don't quite know what to do with you."

"I won't run," she said, craning her head up to look at him. "You will not be worse than Maon." She added a wicked little motion with her fingers that he took to be some curse to follow the High Priest into the next world.

"Very well then." He took her to his tent, made her a bed of sorts with two rugs and Boreas's saddle pad, and went with the Victrix optio to certify death as each name was crossed off the legion's rolls, while the carrion birds waited hopefully in the trees. There were too many for individual pyres, but each legion's ashes would go home to their respective fortress for burial in the graveyard outside the walls. The moon was up but they bent low over each one by lantern light to be certain. When they came to

Tertius, Postumus spilled out the small flask of wine he had brought for the purpose and ordered the wolf's-head hood and cloak burned with him, testament to a return to his rightful place.

XX. Otters

In the morning, the army bathed in the river, in preparation for parade and the sharing out of spoils. Postumus woke Teasag from what was clearly the sleep of exhaustion and gave her a spare undertunic for a gown. Then he took her to the armorer to have the slave collar cut off and led her to a decently secluded spot to wash, both kindnesses that seemed to surprise her. The procession of half-naked soldiers was still filtering back into the camp and she looked afraid, so he stayed, back tactfully turned, while she bathed. It occurred to him that a female slave was going to be a lot of trouble.

The governor and his generals made the rounds of the hospital tent in full parade dress, congratulating the wounded on their valor and distributing such honors as their commanders had suggested. Afterward the medical staff followed the rest of the army to form up on the parade ground within the camp. In the valley below them, the smoke of the Roman pyres still lingered, and the carrion birds had already come for the enemy dead.

Lollius Urbicus, resplendent in his purple cloak and gilded breastplate, praised his army for its valor, its discipline, and its tenacity, and presented the awards of a successful campaign in the same fashion as the grass crown given after the winter battle for the wall – now embodied in a gold wreath on the standard of the Sixth – as promissories to be redeemed later in gold and silver. They cheered him while one by one commanders and individual soldiers were called before him to receive honors, Postumus among them.

"For your impromptu audition for the Centuriate, Surgeon Corvus," Urbicus informed him. Instead of a grass or evergreen wreath from the basket on the table beside him, he slipped a gold circle from the honors on his own breastplate. "You may give this back to me when your own arrives," he said. "I think that Rome lost a natural commander when you opted for the Medical Corps. Inform me, please, if you should change your mind about that."

Postumus turned the gold circlet over in his hand. A Corona Aurea, given to an officer who had held his ground. He smiled. "I will, sir, but I doubt it."

–

The Sixth Legion Victrix marched home to Eburacum and its senior surgeon returned to his usual assignment. The Picts would likely be no more trouble for a generation. The peace imposed on the Brigantes was harsh: conscription of men and of horses, and hundreds of time-expired veterans settled on their land. Postumus had suggested to Lollius Urbicus that if he wished to install a vassal king of Rome's selection among the Brigantes, Dawid was cousin to Bran and would be a good choice. He had no idea whether Dawid would be willing. Dawid was perfectly capable of telling the governor to fly his Eagle up his ass and let himself be conscripted into the auxiliaries instead, but Postumus suspected that like Galt,

Dawid might shoulder a burden he didn't want to keep the remnants of his tribe intact. And, perhaps, not to leave Brica. It was a pity that this foster son of Galt had not been king rather than Bran.

Teasag, however, was a more immediate problem in Postumus's life than whatever the governor decided about Dawid and vice versa. For one thing, she was much younger than she had looked with filthy hair and tattered clothing, probably no more than fourteen. She had red-gold hair and green eyes and a small, sharp chin that made him think of a fox. Clean, she attracted more interest from the men than he liked. He taught her to say "I belong to Chief Surgeon Corvus" in Latin, and had her take Finn about with her but she was a constant worry. She was also a troubling combination of curiosity and ignorance. She thoroughly cleaned his quarters and polished his armor until it shone but he really didn't have enough for her to do to keep her occupied. Her belief that Claudia as Aifa had employed some form of Roman magic to bring the stone tower down prompted her to investigate the catapults' mechanisms, trying to figure out the spell that worked them, and nearly got her hand snapped off. She climbed up to drop offerings of small stones and flowers into the hot air ducts on the roof, which clogged the hypocaust. Postumus tried to explain the difference between magic and engineering but it was heavy going. She didn't have the vocabulary in her own tongue.

The garlanding of the standards at the Rosaliae Signorum perplexed her. With Postumus, she watched the Eagle and the cohort standards brought out from their chapel in the Principia as the junior officers handed wreaths of roses to the legate and First Centurions. The standard-bearers, in parade armor beneath their wolf and lionskin hoods, dipped their poles to receive the garlands and planted them upright again.

"Are they your gods?" she whispered to him.

"They are the heart of the legion," he whispered back.

"Gods, then."

"No."

"They have just sacrificed a pig to them," she pointed out.

"That's for the god Mars. And for the shades of the ones of us who have died."

They watched the rest of the sacrifice as the garlanded bull and the sheep followed the pig. Postumus was silent, his own lost ones on his mind, until he saw that she was weeping.

"You are missing your own kind," he said. "I am sorry."

"I am not," she said. She scrubbed her fist across her eyes. "I am crying for the pig."

At least, he thought, he had had, and still did have, someone he could miss. That did not seem such a bad fate, compared with Teasag's. The only person for whom she had ever expressed an affection was Claudia Silva, in her guise as Aifa. Which was a thought.

> To my good friend, Claudia Silva,
>   This is Teasag. I bought her from the battle spoils because she asked after you and dosed the trackers who were on your trail with your purgative. Also my dog knows her.

Claudia read the message again while Teasag, delivered by a wagon driver from Eburacum, stood before her, staring about at Claudia's private reception room. It was furnished with cushioned wicker chairs and couches upholstered in silk, with elaborate scrolled arms at each end. The floor was made of tiny pieces of glass arranged in a picture of winged babies riding a big fish, and the walls were painted to look like open arches with gardens beyond them, so much finer work than Teasag had marveled over in the surgeon's quarters that at first she thought she could step through them. An ebony table held a silver animal rising open-mouthed from silver waters. It took a moment for Teasag to realize that it was a lamp.

Claudia read the message a third time and appeared to be trying to decide what to do about it.

"If you don't want me," Teasag said morosely, watching her, "you can send me back again. I was learning to make salve for the surgeon."

"Were you? And what were you doing following Dergdian's army?"

"I belonged to Maon High Priest, who is dead." Teasag's expression indicated her satisfaction at that. "I went where he did."

Including into battle where she would be no use at all, just so that he didn't have to lift a finger for himself. "It is possible to be both a priest and a fool. Druid or not," Claudia said.

"That was what I thought," Teasag said. "I threw my amber drop into the tarn to make him die."

Not perhaps what one wanted to hear from a new slave, Claudia thought, although she had a good deal of sympathy for her. She read Postumus's letter a fourth time. He had sent Teasag's sales contract with the note. Was he wooing her with unsuitable slaves? Or did he just not know what else to do with the girl?

"I think you had better stay with me," she said, and Teasag's face lit up while Claudia thought, *Oh Juno.*

"For the time being, at any rate. As it happens, I have need of a new maid." That was conveniently true as the current one had recently married one of the grooms from the stable and was now pregnant and throwing up every morning. Teasag offered an excellent opportunity to assign Coventina to more suitable work, such as not throwing up in the mistress's bath. Except for the fact that she spoke no Latin, had none of the knowledge a lady's maid required, and was fourteen.

Claudia sighed. "We'll try it."

Postumus, my friend,

The girl is very bright. I am teaching her Latin and to read because after I explained that it was not sorcery that told me that Dergdian's wall might collapse, she asks so many questions about how things are built and how they work that she is driving me mad. I allow her one question a day in the morning while she dresses my hair, which by the way she is very bad at.

You were wise to get her out of an army camp. She has never learned to negotiate a large household where the female slaves have any say at all over their own persons. She came to me half in tears and asked if she absolutely had to go with the head groom when he wanted her to. I informed her that she did not and she was free to dissuade him in any way she saw fit. Whereupon she took her new cloak pin (I have given her some decent clothes since she arrived wearing what I took to be your undertunic) and said that the mistress had

342

told her to stab him through the balls if he touched
her. The stable boys are terrified of her now.

Postumus smiled and laid the letter down. It seemed he had done the right thing, which was something pleasant to keep in his mind while he watched the new king of the Brigantes come to pay the tribe's taxes. Dawid, like Galt before him, had negotiated the best peace that he could, and now he came to kneel before Lollius Urbicus and Aelius Silanus, not at the court at Isurium Brigantum, but in the Principia of Eburacum Fortress. To make his vassal state entirely clear, only ten warriors were allowed to accompany him. To make it even clearer, they were allowed to bring their weapons because such weapons would be useless in the face of Rome.

The Sixth Legion formed up on either side of the Via Praetoria while Dawid's men marched between the Roman ranks, followed by the wagons of grain and gold that would leave the Brigantes nearly impoverished. They were either old or frighteningly young, Postumus saw, boys barely out of their initiation. He wondered sadly what had happened to young Evan, and Colin. Dawid gave no sign of recognition as he passed ten paces away. He simply looked straight ahead and disappeared into the Principia.

Maybe, Postumus wrote to Claudia, it would stick this time. Maybe they wouldn't just wait until they had enough young men and horses to do it all again, and again, and again, beating their heads against the Roman occupation. Maybe.

"I'll have the blue gown today, Teasag."

"Yes, Mistress. Mistress, what makes the water come out of the pipes in the bath?"

343

"In Latin, please. Gravity, mostly. That force in the earth that pulls everything toward it. And pumps."

"What is a pump?"

"I don't think your Latin is ready for pumps and I also don't think I can describe one in British. My gown, if you please. And then I want you to take this to Brys and tell him that it is to go to your surgeon at Eburacum."

"That is many messages to him," Teasag observed.

"That is not your business," Claudia said repressively.

> *You did not ask me what I think, but what I think is that you cannot help Dawid and were right not to try to speak with him. He must know that you were behind the governor's decision.*
>
> *In happier news, I hope, your Aunt Felicia, with whom I have become fast friends over roses, has invited me to her daughter's wedding to your brother next month. I am looking forward to showing you how Teasag is progressing and hope that you will explain catapults to her, which is beyond me.*

Postumus found himself unexpectedly lighthearted at that. There was, for the moment, peace, and he had leave. He headed south to the Silure Hills of his childhood with Finn at his heels, to watch Justin get married.

–

"I have had your toga cleaned and pressed," Gwytha informed him. "It's laid out in your old room."

"And don't even think of trying to weasel out of wearing it," Justin said. "Your doom is sealed. Papa has

344

been trying to teach Marcus how to wear his without losing control of it all morning."

Postumus didn't think any of the boys had worn a toga since their coming of age. "Mother, we'll trip over our own feet. Why not our parade uniforms? I brought mine."

Justin grinned at him. "You can blind us all with that Corona Aurea afterward. Congratulations, by the way."

"It cemented my desire to remain a surgeon," Postumus said. "Is Uncle Licinius putting on a toga?"

"Indeed he is, as is Felix, over protest," Gwytha said. "If Felicia didn't make them, Theodore would have. Theodore, as you can imagine, is beside himself. He's ordered a wine that Licinius says will require him to sell half the horse herd to pay for, and acquired a peacock from somewhere. Cook is determined to compete since the guests will eat again here, and I have had to put my foot down on the subject of peacocks. 'A flamingo! That would put him in his place!' she said, and I had to go lie down. I am counting on there being no available flamingos in Isca."

"I think you're safe," Justin said. "She doesn't have Theodore's connections."

Postumus and Justin shared a room for the last time that night, as in the morning Justin would go to be married and bring his wife back to the newly decorated guest chamber. Their mother seemed to have adopted this one as a sewing room in their absence, and Constantia as a place to stash assortments of dried, pressed plants, preserved insects, and whatever else had lately caught her eye. Constantia showed no sign of wanting to get married herself yet but was compiling a *Natural History of West Britain*. Marcus, on the other hand, was courting a girl from the village, although listening to him extol her virtues at dinner,

Postumus had concluded that her main charm for Marcus was the fact that she "understood goats."

In the morning they set out for the bride's house, toga-clad and respectable, in a carriage hired for the occasion. Gwytha and Constantia both had new gowns of bright diaphanous silk and new mantles. Januaria, as Justin's old nurse, had a place of honor in the carriage with them, and a new gown of her own. Multiple prayers against rain had prevailed and the sky was clear.

A small slave waited beside the flower-decked gatepost of the bride's house to direct them. Carriages and litters filled the grassy meadow below the barn, and at the house another slave welcomed the wedding guests and directed them to the inner courtyard, while Justin and Constantia, who was to serve as bridesmaid, were taken off to meet with the priest for last-minute instructions.

In the courtyard, a small flower-draped altar under an arbor supported statues of Juno and Jupiter, with stools before it for the bride and groom, and a ring of chairs for the guests. Slaves circulated with trays of nuts, shrimp, and small pastries, and cups of wine. Postumus saw Claudia among the guests, the sleeves of an elbow-length under-gown covering the marks he knew she still bore on her arms. Over it she wore a deep blue gown caught at the shoulders and sleeves with pearl and silver pins and a mantle of pale green silk with dark leaves embroidered along the hem above green kid sandals. Her ruby ring glinted on her finger and she wore matching drops of ruby and pearl in her ears.

"You look very fine," he told her.

She inspected him. "So do you."

"Not like a man fighting his own bed linen?"

"A little bit. Loosen your death grip on the folds a trifle and just use your left arm to hold them in place."

"This is why I joined the military, to wear clothes that don't fall off if you let go of them. Have you forgiven me for sending that child to you? I didn't know what else to do with her."

"Of course. She actually did my hair this morning and made it stay up."

"Did you bring her with you?"

"Yes. I was rather afraid to leave her to her own devices." Claudia gestured to the far end of the courtyard where the household servants were gathering to watch the proceedings. He saw Teasag among them, looking remarkably Roman in a pale blue tunic and the silver armband of Claudia's household. Her red hair was pinned on her head in imitation of Claudia's.

A trio of flute players emerged from the house and circled among the guests, herding them politely toward the altar. The bride's parents and brother followed, Felix uncharacteristically cowed by the folds of his toga, and then the priest and Justin with a wreath of roses in his hair. Constantia came next, carrying a silver plate of honey cakes for the offering, followed finally by Aurelia in a trailing white gown with a wedding knot at the waist. A diaphanous veil anchored by a wreath of roses to match Justin's covered her face and bright yellow shoes gleamed like little bursts of light as she walked.

"She's lovely," Claudia said, and Postumus thought she looked wistful. Aurelia was enchanted to be getting married, whereas Claudia, in a far more elaborate cere- mony than this no doubt, must have had a different outlook.

The ceremony itself began with the bride giving her consent to the marriage. Justin took her hand, vows were said, and they sat facing each other on the stools while the priest offered the cakes to Jupiter and lengthy prayers for domestic harmony to the imperial deities, as represented by the Emperor Antoninus and his wife. He called upon the parents of the bride and groom to bless the union and then opined at some further length on the institution of marriage as the foundation of the Empire. Just as an elderly guest was beginning to snore, he offered the final prayers and Justin put Aurelia's veil back from her face. The two of them ate the honey cakes, and they turned to be congratulated by their guests.

They went in together to the dinner where extra couches and tables had been arranged throughout the dining room. Theodore had indeed acquired a peacock, which had been roasted and then placed on a silver platter with its tail plumes reinserted. It was dressed with apricots and three different kinds of lettuces trimmed to look like feathers. A pastry temple of Venus held tiny figures of the bride and groom, surrounded by an "ocean" of veal aspic and billows of whipped cream. There were larks, eels in more pastry, stuffed hare in white sauce, stewed fruit with violets, a hollowed-out melon stuffed with cheese and olives, and on another silver platter the molded Capricorn emblem of Justin's new command, made of sausage and goose liver.

"Cook isn't going to outdo this unless she found the flamingo," Constantia whispered to Postumus.

When the last dish had been consumed, it was late afternoon and the entire party began the journey to the groom's home. Household slaves followed the wedding guests with villagers who had gathered outside the farm gates, amid much laughter and singing and throwing of nuts. Justin rode in a carriage with his bride but most of the rest of the party elected to walk.

"This is lovely country," Claudia said, as they made their way down the lane, through a grove of aspen and birch and then past Hilarion's pear orchard.

"Come out on the river with me tomorrow and I'll give you a tour of my childhood," Postumus suggested.

"I should like that."

At the house, Justin lifted down his bride, with her veil draped over one arm and clutching the ceremonial spindle and distaff that was indicative of her new status. His roses hung over one eye as he dodged the spindle to carry her over the threshold. Everyone cheered while the wedding party and houseguests followed them in and Theodore expertly filtered out everyone else with the exception of a few of Hilarion's old comrades from Isca Fortress, including the legate of the Second.

More wine and small biscuits in a digestive sauce were passed around to settle the stomach for the next meal, while the entertainers hired for the occasion trooped into the atrium: a trio of jugglers and tumblers, two dancing flute players, and an animal trainer with a tame leopard on a leash.

A wedding celebration was an all-day affair, but the second, private meal was not as elaborate, despite Cook's ambitions, and a time more conducive to actual conversation. When the entertainment ended, Justin and Aurelia said suitable prayers before the family altar, ate some of Cook's roasted goose and turtle soup for form's sake and then quietly disappeared.

"How long until your boy's leave expires?" Claudius Charax asked Hilarion.

"They have two days before they sail," Hilarion said, signaling to a slave to pour more wine. "Do you know something?"

"Only that there's another shakeup coming, I think," the legate said. "He tells me they are short of troops on the Rhenus, so naturally I am extrapolating to Britain, Britain being my business. The thinking may be that we have settled the north, so now of course we won't need all those cohorts."

"Do you expect they'll recall the governor?" Postumus asked him. "Now that the emperor has his victory."

Charax wiped his fingers on a napkin. "You've met the governor. What do you think? Yes, I expect so, he's much too popular with the legions, and that always makes an emperor nervous."

It had been over sixty-five years since the last sword-made emperor, or only fifty if you counted the assassination of Domitian by his own court. Neither was long enough to reassure an emperor who was without military experience and who had powerful generals holding his territories for him.

"And there's a revolt brewing among the nomads in Mauretania, I hear, that has the Senate worried," Charax added.

"Plenty of senators with farms in Mauretania," Hilarion said.

Rome had invested heavily in northern Africa once the nomads – relatives of Lollius Urbicus, ironically – were under control, which meant driven off, and it had become the Empire's main source of staples. There would be trouble without African grain and olives.

"We mustn't let the local inhabitants get to thinking that they own the place," Licinius said. He picked a stuffed plum from a dish as it went around.

"Certainly not," Hilarion said. "There might be a shortage of hippopotami for the circus, not to mention a number of senators' personal fortunes."

Claudius Charax snorted in amusement but remarked pointedly that it was as well that they had both retired, since they were so clearly lacking in the appropriate attitude toward both Africa and the dignity of the Senate.

–

The meal went on well into the night, and Postumus called for Claudia at mid-afternoon the next day wondering if she would even be awake yet, but found her sitting in Felicia's rose garden in a plain linen gown and well-worn sandals, with a wicker hamper by her feet.

"Felicia says I am bound to get wet, and so she lent me these," she said. "And Theodore has packed up the remains of last night's feast in case we are marooned."

Postumus hefted the hamper. "I shall decrease the chance of both by leaving Finn here with your unsuitable lady's maid." He whistled and Finn stopped nosing at a burrow in the grass and came to heel. Postumus deposited him with Teasag and they set out down the path that cut through Licinius's pasture, where a black mare and a gray stood nose to tail, switching flies. The river ran along the edge, just below the pasture fence. A series of weirs and channels formed the water supply for the house and outbuildings here, and a small currach was drawn up on the bank below the weir. It was a flat-bottomed affair of willow rods and tarred hide, and Postumus stepped in first and handed Claudia carefully in after him. They settled the hamper at their feet and Postumus pushed away from the bank with the oar.

"My brothers and sister and I ran tame on this farm when we were children," he told her. "Partly because this is the best place to get onto the river. It's often too shallow where it runs past our farm."

"Is this the Isca?"

"It's a side branch. The water is calmer here, and good for trout." A man in a straw hat and a tunic hiked to his thighs was fishing just downstream, knee-deep in the current. He glared at them as they paddled past, and Postumus made apologetic motions.

Willow and alder overhung the banks past the landing and the air beneath them was cool and smelled of mud. A fishing heron stood motionless in the shallows as they slid by, and a family of otters popped whiskery faces up at them from the tangle of scrub willow outside their den. Claudia trailed her hand in the water, the edge of the currach pushing her sleeve up so that the tattoos showed against her white arm. She saw him looking at them and smiled. "They have healed nicely," she commented. "All of them."

He recalled her earlier invitation in the cave to inspect them for himself, and laid the paddle across the currach's frame. They were close enough together that he only had to bend his head to kiss her. The currach rocked wildly, taking on water.

"Be careful! You'll have us in the river."

He grinned at her. "As predicted."

"I should prefer to get in of my own accord."

A small island rose in the middle of the water and Postumus edged the currach onto its shore. Willows screened the spot and an impressively engineered beaver dam downstream made a still, secluded pool. "We used to swim here," he said, "when we were children. Probably the same beavers. The otters come here too. They like to fish around the dam."

Claudia stepped out of the currach and tested the water with her foot, sandals in her hand. She smiled at him. "There's quite a depth. Let's swim."

"It's cold," he warned her.

"It's lovely. We'll be otters."

They stripped off tunic and gown and Claudia hesitated only a moment before also discarding a pair of minimal silk breeches and her breastband. "I think I prefer to come home in dry underthings."

Postumus shrugged and followed suit, aware that his interest was becoming more than evident. They dove in naked, and it was indeed extremely cold. Postumus surfaced, spouting water, and reached for her. They clung together, shivering under the willows, until their skin adjusted to the temperature.

"I am most glad to see you again," he told her. The water was clear and he could see the marks on her breasts and thighs, shimmering and distorted by the current as if they were live things.

She turned in his arms and he kissed her, sliding his hands down her hips. He wasn't entirely sure how far this would go, but knew from a youthful experiment with Licinius's kitchen girl that it wasn't going to go very far in the water. She slid out of his arms and dove, a quick fluid motion like the otters, and he followed her, exploring the pool above the dam. Then they floated on their backs, watching a red kite overhead.

"I suppose Antoninus is bound to recall the governor," she said.

"You guess is as good as mine, maybe better. But it's probably inevitable. Every successful campaigner gets recalled." He thought about what Urbicus had said about settling in. "In the long run, I think it won't matter. I don't know if this peace will last, most likely not, but Rome has put down too many roots and they keep growing deeper."

She paddled a bit with her hands to keep from drifting downstream. "We are the roots, I suppose, however the leaves turn out. And our great-grandchildren will still be Roman, in their fashion."

"Grandchildren?"

"Hypothetical ones. Generic ones. Someone's grand-children."

"If we were careful not to make grandchildren, would you get out of the pool with me?"

She smiled at him over her shoulder and he caught her under the ribs and boosted her up onto the bank. Behind the curtain of the willows was a grassy patch nearly invisible from the river. He spread his cloak on it and she stretched out and held up her arms for him to come to her. He put his hand between her legs and she made a contented little sound like a coo that made his heart turn over.

Afterward, belated good sense crept over them both in the realization that they might not be the only ones inclined to swim in this pool, and they regained their clothing and inspected the contents of Theodore's hamper.

"There's a cloth in here," Postumus said ruefully. "We could have lain on that."

"I'd rather not take it back to Theodore in the state your cloak is in," Claudia said.

"Theodore has impeccable manners," Postumus said. "He would never call attention to the fact that the guests have been making love on the picnic cloth."

He swirled the mud-stained cloak in the slow current above the beaver dam and hung it on a bush before they unpacked a box of small meat pies, a loaf of bread, the remains of the Capricorn mold, olives, a jar of apples in honey, and another of the wedding wine.

Claudia handed him a piece of bread spread with the apples and licked her fingers clean.

"I may be transferred to Africa, you know," he said. It was more than likely. The Army tended to move its officers about as often as its generals.

"Possibly." She cut a piece of the Capricorn mold and nibbled it. "This is clever, but it isn't any better the second day. Would the otters eat it?"

"Otters eat anything."

She rose and laid what was left of the Capricorn's tail under a willow on the bank. "Augury by otter. We shall come back and read the pattern of the crumbs."

Postumus wasn't sure whether the otters knew anything, but the little island had always given him the feeling of possibility. Whatever the future held, it was no doubt already on its way.

When they walked back through Licinius's pasture in the dusk, a trio of girls in the next field were cutting wheat stalks with a bronze knife to make a Corn King. They would be lighting the Lughnasa fires in the village tonight. The residents of the combined households were already streaming down the road between the farms, toward the flames, and they followed. A little scuttering wind rustled the trees and they could hear a nightjar in the woods by the river.

By Roman reckoning, it was the Kalends, the day for payment of debts. Postumus couldn't help hearing an echo of the Corn King in that. He remembered again that a king from his own west country was supposed to have died that way, to seal a treaty. That was a generation before Postumus's parents had been born and so it was all firelight tale and gossip, as history tended to be.

The flames sank to ember in the dark field, and Justin and Aurelia ran toward them, laughing, wearing yesterday's rose wreaths, to leap the coals for luck. They had grown up watching these same villagers light these same fires, always somehow on the edge of things, too Roman for the village and not quite welcome in the Army, but it hadn't galled Justin the way it had Postumus. Now he thought that if he had sewn together more than he had taken apart, that might be a good enough equation.

He whispered in Claudia's ear, "We could go jump the fire."

She cocked her head up at him. "So I can bear you many children?"

"Possibly."

"You don't like what I do."

"You don't do it anymore."

"Possibly."

He was silent at that. How much was he willing to risk?

"Should we consult the otters first?" she asked him.

"No." He held out his hand.

She took it and they walked through the rustling night wind toward the fire.

Author's Note

This novel is a sequel, of a sort, to a book written many years ago, and I owe considerable thanks to the people who helped me venture back into the Roman Empire, and particularly into the weirdly counterintuitive world of Roman medicine. Dr. John White kindly walked me through all the symptoms of lung cancer and how to describe its process without ever actually saying what the patient had, because my hero didn't know. The Romans knew a lot but because they were forbidden to conduct autopsies, they knew how to operate for cataracts, for instance, but didn't recognize cancer or appendicitis. Regarding the pharmaceutical remedies contained in this novel, I don't recommend trying any of them, but they are all genuine, and I have attempted to use mainly the ones that might actually have worked.

I would also like to thank the fine people at Canelo Publishing, in particular Michael Bhaskar, Kit Nevile, and Iain Millar, who decided that my earlier Roman novels deserved another appearance, and that this one should follow them.

And finally my husband Tony Neuron and son Felix Crowe, for general support and for putting up with the three-by-four-foot rolling corkboard and map of Roman Britain that seemed to appear wherever anyone wanted to walk.